About the Author

Natasha Jardim is from Victoria, Australia and holds an M.A. of Cultural Heritage and an M.A. of Secondary Teaching, which she puts to full use while writing. Her fantasy work is evocative, fun and emotional, as you would expect when there are loves to be found and enemies to destroy. Her characters are nuanced and relatable, and while she hopes you love some of them, many are diabolical and there to be loathed. Her first novel, *The Elementals: Sansul* was written aged 17 and published in 2013 to lovely reviews. With tertiary education complete, Natasha decided to republish her work and revise the sequel. She credits having a more solid understanding of publishing and marketing for giving her (mild) confidence in sharing her stories with the public.

When she is not writing or teaching others how to do so, you can be guaranteed she is cooking, travelling or reading crime thrillers with her husband.

To keep in touch, you can find her on the following platforms:
Instagram: n_jardim_writer
Tiktok: n_jardim_writer

Also by Natasha Jardim

<u>Murder Mystery</u>

The Deaths at Mansfield Grammar (2024)

<u>Fantasy</u>

The Elementals: Sansul

A Spy Amongst the Rebels (2024)

THE ELEMENTALS: SANSUL

NATASHA JARDIM

THE Q QUARTER

Acknowledgements

This novel would not have been possible without the endless and unwavering support of Christopher, Joáo, Marilena, Tatiana, Jordan and Keanu.

Also, I would like to express my deepest thanks to Heather H. Howard. Without your belief and encouragement, this journey would have been far less bright. Thank you for your guidance and love.

Lastly, I thank the wonderful people who have come with me on this beautiful journey.

To the family we make -
because blood does not define that bond.

Contents

Chapter One

Sansul

THE VILLAGE OF WILMOTA was alight with fireworks, dancing, music and laughter as its residents celebrated the Samhain Sabbat.

Adrianna stood at the centre of the flamboyantly dressed crowd and watched as red and gold fireworks erupted against the backdrop of night sky. As silvery glitter rained down, the clan clapped enthusiastically, cheering out for more. Adrianna watched as her guardian, Fradrik, a master trickster, bowed before his admirers. "My next show will be after the bonfire," he announced, before edging his way out of the crowd.

A tall witch of ten and seven summers, Adrianna had long, dark and wavy hair that was adorned with a floral wreath for the evening. A Samhain tradition, women created wreaths out of the last of the summer flowers in honour of the transitioning seasons. Her deep green almond-shaped eyes lined with thick eyelashes and dark eyebrows, and her honey-coloured skin made her immediately recognisable amongst the crowd of fair-skinned Wilmota clansmen as a child of foreigners.

Adrianna linked her arm with Fradrik's. "How *ever* did you manage to get your hands on those prohibited fireworks?"

"I have my ways," said Fradrik with a wink. "I've not traded on the international seas my whole life without learning a few tricks of the trade."

Adrianna laughed.

"And you, my girl? What are your plans for this evening? No, boys, I hope."

"Not for me," said Adrianna. "But I have a feeling that Kenna and Ralphus will soon take a big first step tonight."

"And what big step might that be?"

"Talking."

It was Fradrik's turn to laugh. "What a tragic romance they weave for themselves."

A group of warlocks nearby roared a toast before downing pints of beer; faeries scattered at the sound. A tall, cherry-haired nymph in a see-through gown walked by and smiled at Fradrik. Adrianna held back a laugh as Fradrik craned his neck to watch her. *Once a sailor, always a sailor!* she mused.

Adrianna kissed his cheek. "See you soon! Rosamunda was helping Kenna with her hair. They should be finished by now."

Wilmota was the largest witchery village in Sansul province. Located outside the Sleeping Forest, it encompassed both mountain land and pastoral valleys, and was overlooked from the north by a domineering fortress perched upon Whistlers Knoll less than a league away. To the east was the seaside.

Six wooden poles, each of which supported white fire-spheres hovering at its top, illuminated Wilmota. Faery glow emanated from the trees and fireworks blasted out from the chimneys whenever the big band started a new song. Large marbles strung together, each filled with a firefly, lined the rows of neat multi-coloured cottages leading to the village centre.

Far from the dancing, a boar roasted over a great bonfire.

Witches and warlocks in magnificent gowns and jackets continued to arrive from the neighbouring villages of Aires, Bruniér and Collusus through the Dial Doors and were greeted by signs that read: *Welcome to the highlands. You are in Wilmota.*

Dial Doors, the primary mode of transportation for witches and warlocks, allowed them to travel across vast distances in seconds. The dial on the side of each door had multiple points of destination, most of which were other major cities.

Beneath a red marquee stood a long table laden with the most colourful and delicious food and drink. Barrels of mead were stacked together by the dessert table. Jugs of water, wine, juices and lemonade floated over the crowd, ready to serve the moment anyone lifted a cup into the air. Garlands laced along gates, tables and chairs. Illuminated hollow-centred turnips with frightening faces cut into them shone from windowsills, paths and dining tables around the village.

Sitting casually at a table on the edge of the marquee, Mathias picked up a turnip. "I do not like these things. They look too much like demons." Tall, thin and narrow-faced, Mathias was pristine in his appearance. He dressed in tailored suits of the finest silks and cotton and was always impeccably groomed.

Beside him, Ralphus, a burly warlock with red-hair, was not listening and slowly lowered his mug. He slapped Mathias on the arm. "Look, there they are."

Mathias smirked as Ralphus watched two girls make their way through the dancing crowd. "They are not coming here. Go and talk to, Kenna."

Ralphus leaned back in his chair and finished the rest of his mead. "Don't want to push my luck," he muttered.

The two witches clutched each other and laughed hysterically, as they pushed their way through the dancing crowd. They stopped in front of a tipsy faun who sat on top of the honey-mead barrel singing boisterously to the music. His empty mug danced in the air before him as he waved his arms around as if he were dancing with an invisible partner.

"I think you have had enough honey-mead, Omfridus," said Adrianna, smiling brightly.

The faun gave a short, merry giggle. "Darling Adrianna," he said, "while my tail still moves I know I can have one more pitcher of this *wonderful* mead." He stumbled to his feet, standing on the barrel, and waved his short tail as if to illustrate his words. "And who are you?" he asked of Adrianna's companion as he flopped back down.

"You know who I am," the girl said in a clipped tone, rolling her eyes. "I am Kenna, you silly goat."

Omfridus laughed again. "That I am," he said pleasantly. "So I am what I am, and who I am is what I am, while what I am is who I am, but it does not make me who I will be."

The witches shared a look. "He will regret this tomorrow," said Kenna, pulling her friend toward the table covered with food. Kenna was an ethereal beauty with straight black hair and dark eyes. Though she looked as gentle as a Woodland faery, she was a shrewd, and at times, short tempered witch who expertly cut people down to size when she felt the moment required it.

Kenna glanced around at Ralphus, who was surrounded by a crowd of his friends. He winked at her.

"I think Ralphus wants to dance with you," said Adrianna, smiling over at the boys.

Kenna blushed and turned her attention to the confectionary table. "I will step all over his feet."

Adrianna sent Ralphus an apologetic look. Mathias slapped him on the back, but Ralphus looked away, slightly crestfallen. Before Adrianna could round on Kenna and demand she went over and danced with him, two other witches rushed up to the table and began serving themselves tea, looking eagerly at the sweets. Adrianna made a mental note to speak to the ginger-haired man about his courting tactics before turning to more approaching friends.

"Hello, Jess, Caitriona," Adrianna said pleasantly.

Jess was a pretty, auburn haired, voluptuous girl. Kenna thought Jess 'simple' because she never said a word out of turn, made trouble or caused the kind of mischief for which Kenna and Adrianna were known. Caitriona was a plump witch with wide blue eyes and curly blonde hair. A trademark red ribbon braided with red tulips kept the mass from falling in her face. She and Adrianna had always been close friends, as they both regularly found themselves at the receiving ends of pranks played on them by the boys of the village.

Caitriona shoved a raspberry tart into her mouth hungrily. Jess smiled and sighed with mock disappointment.

"Bless her, she's tried to keep away from the tarts all night," Jess said as a teapot poured steaming tea into her raised cup. "I love your wreath, Adrianna! Yours too Kenna, the colours are lovely."

"Thank you! It took me a whole day to put together," said Adrianna, smoothing the ends of her hair.

"Did you hear there are gypsies coming up from Azria?" Caitriona asked excitedly, looking hungrily at the roasting boar.

"Really?" Adrianna asked eagerly. "Then I am going to buy some more of their quilts. They are so soft."

"I am going to have my tarot cards read," said Caitriona.

"I only care about the gypsy carvers," Jess said with a wink.

Kenna made a face, to which Jess responded by ignoring her.

"You are leaving for Azria tomorrow, aren't you?" Caitriona asked Adrianna.

"Yes, to see my cousin Blanca. Maybe I will cross paths with the gypsies," said Adrianna.

"Is Fradrik taking you?" asked Jess.

"Of course. He would never let me travel alone."

"Blanca should come here," said Caitriona.

"We should all be so lucky as to leave home for a while," said Jess, looking dreamily at the Dial Doors. "My mother thinks I am too young."

"My father thinks so too," said Caitriona. "The other night I told him I would like to visit Adrianna. I told him *you* were going Adrianna, and his eyes almost popped out of his head!" She laughed. "Then came 'the speech'. Complete with the usual: 'dangers of vampires' and the 'vampire freedoms' they have in the south. I had to block him out."

The girls laughed. Adrianna picked at her pumpkin seeds and honey bread and glanced over to Sansul Fortress, which loomed hauntingly on the hilltop. She noticed that torches at the ends of the fortress gates had suddenly come alight and the windows glowed from the inside as though someone had lit the lamps. She frowned as the sweet bread she had been nibbling turned tasteless in her mouth and her skin prickled with a slight chill. Adrianna had only ever seen the fortress alight this way once before. Six years ago on the same festival night.

"What do you think this means?" Adrianna asked Kenna, pointing toward the fortress.

Kenna usually preferred to pay little attention to the fortress. She despised the cursed, evil people who lived there. Enemies by nature and tradition, those of the fortress lived by the Darkness, while normal folk lived by the Light. On that night, six years previously, the fortress inhabitants had invaded Wilmota village and kidnapped several of their friends and family members, including Kenna's brother Tobias, who had not been seen since.

Kenna was alarmed. She stared at the fortress with wide, frightened eyes and slowly began to shake her head.

Adrianna placed her hand on Kenna's arm.

Kenna turned her head only slightly, her face solemn. "They are awake."

Suddenly, the white-spheres hovering on the poles in the village centre went out one by one. Adrianna spun around as each flame extinguished until the only source of luminosity came from the faery-lights and bonfire. The music came to a screeching halt; people cried out in surprise. Dancing couples stopped awkwardly. Laughter faded, card games paused and children froze. Everyone was waiting for the light to return, or fireworks to erupt. The bonfire was snuffed out, sounding as though someone had taken a sharp intake of breath. Kenna grabbed hold of Adrianna. Caitriona screamed and Jess dropped her teacup.

The faeries in the trees began to scatter, leaving the witches and warlocks in darkness. Emitting light from their palms, the witches looked around worriedly.

"Mama! *Mama*!" Children scattered, searching for their parents in the dark.

Adrianna raised her glowing palm and looked around for her guardian. "Fradrik!" she called, but there was no sign of the older warlock. Growing more frightened with each passing second, she moved closer to her friends. *Was this a prank?* she wondered desperately. She knew the warlocks enjoyed playing tricks, but in her heart she knew they would never do anything like this on a Sabbat, and on the whole village.

"It's *them*, I know it is," Jess whispered, her voice trembling.

"I need to find my family," said Caitriona.

An unnatural chill rose in the air, a sure sign that the Darkness was closing in. With every breath, a swirl of warm air flowed from her lips.

"Look!" a girl cried, and Adrianna saw her point to the fortress.

Like a wave making its way toward the shore, the gasps and cries of surprise became louder as more and more people turned to look at the fortress.

"Everyone!" cried one of the village elders. He held a staff high above his head, showering him with the light from the crystal buried in its core. "Please, calm yourselves. The lights of Sansul Fortress have been lit. Our safety has been put at risk. You must all return to your homes. The night-watchers will report to the Assembly. Place protection enchantments around yourselves and your home. Do everything you can to repel any demon . . ."

The old warlock's voice faltered when the six torch lights fired up again. One figure stood upon each pole, the fire licking at their feet. The human-like forms stared down at the crowd with eyes like black pools of nothingness.

"No," said Caitriona tearfully. "No, no . . ."

Adrianna's stomach flipped. The strong energy of the Darkness seeped out from the strangers toward the crowd. People began to cough. Adrianna felt her lungs tighten and itch; as though there was soot in her lungs.

One of the figures stretched his arms out to his sides, smiling. Fangs lengthened past his bottom lip. Adrianna shivered at the thought of those teeth biting into her neck. *The pain must be excruciating*, she thought. His companions were men. All were dressed in black, their attire identifying who they were, or more accurately, *what* they were.

The witches and warlocks huddled together in silent horror and awe, staring up at the evil that had disturbed their celebration.

"I do apologise for interrupting the Samhain festival," said the only one of the six in a grey coat, "but I am afraid the time of peace that followed the end of *The War Against The Angels* has come to a close. *Your* time has come to an end."

"What is he talking about?" Jess whispered to Caitriona.

Kenna's hand moved toward a knife beside a loaf of bread. With trembling hands, she hid the knife within the folds of her skirt, waiting.

"What are you going to do with that?" whispered Adrianna.

Kenna gave her a warning look.

The men jumped elegantly from the poles and landed on their feet. Their eyes glowed as they stared tauntingly at the Wilmota clan.

A few people scuttled closer to the main group.

"They are going to attack," Kenna whispered from the corner of her mouth. "Get ready."

Adrianna's heart pounded painfully in her chest. How did these six expect to attack the whole clan and live? Hundreds outnumbered them! So surely there were more of them in the village, standing by. Adrianna looked around, trying to see. Nothing seemed to be moving, except the odd person sneaking away.

"Vampires are not allowed in Wilmota!" an elder warlock said sternly. "Do you expect us to just let you attack?"

"Do you realise who that is?" whispered Kenna.

"No," said Adrianna. "The vampire, you mean?"

"The one in the grey jacket – I recognise him from my mother's vampire lexicon. He is Morgan, a Commander, I think, in the army."

"They have an *army*?" asked Caitriona, terrified.

"We must use ice-tears against them," Adrianna said to Kenna in a low voice. "That knife will do nothing."

"Using ice-tears goes against our Lore to protect and preserve," Jess whispered behind them.

"I will protect and preserve myself first," Adrianna replied.

"But the elders . . ." Caitriona began.

"The elders can bite me," said Kenna. She looked at Adrianna and nodded. "I am with you. Use fire-spheres too."

The vampires laughed at the crowd. "Touching as your courage may be, it will do nothing against us," said Morgan. He opened his palms and a silver light in the shape of a sphere hovered there. He faced the elder, glancing down at the staff being pointed at his chest.

"It is unnatural," whispered Caitriona pleadingly in Adrianna's ear. "We cannot manipulate nature in order to harm. It destroys the balance!"

"There is no proof of that," replied Adrianna.

"But there are only six!" said Caitriona tearfully. "Why such drastic measures? I cannot do it! I cannot use the wind or earth to kill. What would become of the balance in my soul?"

"The rest are hiding in the buildings," Adrianna heard a witch murmur from the other side of the table. "Open your senses, witches."

Adrianna closed her eyes, reaching out through the earth, and searched for any singular vessels of the Darkness. They would be easy to find in a village that lived off the Light. The witch was right. Vampires were hidden all around the village, waiting for the command to strike.

Morgan's dilated eyes slowly travelled from the warlock's staff to his face, his lips curling back from his teeth. "You think you can fight me, old man?"

"I was around during that war, vampire," the elder said tartly. "I destroyed many of your people. Leave this place now."

"Generous," the vampire hissed, his lips twisted into a mocking smile. "But no." With a blast, he launched the sphere.

There was a collective cry of horror. Jess grabbed Caitriona's arm as the elder fell to his knees with a hole in his chest. As blood gushed onto his shirt and coat, the elder stared defiantly at the vampire.

Sneering, Morgan kicked him onto his back. "That was boring."

Adrianna watched Renauart, her closest neighbour, pull his wife into the shadows. Mathias motioned for Adrianna, Kenna, Caitriona and Jess to come to him, but there was no way to cross the distance without being seen. Adrianna looked around and saw the vampires spreading out.

"Submit and you may live," Morgan told the crowd.

Then, the lights disappeared, casting them once again into darkness.

"No," Adrianna whispered in protest.

Her voice was drowned by the eruption of screams.

Immediately, Kenna tugged her arm and they ran around the table. Caitriona shrieked when Adrianna grabbed her wrist in the dark. She pulled her along hoping Jess had the sense to hold onto Caitriona. They ran down the winding Main Street away from the village centre where people ran for their lives and frantically searched for family members. Dozens sprinted for the Dial Doors while others, members of the Warlock Myriad, night-watchers and elders waited in full view, their palms glowing with fire-spheres, ice-tears and fire-whips.

Suddenly, a light was upon them. Adrianna and Kenna froze, looking back. The Wilmota watchtower light was focused on the square. There was an outburst of colour and fire: dozens of uniformed vampires stood amongst the people, casting fire-spheres in all directions. Adrianna's stomach lurched and dense fear rose up in her throat. The vampires fought with such viciousness she barely believed they had once been part of the people they now cut down. Witches and warlocks fell, bloodied and screaming. A row of warlocks with beards down to their stomachs threw themselves into a band of vampires, throwing punches and fire. One warlock slashed through the vampires with a lightening-whip.

Adrianna watched as a particularly nasty looking vampire with a patch over his left eye set the flower shop alight and watched it burn.

"Soldiers!" Kenna screamed.

"We have to get to the Dial Doors!" cried Adrianna.

"Adrianna!"

Relieved, she spun around upon hearing her guardian's voice. "Fradrik!" she screamed. But they were too far apart. Fradrik was in the midst of a group of warlocks being surrounded. "Look out!"

"*Run!*" he said, opening his palms. "Get out of here!"

"Get down!" Caitriona shouted, falling to her knees as an enormous sphere of fire hurtled toward them.

In a massive explosion, it landed only a few yards away. Blown off her feet, Adrianna lay flat on the ground with her hands over her ears. Her head reeled. Kenna pulled her up. Adrianna staggered to her feet, dragging Caitriona with her. Jess, on all fours, shook her head in a daze. "This is not happening." They looked to the village centre.

"The vampires are not here for a mass feeding," said Kenna. "They are here to capture us!"

Witches were being bound and knocked unconscious. "Peruva!" Adrianna called out to the sorceress, watching as she trapped her assailant in a small tornado, only to be attacked from behind and wrestled to the ground. Pinned face down, the vampire tied Peruva's hands behind her back. When he was done, he pulled her head up by the hair. "Let him out!"

Peruva looked at the tornado. The vampire inside struggled against the tightening vortex. "No," she said.

The vampire yanked her to her feet. He slammed her against a shop door. "You cannot control the air if you are in pain," he said, opening his palm. An ice-tear formed.

Peruva's eyes widened. "I cannot release him with bound hands."

"Liar!" He cast the ice-tear into her arm.

"No!" Adrianna screamed, making to run and help.

"Stop! We have to go," said Kenna desperately, pulling on Adrianna's hand. "They are coming this way!"

Adrianna looked over her shoulder as she ran in the direction of the Dial Doors. "Why are we not fighting back?" she asked, searching for Fradrik. With the power to control the elements, surely the older people would have the sense to merge with their Element and create waves of water of waves of fire big enough to wash away the vampires. The earth elementals could easily form a wall to block them; yet barely any witch or warlock was using anything more than fire-spheres and close combat to fight.

Warlocks were being beaten down; some were left to bleed on the ground while others were dragged away. Adrianna watched as Johan the painter was thrashed on the back of his legs. He fell to his knees and was clubbed on the back of the head by a small, spindly, greenish creature with an oversized head and pointed nose.

Caitriona gasped. "Goblins!"

Goblins were one of the most evil creatures native to the Elemental Plane. They were the loyal servants of vampires and Black Magick conjurors.

Adrianna saw children were being snatched by vampire soldiers and thrown into cages, which were then dragged off by goblins strapped to the cage fronts. Adrianna caught the broken scream of a child and spun around in time to see a young boy being dragged by the hair into a cage already filled with sobbing children. The goblin slammed the door shut and sneered at the terrified young ones.

"We must stop them!" cried Adrianna, turning to run back.

Suddenly, a roar split the air and beasts in the shape of wolves descended upon the village. These were creatures unlike any Adrianna had seen before. They were not the grey highland wolves that roamed the forest outskirts. There was something strange, unnatural about these gigantic animals. Each face was contorted in violent focus. They crawled over homes, ransacked gardens and shops as they made their way to the square like an unstoppable landslide, unleashing their brutality upon the people.

"*What are they*?" screamed Caitriona, her voice going hoarse.

"I have no idea."

Adrianna's heart clenched. She stood rooted to the spot as one of the beasts cut down a warlock, pinning him to the earth with its heavy front paws before it ripped out his throat. Blood splattered across the ground like rain. The wolf howled and turned, searching for its next victim. Swiftly hit with an infusion of courage she did not know she had, she sprinted to the children who had just been snatched and imprisoned in the goblin-guarded cage. Raising her hand, palm open, she released a fire-sphere, hitting a goblin in the face. It shrieked, clutching its face in agony and fell into the grass. With her adrenalin rising, she cast an ice-tear into its chest. It gave a short cry and went limp.

Taking Adrianna's lead, Caitriona ran around to the goblin strapped to the front of the cage and cast a fire-sphere into its face. It raised a long-fingered hand to scratch at her as Caitriona jumped back. "You evil little cretin!"

Adrianna unlocked the cage and the hysterical children tumbled out.

"Run into the Sleeping Forest!" Adrianna told them. "Hester, you lead them. Find the faeries!"

"Run quickly!" Kenna yelled when they hesitated.

Adrianna yelped as a vampire descended upon her from the sky. Caitriona froze, staring at him with wide eyes. The vampire raised his arm and Adrianna ducked instinctively.

"No!" Kenna screamed. She threw an ice-tear, hitting him in the shoulder. "Come on!" she said as the vampire groaned, disappearing into a vapour.

They sprinted toward the Dial Doors. They were only metres away from the threshold of the first door when there was a massive blast. One by one the six Dial Doors exploded. Adrianna watched as their only means of escape disappeared before their eyes in a pile of splinters and fire.

"More are coming!" Jess cried, pointing to the vampire's emerging from a burning turret-house.

"Head for my cottage!" said Adrianna.

"We'll never make it that far!" said Caitriona.

"I have a cramp," said Jess, holding her side.

A house exploded in the village centre and the ground shook. Soldiers made their way through the village in hordes. Nothing stood in their way. They blasted, trampled over, set ablaze, crushed and imprisoned everything in their path.

Needing to take cover, Adrianna crouched behind the wishing well and opened her palm, ready to strike. She saw Ingrid, a Spellmaker's apprentice, captured as she ran through a cloud of smoke, making for the port to the east. The vampire did not wait before plunging his fangs into her throat, drinking deeply. Sickened, Adrianna tried to look away but the nightmarish scene had captured her focus. When he was finished, the vampire lifted his face, licking Ingrid's blood from his lips with a look of deep satisfaction. He dropped her body into the fountain, discarding her as though she were inconsequential garbage, unworthy of a second thought. The water ran red with what remained of Ingrid's blood.

Adrianna turned to her friends when Caitriona screamed for her brother. "Cedar!"

"It's a demon!" Jess wailed hysterically.

Adrianna looked up with a gasp. Close by, on Fellowtop Hill, Cedar was being circled by a Rakasha demon. A hairless, thin, scaly, humanoid being with unnaturally long limbs and razor sharp nails, its mouth was full of long, sharp yellow teeth dripping with venomous saliva. The narrow slits it had for eyes were black with yellow irises, and focused on the young warlock it was preparing to strike down. The demon moved smoothly with hunched shoulders, tilting its head left and right and baring its teeth.

Cedar looked as though he had battled at length. His shirt was bloodied and hung off his chest in shreds. His normally perfect kempt blonde hair stuck to his sweaty, dirty face.

"It is going to kill him!" said Caitriona.

Adrianna leaped up from her position by the wishing well and ran up the small hill. Cedar took a step back from the demon as it opened its mouth wide. Adrianna saw her opportunity: she opened her palm and cast a fire-sphere directly into the demon's face, blocking the rising shrill cry in its throat. Cedar followed her lead, casting another sphere before the demon released an ear-piercing scream and burst into flames. The scream of a Rakasha was its primary weapon. A few moments of exposure to the sound hit sensitive nerves in elementals that sent them mad.

"Run, Cedar!"

Cedar spun around and grabbed Adrianna's arm. They ran down and joined Kenna, Jess and Caitriona by the wishing well. Caitriona flung her arms around her brother.

"Go, *go*!" he told them. "Into the Sleeping Forest. The nymphs will give you shelter."

"Where are Ralphus and Mathias?" Adrianna asked desperately.

Cedar shook his head. "We were separated."

Kenna screamed. "Cedar! They are coming!"

Adrianna's arms began to itch and a strange burning sensation spread along her palms. She had never conjured so many ice-tears and fire-spheres in her life and wished more than ever that she had her Elemental power. She and Cedar spun around in unison and blindly cast fire-spheres at the oncoming soldiers.

The soldiers blocked their attacks with ease, dodging and deflecting. Once Kenna and Jess joined in, Adrianna called out to Caitriona. "Curse them!"

Caitriona's eyes widened. "I cannot!"

"Do it!" she screamed, casting an ice-tear into the nearest soldier's leg.

Shaking, Caitriona looked tearfully around at the vampires descending on them. They had waited too long. If they had run directly into the forest, they would have been safe. There was no place of safety now. She opened her mouth to speak, blinded by tears, but no sound came forth.

Adrianna knew she had to kill the soldier in front of her before he took the form of his demon. As a vampire, she had a hope of killing him, but as a demon he was twice as powerful as she, a mere underage witch yet to complete her studies. She locked eyes with the vampire and stepped back, moving away from the group.

"I think I will keep you for myself," the vampire said, pulling the ice-tear from his thigh.

"I will kill you first."

"You will learn to obey," the vampire said, a cruel smile forming at his lips. "I will enjoy teaching you."

Behind her, Jess cried out, having been struck across the face.

Adrianna's chest swelled with fury but before she could retort or even prepare herself for his attack, the vampire faded into mist. She blinked stupidly, thinking her eyes were playing tricks on her. Her body tingled with anticipation of his attack. The mist before her was dense and black, like a fog. "Wraith!" she bellowed in warning, stepping away.

"A Wraith?" Kenna lost concentration and the fire-sphere intended for the vampire before her veered off course. The vampire moved swiftly, pinning her hands behind her back.

Kenna kicked at him madly.

Another had overpowered Cedar and he was fighting with difficulty as the vampire attempted to tie his hands behind his back.

Adrianna cast a fire-sphere into the fog but it moved too quickly for her. She was grabbed from behind and spun around to face the vampire who had re-formed solidly in the blink of an eye.

"Let go of me!"

"Be silent," he said.

Adrianna shoved her knee to his groin as hard as she could and pressed her hand to his chest. Only a direct hit to the heart would kill him. An ice-tear formed in her palm and plunged into his chest, and she hoped, his heart. The vampire froze, staring at her. Trembling, he fell to his knees and fell on his face.

Kenna bit at the vampire as he tied her hands. Adrianna cast a well-aimed ice-tear into his heart and pushed him away from her friend. She looked away as Kenna cast a fire-sphere into his face. "Animal."

Kenna swung around and kicked the vampire pinning Cedar to the ground. The two men scuffled, beating each other. Adrianna threw an ice-tear at the soldier's leg, debilitating him. Cedar immediately took the opportunity and forced the vampire's mouth open, holding him to the ground by grinding his knee in the vampire's chest. "Adrianna! Fire!" he yelled.

The vampire struggled. Cedar's fingers dug into the sides of the vampire's cheeks, keeping him from closing his mouth. Adrianna cast a fire-sphere into the vampire's open mouth and Cedar clamped his jaw together.

The vampire's eyes faded to black as his chest glowed from the inside as the flames spread. With each violent spasm, Adrianna felt a rush of pity for his suffering. This man has been a warlock once, perhaps even from Wilmota. The heat from his body touched Adrianna's face but she did not step away. Engulfed in fire, the vampire was no more.

By the time Cedar got up, ripping off his torn shirt, Jess and Caitriona were gone. He used the shredded garment to help stem the flow of blood from his nose.

"What happened?" Adrianna asked, panting. Her flower wreath had been lost on the trail and her hair was a mess of pins and waves. Although her dress was patched with soot and dirt, it was nowhere near the disastrous state of Kenna's dress. The skirt had been ripped up the front, forcing her to hold it together with her hand to cover her thighs.

"Jess! Cait!" Kenna screamed, looking around, terrified. "Jess!"

Adrianna held back tears as Kenna's desperately screamed for their friends.

"Keep moving," Cedar demanded, pulling them both away from the massacre.

"Stop!" It was another soldier.

"Keep running," said Cedar, pushing them forward.

Adrianna grabbed Kenna's hand and sprinted for her cottage. They were halfway down the winding path that ran parallel to a small lake when Adrianna tried to stop her. "We have to go back to the village!"

"We cannot. We have to hide. No one can help them now," Kenna said breathlessly.

They continued to run down the path. Finally, Adrianna's cottage was visible. Never in her life had she been so happy to see its manicured garden. The screams from the village were distant echoes and the blasts still resonated through the earth. Overcome with relief, Adrianna grabbed the front gate and made to open it when Kenna stopped her.

"Hello, witches."

Two vampires emerged, one from either side of her cottage.

"Don't bother running," said the vampire nearest to Kenna. He unsheathed a curved bladed sword and blocked Kenna's fire-sphere. Leaping through the air, he landed behind her. "Be a good little girl," he hissed, snatching her throat.

Adrianna kept her eyes on the vampire circling her. He was toying with her, taunting her into begging for her life. By the look in his eye, she knew he had no intention of killing her, at least not just yet.

"Scared?"

"Never," she spat. She followed his movements and extended her arm, holding out a fire-sphere.

"So she knows how to play," the vampire said provokingly. "Take your best shot, pretty."

Adrianna glared at him. "Do *not* call me that."

The vampire laughed, holding his arms out. "I'll give you a free one. Right here." He pointed to his heart.

Seething, she hit his arm but he did not even flinch.

The vampire struck. He grabbed her face and twisted her arm painfully behind her back. "I suggest you become afraid, witch."

Adrianna cried out as his grip tightened.

Her heart skipped a beat as the vampire's fangs lengthened. His brown eyes darkened; the blackness of his pupil enlarged and seeped into the whites until she found herself staring into a dark abyss. "We have won," he promised before striking her. Before she could even register the pain, her world went black.

Chapter Two

The Underground Chambers

ADRIANNA WOKE WITH A start.

Her eyes snapped open, staring ahead. *What happened?* There was a dull pulsing in her head, and her whole body buzzed with energy. Her palms felt as though they were burning.

Someone screamed.

The attack! She sat up and immediately regretted it. Her vision blurred and a blistering headache forced her to lie back down. The distant cries for help were terrible to hear. Feeling around, she ran her stinging hands over the surface around her. A bed? Her heart lifted. Someone must have found her and brought her to an infirmary. *But . . .* another scream sounded in the distance, and her mind returned to the attack. The last thing she remembered was being knocked unconscious by a vampire. As icy terror gripped her chest, she opened her eyes and stared blurrily at the ceiling.

Slowly, Adrianna forced her tender muscles to move and she slid off the bed. She groaned softly and blinked rapidly in an attempt to clear her vision. The chill of the room set in. She hunched her shoulders, bringing her arms around herself. The tenderness of her hands was soothed mildly by the cold air. Balancing against the bed for a moment, her vision slowly cleared before she took a few steps.

The screams were awful. Terrible and gut wrenching, they were more cries of sadness than of pain. *This is a bedroom*, she told herself. She stood still for a moment, listening for any sounds. When all seemed to be clear, she pulled the door open, quietly stepped over the thresh hold, and returned the door to its exact position. She found herself in a spacious, majestically decorated dark blue room. A welcoming fire was alight in the fireplace, beckoning her toward its heat. As she crept toward it, she noticed the floor to ceiling windows to her right covered by heavy, silk drapes.

"No," she whispered, ready to cry. "No . . ."

The vampire had brought her to Sansul Fortress.

Adrianna stood in the middle of the room, staring at the heavy wooden door before her. That was her way out.

The pleading and strangled voices instilled a terror into the very depths of her soul like none she had ever felt or imagined before.

Adrianna's knees gave out beneath her. She fell into a heap, sobbing help-lessly. What had happened to her? The whole world was crying out; the land, the air, the mere energy from which elementals drew strength mourned their loss. On her hands and knees, she cried until her chest burned with the same ferocity as her hands. What was the vampire going to do? Rape her? Turn her? Torture and submit her to endless suffering? "Why?" she cried. "Why? Why?"

Adrianna crawled into the corner of the room, hoping to become one with the wall. She lifted her knees to her chest and wrapped her arms around them. Rocking back and forth, she wept.

"I will not give into them," she whispered finally, tears running down her cheeks. "I will not give into them. I will not give into them." She chanted the words like a mantra.

It was dawn when the muted screams subsided and the fortress stood still. Adrianna was aware that the voices were those of her clan, captured, as she was. But where were they? They were not close enough to be in a neighbouring room. Was she destined to be imprisoned, or was hers to be a blunt end? When would the vampire return to serve upon her his cruel amusement?

Adrianna knew the vampires would lock down the estate, covering windows and bolting the front doors, for they were weakened in the sunlight.

She wiped her face with the back of her hand and leaned her head against the wall. Perhaps the vampire would not come for her so soon. A creak sounded from the far side of the room and sent her heart racing. A bolt of fear shot through her chest as the top of the door opened slightly, casting a sliver of light across the ceiling. Her eyes widened and panic sucked the air from her lungs. Giving in, she fainted.

Two shadowed figures entered and the oil lamps around the blue room came to life. In the dimness, the men looked around for the witch they had hidden.

"Liam," the fair-haired vampire said suspiciously, eyeing the open bedroom door. "Where is she?" He went directly to the bedroom, yanking back the bed-covers only to find the bed empty.

"We left her here. That is where I put her. You saw me, Daniel." Liam felt behind the curtains. He could not look, as the sun was rising outside. He checked beneath the couches, around the sitting room and found nothing.

"Here," said Daniel, carrying the unconscious girl from the corner of the room.

Liam watched as Daniel put her on the bed. Her face was pale and her lips had lost their colour. Daniel looked at her tear-streaked face and turned her dainty hands over. Her palms were bright red. She had fought like a lion for her life. For now he knew she was at peace, but she would wake before long. "We cannot keep her here in secret," Liam said in a soft voice. "The coven will sense her."

"So we just say we caught her to keep her for our own private use," Daniel justified.

Liam's eyes turned black. His face contorted in an ugly sneer. "She isn't an animal, Daniel!"

"If you want her to become a blood slave then so be it, Liam," Daniel snapped. "They'll put her with the other captives in the underground chambers. I agreed to do this because you insisted."

Liam shook his head. "So it has come to this?" he asked softly. "We have conquered the witches – the people of which we were once a part."

Daniel leaned against the bedpost. "We are different now, *better*," he hissed. "Try not to dwell on the past." He looked down at the sleeping witch. "Don't even dwell on *her* – once she sees what you have become she won't remember who you were."

"She was our friend," Liam argued.

"And now she's our prisoner," Daniel replied indifferently.

Adrianna shifted at the distant sound of voices. Her hand went to her head and she opened her eyes, staring around vacantly. *Perhaps he will not come.* When she sat up, she saw them; two pale-faced vampires, reeking of the Darkness. She jumped back, retreating until her back hit the headboard. Her palms ached but she knew she could conjure more fire-spheres if necessary.

The vampires remained at the foot of the bed. Neither was in the uniform worn by the soldiers who attacked her clan. The blond vampire wore a waist-length deep blue jacket and the shirt beneath it was untucked. Vampires were known to present themselves immaculately, down to the lowest-ranking soldier. The dark-haired vampire stared at her strangely.

Adrianna fixed him with a glare. "You are not the vampires who attacked me."

"No, we are not. We are not going to hurt you," said Liam.

"Yet," Daniel muttered.

"Don't lie!" she snapped. "You didn't attack my home and kidnap me to keep me alive."

"Adrianna, we brought you here so the others wouldn't get you," Liam said.

"How do you know my name?" Adrianna looked from one to the other confusedly.

It was clear she did not remember them. Liam understood. It was six years since they had been turned. She must have thought them dead.

"You do not remember us?" Liam asked.

Adrianna sneered. "I am not friendly with vampires."

"I am Liam," he said. "And, this is Daniel."

Adrianna studied them, wanting to catch them in their lie. *Impossible,* she thought. They looked far too old. Daniel and Liam had been mere children of ten and four summers the night of their kidnapping. Liam was a quiet and easily led boy, and Daniel, confident and canny in his thinking.

The Daniel before her was very tall, broad shouldered, well-built and lean limbed. His long blond hair was tied back from his pale face. He had an air of charisma, yet condescension shined through his silver eyes and demeanour. Liam was a powerfully built vampire, his hair short, black and wavy. But he was more of a dark, shadowy figure. Instead of being confident in his vampiric power he seemed to withhold it, almost as if he were ashamed of it. Something about him made Adrianna uneasy, more so than Daniel. Liam's eyes were cold, void of emotion.

Adrianna swallowed. Her eyes lingered on Daniel for a moment, until she looked away sharply. The past did not matter. She may have known Daniel the child, but Daniel the vampire was somebody quite different. If they were indeed who they said they were. They were vampires and part of the coven that invaded her quiet village and subjected them to murder and slavery. "So?" she asked bluntly.

"She is going to be trouble," muttered Daniel.

Adrianna glared at him.

"We don't want to send you to be with the others," Liam said calmly. "You can stay here."

"And be your personal slave?" she asked coldly. "I would rather be drained."

"I can do that," said Daniel, his fangs lengthening. "It will teach you to hold that snake tongue of yours."

Adrianna grimaced at the sight of his fangs. She looked him in the eyes and paled. His eyes were no longer silver but black.

"Restrain yourself," Liam told him.

"You have no idea what you have done," she said, finding herself slightly breathless. "Or perhaps you do . . . all those people . . ."

The fall of her clan was absolute. It could never be undone.

"We cannot be away too long," said Liam. His eyes faded to black and he tilted his head. Adrianna felt him using his senses to feel beyond the walls, outside of the fortress. "They have almost all returned. Reports must be made to the Council."

"Just put her with the others," said Daniel, his eyes reverted from black to silver. "She's as stubborn as a wild centaur."

"It's better than being a blood sucker," she snapped.

Daniel grabbed her arm and yanked her off the bed. "Did your mother teach you that?" he shot back. "Why don't you think of a few more petty insults while you're branded, chained and forced to give your blood?"

"I will," she replied confidently.

"Let her go," Liam told Daniel, his own cold hand going around Adrianna's other arm.

Adrianna immediately snatched it from his grip. "Do *not* touch me!" The impact of Liam's hand felt as though a red-hot poker singed through her arm. Liam's expression faltered, as if he was sorry for touching her in the first place. She could not release herself from Daniel's grip so easily.

"We should teach her a lesson," said Daniel. "Respect," he hissed in Adrianna's ear, "for her *masters*."

A hot, tingle ran down her spine the moment his breath touched her skin. Was it fear or perhaps disgust that bubbled in her stomach? "Do not get used to that title," she replied darkly. She stared ahead at the door, not daring to meet his eyes.

Daniel continued to stare down his nose at her. His grip did not tighten nor did it relent. Instead, he shoved her forward. "Your lesson starts now."

Daniel pulled Adrianna down the many long, meandering halls until they reached the centre of the fortress. It was eerily silent. The voices of the imprisoned witches could no longer be heard, they were replaced by an uncomfortable quiet.

Momentarily engrossed in the surprising beauty of her surroundings, Adrianna allowed Daniel to lead her without argument. As a child, she and her friends would imagine cold, drafty halls that ran with blood, moth eaten, blood-stained carpets and rat infested dungeons beneath, but their imaginings had been quite different from the reality she now faced.

Beautiful gilded mirrors hung from the deep-toned walls that varied in greens, blues and reds. Nothing seemed worn or used; the carpets looked like the work of the rug-makers from the City of Tents. The high ceilings were mostly painted. Some halls were lit with torches on the walls, and others had chandeliers. The scent of sandalwood lingered in the air.

It was the perfect abode for people who prided themselves on beauty and perfection.

Daniel walked her down what she took to be back corridors because she saw nothing but doors, stairs and the odd window. She saw no foyer, reception rooms or any other people for that matter. Where were the witches? Had the vampires killed them all, or were they being kept in the infamous underground chambers? Had they been slaughtered? *No*, she told herself. Her mind could simply not imagine such a thing and refused to acknowledge the possibility that it too would be her fate.

"What did you do to my clan?" she demanded as they walked toward a black-clad guard standing in front of a bolted door.

"I have another one," Daniel spoke to the guard.

The door was immediately unlocked.

"I *said*, what-did-you-do-to-my-people?"

Daniel shoved her inside.

Adrianna grabbed onto the wall to keep from falling as she stumbled on the stairs. She straightened, and with a gasp, found herself staring down at a mass of witches. Well over one hundred witches stood, sat and paced the cold chambers. They turned toward the opening door with expressions of angst and surprise. Realising who had been thrown in to join them, they looked at her with pity. The witches' beautiful dresses, most made especially for the festival, were ripped, burned and dishevelled from the fight. Adrianna scanned their faces through the dim lights but could not find Kenna. All were covered in cuts, bruises and minor wounds. Why were there no men? Where were the warlocks? The children?

Daniel smirked behind her. "Glad to see you are finally holding your sharp tongue."

Adrianna turned to the door as it slammed closed. "You cannot do this to us!" she screamed, banging her fist against the wood.

"It is no use," said a voice close behind her. "There is no way out."

Adrianna spun around. "Rosamunda!" she said, throwing her arms around her neighbour. "I thought you would have escaped. You knocked down so many vampires when I saw you."

"Thank goodness for you, Adrianna," Rosamunda said softly. "Come." She led Adrianna further into the room and they sat in a free space against the wall. Rosamunda smiled ruefully as the others began to settle into their prison. Her usually neat, shiny red hair was tied back from her flushed face but her green eyes had yet to lose their spark. Her gown, a mass of patterned satin and lace, was scorched and ripped, her striped stockings torn and nicked. Adrianna knew it had taken a lot out of the vampires to finally overpower this voluptuous witch.

"Well, I fought my way through a group of those *beasts*," she said, savagely pushing out the last word, "and was able to pass the girls to Renauart before I was caught. Ren tried to come back for me, but I told him our girls were more important. He continued to fight the vampire who had tied me up and was wounded." She shook her head sadly. "I just hope he escaped with the children."

"Oh, Rosa," Adrianna said sadly. "Renauart will have taken them somewhere safe."

"By the blessings of the Light I hope so," Rosamunda said tearfully. She took a deep breath and shook her head as if trying to free herself from the sadness.

"Have you seen Kenna?" Adrianna asked.

"She is probably in one of the other rooms," she said. "They have many others like this one."

Adrianna shivered. As she looked around, she realised why this was the perfect prison for witches. There was nothing in the room except the flames from the chandelier and torches from which they could take energy. The walls were made of perfectly cut, equal-sized bricks of limestone, in which there was no natural energy. Unlike a substance such as wood or dirt, limestone was void of power.

The room was long and narrow, illuminated by a lone, flickering chandelier and torches. Unfortunately, the floor was made of marble, another dead energy. Marble was widely used by vampires for decoration because it had a substance in its small veins that connected with the Darkness. For witches, it was useless. With no windows, all those whose Element was air were left with nothing from which to draw. Those of the earth Element would slowly suffocate with the limestone and marble surrounding them. Earth elementals needed to be surrounded by nature to be empowered. Grass, dirt, wood, air, sun, the moon, and water – all provided them the power and energy they needed to not only conjure magic and meld with the Elements, but also to survive.

"They put all the fire Elementals in a different room," Rosamunda told her. "They are most likely locked up in complete darkness."

"The vampires do not miss a thing, do they?" Adrianna muttered, staring at the marble.

Unfortunately, the only way out was through the bolted door. None of the witches seemed in any way able to fight anymore. Many had collapsed from utter exhaustion.

Adrianna was glad to sit beneath one of the torches. The heat soothed her skin. Basking in its warm glow, she stared around at her clanswomen and recognised many of them as immediate neighbours. Others were from Upper and Lower Wilmota and a fair few were from other clans. She smiled at Mada Brune, a witch who ran the poppy farm, and sent a small wave to Annie and Collette the identical twins who read messages through fire. Collette was trying to get Annie to sleep, but the trembling witch sobbed. Margarithe, a witch married to a tradesman from the City of Tents had made herself a pillow using her skirt. Three of the four village elders, Lizzette, Mara and Adalina, walked amongst the youngest witches in the room, attempting to soothe their fears.

Only hours ago we were dancing and singing in the village, Adrianna thought sadly. Her thoughts turned to Fradrik. What had become of her guardian? Had he been killed? Or perhaps forced to the same place all the warlocks had been taken? *Wherever that was.* Wishing she were safely tucked into her warm bed,

Adrianna tried to keep from crying again. She took a deep breath, allowing her lungs to swell as far as they allowed and swallowed, forcing tears down.

"What do you think they are going to do to us?" a woman asked, staring ahead with defeated eyes.

Blonde and freckled, the witch sat cross-legged next to Adrianna, her back against the wall. She picked at her nails. Her mismatched stockings were ripped and grass stained, but otherwise she looked unharmed. Adrianna did not know if the question was directed at her, and if it was, she didn't know what to say.

"Nothing too horrible, I hope," Adrianna said a moment later. She loosened the laces on her shoes and noticed the knees of her own stockings were muddied.

The witch closed her eyes. "They wouldn't kidnap us like this if they did not intend to hurt us," she said tearfully, her voice quivering.

"Shh," Mara hissed, "you'll scare the younger ones."

"I'm not scared," said Samantha, a girl of ten and five summers. She rolled her cardigan into a ball, looking to use it as a pillow. "Honestly, I'll fight a vampire any day instead of staying locked up in here."

As the women talked amongst themselves, muttering about the girl's inability to understand how grave their situation was, the woman next to Adrianna finally looked at her.

"They . . . they murdered my sister in front of me," the woman said. "Peta was about your age. She had not yet gained her Element. All she had were the fire-spheres and ice-tears. Still she was not fast enough with them. Then when those wolves . . ." Her voice broke and she buried her face in her hands.

Adrianna wrapped an arm around the woman. "It was not your fault," she whispered as the witch sobbed helplessly. "Your sister has gone peacefully to the Spirit Plane."

As the day turned to night, the women finally began to fall asleep. The witch turned to Adrianna, who was still awake, and introduced herself. "I am Orla."

"I am Adrianna. This is Rosamunda."

Rosamunda was asleep, resting her head on Adrianna's legs.

"Thank you for listening to me," said Orla. "I felt as if I was going to burst." She sighed. "I wish I could wipe this whole night from my memory."

"I think we could all do with a memory altering spell right now," she said, "but I doubt any of us has the strength."

"My sister was going to be married, you know," said Orla; her eyes alight with the memory. "She had only just convinced our parents to allow her to marry her sweetheart yesterday. He was from your village. It's why we are here. She was so happy. She was different from me, always happy, always saw the good in all beings and was a friend to everyone. Peta was *my* best friend."

"I know what you mean," said Adrianna, thinking of Kenna.

CHAPTER THREE

The Rise of the New Regime

"**K**ENNA! GET AWAY FROM there!"

As Renauart implored, Kenna shrank back from the window. Trembling, she knelt in the corner. Her brown eyes darted from Renauart, who sat on the opposite side of the corridor, to the window. He motioned for her to remain quiet as he crouched, bouncing lightly on the balls of his feet ready to lunge at anyone who passed through the front door.

They were in the abandoned home of Celeste, the herbalist. Kenna had taken refuge here when she escaped the clutches of a vampire soldier. After Adrianna had been knocked unconscious and carried away, Kenna was left to battle alone. She fought off and killed many vampires in her attempt to find Adrianna, but no matter how many times she screamed for her best friend or where she looked, Adrianna was gone. Like Caitriona, Jess, Rosamunda, Cedar and even Ralphus, she would likely never see them again.

The Gordgáin, a rebel group made up of the folk of the Light, found her in the midst of the smoke and dying embers and brought her to the safety of the Gordgáin sanctuary, an underground city created as a refuge during *The War Against The Angels*. It was there that Renauart, with his daughters Jane and Iona, saw her trying to sneak back above ground. They had barely escaped with their lives but Kenna was fighting tooth and nail to return to the village and find her beloved friend. Renauart knew Kenna's tempestuousness would get her into trouble or killed. Bloodied, bruised, and with her clothes torn and singed, Kenna had stood at the sanctuary entrance and demanded to be allowed to leave.

Renauart left his daughters in the care of a survivor and accompanied Kenna, refusing to let her leave the sanctuary alone. "Besides," he confided, "I may find Rosamunda."

During the night, all those still able engaged in battle against the invading vampires of Sansul Fortress. But they were no match for the vampires. Refusing to use their Elemental powers to destroy, the witches and warlocks were left with no defences but fire-spheres, ice-tears and spells, and against the strength of the Darkness, they were far inferior. Still, as all hope seemed to fade, members of the Warlock Myriad, those left in Wilmota, assembled in the daylight hours when the vampires had retreated to the fortress. On this second night of fighting the Warlock Myriad spilled the blood of their enemy.

Kenna clamped her hands over her mouth, stifling a gasp, as footsteps sounded outside. They were slow, deliberate, taunting. Her senses told her it was a soldier, one of those conducting a sweep of the village for stragglers. The vampires knew the witches had Disappearing Cupboards, Staircase Trunks; trunks that when opened with the right key, would lead you into an underground bunker, hag disguises and some even had their own Dial Doors. Vampires had taken to burning homes; smoking them out of their hiding places.

Kenna's eyes widened as the footsteps came closer, up the front steps, until – silence. Renauart stared fiercely at the door; beads of sweat covered his face. Kenna's fingers curled around her mouth as she fought the urge to scream. She took a deep, shuddering breath through her nose and glanced up at the window. From behind the flimsy, white curtain, a slight shadow loomed. The hairs on her arms stood on end.

Her eyes snapped to the door handle. It turned, right to left and back again. Suddenly, a great explosion sounded. Splinters of wood, fire and smoke flew into the air. Kenna screamed and covered her head to protect herself from the debris.

The soldier looked directly at her as he stepped through the threshold.

Renauart launched himself onto the vampire. Kenna watched as he wrestled the vampire to the ground, expertly twisting one of the vampire's arms behind his back as he dug his knee between his shoulder blades, pinning him down. The vampire released a low growl and rolled sharply onto his side, taking Renauart with him.

Kenna sprang into action. The soldier almost managed to overpower Renauart when she grabbed onto the ladle hanging from the kitchen dresser and swung it into the vampire's face. There was a *crack* as the ladle struck his skull. The vampire groaned, clutching his temple. Kenna took the vampire's gloved hands by the wrists and held them down as Renauart opened his palm. A fire-sphere hovered above his hand. "Get ready..." Renauart sent it into the soldier's mouth and pushed his jaw closed. The vampire's body thrashed and shuddered. "Now!"

Kenna and Renauart jumped away just before the soldier's body burst into flames and faded to ashes.

"Let's go," said Renauart, pulling Kenna to the back of the house.

"We must go to Adrianna's cottage," Kenna panted as she followed.

Renauart stopped. "Kenna," he said sternly. "Adrianna is *not* here. If she were, we would have found her. All survivors are with the Gordgáin or fleeing to Aires. We need to go back to the sanctuary and connect with the neighbouring clans. That soldier was easily killed because he was weak. We were lucky. Any other would have killed you on sight and overpowered me without much difficulty."

"I am not giving up on her," Kenna protested.

"And I am not telling you to. I am telling you to cease risking your life to find her here," said Renauart. "She *is not here.*"

"Why has this happened? Are we at war?"

"If you want answers, we must return to the Gordgáin. And we are most certainly at war."

~

The witches woke with a start as the prison door burst open.

"Stand up, witches! Now!" the guard barked, striding in with a line-up of masked, gloved soldiers.

Adrianna lifted her head off Orla's shoulder. Rosamunda rose slowly to her feet. She blinked rapidly and tried to adjust her eyes to the minimal light of the room.

A dozen soldiers entered, spreading out from one end of the room to the other. They wore uniforms of black, gloves and masks over their eyes.

The witches were ordered to stand against the walls and put their hands behind their backs.

The vampire in the doorway disdainfully scanned the women with his protruding blood shot eyes. He had the distinct air of a man who enjoyed seeing others suffer. Adrianna cringed at his harsh, goblin-like voice.

"Separate the older ones from the others," he growled. "We will find another use for them."

"What? Why?" Adrianna whispered to Rosamunda.

"They are more powerful," she whispered back, trying not to move her lips.

Margarithe refused to let go of her grandmother and shouted at the vampire who ripped her away. "What are you going to do with her?"

"There is no point in arguing," the guard said with finality. "If you put up a struggle you will be eliminated."

"Be calm, my child," Margarithe's grandmother replied gently. She did not physically look much older than many of the other witches, and was therefore not one of the few who had chosen to age with time, like Lizzette the elder. Still, the vampires were able to sense her age and the life in her blood. It was richer, better for a vampire to drink.

Rosamunda and Orla were sorted into the same group as Adrianna. Their hands were bound before they were led out of the prison and down a series of empty, limestone passageways on the far side of the fortress. They walked in silence; nobody dared to even cry for fear of being killed on the spot.

Adrianna felt dizzy and ill on the journey to their new prison. The surrounding Darkness would slowly suffocate them until the Light no longer existed within and they died. The lack of natural elements, especially water and earth, made it difficult for the witches to repel the Darkness. She felt the weight of the walls bearing down on her like a thousand boulders.

The line came to an abrupt halt. Adrianna felt Rosamunda stiffen behind her and Orla began to quiver. Footsteps came toward them. Adrianna watched two pairs of black, buckled boots stop in front of her.

"Is this her?" asked the guard.

"Yes," the other replied. "I have a personal interest in this one."

"All right, Liam. She's all yours. Make sure you brand her."

What? Adrianna thought as Liam pulled her out of the line. She felt the same burning sensation on her skin as she did when he had touched her before, but she ignored it. Glancing back to Rosamunda and Orla, the line began to move again. *Where are the others going?*

She yanked her arm from his grasp. "Let go. I am not going to run away."

Liam did not say anything and continued walking. Leading her down the same corridor Daniel had taken her through, he opened the door to his quarters and motioned for her to enter, closing it sharply behind her.

Adrianna stood back as he removed his long coat; having no wish to bring herself closer to her impending death. *He is going to use me for blood. What a disgusting way to die,* she lamented.

The dimly lit circular room was much warmer than the rest of the fortress due to the fireplace nestled in the wall. Silk drapes covered the windows to her left. She made a mental note to check if they were locked. Two elegant wingchairs stood on a green rug in front of the fire, and after a night of sitting on a marble floor with aching muscles and a terrible headache, she wanted to collapse on them and sleep forever.

The richly decorated room was dark despite the dozens of candles. She wondered how vampires could possibly see in such little light.

"Why did you bring me here?"

"Believe me when I say, you do not want to go where the others are headed," said Liam, opening the curtains to reveal a ceiling-to-floor window. In was night and judging by the flecks of water on the glass, it had recently rained.

"That is not an answer."

"Sit down," he said, pouring a steaming, clear liquid into a small cup.

Adrianna moved slowly and did as she was told, choosing the wingchair closest to the fire. As he put the cup down in front of her, she looked at him expectantly and lifted her bound hands. The rope and cloth around her fingers had made her hands stiff. Liam hesitated in releasing her.

"I will not try to escape," she said, looking him in the eye.

Liam's ice-cold hands untied hers and threw the rope into the fire. Adrianna flexed her long fingers and rubbed her wrists as he sat opposite her. She looked at the steaming cup suspiciously.

"I am not planning to poison you," he said. "You know what it is."

Adrianna took the cup and smelt the liquid. Her stomach squirmed, reminding her of how hungry she was. She had not eaten in over a day. It smelled of mint and honeysuckle. "Purifying Solution?" she asked, finally understanding why he made the potion. It would kill the small remnants of the Darkness that were beginning to build in her body, making her feel ill and tired.

Liam nodded. "I cannot have you fainting again."

Adrianna downed the potion in one gulp and instantly felt lighter. She did not try to perform any enchantments though, not in front of him.

"The fortress can sense any kind of witchery being performed," Liam said in warning. "Healing, spell casting, escapes...you won't even get out of the window without someone catching you."

"Why are you doing this to us?" she asked. "Your mother would die of shame if she were alive."

"Because we can."

"You do not have the right to enslave us," Adrianna replied coldly.

"But we have the power. In war that is all the matters. Right and wrong is all semantics. The stronger beast always wins," said Liam, arching an eyebrow as though to underline the point. "True, we caught you all unaware – but we have a fair number of you. However, I heard it took three vampires to take you down."

His answer made no sense. Vampires would not murder and enslave an entire village without a reason, even if it was to expand their numbers. Logic, order, rules and power were the very essence of vampire life. They were not there just to be blood slaves, vampires loved to hunt. The blood-hunt was what made their feeding more gratifying.

"Oh, it was more than that, believe me," she corrected. "Where are all the children? I suppose you killed the warlocks?"

Liam tilted his head. "I have not killed anyone personally; but the warlocks are not in the fortress. The children are in a chamber with the witches and the Black Annis has kept her teeth sharp for any one of them who misbehaves."

Adrianna had a vision of a bright blue eye, glowing out of an emaciated, colourless face. The Black Annis was a legend told to children in order to frighten them. Unfortunately, she was very real and more of a danger than she was ever given credit.

"Why-am-I-here?"

"Because I do not want you to die," said Liam. "That will be a good enough answer."

Someone knocked hard on the door and entered without waiting for permission. Daniel took no notice of Adrianna as he strode into the room, dressed in full travelling attire. "The warlocks are putting up a fight. Nikita wants to see you."

"Have any escaped?" asked Liam.

Daniel nodded. "A few. We set the Fourth Vanguard on them."

"Let's go," said Liam, following Daniel. He paused at the door. "It will be locked. That is where you will stay." He nodded to the door on the far right. "Nobody knows you are here."

Adrianna glared at him. When the door slammed closed she kicked the table leg in frustration. Dread and helplessness washed over her. Whatever reason Liam had for taking her away from her people, it was a big mistake. She was going to find a way out of this prison, even if she had to burn it to the ground.

~

Adrianna pressed her ear to her bedroom door when a group of vampires thundered into Liam's quarters and began speaking at once.

"Those witches are putting up a fight!" one of the vampires roared furiously.

"What did you expect?" Daniel's voice asked amusedly.

"You could be less calm about it all," a woman snapped. "It seems to me as if you do not even care about what is happening!"

"Of course I care," Daniel replied. "Just not as much as you."

There was a long silence.

"Do you sense that?" another voice said.

Adrianna gasped, her eyes widened. Could they sense her?

"Leave it!" said Liam.

"If I did not know better, Liam," the woman said, "I would say you had a play thing."

"I am within my rights, Pandema," Liam replied sternly. "Stay away from that door."

"Moving on from your personal tastes," said a deep, raspy voice. The hairs on Adrianna's arms stood on end. The man sounded as though he had gravel stones stuck in his throat. "Liam you should propose measures to the Council that would certify that none of the witches use their powers against us. Punishments must be severe if they do. Understood? And make an example of a few."

"It will be done," Liam replied.

You disgusting, murdering coward! Adrianna clenched her fists until her knuckles turned white. Her fury only grew as the vampires continued to speak of punishing the witches in the same casual way Adrianna would gossip with Kenna over a cup of tea. *I have to get out of here!* If she died trying, then so be it.

After a while, their voices became muffled and finally, just as she was falling asleep, the vampires departed. What were they planning? They would kill them all in due time, she was certain of that. But how could they forget that they too were once part of the Light? Why did the vampires seek to destroy their kin: their families, old friends and neighbours? No matter how she tried to rationalise it, what the vampires were doing made no sense. There were so many questions and so few answers, and the worst of it all was no one was there to answer her questions. No one at all.

~

A week passed and Adrianna began to fall heavily under the pressure of the Darkness. Night after night, she dreamt of the screams of suffering people, the cries of mothers, distant, frightened squeals of children and the howls of dying people being massacred and suffocated by the Darkness. But were they dreams or reality?

There were evenings when Adrianna lay in bed and imagined their torments. Were the soldiers masked when they drained innocents of their blood? Did they laugh in the faces of the dead? She imagined the pain of vampire fangs, piercing throats and ripping open veins. What would it feel like to have them pull at blood? It must have been agony, but the vampires themselves enjoyed being fed from. Perhaps it was only agony for those of the Light.

Are others trapped like me? She often wondered how many witches vampires were keeping in their private quarters. There was no doubt that they were not being left alone as she was, but perhaps they were spared the discomfort of the underground chambers. When the dark corners of her imagination put terrible pictures in her mind's eye, she forced herself to think of summer days by the beach, sipping lemonade with her friends; strolling through the tulip fields after dinner. Tears rolled from the corners of her eyes. She wished her parents had been there; fighting with her, even to hug her to sleep. But they were gone, long ago.

On her darkest days, she could not face Liam. When he knocked gently on her door to ask how she was, she ignored him. He was a daily reminder of how weak she was becoming. There were times when simply raising her hand was like trying to pick up a boulder.

It was not long before she was able to sense the vampires when they were in their demon forms. The pressure of their presence was a terrible weight to bear, worse than the Darkness. The fortress was home to demons that even she was too afraid to read about in her family's lexicon. The most common was a Rakasha; a long-limbed demon whose scream scrambled the mind. There were Baál; enormous, horned, bull-like humanoids that were used as hunters in the Demon Plane. Also Lasé; though rare, were very much sought after because they turned their hosts into blue-skinned, faery-like beings with vertical shaped pupils. On one occasion, she saw a Wraith; a black-skinned, soulless, flesh consumer that moved in fog.

Vampires rarely released their demons; it was too dangerous. When transformed, the vampire was not in control of their demon, and if they were not strong enough the demon could, on rare occasions, begin to influence its host. As far as Adrianna knew, there was no order or rule as to what demon was placed with which vampire. But then again, that was not the vampire way. They were meticulous in their planning; every step calculated, studied from all potential angles for possible faults before it was acted upon.

So why were we attacked? No matter how many times she tried to understand, an answer never came.

Adrianna wondered what demon essence Daniel hosted. She hoped he was not host to a Knor or a Vermillion; every demon race was dangerous, but Knor and Vermillion's were, as Kenna put it, 'evil, wrapped in power, smothered in strength and stewed from the Darkness's own black blood'. *But then*, she thought, *he just might be that exact work of evil.*

Adrianna had hoped, year after year, that Daniel had survived and somehow found peace after that terrible night when he, Liam and so many others were kidnapped. Though he had been her childhood nemesis, she was fond of him and missed him terribly when he was gone. She never forgot to place flowers outside his old home in memorial to him on his birthday and sometimes, when she least expected it; she could almost feel him with her at night. In her dreams he would sit by her bed. Never speaking, never moving much, but he was there.

She had not revealed her feelings to anyone, not even Kenna, and was certain now that they were just dreams. The man he had become was not the Daniel who sat beside her in her dreams, and he was certainly not the boy she remembered from childhood.

One night, as the fortress lay unnaturally still, Adrianna decided to collect her rejuvenation potion, which was usually left in the sitting room. When she opened the door, she was met by a wave of thick, heavy air that made her skin feel tight and raw. She coughed as each intake of breath scraped her lungs. She made to go back inside the cramped room when she noticed a long, horned shadow against the wall. Her heart skipped a beat and what felt like a heavy stone settled in the pit of her stomach. The palms of her hands tingled and grew warm...

With its back to her, a colossal, bull-horned demon stood before the fireplace.

Adrianna's eyes followed the length of it, horrified. *A Baál!*

The demon was almost twice the size of a man, both in height and breadth. With ridges running down the spine, its arms and legs were long and muscled, with hands three times the size of a man's. Small horns hung from the elbows and heels, and long, smooth bull-like horns protruded from either side of its head where a mane of black hair cascaded down its back. The *Baál* was a pure beast made to kill.

Fire-spheres formed in her palms. Adrianna struggled to breathe. *How do I get out? Walk slowly, backwards.* There was no way to escape the demon if it wanted to kill her, but luck was on her side and it had completely disregarded her. *But why?* The fire-spheres would slow it down, but she was sure to be dead before the third launch hit it. She was finally about to take a breath and step back toward her room when, by way of the shadow, she saw its head snap toward her.

No! Adrianna leaped back so far she hit the wall. Pain shot through her shoulder and both fire-spheres shot from her hands. One hit the ground and released a deafening bang, sending flames rolling across the carpets, while the other narrowly missed the *Baál* and collided with the wingchair by the fireplace.

It whirled around, giving a loud, bull-like snort and she screamed. Upon seeing its blazing yellow eyes she retreated into her room and locked the door, pressing the full weight of her body to fortify it. *What am I doing?* With one swift kick the demon would have the door in splinters.

"Do not come in," she whispered. "Do not come in. Please do not follow."

It did not. After almost an hour of sitting by the door, half hoping it was gone and half waiting for it to pounce, she heard Liam's voice.

"Adrianna, are you there?"

"Is it gone?"

"Open the door."

"How do I know it is not with you?"

"My word. You should have sensed it before you came out."

It was true, she should have but she was growing so weak her senses were dulled. She opened the door an inch.

"I did not think you would come out this evening. Don't be afraid . . ."

"I am not afraid of *you*," she said, opening the door wider. "How did it get in here? Who was that?"

"How much do you know about vampires?" Liam asked walking across the room to the bookshelf.

Adrianna frowned. "Obviously not enough. Why?"

Liam pulled a black, worn book from the shelf and handed it to her. The moment she touched the cover her skin pinched and burned. She dropped it.

"I cannot touch anything made by the Darkness," she said, stepping away from the book. The cover had felt like dried flesh. "What is it?"

Liam placed the open book down on the table. On one page was a sketch of a vampire and on the other page was a demon. There were carefully written notes in the margins of the pages. Liam turned the page, revealing a gruesome picture of a vampire's physical transformation into the form of a demon. Adrianna cringed and leaned in closer. She tried flexing her stinging fingers and immediately regretted it. They burned even more. She was torn between wanting to read more and going to her room to put her hands under water; her curiosity won.

Liam went into his room.

On half a page, beneath the image, was further detail. "When a being is bitten by a vampire and the blood is transferred, a demon essence is able to inhabit the body through an inauguration and walk the same path as beings of the Light," Adrianna read aloud. "The demon cannot control the vampire's body, but is a source of power and with the consent of the vampire can take its natural form for an unknown amount of time."

Of this Adrianna was aware. The only way for a demon to walk on the Elemental Plane was through a vampire. It was the only reason the Elemental Plane had survived for so long. If demons were free to roam the elementals would cease to survive and the angels would be forced to either declare war or fortify the Celestial Plane against them.

Liam returned with a damp cloth.

"Thank you," she said when he held it out. She placed it between her hands and felt the instant effects of the cold water.

"I put ointment on there too."

"It is working. Do all vampires have a demon essence inside of them?"

"Not all," Liam said, closing the book. "Some are fortunate enough to be free of a demon."

"So . . . that demon, the *Baál*, you are its host?"

"Yes." Liam raised his eyes to hers. "Jeith. He is a famous Bounty Hunter across the three Planes."

"Bounty Hunter? Of other demons?" She had a sick feeling he was going to say Jeith hunted witches.

"Not only other demons. They hunt whomever they are hired to hunt. Before me, Jeith inhabited the body of another vampire. Back then Jeith was infamous for his witch-hunts. He used to auction those he captured. Not the most respectable trade, I admit," he said coolly. "When that vampire was killed, Jeith survived – purely because the killer was slow in capturing his essence – Jeith moved to me when I was...bitten."

"Why did you take the form of your demon just now?"

Liam lowered his eyes. "At times, the pressure of such a powerful entity becomes too much. It needs releasing. Do you know what that feels like, Adrianna?" He looked at her face. "To know you cannot control the things around you? The things you want?"

Adrianna stared at him. Liam was now part of something else, no longer just himself, but a portion of a being that had the proven ability to do great evil. The demon was sharing Liam's body and he let it walk freely. She could almost see the life of the demon in Liam's eyes. Jeith certainly had an influence over him, but whether Liam knew it or not, she was not sure.

"You did not have a choice, did you?" she asked.

"None of us does," he replied, going over to the shelf. He slid the book into place slowly, running his thumb down the spine. "But we are all greatly misunderstood . . . vampires, the demons, even the Darkness."

Adrianna struggled to understand. "All creatures are misunderstood," she said, looking at the fire. "That is the way things are." As a servant of the Darkness, of course he would believe he was misunderstood. It was something she had to stay away from – that was all she needed to know.

"I want to be with my people."

"You will be, soon enough."

"Why are you keeping me here?"

Liam ignored her and went to his room, closing the door on her and the question.

After two days of relative silence, Adrianna woke from a nightmare with screams ringing in her ears and the pressing feeling of slow suffocation upon her. She tugged the covers up to her chin and curled herself into a ball.

"*Please*, have mercy on her," a woman screamed hysterically. "Please!"

The woman's cries were directly outside of Liam's quarters.

Adrianna sat up and kicked the covers off, ready for a fight. If Liam was hurting the woman, she would demand to be sent with the others in the underground chambers; that was, if he did not kill her first.

She tiptoed from her room and grasped the handle of the heavy, bolted door that led out of Liam's quarters to the residential halls of the fortress.

"No! Please, hurt me . . . do not hurt my sister. She is innocent!" the woman pleaded.

Adrianna's hand froze over the handle. She knew that voice. It was one of the twins from her village: Collette or Annie. One was crying out for the other. A loud thud sounded against the wall. Adrianna stared at the door. Someone had been thrown. "This isn't happening."

Suddenly, a severe pain filled her chest. A terrible scream sounded and Adrianna collapsed, clutching her heart. She could feel their pain. Taking a few deep breaths, she grasped the door handle, determined to get out there and help. It would not budge. "No, no, no!" She shook the handle, twisted, pulled, yanked, and banged against the door. "Stop it!" she screamed. "Do not hurt them! Stop!"

The door remained unmoved. She slammed it with her body.

"Annie . . . What-did-you-do-to-her?" said Collette, her voice shaking with desperation and grief. "Oh no! *Annie!*"

Adrianna burst into tears, pressing her forehead against the cold wood. Liam had sealed her in. If there had been any chance to save them, it went when Liam locked her inside his quarters.

Collette screamed hysterically. "Annie!"

Adrianna slid to her knees weakly and cried. Annie was gone. "May you travel a safe passage to the Spirit Plane," she whispered, wanting to reach through and hold the broken sister. Her chest compressed. Visions of Collette clutching at Annie's battered body as demons dragged her back filled her mind's eye.

As Collette's agonised cries faded, Adrianna struggled for air. The heavy feeling of soot in her lungs made her wheeze. She closed her eyes, moving onto her hands and knees and tried to regain control. But her shock and terror were not what was keeping her from breathing; it was the Darkness.

She rolled onto her back, gasping and felt two cold hands on her face just as everything went black.

Chapter Four

The Wrong One

"Mark me, Liam. She is not going to last much longer. The witch is *far* too sensitive to the Darkness. She used magic to try and pry open the door and save that girl, but it ended up suffocating her. You are fortunate no one sensed the energy blast."

"*I* sensed it," said Daniel, crossing his arms. "She is careless."

"No, she is a witch. Her reaction was natural."

Daniel watched the Librarian somewhat reservedly. Standing at the foot end of the sofa on which Adrianna lay unconscious, he observed Sergus, more commonly known at the Librarian, as he ran his hands slowly over Adrianna's face without touching her.

"Her body went into a deep sleep to protect itself," said the Librarian's elderly voice. "She has a . . . very sick. Very sick she is. Her consciousness is being protected. She will not begin to awaken until she is healed or coerced."

A three thousand year old vampire, Sergus the Librarian was completely fallen to the Darkness. Already an established alchemist, he was seven hundred years old when turned into a vampire. Infamously known for mixing Darkness and Light and testing the usage of both energies beyond their known limits, his experimentation with Black Magick had shaken the witchery world and made him an outcast; it was then that the vampires had come calling.

Having abandoned the Light soon after his transformation, three thousand years as a servant of the Darkness had made him a shadow of his former self. Once strong, vibrant and loved for his multi-coloured hair, he was reduced to mere wispy patches around his ears and black soulless eyes that protruded slightly. His grey skin seemed tight and stretched over his face beyond its capability, so that if he spoke it looked perilously close to tearing.

"*Why* is she so sensitive?" asked Liam.

"You have forgotten your old ways," said the Librarian, straightening his small, emaciated body. "Caring, helping, nurturing, friendship . . . love, it is all natural to her. It is an *instinct*. To die in the course of saving someone else, even a stranger, is in her nature. Her temperament is to care." The Librarian shook his head. "I have seen it too many times. Women like this usually die quickly . . . they fall prey to *hope*." He stared down at Adrianna assiduously.

Daniel rolled his eyes. "Are you going to wake her?"

"If I do it will only accelerate the rate of her death. The Darkness in these walls is smothering her. Since she is untainted by life, she is weak. She has no ability to protect herself from what surrounds her, except cocooning her soul. She feels it, senses it in her sleep, but knows not what it is. And since there is no pure natural element to draw energy from, the witch is merely defying the inevitable with every day she remains alive," said Sergus. "I will give her this, but only this once. Liam, you must learn that witches are not our friends. Accept that she will die." He placed a small bag between Adrianna's hands. "They all die in the end."

Daniel and Liam shared a look.

"Liam, see me out," said Sergus, rolling down the sleeves of his shirt.

As Liam walked the Librarian to the door, Daniel watched Adrianna's sleeping form. It was only a matter of time before she died. Trapped inside stone walls, a slave, her last breath would come after the Darkness smothered every bit of life out of her. A sickly feeling formed in the pit of his empty stomach.

Things were not going to plan.

~

Adrianna woke slowly, pushing through the drowsy layers of her mind. She lay in bed, gradually opening her heavy, sticky eyes and tried to remember what had happened before she fainted. *No,* she told herself, *I did not faint.* The last thing she remembered was a terrible, dense itchiness in her lungs, making it impossible to breathe and drained her of every ounce of strength she had.

A small, cotton pouch lay in her hand. The memory of the previous night returned, as did the sound of Collette and Annie's screams. Annie was certainly dead. Had Collette suffered the same fate as her twin? Tears came to her half opened eyes but she did not wipe them away; they were the only real things she had at that moment. Who killed Annie with such brutality? She had certainly been beaten. Was it because she fought against her captors, or because they found it amusing? If the sisters were being taken to become blood-slaves, then Adrianna was certain they would have fought. The prospect of servicing a vampire through blood was nothing less than a nightmare, and inconceivable in many minds.

Why live, if this is life? I have to get out.

She clutched the pouch tightly. From the outside it felt hard and lumpy. She pulled the strings and peered inside. *Miracle . . .* It was filled with bark, roots and earth. Lifting it to her nose, she breathed in deeply: sandalwood and barley. A soothing calm replaced the sickness in her stomach.

Adrianna closed her green eyes and tried to remember what she had seen of the fortress.

The witches had been moved from their initial holding rooms and put in what Liam had called the underground chambers. She needed to find them; the underground chambers, her people and talk to them. It was the only way to escape.

The earth in the pouch was beginning to take effect. As her eyes became heavy, Adrianna fell into a dreamless sleep.

~

It was daylight when Adrianna woke. Knowing this was the safest time to sneak around the fortress, she ate the food left on the table by the window, bathed and dressed. Adrianna slipped out of her bedroom, glancing quickly to the closed door to Liam's bedroom and tiptoed to the sitting room. If the door was bolted, as it had been the other night, she was doomed.

It was.

Adrianna gripped the handle and tried to sense what kind of lock he had placed on the door. *Weak,* she thought, looking over her shoulder to his bedroom door. Trembling, she forced her energy through her arm and snapped the lock inside the door. It was a conventional silver lock. Fancy and impractical. What had kept her inside the night of Annie's murder was the Black Magick he had used to secure the door.

Carefully, silently, she slinked out. As he was in his bedroom, hopefully asleep, she trusted he would be there until sunset, provided he did not notice her missing.

Adrianna looked to both sides of the corridor before closing the door. It was completely empty. By the silence, Liam was not the only vampire sleeping. This was a rare occasion. Liam mentioned that the vampires merely closed the shutters during daylight hours since they did not need to rest as constantly as witches did. Perhaps, Adrianna thought, this was a communal day of rest.

Tiptoeing along the deserted hall, she ran to the only window and peered outside. The sun shone brightly but a mass of grey clouds was moving in from the east. The leaves were usually different shades of golden brown in the autumn, but like the grass, they were turning white. Winter had begun. From this, Adrianna calculated that she must have been in the fortress five weeks.

Her eyes followed a small, dark shape in the garden. It moved unevenly, as though limping, and came into view as it passed a willow tree.

Goblin. Adrianna sneered at the sight of it. A shadow passed over the window, fast followed by another. She watched as a pair of gargoyles flew up and around the side of the fortress, squawking at one another. Their leathery wings spanned far on either side of their heavy, demonic bodies.

"Enchanted," Adrianna whispered to herself. Gargoyles were only supposed to wake at night upon their master's command. During the day they sat as stone statues, with the rising of the moon to give them the breath of life. They were the guardians of the vampires, created in the image of demons to serve as protectors, guards and spies.

It was obvious that someone had cast a spell, which enabled the gargoyles to remain awake during the daylight hours. Perhaps this was why the vampires all slept; they knew they were well guarded.

Still, she could not take the chance of being caught if all the vampires were not asleep. She ran down the staircase to her left and arrived at a darkened level of the building, underground. As her hand brushed against the sandstone wall, her stomach gave an excited leap. Sandstone had no useful elements; therefore a witch could not draw energy from it. Was this a prison? She could not believe her luck if it was.

A large wooden door appeared to her right. "Yes!" She pressed her ear to it. There was no sound. She debated with herself on whether or not to knock. What if vampires were behind the door? Would she wake them? She bit her lip, sweating with nervous excitement. There could be witches, tied down or dying.

She listened again for a long moment before deciding to knock.

"Please, please," she whispered.

Instantly, she heard movement. "Please, not vampires." Her heart thundered and with sweaty palms she knocked again. This time there was a reply. Three knocks. "Yes!" Too eager to stop, she grasped the handle, turned it sharply and pushed on the door before having second thoughts.

It was not even locked! Adrianna opened the door slowly, expecting some kind of hex or booby-trap to be launched. The vampires were terribly arrogant to leave the area unattended.

The guards could be returning, she told herself.

"Hello?" called Adrianna, distinctly hearing gasps and shuffling through the dim light.

The light formed upon her arrival, allowing her to see the full scope of this enormous chamber. There were beds and sofas lined against the limestone walls and witches surrounded a fireplace to the left, but it was otherwise bare.

Many were roused from sleep by her presence, and others seemed momentarily dumbfounded.

"*Adrianna!*"

Snapping out of their trances, they ran forward excitedly. Adrianna closed the door quietly and smiled, enveloped by the dozens of arms.

"How did you find this place?"

"Are we being freed?"

"Are we being attacked?"

"She could be a vampire!"

One voice stood out in the flurry of women. Rosamunda fought her way through the group, pushed everyone out of the way and threw her arms around her young neighbour. Adrianna held onto her. She was the last and closest reminder she had of home. Her body shook with the emotions that were bubbling inside: fear, relief, and sadness.

"It is all right girl," whispered Rosamunda, stroking her hair. "You can cry."

"I thought so many terrible things," said Adrianna, her voice shaking.

"I thought they had killed you," said Rosamunda. She pulled back, holding Adrianna at arm's length to survey her. "My goodness, you look worn out."

"So do you," replied Adrianna, seeing the dark circles under all their eyes. They looked half dead. "All of you." She wished with all of her might that she had remembered to bring the pouch of bark with her. They could have passed it between them to keep whatever strength remained. A little bit of something was better than nothing. "I am a fool," she whispered, looking into their withdrawn eyes.

"We have not seen the sun in weeks," said Margarithe, running a hand through her unkempt hair self-consciously. "How did you get down here, Adrianna?"

"Pure luck. I do not know how long I can stay," said Adrianna quickly. "I am trying to find a way out – is there no one here who has seen the fortress?"

"No," said Rosamunda. "Only those who have been taken away, but some do not return and others never speak when they do. What about you?"

"I have been cooped up in a room for over a month," said Adrianna.

"A room? What room? With a vampire?"

"There is nothing sinister," said Adrianna quickly. "I am merely a prisoner of someone from our village. But the only harm that has come to me has been through the Darkness. It has made me weak and ill. I know I will die soon. It is so strong in this terrible place. The tortures . . ." Her voice faltered when her eyes landed on Collette. She was covered in bruises, her dress ripped and strips of her skirt were used to make the bandages around her wrists.

Adrianna placed her hands on the side of Collette's puffy face. "I heard everything," she said, looking into the witch's dead eyes. "It happened right outside the door to my prison."

"You heard them murder Annie?" asked Rosamunda.

"That is so sick," said Jess from behind her. She looked paler than the others. She offered Adrianna a small smile, but it disappeared as fast as if came.

Tears formed in Collette's eyes but she did not sob. She was in an empty place beyond grief. "They murdered my sister...one of them tried to turn me, but Annie begged them not to. She said they could do anything with her, just as long as they did not hurt me." She shuddered, her cut lips quivering. "Then they killed her...and they beat me."

"We are going to get out of here," said Adrianna, gripping her shoulders fiercely. "I promise you."

Collette closed her eyes. The promise was cold comfort, but witches never allowed themselves to be bested. "We can only try."

"And we will have revenge," a large woman said, her deep voice dripping with determination.

Adrianna nodded, going to the door. "Where is Orla?"

"One of *them* came and took her right after you. I have heard nothing," said Rosamunda.

"And Caitriona?"

Jess released a dry sob and pushed her way out of the group. "I can't, I can't . . ."

"Caitriona . . . comes and goes," said Rosamunda, obviously uncomfortable about speaking so openly. "She has not been turned," she added quickly, "but it is obvious one of the vampires keeps her."

"How can she stand it?" asked Adrianna, knowing Caitriona would never suffer being in the presence of a vampire willingly.

"She *never* speaks of it."

"I have to go. I do not think the vampires will leave these rooms unguarded long. I will be in touch soon," said Adrianna. "In the meantime – try to listen out for anything that could help find a way out."

"We will."

"Child." Lizzette, one of the elders, stepped forward. "You must not return here. It is too dangerous."

Adrianna raised her eyebrows. "I am going to help get us out."

"You risk too much. At this point, we have been treated . . . reasonably well, considering the past history of the vampires and their treatment of witches. Remain alive. Let that be your primary goal."

"But if she can help us get out . . ." said one of the others.

Lizzette's sudden turn toward the group silenced the speaker at once. "Phyllis, we are deep beneath stone, embedded in enchantments and magic you would not understand. We are weak and growing weaker every day we spend here. How exactly is this one child supposed to find a way out, when she herself is trapped?" Her tone did not invite a reply.

"If I find an opportunity, I will do what I can," Adrianna promised.

Lizzette nodded. "Good luck, child."

Rosamunda kissed her. "Please, be careful."

"I worry about you."

"No. Do not. We will deal with trouble as it comes," said Lizzette. "Now go."

~

Adrianna had only just made it to the wingchair in front of the fire in Liam's sitting room when the locked door gave a soft 'click' and opened. Believing it to be Liam, Adrianna looked up expectantly.

It was not Liam. The door that opened was not his bedroom door, but the front door, which led from his quarters. The door she had only just run in from.

The casual greeting she usually spoke to Liam slipped from her mind the moment she lifted her eyes to Daniel's icy silver ones. Every nerve in her body came alive. Her mind told her to back away but her legs felt like weights, holding her in place. Her eyes followed the door as it closed and locked itself behind him.

She could not breathe or move, and her mouth felt as though it was filled with cotton. There was a sofa and many feet between them, if she could only get her legs to move, there was a chance to evade him.

Daniel moved with purpose. He took slow, calculating steps toward her, almost as if he was placating her fear. But she was afraid, terribly so, and he could smell it.

When he reached the sofa, Adrianna felt jolted. She stood up in a flash and backed away.

"L-Liam is not here," she said nervously, not realizing she was backing herself into the shelf.

Daniel's silver eyes narrowed and his signature sneer appeared on his pale face. "I was not looking for Liam, *witch*," he said harshly. "I have found exactly what I wanted."

"What do you want with me?" she asked, her heart beating rapidly. Clenching her skirt tightly in her fists, she tried to steady her trembling hands. When her back hit the shelf, she whirled around and made her way around the sofa but he continued to follow.

Daniel smirked, exposing his fangs. "I can sense your heart beat," he jeered. "You are scared – as you should be."

Her legs hit the footstool and she pitched backwards, landing on her backside with a shocked squeal. She could not help but huff in frustration as a blush appeared on her cheeks. It had always been this way with them. He intimidated her as a child as he intimidated her now. Things had slowly begun to change just before he was kidnapped, but it was terribly obvious that none of the past affection they held for one another as children had lasted after he was turned.

"That is exactly where you and your kind should be – on the ground. *Don't* look at me like that," he growled at her furious expression. "This battle between our people has proven who truly is more powerful."

"You are disgusting!" she shrieked as he yanked her up to her feet harshly. "Your mother is a witch! You should be so lucky she was not in the village when you attacked us. She would be so ashamed of you! Do not touch me!" She slapped his hands off her.

Daniel put his hand to Adrianna's thin throat before pinning her to the wall. Adrianna could only glare. Her nails dug into his skin, trying to relinquish his grip through pain. Blood appeared beneath the welts she created but it seemed to make no difference. There was no humanity in his eyes. As the force of his hold refused air into her lungs, she searched, desperately, to find a trace of life in the steely, narrowed eyes that would have been so beautiful had they not been filled with hate.

"Feel trapped?" he asked tauntingly, his eyes turned black. He watched amusingly as she struggled. Droplets of blood ran down his hand. His nostrils flared, and as his lips parted, she caught a glimpse of the tips of his fangs.

She gasped, trying so hard to breathe. Perhaps this was how she would die. *How long is he going to make me suffer?* As tears blurred her vision of him, she released her death grip and touched the edge of his jaw.

Air. The pressure on her neck lessened and air filled her desperate lungs. Tears of relief ran down her face. Her body shook of its own accord no matter how she tried to remain still. Warm breath tickled her neck; hair touched her face. She stiffened as he pressed his body pressed up against hers, holding her in place.

She whimpered as Daniel's fangs lengthened, nearing her throat. "Daniel, don't . . ."

Daniel's eyes flashed. His hand slid from her throat, down, over her collarbone and rested over her heart.

Adrianna stared as his hand rested between her breasts, taking in the beats of her heart. She opened her mouth to speak, to have him stop touching her, when the fangs came toward her again. Slowly, his face neared hers. His shoulders slumped in order to reach her, and as his mouth neared her neck . . .

Liam strode through the door at the very moment Adrianna became weak at the knees.

"Release her!"

Adrianna slid to the ground in a heap when Daniel relinquished his grip.

"What are you doing?" Liam asked irately.

Daniel glanced down as his eyes faded to their natural silver. "Teaching the little *slave* a lesson in respect."

"I think it would be best if you left now," he said tightly.

"Fix her up," said Daniel. "She looks a bloody mess." He strode from the room without looking back.

Adrianna felt a surge of emotions and closed her eyes as the door slammed shut. Death had been so close a moment ago. As Daniel had robbed her of air, he felt she deserved to die. She sensed it. They were close enough that she could feel his emotions: his hate, rage, and lack of empathy. He had wanted to kill her to see how he would *feel* afterwards, his own little experiment. But then, something had changed. The moment she touched his face, his will to kill her stopped only to be replaced by something she did not recognise.

Liam moved to stand in front of her. "Are you all right?"

Trembling, she shifted away. "Stay back. I thought . . ." she choked tearfully. "I thought I was going to die."

"Calm down," he said. "Your emotions will be felt by others if they overpower you."

"He would have done it," said Adrianna. "Would not he?"

"Yes, he would have killed you. And afterwards he would have thought nothing of it," replied Liam. "That is how we are."

"You are all evil," said Adrianna, rising on her shaky legs. "I do not know why you are keeping me here, but I would rather be with my people."

"Yes. Better to die with your own."

~

It was a week before Adrianna found the will to leave her room. Her fear of seeing Daniel and her failing health forced her to remain in bed, clutching the earth-filled bag. She was by the fireplace when Liam returned from his weekly 'meeting' with Nikita, of whom Adrianna had heard horror stories. Nikita's ruthlessness and blood-thirst, coupled with his status among his own people made him one of the most feared vampires in all of Sansul.

Liam and Nikita joined one another on blood-hunts. Adrianna had over-heard one of the resident vampire women mentioning it to a companion outside her door one afternoon. Blood hunting was a vampire sport. They stalked their prey: witches, warlocks, centaurs, faeries, nymphs, sometimes for hours, even days before feeding upon them. Now that more beings of the Light - those not kidnapped - were moving out of Wilmota, the vampires tracked them down and killed them off one by one.

Liam was not alone when he returned. His companion entered but remained by the door. Adrianna was ashen faced, her eyes watery and blank. She sat on a sofa with a blanket over her thin legs.

"I have brought someone," said Liam. "She insisted on seeing you."

Adrianna frowned. "Who?" she asked weakly.

Liam nodded to the woman and disappeared into his room.

Adrianna waited quietly as the woman neared. She blinked, trying to see the stranger's face through the dim light. There was something so pleasantly familiar about her.

The vampire was graceful, mature, with a long, thin face that was softened by her brown eyes. There was something childlike about this woman, Adrianna sensed. Her blood-red lips were pressed together tightly. Straight dark hair cascaded down her back, the colour contrasting her blemish-free, pale skin. Adrianna was surprised at her boldness when the vampire crouched down beside the sofa, looking at her with pity.

"What have they done to you?" the vampire asked softly, her sweet voice all too familiar.

Adrianna stared, too shocked to speak. *How could this be?* She reached out her weak hand, her cold fingers touching the cheek of the vampire whose brown eyes she knew better than anyone else's. A lump rose in her throat.

"Kenna?"

Kenna wiped away Adrianna's tears. "Do not cry for me, not like this. I am still alive. They did not catch me until a week after the attack," she said, looking toward Liam's door anxiously. "I was helped by some members of a group called the Gordgáin," she added in a lowered voice.

How Kenna was helped was the furthest thing from her mind. Her best friend, her sister, her greatest love was turned. She was the Darkness, yet Adrianna did not sense it in her. "You look so different . . . yet, exactly the same," she said, feeling weaker.

Kenna kissed her cold hands and placed them beneath the blanket. "I will lament my change when you are safely out of this place. I will not tell you all that I know, not while you are so weak."

"Tell me," she insisted.

"You must be strong for what we must do. I am still learning myself, but I will reveal what I know when I am sure your soul can take it. Now, the Gordgáin . . ."

"The rebellion group?"

"You know of them?"

"The elders used to speak of them, remember? When they spoke of *The War Against The Angels*, they told of a group called the Gordgáin," whispered Adrianna. "Were they able to save anyone?"

"Oh, yes," said Kenna. "The Bruniér and Aires clans were warned far before the vampires crossed their borders. Now the vampires are working on catching those of us who got away, and there are many. Aires and Bruniér have blocked their borders. They are safe but only for a short while."

"And how did they find you if you were with the Gordgáin?"

"I went looking for you," said Kenna. "I was taken by the vampires near your cottage."

"You should not have done that," said Adrianna reproachfully. "Look what has happened."

Kenna was unapologetic. "You would have done it for me. Now, look at you," she said, running her hand over Adrianna's hair. "I sensed you the other week when you were in the underground chambers. I know you want to find a way out."

"We are dying every day," Adrianna interrupted. "I am not going to last another week. I can barely stomach food and I fear Liam has plans for me. I do not know what they are though."

"I know," replied Kenna. "Which is why I am going to help you. Liam is the least of your worries at the moment. He is high up in this coven, though how high I am yet to find out. He is not the docile vampire he makes himself out to be. Liam is very mercurial, very short tempered and I have seen him kill one of his own men for failing a mission. What you are doing seems to be working for now, stay as you are."

Adrianna's eyes flashed. "*I want to get out of here!*"

"Shush." Kenna glanced behind her, worried. "I will not be able to sneak you out. That will take a little while. A plan must be made because there are guards *everywhere*. In the meantime..." She pulled a small satchel from beneath her skirts. "Drink the potion in the blue vial when I leave. Hide the satchel behind stone; they will not be able to sense it there. Inside is a basalt rock. Sleep with it in your hands every night, as it will keep the Darkness from touching your body. That is what is making you weak. You must get better or else you will not be able to save yourself or anyone else."

"Kenna, whatever you are planning, will you come with me?"

"That may not be possible. I may be a vampire now," said Kenna, "but I do not want to see our people extinct. I will never forget, Adrianna. You are my family."

"Do not do anything stupid. I do not want you to be killed."

Kenna smiled. "You mean 'Do not do anything *you* would not do'," she corrected. "I will come back soon, but you must rest and get better."

"Wait! The women in the underground chambers," said Adrianna, "they are weaker than me. Is there anything to give them?"

"I do not know. I will try to think of something."

"Has anyone else been . . .?" Adrianna stopped. "Do you know anyone else who has been turned?"

Kenna nodded. "But they all succumbed to the Darkness," she said. "You are the only one who is up here and not a vampire. It is a near-miracle that no one has sensed you."

"All right . . ." Adrianna leaned back on the sofa, her eyes feeling heavy.

Liam came out from his room just as Adrianna finished shoving the satchel under a pillow. "We are expected outside."

Kenna nodded and followed him to the door where she paused, looking back to her best friend. Adrianna knew now that everything would be all right. With Kenna helping her, just like always, she could succeed.

~

Adrianna sat on the soft, deep green rug by the fireplace at peace for the first time in weeks. Daniel had not been around to taunt her, Liam was barely present and with Kenna's potion she had slowly regained her strength.

She was gaining a deep insight into the world of the vampires through a curious book she could no longer ignore. The vampires, though still as repugnant to her as always, were a fascinating race. She hoped that by learning more about them she could find a way to fight them one day.

The door flew open unexpectedly. Adrianna jumped when Daniel strode inside, a long fur-collared coat around his shoulders, and looked around with an expression of deep displeasure on his face. When his eyes fell on Adrianna his expression softened.

Adrianna was surprised but remained silent.

"Liam, where is he?" he asked, his voice stern.

"Probably on another blood hunt," replied Adrianna casually.

Daniel looked disgusted. "Playing more games," he muttered. "When did he leave?"

"Yesterday," she replied, not wanting to heighten Daniel's anger. "He said he would return today."

"Why would he be so precise with you?" snapped Daniel.

"He was not," said Adrianna, going back to her book. "I overheard him telling that Nikita creature that he needed to be back today for some ceremony." She flipped the page casually, seemingly ignoring him.

"Since you are so sure," said Daniel, waving his hand to the door. It closed and locked. He pulled off his cloak, threw it on the sofa furthest from Adrianna and sat down.

Adrianna looked at him curiously. Sitting with his legs crossed at the ankles, his elbows resting on the arms of the chair, and his fingers laced together, a strange, unexplainable emotion surged through her as she looked at him. He looked both confident and displeased; they were a wicked mix in a vampire.

Adrianna turned back to her book and began to read but only made it a few lines through when Daniel broke the silence between them.

"So, your strength is growing," he said, laughing humourlessly. "I wonder what his game is. Soon he'll allow you to eat at the same table as us."

"I doubt you eat anything which would appeal to my taste," she replied, closing the book. She decided to go to her room before he was tempted to try and end her life again.

"Stop!" he ordered.

Adrianna obeyed.

Daniel grabbed her and turned her around to face him. His grip forced her stand with her back against the wall where he had almost taken her life.

Not again!

"What were you doing in the underground chambers?" he asked.

"I do not know what you are talking about," she replied, looking at him nervously.

"Oh, I think you do," he said icily. "Do not make me ask again."

"I . . . was seeing if they were all still alive," she replied steadily.

"Not planning any escapes?" he asked, his eyes directly on hers.

Adrianna blinked. "No," she lied.

"You are an unconvincing liar. Does Liam know you were down there?"

"No."

Daniel arched an eyebrow. "I think Liam should be informed of this little bit of news, don't you? He should know that he is trying to save a conniving spy."

"Prove it," she spat, fighting against his grip.

"You are in no democracy anymore, witch. This is your prison. I could snap your neck right now and no one would think twice."

"I am just trying to survive."

Daniel smirked. "And how far would you go to do that?" he asked, placing each of his hands on the wall beside her head.

Adrianna stared at him calculatingly for a long moment. "I may be a prisoner now," she said, "but I maintain my dignity. I will die with it, and you will *never* take it from me."

Daniel narrowed his eyes. "You know how to anger a man."

"It is a fault of mine," she snapped. "Is there no one else you can bully? Why don't you go and sharpen your fangs on somebody more important? Let-me-pass!"

"*I* will tell you when you can leave my presence," he hissed, grabbing her hair roughly. He turned her head to the side, exposing her neck. "Be grateful Liam walked in when he did. I would have gladly feasted on your blood. Shall I sharpen my teeth on you?"

Adrianna pressed herself against the wall in a vain attempt to get away. His fangs were so close to her throat his breath was beginning to warm her neck. With a tug on her hair, he tilted her head back and kissed her hard on the mouth. A fever rose in her, flushing her instantly, mingling with shock. His bruising kiss made her whimper in pain. There was no tenderness in his touch. His kiss was harsh, just like a vampire, cold and sharp. But instead of repulsing her, a warmth spread through her body. She could not pull away; she did not *want* to pull away. At least, her body did not. Something other than his hands was keeping her still.

A sharp pinprick-like pain on her lip brought forth a split second of clarity and forced them apart.

Panting, Daniel raised his fingers to his bloodied lip. Adrianna did the same and was horrified to find blood. Was it his? Was it hers? Had their blood mixed? Daniel's cut lip healed instantly. Adrianna dabbed her mouth with a handkerchief, making sure not to allow any blood in her mouth. It would kill her.

"You dared?" he said hoarsely.

"I do not know how it happened!" she cried. She looked at the droplets of blood on her handkerchief. A sudden thought occurred to her. The unexpectedness of his kiss, the lack of resistance, and the spark that caused them to pull apart; she had read about it so many times. It was inconceivable that this rare occurrence could have anything to do with her. This divine, untameable magic could not occur between a vampire and a witch who loathed one another surely.

"No," she whispered to herself, horrified. She moved away from his reach, disgust rising as quickly as the flush of heat only seconds ago.

"Stop," he ordered. "Explain this!"

Adrianna looked at him with teary eyes. "No," she said, walking backwards toward the door of her small bedroom. "This is not supposed to happen. Do not come near me ever again. You are the wrong one . . . it is not you."

"You are rambling," said Daniel, following her. "What did you do?"

Adrianna burst into tears and hastily retreated to her room, slamming the door closed. "This cannot happen to me," she whispered, still very aware of the feeling of his lips upon hers.

CHAPTER FIVE

The Spellmaker

O N THE FAR SIDE of the room, where the light of the candles did not reach, Nikita, Daniel, Kenna and Liam stood silently, watching the torture of a Spellmaker.

The underground holding rooms were located in the northernmost tower of the fortress, deep beneath the tower itself. During daylight hours, the gargoyles were responsible for guarding the tower, and by night, vampire soldiers took the responsibility of keeping the coven's most dangerous enemy prisoners from escaping.

Nikita looked particularly unmoved by the agonised screams that filled the room. His waist-length black hair was loose about him, acting as a curtain around his hollowed face and aquiline nose. Kenna stood as far away from him as possible without being obviously disrespectful. This being of legend, infamous for being a cold-blooded killer and serial blood-zealot had one of the darkest auras she had ever sensed.

"Is this going to take long?" he drawled in Daniel's ear, his dilated eyes on their victim.

Sitting in a low chair in the middle of the stone room, the bearded Spellmaker blinked away the sweat that rolled down into his withdrawn amethyst eyes.

Kenna bit her bottom lip to keep from visibly shaking. Hiding her trembling hands behind her back, she watched as the Spellmaker visibly prepared himself for the next onslaught of pain. Beside her, Liam looked thoroughly entertained.

That Liam, someone she had known since birth, grew up with, played with and mourned, was enjoying the suffering of another being made her feel ill.

Daniel, she noticed, was stoic. From the moment she met them at the base-door of the tower and throughout the torture, he did not move nor speak. At one point she wondered if he had turned to stone, until Nikita whispered something in Daniel's ear in his baritone, gravel voice and a knowing smirk appeared on Daniel's lips.

She cursed her Maker, Thomas, for forcing her to watch this terrible abuse. "It is to accelerate you emotional changes," he had told her when she argued with him. According to Thomas she was 'desperately holding onto her most deep set emotions, primarily because she was yet to discard her empathy for her former race'. How she was supposed to suppress her most basic emotions by witnessing the torture of a Spellmaker, she did not know, but she had told him to burn in agony far too many times to get away with it any longer.

Unable to help herself, she closed her eyes as one of the guards placed a fist-sized, smooth, white stone over the Spellmaker's chest. Through it they unleashed deep, unadulterated pain in short intervals. Yet another strained cry of agony followed, morphing into a scream. Kenna recognised it not so much as a cry of pain, but a scream of determination not to give in. Holding her breath, she forced herself to stare at the far wall, as his voice became white noise in her ears.

Anguish, pain and sorrow had been captured and stored in what the lexicons called Torture Stones. They were tools accidentally created by the Spellmakers, those who invented new magic and experimented with the old. After *The War Against The Angels* Black Magick lexicons along with books and scrolls that listed, described and taught the artistry of Black Magick were hidden or destroyed. Torture Stones, amongst other devices of torture, were outlawed by Witchery Clans as they were harmful and went against the first Witchery Lore: to protect and preserve.

"Where did you hide your lexicon?" the second guard asked the Spellmaker for the hundredth time.

Every family had a lexicon of spells, charms and potions. Extended with each new entry, every book was unique, catering to the requirements and individuality of each family. There was never just one large lexicon in a household; instead volumes were separated according to their specialties. Household spells and charms, potions and spells for healing, decorating, hexes and curses, also tutoring volumes ranging from basic spells for children to study about demons, angels and destructive elemental beings like goblins. Still, every family had one main lexicon in which the most important spells, charms, hexes, curses, potions and information was stored.

Many lexicons were made purely to store Black Magick, but under the Clan Protection Edicts, they were to be destroyed or given to a Spellmaker as only they had the full knowledge and comprehension of magic and the power to fix the wrongs.

"Where did you hide your lexicon?" the vampire repeated.

"In a place," said the Spellmaker, holding his pained chest, "you will never find."

The guards turned to the four.

"Maybe we should bring one of the witches," the first guard said to Nikita. "Let us torture her and see how he reacts."

Nikita stared at the Spellmaker for a long moment. "It will not make a difference. He knows the importance of his lexicon."

"You think torture will make me reveal the location to one of the most sacred books of my people?" the Spellmaker spat.

"Try his blood," said Liam.

"I take the strongest Blood Purifying Solutions available on this side of the Pearl Line," he said weakly. "You will never read my blood, vampire scum. The truth . . . the truth lies not in my veins."

Nikita sized the Spellmaker with a look. "You lie."

"He is not lying," said Daniel. "They have long known how to protect themselves from us."

"Not enough," replied Liam. "He got himself caught."

"The life of my daughter is more important than my own," the Spell-maker said between shallow breaths. "But you would not know the meaning of such sacrifice. You would not have caught me, had you not attempted to defile my . . . my greatest creation."

Kenna pushed herself off the wall. "I have had enough."

"More?" asked the guard, turning to Daniel for permission to continue his torture.

Daniel and Nikita followed Kenna to the door. "Report before sunrise," said Daniel. "If he does not give up the location by then, send him to be with the warlocks in the mines."

The Spellmaker laughed humourlessly. "Fools . . . the lot of you."

~

In the middle of the twelfth moon cycle of the year, Liam was called away. Adrianna was trying to remember the path she had taken to the underground chambers when a knock sounded at her door. It was Liam but the sight of him made her keep the door open only slightly. His eyes were black and withdrawn; the skin around his eyes was darkening also.

"I am leaving tomorrow evening. You have to remain with Daniel," said Liam.

"Why are you leaving?"

"My scouts are being outwitted by those half-breed nothings the Maquis," he said, going back to his desk. Adrianna opened the door further and stood in the threshold. "The Council has ordered that I take another group and track them down," he continued, thrusting papers into his desk drawers.

Seeing those papers would have been useful, if she were allowed to remain here alone. It would give her the time and freedom to better plot an escape without being interrupted. There was no chance of Liam allowing for that.

"Are the Gordgáin not your biggest problem?"

"The Gordgáin and the Maquis work together," Liam replied, "to free you and your people no doubt."

~

Daniel's quarters were in a small, detached stone building within the fortress boundary walls, overlooking the sea. The foyer and its halls were as lavishly decorated as the main stronghold. The corridors were empty and filled with sounds of the ocean when Adrianna arrived. She hated the idea of being shuffled from room to room like a package of dangerous goods. Worse, she was weakening once more and barely had energy. She was desperate for news on her people but neither Liam nor Daniel ever spoke to her of them.

A mild salty scent lingered in the air. The ocean was rough this night. She was dangerous, angry, and as her waves crashed against the cliffs, Adrianna sensed her rage. As the daughter of a sailor, she knew the ocean was alive. The ocean was all things good and terrifying. If she was treated with respect and piety, she protected and honoured, but if disrupted or angered, she destroyed without mercy and dragged her enemies to her abyss. The merchant ships of Wilmota no longer sailed through her waves, nor did the magic of the land grace that of the ocean. There was great unhappiness and unbalance.

When in Daniel's quarters, Adrianna peered out of the window and saw that they were perched on the edge of the cliff. The salt in the air provided her with cleansing nourishment, though it was rather mild. From Wilmota, it had been impossible to see the true expanse of the fortress. A vampire residence built on hills and cliffs was not how Adrianna imagined it, though it was fitting. Curiously, she noticed that the ocean waves would not hit a particular part of the cliff, but ride on as if there was a cave.

She stepped back. *He might throw me out the window one of these days.* She resigned herself to stay out of Daniel's way. The less she saw him, the less chance she had of testing his temper and finding herself hurtled to her death.

Daniel had no spare room, unlike Liam. "Stay out of my way at all times, witch. You may stay in this sitting area during the day, unless of course I have guests. There is a bedroom through that door," he said, nodding to the dark wood door behind her. "You sleep in there."

"Where do you sleep?" she asked suspiciously.

"I do not," he said dismissively, waving her away.

A vampire did not sleep nightly like witches and warlocks. They lasted moons without recuperation, provided they fed often. When the time came for deep rest, they went into the necropolis. Every vampire coven had a necropolis. As Adrianna understood it, it was a communal place of rest deep inside the coven strongholds. Nobody outside of the covens knew their locations, as they were guarded with the utmost secrecy.

That night, as the wind howled outside, Daniel was busy at his desk when he sensed fear coming from his bedroom. His hand stilled over the orb floating above his papers. His ears focused on the bedroom: the bed sheets rustled, a whimper sounded. It was impossible for someone to be in there but he did not take the chance. He opened the door without knocking and looked at her through the dark.

Adrianna thrashed around beneath the covers as though trying to get away from something. As a vampire he could see in pitch-black. Her veins glowed white and he could track where her body was warmest. The clothes Liam had acquired for her were in a small trunk by the window. Her nightgown slid up her legs as she rolled over onto her side, her face tense and her chest rising and falling heavily.

Daniel went to her side and drew the covers over her. He was careful not to touch her in case she woke, but his fingers accidentally brushed her arm as he lifted the soft bedcover to her shoulder. Her body stopped moving. When she did not wake, he moved her hair from her face.

Adrianna's breathing slowed. Surely he was not able to calm her down like this. She feared him. She did not want his comfort.

He caught sight of her hand. It was resting against the pillow, but it was clenched. He tilted his head. There was a brown rock in her palm. He leaned back, staring down at her. Then it dawned on him.

"Basalt rock. Clever witch," he said softly as he left.

On the second evening of her stay with him, Adrianna sat by the window, her book forgotten on her lap as she watched the rough sea crash against the cliff-face and retreat. An owl flew by the window, pushing its way strenuously through the wind. At his desk, writing endlessly, Daniel had not noticed her for hours.

Adrianna was grateful he was so engrossed in his work as there were no snide remarks, no embarrassing glances, no questions about what had passed between them a few days past and no threats against her life. They simply went about their business. Boredom was her business. She traced a drop of water against the windowpane and wished she could feel its purifying energy. That was until the rain, which splashed against the glass, began to concentrate on the spot on which her finger was pressed. A wave of excitement filled her as a small sphere of water formed, its energy slipping through the fortress defences and into her skin. Through this tiny doorway, she concentrated on what little energy she had left and poured it outside, feeling around, going with the gale winds.

The peace of Wilmota was long gone, replaced with devastation, ruin and secrecy. Something was moving in the highlands, something neither Light nor Darkness. Adrianna took a deep breath, steadying her energy. Her eyes glowed bright green. There were voices in the winds, too many to concentrate on one in particular but they were growing louder.

We are coming...

A warm hand covered hers, blocking the connection. Adrianna jumped, her eyes dimmed. Daniel stood over her. He glanced outside then at her hand. "They will have sensed you."

"Who?"

He dropped her hand. "Do you have your Element yet?"

Adrianna shook her head. "No, I am too young. You know we have to reach full maturity to discover which point of the pentacle we will stand on."

"I watched you. Either you have your Element or you are something more than a witch. You just wrote your own Death Warrant if anyone of the coven sensed you reaching into the wind."

"It will be no great loss."

Daniel's eyes narrowed.

"Do you have yours?" she asked.

Witches and warlocks were obsessed with gaining the ability to control an Element. Usually they obtained the skill by growing into adulthood, generally between thirty and fifty years old, but if one was powerful enough they could receive the power beforehand. "Vampires grow to maturity within days of being bitten; if we are strong enough we receive our Element too," he answered.

"So not all vampires can control an Element?"

"No. If you are not strong enough you cannot go into the *Seline* to draw the Elemental power," Daniel explained. "Besides, the Darkness can corrupt the Elemental balance so it's probably a good thing not all of us can."

"It would not really make a difference," said Adrianna. "All your powerful leaders can control an Element, can they not?"

"Of course."

"Can you still produce fire-spheres?"

Daniel lifted his hand and uncurled his fingers. A sphere of fire hovered above his open palm, then an ice-tear formed in the place of the fire-sphere. Adrianna clenched her jaw. She had been trying to do that for moons. She wanted desperately to be able to create them simultaneously in each hand but also make a fire-sphere and then an ice-tear without having to close her hand each time.

"Can you do one in each hand?" she asked.

Daniel opened his other palm and formed a fire-sphere. He smirked at the annoyed look on her face. "You are having trouble with it?" He closed his hands.

Adrianna squared her shoulders. "I am practicing," she said in a dignified voice. "At least I *was*, before I ended up here." She opened her book and turned away. There was no way she was going to let him have one up on her and allow him to rub it in her face.

Daniel held back a laugh and went back to his desk. "Tell me about the Spellmakers," he said casually.

"No," she replied without turning to him.

"Do you have a lexicon?"

"You know I do."

"Did you hide it?"

"I did not have time," she replied, casting him an annoyed look. "You attacked us without warning, remember?"

Daniel smirked. "Do you know any Spellmakers?"

"Maybe yes," she said slowly, "maybe no. Why the questions?"

"Why no answers?"

Adrianna rolled her eyes and sat closer to the fire.

"How did you get better so quickly?" asked Daniel.

Adrianna shrugged. "Good fortune, I suppose," she replied softly, staring at the cracking flames.

Daniel crouched down in front of her, his elbows on his knees. He stared at her in silence until she began to blush and looked back at him.

Adrianna raised her eyebrows. "What is so interesting?"

"Uncomfortable?"

Adrianna groaned in frustration. "*Why* do you answer with a question?"

"Why do you not answer my questions?"

"Oh, goodness, perhaps, because you're my enemy!" she said sarcastically. "I cannot spill my secrets to you."

"Fine. Forget about the lexicon and Spellmakers," he said. "Explain what happened between us the other day."

Adrianna looked at him as if he were joking. *What is he playing at?* "W-well, I do not know," she said.

"Yes, you do. You knew exactly what happened after you saw the blood," he said.

"You would not understand," she said, frustrated. "You would not like what you hear; *I* do not like what's happened. You are better off not knowing."

"Am I?" he asked. "Or are you just better off not telling me? Afraid it will change something? Because *nothing* would make me see you as anything more than a slave, that I hate, that I own, whose life is in my hands."

With every word, her heart pained as though being pricked with a pin.

"Believe me when I tell you that I am not afraid of much and that I do not care about how you see or feel about me," she said, her voice shaking. "You are nothing more than a heartless upstart, self-centred, murdering, waste of space, which goes well with how you see me." She made to leave when Daniel stood in front of her like a wall before she could even take a step.

"Obviously I did not teach you anything last I was here," he said in an icy tone. "You have some audacity, little girl, to speak to me like that."

Adrianna felt the familiar tingle between them and stepped back. "It is a fault of mine."

"You seem to have many of those."

"Well, since you believe yourself to be utter perfection I suppose I must be full of faults," she said facetiously. "I have never killed anyone, or drunk their blood to satisfy my own personal hunger, or enslaved anyone, but yes, *I* am the one with the faults."

"You really are obtuse. You think everything is the way you see it."

"Oh, do not be cryptic," she said impatiently. "Move please . . ."

"No."

"I do not want to talk to you anymore!"

"No one asked *you* to talk more than you should," he replied, grabbing her arm to keep her in place. "Tell me what happened or you will see just how *evil* I can be."

"No!" Her arm began to tingle, spreading to the rest of her body. "Let me go. You do not know what you're doing."

Daniel pulled her forward. "I usually give the orders, witch," he said coldly, his eyes turning black.

Adrianna began to tremble, trying to shrink away but the magnet force between them pushed them closer the more she resisted. She looked into his blackened eyes. "Deep down inside, you're still the same," she said softly. "You did not really change when you became a vampire."

Daniel's grip loosened.

"I will kill you if you do this to me," said Adrianna. "The Pull is not something you would want. It would eventually destroy us both, but I will get you first. I promise."

"The Pull?"

Adrianna stepped back, shoving him away. "It has nothing to do with *your* kind. Is it not bad enough I have to suffer being here? Do not put this shame upon me."

Daniel's eyes slowly turned back to normal.

"Can I go to bed now?"

Daniel nodded, stepping aside. When Adrianna disappeared into his room, he picked up his coat and left, locking the doors securely. Answers were needed and if she would not give them, he would find them.

~

Nikita was making his way up the hall. He looked livid. "We need to talk."

"I was on my way to . . . actually, you may know something of this," said Daniel. "I cannot speak in my quarters."

Nikita led him two doors down. "In here. It is always empty."

The indigo room came to life as they entered: the curtains opened, allowing the moon's light to pour inside; the fire burst to life and the orb-lights glowed dimly.

"Did you lock her in?" asked Nikita.

"Yes, she is sleeping."

"It will not be long, Daniel," said Nikita, taking a seat at the small mahogany table. "The longer this takes, the closer she is to being cast to the underground chambers."

"I know. I am trying to move as quickly as I can, but I cannot arouse suspicion. The Council is pushing for a fight and Liam is very close to the end."

"Yes and when he is lost, *completely*, how long will it be before he kills that girl?"

"It could be any day."

Nikita laced his fingers together. "Sit. What is it you wished to ask me?"

"What is The Pull?"

A deep, rough laugh came from the black-haired vampire. "Daniel, why are you bothering with such annoyances? If you wish to bed the witch, do so, but do not let her cloud your mind. We have work to complete."

"Just answer me."

"Very well. The proper name is *Eriseda*. It is the effect of finding one's soul mate outside the Spirit Plane. It constitutes the joining, binding of the two souls in love and purity. Once the two souls have been reunited they must consummate *Eriseda* or part, so as not to feel the continuing surge of emotions they feel when in close contact."

That was why Daniel was always angered when he saw her. A vampire's primal emotion is anger; therefore, he felt what was more natural to him.

"What happens after consummation?" he asked.

"The two bond. Emotionally, mentally . . . time allows for the two to become one in harmony, in mind and spirit."

"If one dies, what happens?"

"It would not break the spiritual link, nor will the death of one cause the death of the other. They simply continue to the Spirit Plane."

"If one is of the Light, and another of the Darkness, what does it change?"

"I do not know. Nor do I care to. This is too far from my interest."

Daniel laughed. "It sounds like the writings of those novelettes."

"Then why ask?"

"It was a term I came across."

"Can we return to real work now?"

"By all means," he said, allowing for Nikita to explain his business. He decided that she was a beautiful woman whom he was attracted to purely on a carnal level. It had nothing to do with *Eriseda* or anything else.

~

It was almost three weeks after Liam's return when Adrianna saw Daniel again. He did not visit Liam's quarters in all that time and Adrianna knew it was because he was either afraid of what they had discovered in the Pull or he was angry with her. Perhaps it was both, but she was grateful for the distance.

Daniel's mood had been slightly short of foul the last few days of her stay with him. He hardly looked at her and when he did, he stared at her so long she thought he was trying to read her mind. She ignored him for the most part, but on the last night, she could not help but wonder what she had done to make him ignore her and distance himself as though she were a toxin.

Finally, when she reached the end of her ability to disregard his presence, she faced him. "What?" she snapped. "You are annoying me! What did I do?"

Only to be infuriated more when he simply replied, "Do not talk to me."

Liam returned a different man. He had become temperamental and was often in his demon form. Adrianna locked herself in her room for two days when he transformed into the Baál and did not speak to him afterwards because he was always preoccupied. She was grateful for Kenna's visits, however short they were. With every visit, she whispered bits of information that she had gathered over the weeks. Nothing was solid, but it seemed that Sansul coven was about to awaken an ancient vampire, the leadership was in question, and the Maquis had made yet another demand for the release of the Wilmota clan.

"*Why* all this talking? Why has no one just . . . bombed the place?"

"If what I am hearing is true, then they will, and very soon," said Kenna. "I think they are afraid that if they do attack, you will all die as well."

"It is better than rotting slowly like this. Kenna, if I am not out of here soon I will go mad from it. I know nothing of the world outside . . . it is torture. I would rather be fighting out there every single day than remain imprisoned here."

"As would I."

Kenna's remedies helped. The basalt rock kept the Darkness away when she slept and the potion had cleared her body of the decay the Darkness was creating. But it was not all good for her to be so strong; the hurt and torment the witches suffered at the hands of the vampires was even louder in her ears. She felt the pain even more strongly. No matter where she stood or how much she tried to block them, the suffering of her people often overwhelmed her.

Adrianna wondered how long it would be before the Darkness began to suck the life from her again. The basalt rock would continue to protect her body, but it could not shield her heart and soul from the grief of knowing her people would soon cease to be.

She wondered if the villages further south had been affected. Was Aires still standing? Had Bruniér been invaded? Collusus would only fall if the others did, and Azria was protected not only by the nymphs who patrolled the border, but also by the Azria coven, the largest and most powerful vampire coven in the lowlands, and oldest rival to Sansul.

Adrianna often wondered how many Wilmota witches and warlocks had escaped. Was Renauart gone? Had Ralphus and Mathias found safety, or were they imprisoned somewhere in the fortress? Was the Gordgáin providing sanctuary to those who escaped? She hoped they would soon outwit the Sansul vampires.

Wild gale storms raged outside the fortress when Adrianna saw Daniel again. She was sitting in her room, the door slightly open, when he barged into Liam's quarters. Her heart fluttered as his elegant form passed her door.

"The Gordgáin is on the move," he announced when he entered.

"What?" Liam turned away from the map of Sansul hovering in front of his desk. "How were they able to regroup?"

"We did not capture all the people. Many escaped," said Daniel. "Apparently, they have a large number hiding in their sanctuary."

"Likely all of them are gypsies," Liam said dismissively.

"Which means they will be able to quickly notify villages in the southern provinces," Daniel replied sternly. "You know how far their connections go."

"The Gordgáin will not get far," said Liam.

"No?" Daniel snapped. "The dhamphir are helping the witches. They have allied themselves with their mothers' peoples – it will not be long before they come crashing down these walls to release their kin."

Adrianna knew what Liam was thinking. Dhamphir were double the threat to vampires. They were the children of a woman and vampire. More often the progeny of a witch and vampire but the dhamphir were also known to be a mixed group of faery and nymph. The dhamphir, almost all of whom were Maquis, would have the power of each parent, light and dark, the knowledge of witchcraft and the knowledge of vampirism. Having refused to fight against their mothers in *The War Against The Angels*, it seemed that now they were allied with their Light side again.

After a long silence, Liam said, "Then we will make an example of them."

"Get twenty of the weakest witches and kill them," said Liam.

Adrianna gasped and put her hands over her mouth to keep from crying out.

"Is that you speaking?" asked Daniel. "Or is it Jeith."

Adrianna stared at the partly open door in horror.

"My demon is strong," said Liam. He was breathing heavily. "But you know it has no hold on me."

"Yet."

Daniel did not look in her direction as he followed Liam out. Adrianna felt cold and frightened. Dread rose within her, tickling between her ribs and spreading across her chest and neck. Twenty witches would lose their lives – would their bodies be left outside the Gordgáin sanctuary as a warning? Would the Gordgáin heed that warning?

Chapter Six

The Gordgáin

KENNA FROZE WHEN THE stoic voice of her Maker called her name. Her hand hovered over her black embroidered coat; she turned her head toward the door. He was the last person she wanted to be near. His attempts to devoid her of all emotions had not worked; it only made her more determined to rebel against the Darkness and her changing form.

Standing in her doorway, the narrow-faced man stared at her with eyes as emotionless as his voice. His black hair was immaculately brushed back; his clothes of the usual clean-cut style of the vampires, separating themselves even further from the warlocks by abandoning the flamboyant flairs and colours of the Light elementals.

"Yes, Thomas?"

"Where are you going?" he asked, stepping into the room.

"Away from the screams," she replied, picking up her coat. "I am fed up with the constant noises coming from the underground chambers." She felt pleased with herself, surely she sounded arrogant enough.

"Yes," he said, his tone unchanged. "I do wish we would put the witches out of their misery. But the Council has plans for them."

Kenna arched an eyebrow. "Well, seeing as you enjoy it so much . . ." She made to leave.

"And what about your friend?"

"Who?"

Thomas looked slightly pleased at having caught her so surprised. "The young witch Liam keeps hidden in his rooms. He thinks nobody knows. I know he brings you to see her."

"So?"

"So, I hope you are not trying to help her, Kenna," he continued. "I do not want to have made a mistake when I turned you."

"You did," Kenna assured him. "What did you think would happen when you turned me? I told you before that I would not give in to you. Did you think I would learn to exist within the confines of this prison? Become your lover, maybe? Turn my back on my people, my family?"

"You are resisting the Darkness with every fibre of your being, aren't you?"

"Make no mistake of it. I will *not* be like you."

She could not comprehend why Thomas found amusement in what she said; his usually expressionless face smiled, but it did not meet his eyes.

"I know you will not." He stepped out of her way. "Do not be gone for long."

Kenna nodded and made her way quickly through the halls. The torch flames cast her shadow along the pale yellow walls. She avoided looking at the couple standing, entwined, outside their bedroom. They broke their kiss and watched her pass, their eyes luminescent with desire. Walking out the front doors, she ran to the fortress gates. Piercing her thumb with a fang, she ran her blood over the lock. Sensing the Darkness in her, it opened.

"Where are you going?"

Kenna spun around. "Daniel."

By the amount of snow that was dusted over his fur-trimmed coat, she surmised he had been outside a while. His blonde hair cascaded down around his shoulders, giving him the appearance of a white angel.

"I was just going to . . ." She looked out toward Wilmota and sighed. "Walk through it all."

"You are Adrianna's oldest friend," he said. "I do not think for a moment that you are just going to 'walk through it.' That is not your style."

"Does anything pass your attention? You seem to know everything."

"I keep myself informed," said Daniel. "It's the only way to survive."

"So you must know that one of these days, Adrianna is going to snap. She is either going to die or get out."

"Indeed she will."

"So why do you not let her go?"

"Because if she is gone, I cannot protect her as easily," he said.

Kenna's eyebrows shot up. "What do you mean?"

"Do not be long," he said, turning away. "Vampires are not welcome in Wilmota. The Maquis will kill you if you are caught."

Kenna stared after him. "I do not understand!"

"Step lightly, Kenna," he said without looking back.

When Daniel passed through the wooden doors of the fortress, she covered her head with the hood of her coat and stepped out through the gate.

~

Wilmota had become a ghost town after the attack. An eerie silence hung in the cold night air as Kenna walked swiftly through the empty village toward the small temple located on a detouring path off the main road.

Knowing there could be no immediate rebellion, the survivors were forced to abandon any rescue plans and remain in hiding. In the days after the attack, vampire soldiers had returned to Wilmota, killing those who had not hidden themselves well enough, while others, who would prove useful to the vampires, were taken to the fortress.

Disappearing Cupboards and Staircase Trunks could only keep people hidden for a short time. Most of those who hid were forced to escape the flames of their burning homes after soldiers came looking for stragglers; braving the decimated, vampire-run village in an effort to reach the hidden sanctuary entrance. The Dial Doors were the first things the vampires destroyed, keeping anyone from escaping to neighbouring villages.

Now, Kenna was the only moving living thing in the village. Even the birds had fled. She passed empty houses on her way to the temple. Some had been burned to the ground, others desecrated; not one was left untouched. The water fountain on the village green was now dry and stained with blood, and even the temple had been denied mercy.

On the night of the attack the vampires had violated the commanding and formerly welcoming structure. The doors were barely hanging on their hinges, the basilica-shaped interior was scorched and gutted, windows were shattered, and the altar was reduced to a mere upturned burnt table.

Kenna knelt before the altar.

"I am Kenna," she spoke, "Daughter of Sandra and Junes of the Wilmota clan. I am a vampire without a demon soul, turned against my will at Sansul fortress. I seek the help of the Gordgáin members who sought me three weeks ago. I have information that will help with the effort to release the witches."

She did not have to wait long for a reply. The ground shook beneath her knees.

"Get off the door!" said a gruff voice, as the speaker knocked heavily.

Kenna shuffled aside, watching as the stained carpet flipped up and a trap-door opened. A pleasant-looking man with greying hair and a lilac beard poked his head through the hole.

"Hello Simo."

"Ah, Kenna," he said coolly. "I am glad you came."

Simo, the Gordgáin leader, was Chief of the Rhoxolani gypsy tribe. He had been in Wilmota for trade when the vampires attacked. Duty called for him to take up his former post and he was once again in command of hundreds of witches, warlocks, nymphs, faeries and other elementals, fighting against the Darkness.

"I cannot stay long," said Kenna. "I suspect someone is following me."

"The temple is well guarded against spies. It may look like a pile of old ruins, but we are still protected," he said. "Come inside."

Kenna followed him down a flight of steep steps. Before them was a bolted oak door, the official entrance to the sanctuary. She would never pass that door again, not now that she was a vampire. They entered a bunker-like chamber. Ten people were waiting in the cramped area. They did not come near her, preferring to stay back. Only Renauart came forward. His eyes spoke more than any words could have expressed.

"It's all right," she told Renauart. "I found her. I did what I set out to do."

"I failed you," he whispered sorrowfully.

"No! You did everything you could and more. Now it is my turn to help you."

Renauart pinched the bridge of his nose and blinked away the tears that were threatening to fall. Kenna squeezed his arm and turned to Simo. "As I said, I cannot stay long," she said. "You must leave if you wish to remain alive. There is no way to know for sure that the vampires will not scour the area again."

"The village is deserted," replied Simo. "Those who were not captured could only stand to live here a few weeks before travelling south through the tunnels. Only members of the Gordgáin remain."

"That is a relief," said Kenna.

"The old curses and protections still remain. We have some nice additions, thanks to Allan the Spellmaker," said Simo, looking at the walls fondly. "Any vampire that tries to pass," he turned and nodded to the bolted door, "will meet with a nasty surprise."

"How many are you?"

"Don't tell her that," said a man harshly from the corner of the room. He looked very distrustful of Kenna. "Don't speak like you're not one of *them*, girl."

"I do not think like them," Kenna snapped. "I was bitten against my will, Gralam, as were so many others. You would do well not to judge so quickly."

"She knows our secrets," said Renauart fairly. "If she wanted to betray us, she would have already."

Kenna inclined her head gratefully to Renauart. "You wanted to know the status of the prisoners," she said to the group. "They are weak, tormented by the Darkness. Many have been turned. Others have been branded. But there are many who can be saved. You must do something soon if it is to be done at all."

"Branded?" gasped a blonde woman. "Just like the old days."

"I do not want to sound heartless, but there are more to be saved than those being taken by vampires," said Kenna. "Once Henry is awakened there will be no hope for any of them."

"*Henry?*" cried the woman in horror.

"We are truly cursed," said a warlock.

"When is he to be awakened?" asked Simo.

"Soon. Once the infighting stops in the Council, it could be a fortnight, perhaps less," said Kenna. "Make haste with your plans. Have you called upon the Maquis?"

"We are waiting for a reply," said Simo. "I know they will help us. The question is, when?"

"They are working independently at the moment," said Renauart.

"How are you faring Kenna?" asked Simo. "Have you," he paused, "accepted the change?"

"I can do nothing else," she replied. "I do not want others to have their lives torn away from them. I do not want . . . I do not want Adrianna to die or end up like me."

"We are trying our best," Renauart assured her.

"Can you tell us how many are being held in the fortress?" asked Simo.

"I think there are at least two hundred witches in there," Kenna said. "Dozens were killed and I know a few dozen children have been taken to a guarded place nearby. They are likely in a separate building behind the wall. The warlocks, I know nothing about. Some say they are in the mines beneath the sea . . ."

"And I know for sure that one hundred people escaped to the south the night of the attack," a blonde witch replied.

Kenna nodded. "Those turned to vampires will no longer be willing to leave."

"*Leave*?" asked Gralam. "They are changed. There is no hope for them."

Kenna narrowed her eyes at him. "You are very quick to discard others, aren't you? I thought I was supposed to be the cold one."

"Gralam," the blonde witch said reproachfully.

Gralam glared at Kenna and crossed his arms. "The Immortal Damned," he said confidently. "That was the name for your kind in the past. Damned you all are. Damned to walk in the shadows. Damned to drink the blood of the innocent and damned you are to live with the energy of the Darkness. Once you are lost, there is no returning."

The Gordgáin members stood silently. Their stillness only confirmed their agreement with Gralam's words.

Kenna squared her shoulders. "We are not immortal. This 'damned' vampire has come to this hole in the ground to aid you," she said. "You have an unusual way of showing kinship, or at the least, gratitude. I have collected information in the hope it would aid *your* cause. The way you discard my existence, and those others who have been unmercifully turned, is appalling. For a man whose duty it is to spread words of forgiveness and caring, you purposely forget those words because of a difference in race. That is why war between vampires and warlocks has lasted so long; you cast aside your love for your former sons and daughters so quickly." She looked around at the group grimly. "I did not come here to be insulted."

"Kenna . . ." said Renauart.

"I hope someday you see beyond the orthodox world you live in," said Kenna. "And that you can embrace those who return to you; no matter how much they may have changed. Goodnight."

~

Daniel sat at his desk, fiddling with his pen as Nikita spoke.

"You can give Rasmus the briefing when we get back," he said. "You are better with the finer details than I."

Nikita paced back and forth. Graceful in his movements, like most vampires, he had a confidence that was difficult to ignore. He did not speak to those he deemed unworthy of his time and *never* repeated himself; many learned the latter the hard way.

Daniel was hardly listening to his friend; his mind was on Adrianna. He often found himself thinking about her, sometimes at the most inopportune times.

"Daniel," Nikita said sternly. "Stop thinking about the witch."

"I am listening," he replied.

"Rasmus wants you to send Erik a message directly, informing him of the number of guards, spells and gates around the fortress," said Nikita. "He said it would help sharpen the point of attack."

Daniel nodded, noting it down.

"We must overthrow Liam and the Council, to stop them from waking Henry," said Nikita. "This is crucial."

"So is our cover. If Liam even hears a whisper that something is off, he will put our plans in jeopardy."

"Have you noticed him lately?" asked Nikita. "He is losing his mind."

"Losing? His sanity is long gone," said Daniel. "Jeith has seeped into his consciousness. Liam is dying and being replaced by his demon."

"This has happened too quickly," said Nikita disapprovingly. "There must be a way to stop it."

"Other than killing him?" asked Daniel. "No. Jeith is too powerful. He cannot be stopped."

"Which is why we must aid Erik and launch the attack sooner," said Nikita, pulling a pipe from his pocket. He took a deep breath and blew into it, casting a flame into the tobacco. "Then we can finally go home."

Daniel nodded, discarding his pen. "How did we get trapped here?"

"Wrong place," said Nikita, releasing a smoke ring, "wrong time. Last I took Liam on a blood-hunt, he told me more about the witch he has in his rooms."

Daniel raised his eyebrows. "I am waiting with bated breath," he said wryly.

"He says she used to be a friend of yours, when you were children," said Nikita, watching Daniel closely.

"A minor fact."

Nikita took his time, taking a long puff of his pipe. "Apparently, she is more than just a witch. When you were children, she performed magic so beyond her years he was convinced she was something of an angel."

"I think Liam has been smoking some of your weed, Nikita," said Daniel.

"It would not be beyond the realm of possibility. If she is celestial . . ."

"She is not."

Nikita held his gaze. "Maybe not, but the reason for his keeping her quiet is that he intends to give her to Henry."

Daniel squared his shoulders. "A very calculated move. If she is pleasing to Henry, Liam rises in his esteem, and likely, position."

"Exactly. But what he fails to understand is that Henry does not give and take power for tokens like women. Henry is an old-fashioned dictator. So, what do you plan to do with her?" Nikita asked pointedly.

"I don't know," Daniel replied honestly.

"You cannot save her, my friend," said Nikita. "She is lost. I have seen many a beautiful creature and at times I have wished that my life had turned out differently. But they all die. They are all losses and we cannot afford to be blindsided. Especially at a time like this, in a *place* like this."

"Maybe."

"Have you had her?" Nikita asked, blowing a ring of smoke. When Daniel laughed, Nikita added, in disbelief, "She stayed with you almost a week in your private quarters and you did not take her to bed? Not once . . .?"

"I was too busy trying not to kill her," said Daniel. "She is infuriating. She has no fear."

"Which is why she tempts you," said Nikita. "You call yourself a vampire."

"If I did bed her, I'd have to tell her the truth. There are consequences to getting involved with witches," he said, staring at the corner of his desk. "How did she *bloody* end up here?" he demanded, speaking more to himself than Nikita. "She should have gone to Azria with her cousin when her parents disappeared."

It was Nikita's turn to laugh, though it sounded sinister. "Daniel, we are all trapped here. I'll tell you what, when all these plans are done and it is time for us to leave, bring your witch."

"She is not my witch," Daniel muttered.

Nikita arched a brow and stowed his pipe in his pocket. "There is still time."

Daniel smirked. "Have you heard from Christopher?"

Nikita nodded. "Yesterday. He is with the Maquis."

~

Sweet, warm, crimson liquid dripped into the snow, tainting the white beneath his heavy, black boots.

With a growl, Liam pulled his mouth from the witch's throat. She was limp in his grip; her wide lifeless eyes stared up at him. He released his hold and watched, blood dripping from his fangs, as her body crumpled to the ground.

Liam's chest heaved from the force of his feeding. He had taken mere mouthfuls of her blood, and his hunger still burned like an ache in his veins. He needed more. Younger, fresher . . . and next time it had to be one who would remain alive while he fed. A cold smile graced his bloodied lips. The best feedings had always been while his food was alive. He loved it when they screamed in terror; terror he could taste in their heated, saccharine blood. They thrashed and begged, as they balanced on the periphery of death.

Liam glanced down to the dead witch at his feet. His aide handed him his coat. Yes, this one had been too old, at least three hundred years. She was pretty, he had to admit, with her long, fire-red hair and sun-kissed skin, but her blood was too mature for his taste. He preferred fresh witches, the ones who were yet to experience the fruition of womanhood and gain their elemental powers. Their fear of being bitten and dominated by a vampire was irresistibly alluring. He licked the corners of his mouth for any blood he might have missed.

Nikita, dark and foreboding with his aquiline nose and waist-length black hair, strode through the trees toward him.

"Anything?" asked Liam.

"There was movement in the village," Nikita said uncaringly. "Perhaps you will have better luck there."

Liam grinned and motioned for the two soldiers behind him to follow. "Remind me why you don't enjoy this anymore, Nikita."

Nikita glanced at the lifeless witch. "I have been doing this for almost a hundred years," he said. Memories flashed in his mind as he spoke. "It gets boring. I have heard every scream, every kind of cry. At the end, they are all just the same – dead."

"So morbid," said Liam, walking out of the forest. "The blood-hunt is our sacred right, Nikita. Without it we would go wild. We need to dominate."

Nikita ground his molars as they walked toward the village. The snow was thick around his ankles. He buckled his fur-trimmed coat tightly, not wanting any part of himself exposed to the chill. In the past, the fruit had been there for the picking. But since the attack had enslaved most of the witches and forced others into hiding, the only thing they were likely to catch was a hag or a stray nymph outside the Sleeping Forest.

Liam sniffed the air as they passed a once grand house, now reduced ruins. His eyes dilated as he turned to Nikita, grinning. "I believe we have our meal," he whispered.

Nikita breathed in. There certainly was a whiff of witch in the air. They were close. So close in fact, he could hear footsteps.

"She is in one of the cottages," said Nikita, his fangs lengthening.

Liam disappeared around a group of snow-capped buildings. Nikita dawdled to the frozen water fountain in the middle of the square. He motioned for the soldiers to stand on either side of the path. Soon it came – the scream of terror that Liam lived for. The door to the candle-maker's home burst open and a wave of blonde hair flew out into the snow. Liam strolled out, heaved the witch by the scruff of the neck and dragged her to the fountain.

"She was trying to get into a Disappearing Cupboard," said Liam, casting her at Nikita's feet.

The witch thrashed on the ground and tried to run away, only to be thrown down into the snow once more and held down by Liam's boot. He slammed the weight of his foot heavily on her chest, winding her.

"What is your name?" asked Liam.

"Curse you!" she said, wheezing.

"Are you a Gordgáin?"

"I will see you burn, *filth*!" she cried, gasping beneath the pressure of his boot.

"You and your kind are an irritant," muttered Liam.

"If you are going to kill me, then do it," she choked.

Nikita leaned his elbows on his knees. "Look at me," he ordered.

"No."

"Do you know who I am?"

"Yes."

"Are you a Gordgáin?"

"Yes."

"Do you want to live?"

"Yes."

"Then answer any questions truthfully. Or else I will make your death a painful reality," said Nikita.

"I will not tell you *anything*." She cried out when Liam kicked her side. "No!" she gasped, rolling away. Wheezing, she clutched at her ribs.

Liam plucked her from the ground and turned her face to the side. "Where is the Gordgáin to help you now?" he hissed in her ear before burying his fangs inside her neck. After a few mouthfuls, he pulled back with an appreciative groan. Her blood was already warming his body. Every one of his senses had come alive. But this had been too easy; he might well have taken one of the witches from the fortress for all the thrill this brought. This was no challenge. There had been no stalking, no anticipation, and no satisfaction in this laughably easy capture.

The witch's head flopped forward weakly. She whimpered when Liam yanked her head back, pulling her hair.

"Do you want to live?"

"Yes." She squeezed her eyes closed, crying.

"Then go," he said gently, stroking her cheek. "But go quickly."

When he released her, the witch fell to the ground. She scrambled to her feet and ran past them, down the winding path out of the village.

Liam licked his lips and laughed. "They are so simple."

"You are letting her go?" Nikita asked casually.

"Of course not. But a hunt would not be a hunt if it ended so quickly," said Liam. "Let's go."

"I have had enough," said Nikita. "I am going back."

"Without feeding? You must taste her – her blood was untainted," said Liam.

"I will feed at the fortress," Nikita replied. "Maybe a voluptuous brunette this time; those fair sticks do nothing for the appetite."

Liam smirked. "You have changed too much, Nikita. I am not sure Henry will approve."

Nikita's lip curled in disdain as he watched Liam follow the witch toward the tulip fields. "Wait for him here," he told the guards. "Report to me the minute he returns to the fortress."

Liam followed the witch through the tulip field. The flowers, usually a rainbow of colours, had turned white for the winter. He waved jovially at her as she ran, looking over her shoulder at him. *There is nowhere for her to go,* thought Liam with satisfaction. He paused, mid-stride. The tulips were moving, shifting, as if someone was walking through them. The witch was almost to the end of the field now.

"You cannot pass the field!"

Liam looked around for the origin of the squeaky voice. Opening his palm, he threw a fire-sphere into the flowers at his right. There was a yelp and a little pointy-eared figure in a red suit and cravat leaped into the air clutching its bottom. Liam smirked. "Elves."

The elf fell back to the ground and rubbed his backside in the dirt to put out the fire. His fellows growled menacingly at the vampire. Their oversized eyes were globes of fury. At about eight inches in height, they were not tall enough to be seen through the tulips, but that worked to their advantage. The elves walked slowly toward Liam's boots; their little feet made no sound upon the snow. Using the tulip stems as cover and vantage points, they moved into an attack formation. But just when they were ready to strike - fire descended upon them.

Liam rained fire upon the entire field, burning flowers, soil and elves. They fell back. Those caught by the flames squealed and squirmed on the ground, others made their way through the blaze to their injured friends. The elf whose bottom had been burned, leaving him with his backside hanging out of his red trousers, shook the stems of the tulips in an effort to shower his fellows with snow, but the fire had quickly evaporated any moisture in the field.

The elves sped through the burning stems, making for the Sleeping Forest. Their red, green and brown suits were singed, their skin badly burned, so badly that some had to be carried by their fellows.

The witch crouched behind a tree. It was too dangerous to go to the Gordgáin sanctuary. She had to wait for the faeries to confirm that all vampires were gone from the village before sneaking back. She cried as flames engulfed the field, burning each and every flower. The tulip field had been one of Wilmota's attractions. Its flowers had once provided beauty to the landscape, commerce to the florist, healing to the apothecary, and a beautiful setting for parties and weddings.

"You won't be spying for the Gordgáin anymore," said Liam, coming up behind her. He snatched her face, his fingers digging into her jaw. He turned her to face him.

The witch did not fight back. Instead she squared her shoulders. "Upon your death, you will know the pain of all those you have killed, one hundred times over," she said, her eyes on his. "You will stand strong and sustain it or your soul will evaporate into nothing. I curse you and your demon."

Liam bit into the front of her throat to keep her from continuing. She did not scream or whimper. As her life was drained away and Liam drank his fill, her dying breath sealed the curse.

Liam carried her body to the temple where he dumped her at the front door. He wiped his mouth of her blood and left his bloodied handprint on the wall.

"This is for all Gordgáin spies!" he yelled into the basilica. "Worthless," he hissed, looking at the witch's corpse.

His guards were waiting. Lifting his collar around his neck, he motioned for them follow.

"It is time to make some changes."

CHAPTER SEVEN

Baliath

D ANIEL PRESSED HIS EAR against his bedroom door. He sensed little and heard nothing: no sheets shifting, footsteps or even breathing. The previous day, he and Adrianna had passed the time in an awkward silence. Unable to escape her or leave her unattended, when in the same room, he looked at anything but her. Adrianna, he noticed upon quick glances, was doing the same. Her attention was focused firmly on the book in her lap. As evening approached, Adrianna muttered something about being tired and slipped away to his bedroom. There she had stayed. She had not even responded when he knocked on the door that morning to announce the arrival of her food. He suspected she was ignoring him. But by now she had gone too long without sustenance, and he had become concerned about her weakened state.

Opening the door slowly, he peered inside, adjusting his eyes so as to see through the lightless room. Adrianna was curled up on his wingback chair by the window. The candles came alight with a wave of his hand, showering the room in a golden glow.

Adrianna closed her eyes and groaned. She was pale, sweating and trembling involuntarily. Her breath came out in short intervals; sounding as though each was a painful struggle.

Daniel's eyes flashed. He had seen this before. She was dying. The Darkness had finally broken through the last barrier of her resistance and infiltrated her lungs.

"What are you doing?" Adrianna whined weakly when the light hit her eyes. She tugged at a blanket, trying to hide her barely-dressed body. Her dress lay discarded on the bed.

"Do you not realise how ill you are?" he asked, pulling her hands away from her face.

"I will be fine," she said softly. "I am just tired."

"You have a fever," said Daniel. "Take this off."

Adrianna laughed weakly. "I do not think you need to see me naked," she muttered. "I said I am fine. Just go away."

"Do not act like a child," said Daniel, pulling the blanket off her. "Try to get up."

"You cannot do anything for me. The only thing that can help me is nature. Witches do not survive behind stone walls; it's why you put us here."

"So you want to sit there and die?"

She closed her eyes. "I have come to terms with it. I am sure you will miss me."

It was true; she had come to terms with her own death. When she felt her life force ebbing away during the night she knew the time had come. There was nothing to do but wait. She had tried to think about her life, past and present, and the people who had made it so wonderful: her cousin Blanca, her parents, Kenna, her clan. She drew comfort from the memories.

All the while, in the back of her mind, something told her she could not die. Her mother's words repeated in her tired mind. "Death for our people is a chosen path," she had said. Tears came to Adrianna's eyes as she envisioned Irina's beautiful face. Tall and dark-skinned with black glittery hair, her mother had been so full of love for her only daughter. Irina's disappearance had confused and tortured Adrianna for years. The passing time did little to numb the pain . . . perhaps they would soon meet again on the Spirit Plane.

As Daniel stood beside her, the memories faded, leaving her mind in the peaceful meditative state in which she hoped to die.

Daniel scooped her up in his arms. "Be quiet," he said as the blanket floated up to cover her.

"Daniel, please put me down," she said softly.

"You need nature, I'll give you nature," he said, striding out of his room. He raced out of the building from a long unused flight of stairs. As the back entrances were usually abandoned, Daniel was fairly confident they would not be seen. She needed to connect with the earth, to be one with it and draw her strength from its richness.

Witchery had deep foundations in the connection and manipulation of nature. Elementals lived their lives by the turns of the seasons, the days and nights, drawing their energy from the sun and the moon, the earth beneath and the sky above in equal force.

The Darkness and the stones of the fortress had sucked out her strength, and the will that kept her alive was now rapidly destroying her, for the more one resisted the Darkness the faster it strengthened.

Daniel kicked open a small door at the foot of the stairs and ran out into the night air. The heavy Wilmota winter had turned the gardens white. Leaves fell in the autumn and were reborn white on the first day of winter.

He fell to his knees by a group of snow-dusted trees far from view of any windows. Resting Adrianna on his lap, he melted a patch of snow using a fire-sphere and cut out a block of iced soil using the same method. He placed Adrianna in the hollow and covered her chest and legs with the moist earth. He rubbed it on her dainty hands, her neck and then sat back, waiting.

She had drifted off into the *void*, the unknown place on the edge of life, as he carried her. She was barely holding on.

"Wake up, Adrianna."

Whenever the wind blew, Daniel thought he noticed Adrianna moving, only to realise it was his imagination. She lay there as still as the earth itself. Soon, a glow began to surround her. Small golden sparks, flickering like miniature lightning bolts, emerged from the soil. Daniel moved away as he did not dare get too close. The sparks merged, one by one, until Adrianna's whole body was immersed in a white light. It looked like a casing of misty white glass.

Daniel watched from a distance, but his demon had begun to stir, aware of the strength in the power that was now emanating from Adrianna. He did not want to leave her, not as vulnerable as she was. He wanted her to be well, to heal her. So he sat and waited.

"What is this?"

Daniel looked up sharply. Instinctually, his eyes turned black and his fangs lengthened.

A dark-haired vampire stood a few feet away between a snow-covered bench and a flowerless bush. His lips and chin were smudged red and the front of his shirt was stained in blood. He had just killed.

"So the rumours are true," the vampire said, his black eyes locked on Adrianna. "You and Liam have a witch."

"Keep your tongue behind your teeth," growled Daniel, rising from the ground. "Or I will rip it out."

"Really, Daniel?" the vampire asked cockily. "How are you going to do that?"

Daniel tilted his head; his dead black eyes menacing against his pale face. His skin colour began to change. His hair disappeared, retreating into his head. Next his fingernails darkened to black as his skin turned vermilion red. On his face, two black lines ran from the eyebrows, over the crown of his now bald head, and down to his neck. Two thin black strokes, an inch in length, adorned each of his cheeks and the ink markings began again on his shoulders disappearing into his shirt. His now red ears were pointed at the top. Muscles expanded, thickening around his shoulders and arms, making the shirt he wore too small.

Now twice the size of the vampire, the demon rolled his neck and shrugged his shoulders as though having just awakened from a deep sleep. This was no longer Daniel; he had transformed into the demon essence that possessed his body from the night he had been made a vampire.

The intruding vampire was instantly humbled. He knelt on one knee, his head bowed. "Baliath," he said reverently. "I had no idea it was you. Please, forgive my disrespect."

The demon cocked its head to one side. "Forgiveness is not a virtue we of the Darkness possess, Kayman." His voice was a deep rumble that vibrated from his chest. Baliath spoke slowly but powerfully, knowing his words would be heeded without argument.

"Then I request your pardon," said Kayman. "If I had known who you were, I would not have disturbed you."

Baliath motioned for the vampire to stand. "You carry a lowly demon, I sense." He stepped forward, strengthening his connection with the vampire. "There is no need for fear. This witch serves my own . . . personal purposes," he said. "My business is my own."

"Of course," Kayman said quickly. "One as powerful as yourself need not answer to anybody."

Baliath smiled meekly, as though he knew the punch line to his own joke. He put his large, red hand on Kayman's shoulder. "I would like to believe that what you say is true," he said, "but in these tumultuous days I cannot afford the risk." He snatched Kayman's neck, lifting him off the ground. "I have too many enemies on this Plane to risk being seen." He put his other hand over Kayman's heart, burning it from the inside. The vampire's legs shook violently, his eyes widened and rolled to the back of his head, his fangs lengthened but his mouth slacked as he grabbed feebly at Baliath's arm.

Baliath released his grip. Kayman fell limp on the ground. A black, dense smoke emerged from his mouth.

Baliath caught the smoke and set it alight. He stepped back from the body and as he waved his hand, the corpse burst into flame, quickly consumed. A strong wind arose, and the remaining pile of ash lifted high into the air in a swirl and disappeared off the cliff.

It took a moment for Baliath to transform into Daniel. As his bones snapped back into place, his muscles twisted, shrank, and rippled beneath his now fading skin. Daniel groaned, clenching his molars against the pain. Daniel was larger than most men, but Baliath was an enormous demon; taking his shape, especially in the beginning, required great strength.

Daniel knelt beside Adrianna as the white casing around her began to fade.

Adrianna pulled her way out of thick layers of sleep, drowsy but rested. Her mind was spinning, and she was desperately cold. She opened her eyes slowly but they watered. Daniel's face hovered inches above hers. "This is how you wish to kill me?" she asked croakily.

"I'll explain when we get back," he said, lifting her out of the dirt and into his arms. He carried her to his room and lay her down on the bed.

Adrianna felt as though she had just awakened from the best sleep of her life. Her body was energised and powerful, her mind clear. She had not felt this good since before her capture. Yet he had halted the peaceful death she had been expecting.

"I am covered in dirt."

Daniel took the basalt rock from the table by the window and put it in her hand. "I do not want to have to do that again."

"You would do it again?"

"You know I would."

Adrianna frowned. "Thank you."

"I thought you had come to terms with your death," he said facetiously, opening the window.

"Obviously you have not," she replied, covering her icy body with the bed covers.

A strange expression passed over Daniel's face as he turned to her. She had meant it as a joke but his reaction made it obvious she was not far from the truth. Daniel masked his expression, leaving his face as cold and stoic as usual, and they were left once again in an awkward silence.

"Is your demon very powerful?" she asked, grasping for something to replace the quiet.

"You could say that," Daniel answered. "He was a member of the Demon High Council and a great warrior. Baliath fought personally against Phillip, Conqueror of the Angels." He sounded proud to have the essence of such a demon.

Adrianna was not impressed. If anything, she was nervous, but a few things were beginning to make sense. This demon must have influenced Daniel's dark side. Was *he* responsible for almost strangling her to death all those weeks ago in Liam's quarters? Was Baliath influencing Daniel's indifference to the suffering of witches?

"Why did Baliath leave his position?"

"Demons do not *leave* their positions. This is not an apprenticeship at a haberdashery," replied Daniel, sitting in the chair beside her bed.

"If you insist," Adrianna rested her head against the headboard. "There is much turmoil in the earth, you know. It is not at peace. If this goes on, there will be no cycle of rebirth in nature this spring. Do you know what that will mean for the rest of Sansul?"

"Yes."

"Then I do not need to tell you that if nature ceases to live, we also die. Beings of both the Light and Darkness will die, and the strength we need to reincarnate will grow weaker. Which means the Light and the Darkness grow weaker, until it too has no life."

"It will not come to that," he said, looking into her eyes.

"It will. I promise you. I saw it when I lay in the soil. Life is a cycle, Daniel. This coven has not learned from its past mistakes."

"What else did you see as you lay in the earth?"

"Pain. Great pain. Nature is not happy with us; it sees what is becoming of us. But I did sense Liam returning. He is hunting my people," she said, her voice growing tired and hoarse.

"Yes. He will return with the Darkness awake inside of him, his demon no longer dormant, and he will hurt you."

"I know."

"A demon cannot take over a host's body without permission," Daniel explained. "But, if the host is weak it is only too easy for the demon to overpower the host forever. Jeith is awake and controls Liam's body . . . and mind."

"You are saying Liam is weak?"

"Jeith is not a demon of fairy tales."

Adrianna scooted down beneath the covers. "You would not ever let Baliath take over you, would you?"

"No."

Adrianna's eyes fluttered closed. She tried to stay awake, but Daniel knew she still needed rest and closed the curtains.

"Sleep," he said. "A bath will be waiting when you wake."

The next evening, Adrianna was in a light trance when Daniel returned to his quarters. She sat with her legs crossed before the fireplace in the living room dressed in a black skirt and shirt. Using the energy of the fire, she worked to replenish the deteriorating parts of her body. There were too many enchantments on the fortress to use the fire for anything beyond that. The fire would not move from the hearth, nor grow or shrink. If she had any intention of burning the fortress to the ground, it was quickly forgotten.

Adrianna lifted her head and spared him a small smile before turning back to the fire. Daniel removed his jacket and continued to his room. Moments later, he returned with his shirtsleeves rolled back and went straight to his desk.

"I have an appointment with some unsavoury people this evening," he said as he sat down, "and I do not want you seen."

"All right," she replied, rising and separating herself from the fire. "What is so unsavoury about them?"

"For one thing," said Daniel, looking over to her, "they hunt witches for sport."

"Isn't that true of all vampires?" she bit back.

"Did that book not teach you anything?" he asked, arching an inquisitive eyebrow.

He referred to the book she had spent days reading in Liam's quarters. She had read in great detail the history of the vampires and their ways of life.

"It taught me that vampires are very gluttonous," she replied.

Daniel only annoyed her when he smiled, and charmingly at that. "Yes, we are." He picked up his pen and dipped it in ink. "What is the point of living an eternity if you cannot enjoy it?"

Adrianna huffed and turned away. He *always* had to have one up on her. Why could he not let her have a snipe at his people and be quiet?

Almost an hour later, Adrianna's attention was interrupted by a sharp knock on the door. Jumping up immediately, she went into his bedroom. Curiosity got the better of her. She had to see who these *unsavoury* people were. Closing the door, she knelt down, removed the key from the keyhole and peered through.

She could not see from the door to the corner of Daniel's desk, but the fireplace and the open sitting place were in perfect view.

The visitors were two men. One was almost as tall as Daniel and solidly built, his eyes large with eyebrows as dark as his hair. *Creepy.* The other was extremely pale and had deep-set eyes, a thin moustache on his top lip and dark slicked-back hair. *Creepy and oily.*

"You're late, Vascus," was Daniel's greeting to the latter.

"We had trouble getting past them Maquis," said Vascus.

Adrianna recognised his accent as that of the Bruniér people. Bruniér was a township southwest of Wilmota with its own vampire coven that lived deep in the mountains. She watched, squinting, as he put his hand in his pocket and handed Daniel a letter. "It's from Lukaas. Him and his are in Azria."

Adrianna held her breath. The other vampire was slowly making his way toward the door!

"I smell *woman*," the vampire said, sniffing the air like a dog. "Witch!"

"Get away from there, Rowan," Daniel said warningly.

The vampire grinned, looking at the door as if he could see her. "No harm, Daniel. You know I like a good woman and this one must be tasty if she's still alive and in your quarters."

"Would you stop thinking with your second brain for once?" Vascus asked, sitting on the chair in front of Daniel's desk.

"It's my only brain," replied Rowan, making his way to the fireplace.

Adrianna breathed a sigh of relief.

"I do not doubt it," Daniel muttered.

"So when you getting out?" Vascus asked Daniel as he ran his finger over the edge of his moustache. "This place is nothing anymore; it's going to implode."

"I have my orders," replied Daniel. "I will leave when it's necessary."

Vascus shrugged. "Just don't wait until the last minute, is all I'm saying."

"Did you accomplish what I asked?" said Daniel.

Vascus nodded and Rowan laughed as if he held some sort of secret knowledge. "Got so close . . ." said Rowan, rubbing his hands together. "They're masochists, them on the Council. That Hammer . . ." He shivered deliberately, "*Bloodthirsty.*"

Daniel looked to Vascus for an explanation.

"It's nothing you don't already know," said Vascus. "The Council is planning an expansion, they want to eliminate the Maquis and Liam wants to awaken the ancients. Pandema tried to get them to rethink their plans before sending out orders. You see, she's nervous about a fight with Rasmus."

"Naturally," said Daniel.

"Liam wants all them warlocks in the mines executed," Vascus continued. "Seems the Council wants to take over the villages all the way down to Azria, but they're too scared because an Inter-Plane war will break out again, not to mention the trouble they'll have with the other covens, especially Azria and Citron. This Council is shit if you ask me. They're too afraid of their own shadows."

"It's why Liam wants to awaken Henry," said Rowan smugly.

"He thinks Henry will give them victory," said Vascus.

"Knows it," said Rowan. "We nearly won *The War Against the Angels* with his leadership."

"Did you kill Rex?" asked Daniel.

Adrianna perked up.

"No, he was hard to get to. I'll get him before tomorrow."

"Get it done," ordered Daniel.

"It's not easy to kill someone on the Council," Vascus replied. "They're always with someone – *timing* is everything."

"Kill him in his quarters then," said Daniel.

"What if he's with someone?" asked Rowan.

"Kill them too," Daniel said, as if the answer were obvious.

Adrianna looked at the keyhole in horror. Had Daniel truly just ordered the assassination of a Councillor? Who was he? How can he have the power to end the life of another vampire?

"If Rex keeps pushing to wake an entire regiment of the army that means trouble for us," said Daniel. "And at least fifty witches will be used for blood."

"Stupid move, wan'it?" Vascus said tartly. "I'll tell you this though, Daniel, if Henry wakes, them witches are gonna be dead anyway."

"True. Rowan, you are to go and scout along the border. See if you pick up anything interesting. Return in one week," said Daniel.

"And me?" asked Vascus.

"After you have finished Rex, remain here," said Daniel. "I may need you for something else."

Vascus and Rowan inclined their heads and departed. Adrianna raised herself from her aching knees, stumbling slightly, and put the key back in the lock. She rubbed her knees and kicked off her shoes. Was Daniel some kind of assassin? A commander of some sort?

She was just settling against the pillows with a wicked-looking book full of hexes from Daniel's shelf when a soft knock sounded on the door. With a sigh, she set the book aside and went to the door, opening it a fraction.

"Have you eaten?" asked Daniel.

"Not yet," she replied. "Your . . . err . . . helper . . . aide, um person, usually comes after the middle night hour."

"You heard," he said, noticing how she did not open the door completely.

"A little," she lied.

"You do not have to stay in here."

"It is fine for me," she said. "I should stay out of your way."

Daniel looked as if he was going to protest but seemed to catch himself. A strange expression crossed his face. "Suit yourself."

Adrianna looked away. "Goodnight then." She spoke so softly it was doubtful he heard. She began closing the door when his hand slammed against the wood and stopped it.

"I know what it means."

"What?" she asked nervously.

"The Pull," he snapped. "I did my own research."

"Oh . . ."

"You witches are conniving," he said darkly. "You act so humble and pure, but it's a façade; it has to be."

Adrianna felt a surge of fury and squared her shoulders. "*Conniving?*"

Daniel was unmoved. He looked down at her with the same superciliousness and antipathy she had come to expect from him.

"How dare you? You arrogant, loathsome idiot!"

Daniel kicked the door open, letting it slam against the wall and entered the room. Adrianna stepped back nervously. "Watch what you say, *witch.*"

"Or else what?" she asked fearlessly. "You think I am afraid of you?"

"You should be."

"I am not," she snapped, walking backwards from him. "So sorry to disappoint you. I warned you against the Pull. I *told* you that you would not like it. What are you so angry at me for?"

"You are infuriating!"

Adrianna moved quickly, stepping around him and went to stand in the doorway. "What is wrong with you?" What was wrong with *her*? Heat was rising from between her ribs, her chest felt tight and she was so angry the surge was making her dizzy.

"Do not walk away from me."

Adrianna was halfway to the other side of the sitting room when he grabbed her by the shoulders, spun her around and held her to him. "Let me go . . ."

"No."

"Let me go, Daniel," she said warningly as the all too familiar tug formed between then. The heat and tug from the Pull was becoming irritating, like an itch.

"Stop fidgeting, I'm not trying to hurt you."

"Then let-me-go!" she demanded before he kissed her. She felt a rush of relief, like cold water on a burn. The tug strengthened into a hold, but the ache was gone now that they were locked together.

Daniel pressed her onto his desk as she sighed against his lips. He buried his fingers in her dark hair, holding her still as his lips urged her mouth open. The taste of her inflamed something in him he had never felt before. Pure, deep, carnal hunger coursed through his veins, demanding her blood, her body. He needed to possess her, to mark her.

Adrianna heard the distinct sound of papers and heavy objects shifting off the desk. Daniel leaned into her heavily, forcing her onto her back. She clenched his shirt and brought him with her, her leg wrapping itself around his.

Running her hands across his chest, she felt the hardness beneath his shirt as he thrust the hem of her skirt around her hips. Her eyes snapped open. His hands were all over her thighs, sliding up around her hips, at the very same time her tongue slid across his and touched the edge of his lengthened incisor.

Adrianna's head swam; her thoughts were a mess. She only knew for sure that his kiss, though amazing, was making her feel things for him that were a contradiction to how she should feel. She was not frightened of those fangs, nor was she ashamed of lying beneath a vampire who was about to strip her bare and consummate feelings neither of them understood.

Adrianna put her hands to his face, stilling him. They were acting under the influence of the Pull.

"We are not thinking clearly," she gasped as he pulled his mouth from hers. "Neither of us wants to have . . ."

Daniel arched a brow.

"A connection," she said sternly.

"You're very connected," he replied, looking down at her leg that had wrapped itself around his.

"I cannot do this."

"You were doing well," he said, smirking. "And you surprise me, not every woman is willing to be taken on a desk."

"Get off me."

"No."

Shame washed over her. Her eyes stung with tears and her stomach was heavy, as though she had swallowed a boulder. Adrianna pushed against his chest but it was like trying to move a wall. She tried to knee him in the stomach but he caught her in his grip when she went to strike. "Let me up!"

Daniel moved back, but only enough for her to sit up and straighten her clothes. He ran a hand through his hair, suddenly aware of how close he had been to actually making love to Adrianna. On the desk. He knew he should not have goaded at her about that.

Adrianna stood straight and took a deep breath. She felt disgusting, unclean and without morals. "You are clearly busy, so I'll just be out of your way," she said shakily.

Daniel blocked her. "Why do you always want to get away from me? I am not going to bite you, Adrianna."

"What do you want from me? Can you not see that this is wrong? *No*, do *not* touch me." A fire-sphere formed in her palm.

Daniel did not pay it any heed. "What if I want to?"

"*Have you lost your mind*? What are you talking about? You hate me! You told me yourself! Please do not make this complicated," she begged, closing her hand around the fire.

"I wouldn't kiss you if I hated you," he argued.

"You cannot help it!"

"Vampires have more resistance than others," he said. "No one dictates to me."

"Daniel, I know that as a vampire you are proud, sometimes maddeningly so, but no one, vampire, angel, demon or elemental can fight against things like the Pull," she said softly. "I do not want this and you cannot want this. For goodness sake, half my clan is enslaved by *your* people as I am. We would destroy each other or the circumstances would destroy us."

Daniel's face was unreadable, but his eyes told of his pain. It was the first time Adrianna had ever seen him look vulnerable. His cold mask of indifference was gone. He looked as though he had been slapped by reality.

"You've thought about this."

"Not much," she said, her voice breaking. "I have been too scared. Tell me if I am wrong."

"You are not wrong," he said admittedly. "To give in to the Pull would be acknowledging feelings; feelings we do not have," he added determinedly.

"It is all right to have feelings."

"No it isn't," he said harshly.

Adrianna blinked away tears. "All right," she said. "Now we understand each other. I will leave you to get on with your work."

When his bedroom door slammed shut, Daniel almost collapsed from the intensity of his emotions. He gripped the edge of the desk, his knuckles becoming white, and squeezed his eyes closed as he calmed the surging sensations rushing through his body.

Adrianna was wrong; they did not understand one another at all.

The following evening, as Adrianna ate by the frosted window, she made up her mind. Now was the time to act. She would go back to the underground chambers and make for an escape with all those who were willing. She had strength enough to fight.

It was time to be free.

Three hours later, unable to sleep, Adrianna heard the door open. She sat up and brought the blankets up to her chest, holding her breath as shadow moved into the room. Her first thought was that it was Daniel, but the stranger's outline was much smaller than his, and less overwhelming.

The candles came alight, casting a dim luminosity about the room.

Kenna stood in the doorway; a small flame hovered over her outstretched palm. Her pale face glowed, making her once pink cheeks seem hollow. She closed the door and discarded her shawl on the end of Adrianna's bed.

Adrianna breathed out with relief. "You really startled me," she whispered.

"Sorry. I'm not so clumsy anymore."

Adrianna smiled; glad to have her friend with her.

Adrianna did notice that Kenna sat down at the end of the bed, maintaining distance. While she was hurt, she understood. The carefree days were over. Now there would always be a barrier between them, more so from Kenna's side. While Adrianna knew she could protest and assure Kenna that nothing was changed between them, Kenna would forever feel like the outsider. Their innocence had been stolen from them on that Samhain night.

"Where have you been?" asked Adrianna.

"Around. I have to make sure no one suspects me of aiding you. I have been slipping away from the fortress more often than my Maker would like. I think he knows I am giving information to the Gordgáin."

"Then why does he not say anything?" Adrianna asked curiously.

Kenna shrugged. "I think he might have a soft spot for me."

Adrianna looked disapproving. "If he did, he would not have bitten you."

"Do not be so quick to judge," Kenna replied, her voice hinting at mirth. "Now, I have received word from the Gordgáin and they are *finally* in contact with the Maquis."

"Really?" Adrianna asked in surprise. "The *real* Maquis?"

"The very same. They have been fighting off the vampires on the Aires border. After the Sansul vampires attacked us, they moved quickly to Aires. From what I have been able to overhear, the vampires thought they would have an easy time of it. Apparently we were easy to conquer and they are unsatisfied. Still, Aires is keeping the vampires back with the help of the Maquis."

"And what does it mean? This communication between the Gordgáin and the Maquis?"

"That they may be able to get you out."

"How? Negotiation? What could possibly be offered in return for our release?"

"No, not negotiation. You do not negotiate with this coven."

"So..." Adrianna moved to sit up straighter, crossing her legs beneath the blankets. "They are going to demand our release? Take us by force?"

"The Maquis are capable of causing a lot of damage to this place if they decide to attack," said Kenna. "If they do it right, you will be free."

"When is this all going to happen?" asked Adrianna, now filled with excitement at the prospect of escaping.

"Very soon, but I was not told exactly when," said Kenna. "They would never give me complete information; they do not trust me. I do not blame them, so do not pout. I just hope you will be rescued before they start registering."

"What do you mean 'registering'?"

"You do not know?" Kenna asked hesitantly. "I thought maybe . . . Daniel would have told you."

"*What*?" Adrianna demanded a little too loudly, her heart racing.

"The Council passed an order that all witches are to be registered because many have gone missing," Kenna replied. "Thomas, my Maker, believes it is because demons have taken witches they need for feeding, among other things."

Adrianna paled. The image of herself in the hands of a Rakasha demon flashed in her mind. She pictured its long, toothy mouth, as dark and endless as a black hole screaming in her face, piercing her eardrums until they bled.

"Adrianna . . . ?"

"Sorry." Adrianna realised she was staring at Kenna with wide eyes. "This is unbelievable! How could this happen? Why are we still stuck here?" she asked, frustrated. "How can the angels just stand idly by and let this happen to us? Do we not have a Friendship Treaty with them?" She stood up and began to pace around the room. "Where are the other clans? It's as though we have been . . . abandoned!"

"I do not know," Kenna said in monotone.

"I would probably be able to blast my way out of here if I were able to make the right potions!" said Adrianna to herself. "I cannot do anything without the vampires sensing it. Plus I'm stuck in these darned four walls day and night!"

"Well," said Kenna, moving to the window, "be glad you are here and not in the Laboratory."

"I know," said Adrianna. "I just wish life was the way it was before all this evil." She scrunched her nose and squeezed her eyes closed, trying to block the tears, but they came.

Kenna put a hand on her shoulder. "You are going to be all right. The Maquis will free you, all of you."

Adrianna held the basalt rock tightly in her hand. She noticed Kenna's eyes were turning black. As quickly as they turned, they faded once more to brown. "Do you feel different?"

"I feel as though my body and soul have been violated."

Adrianna got up and hugged her. Even though Kenna did not return it, she knew her best friend felt the love she poured out.

"I feel this gnawing hunger all the time," said Kenna. "There is never relief. I am so angry I feel as though I might burst from the intensity of it, but I know I can do nothing to change what I have been forced to become. I fear this place, I fear the vampires, I fear the outside world, and I fear the all-out war that is coming . . ."

"Maybe it will not!"

"Oh, it will. Another regiment is being awakened before the second moon. Do you have any idea what that means? The people here are predicting another era like *The War Against The Angels*."

"Then we will meet it – but I am going to be out there, not trapped in here."

"I hope so too." Kenna gave her a gentle squeeze.

"Is that why we were attacked? Because they want to regain what they lost during *The War Against The Angels*?"

"Sansul was at the height of its power during that war, I doubt they could reclaim it just by attacking our clan."

"It is a start."

Kenna was silent for a long while. Adrianna watched her friend closely, waiting for her to speak. A few weeks ago, nothing was unsaid or unspoken between them, but now Kenna carried knowledge and secrets without wanting to share them all. Adrianna felt betrayed, shunned from the new life Kenna was forced to lead. What hurt was that Kenna was the one shutting her out.

"It all has to do with that war," said Kenna, though she did not look at Adrianna. "When Henry was Supreme Chancellor of Sansul coven, the coven's population was triple what it is now. Henry gave his people everything he promised when he came to be Supreme Chancellor. Power, control, freedom – everything they needed to be out in the open and put the fear of mortality into the rest of Sansul. The vampires and angels were always vicious toward one another, but it started because of the angels not the vampires."

"I hardly believe that."

"History is fact, Adrianna."

"How does this explain why they attacked us now?"

"Be patient. Our village is the closest to here, so our conflicts with the Sansul vampires were the most frequent and most bloody. When the vampires attacked, Wilmota responded. How could they not? Close to the end of the war, there was a party of vampires returning to Sansul after negotiations for peace in Citron. All, but one, were women."

Adrianna had a feeling she knew where this was headed.

"They were travelling under the green peace flag, which we know is sacred. Those who travel under its protection cannot be touched."

"What happened to them?"

"The Warlock Myriad and the angels decided to ignore the flag. After so many atrocities during the expanse of the war, what was one more murder? After all, the vampires had been declared sub-Elementals by the International Cooperation of Warlocks and Witches." Kenna's eyes faded to black and she continued. "All but one in the vampire party were murdered en-route to the fortress. The last one was taken to the middle of the village and tied to a white pillar."

Adrianna lowered her face to her hands.

"They branded her. On her face," said Kenna.

Adrianna shook her head, disgusted.

"This is a diary I found in Thomas's private library," Kenna continued. When Adrianna looked up, Kenna was holding a plain, brown journal. "It is the diary of a woman, a vampire, whose husband was a warlock. She was taken and turned just before the war broke out and hoped to be reunited with him. It was her one and only dream. She wrote, 'I hid like a coward as they crowded around Eleanor. I knew the name and face of every single person who circled her. The smell of her branded skin was vile. The flesh continued to burn until her cheek was almost burnt through. Then a witch, Lizzette, came forward and untied her. I hoped it was the end of it all. Lizzette turned Eleanor around and tied her so that her back was to the crowd and she faced the white pillar. Then a soldier from the Warlock Myriad came forward and formed a lightening whip...'"

"I get the picture," said Adrianna, closing the journal in Kenna's hands.

"When her body was returned to the fortress, there was no skin on her back. But there was a note stuck to it, which read: 'Punishment Hurts.' After we were attacked on Samhain, I was sheltering with the Gordgáin when a note was pinned to the door of the temple. Renauart brought it down to the sanctuary and nobody explained to me what it meant, but they all looked as though they knew the meaning behind the meaning. Everybody refused to tell me why it was sent to the Gordgáin and why it made them so ashamed to see it."

"What did the note say?"

"Punishment hurts."

"So we were attacked, brutalised and captured because the Sansul vampires are avenging unfinished business from a war that ended hundreds of years ago?"

"History repeats until we learn not to make the same mistakes."

<u>CHAPTER EIGHT</u>

The Laboratory

ADRIANNA SCREAMED WHEN THE explosion sounded. One, two, three . . . a dozen bomb blasts from beyond the fortress gates threw her from the sofa as the windows shattered, raining glass shards. She rolled into a ball on the carpet, huddling her head on her knees. The ground beneath shook with a furious rumble, shaking the fortress to its foundations with such violence that the furniture moved. Books fell from the shelves and the chandeliers swung freely, forming cracks in the ceiling.

Voices filled the corridor. Some shouted orders and others cried out in worried tones.

Then everything stilled. Adrianna lifted her head tentatively, waiting for another onslaught of bombs. Blue and white light filled the room for a single second.

"Fire!"

Adrianna ran to the broken window, brushing glass and plaster from her clothes.

Enormous spheres of blue light and fire were being launched at Sansul Fortress. Squinting, she spied four points at the base of Whistlers Knoll, the hill on which the fortress stood, where energy-spheres and waves of fire were hurtling through the night air.

Finally!

Uniformed vampires rushed out from the gates: Rakasha demons, gargoyles, Fire-Lithes, and wisps of black fog amongst them. The Fire-Lithes, waif-like demons of fire, glided alongside clouds of black fog that Adrianna instantly recognised as Wraith. In their solid forms, Wraith became black-skinned bodies that sucked blood directly from the veins of their victims. They were the most feared elemental not only for the painful way they killed, but also because they were almost impossible to track.

From where she stood, Adrianna was just able to see the attackers. The brilliant light of the blue spheres and fire-spheres coming from the base of Whistlers Knoll illuminated unfamiliar faces. These were not witches or warlocks she had seen before, nor were they nymphs. They were quite unusual and carried weapons her own people did not wield.

One of the attackers glided along on a cloud of fire, slashing vampires with a curved sword. Another expertly cut down goblins with lighting-whips, which snapped through the air with a crackling sound every time they met with flesh.

Moving with speed Adrianna had never thought possible, a pixie-haired woman charged at, flipped over and cast two ice-tears into the necks of two vampires before leaping over her spiky-haired comrade. She cast a protective shield as a fire-sphere flew at them. The fire-sphere rebounded off the invisible barrier, and she made for the gate.

"Blast the battlement gate," muttered Adrianna, watching a fire-sphere land right on top of a Baál. *Was that Jeith?* Had Liam just been killed?

Baál were horrifyingly ugly, horned demons who took the most brutal approach to warfare and left none of their enemies alive once captured. Feared even amongst demons, they were infamous for taking delight in ripping off the heads of children while their parents watched.

Adrianna stood on her tiptoes in an effort to see further, but it was in vain. Trees blocked her view and the Maquis were not getting any closer. They seemed to be deflected by some kind of shield. *Of course,* she thought. Naturally Sansul Fortress would have some kind of neo-physical protection, and it was most probably a Protection Shield conjured by the Librarian using the Darkness as its energy source.

A swarm of goblins congregated inside the fortress walls, but the battlement guards were refusing to release them. The goblins stomped their bony feet, screeching and spitting as they worked themselves into a frenzy.

Two warlocks stood before the gates, their arms outstretched and their mouths moving rapidly. Adrianna deduced that they must be trying to lower the shield, but against the strength of the Librarian, it was a useless attempt. The air around the gate shimmered for a moment, and Adrianna's heart skipped a beat in hope, but it led to nothing. The men were forced to take cover as a dozen fire-spheres came at them from all sides.

Adrianna cursed, frustrated. *What in the name of the Light are they doing?* Surely the Gordgáin and the Maquis were not so badly prepared as this.

"Get André to take his men around behind them!" someone bellowed down the halls.

The fighting continued a while longer before the goblins were finally released. Adrianna watched as they scurried off like a stampede of ants down the hill toward the Gordgáin and Maquis. Carrying small weapons high above their heads, they squeaked what sounded like a war cry.

Startled, Adrianna jumped back from the window as something dashed by: a gust of wind hit her in the face. Completely blocking her view for a second, it flew high into the air: Adrianna leaned out, and looked up only to retreat, frightened.

All the gargoyles were now awake. Almost a dozen flew out to follow the goblins, whose teeth-grinding screams were proof that the attackers were strong. The bat-like wings of the gargoyles spanned far on either side of their leathery bodies. Adrianna watched as a grey-skinned gargoyle circled a man from the air. It glided silently above his head, and then suddenly flew down and speared the man's side with the horn of its foot. She blocked her ears as another let out a jaw-clenching, eagle-like scream before descending over the hills.

Beyond the gates, Gordgáin and Maquis were moving away. Adrianna gripped the window frame, glass cutting into her hands. "Please . . ." They were leaving.

It was not long before the goblins and gargoyles returned. Vampires had dispersed all over the fortress grounds, calling for a retreat.

Her heart fell. They had not been saved.

Clearly, even though many goblins had been killed, gargoyles and vampires wounded, the attack had not been successful. What had stopped them? The Protection Shield? Had the Maquis not anticipated the immediate reaction from the vampires?

She backed away from the window, numb. *We are completely lost.*

The doors burst open and a furious Liam bounded inside followed by Daniel, Nikita and a blank-faced vampire who strode in as if he had not a care in the world. Nikita leaned against the fireplace mantle and crossed his arms. Liam took a moment to look around his rooms. His boots crunched on the glass that littered the floor.

"Think about it, Liam, she couldn't possible know," the unfamiliar vampire spoke in a monotone.

"Oh, she knows," said Liam, glaring at Adrianna. "You may have turned that other witch, Thomas, but they are still loyal to one another."

Adrianna did not dare look at Daniel.

"What did Kenna tell you?" Liam demanded.

"Nothing," Adrianna replied. "I do not know any-"

"Do not lie to me," Liam growled. "You're only alive by my choice."

"Then put me back with the others!" she argued, not caring about the consequences. "Even if I knew something, I would not tell you!"

Liam looked as if he was about to slap her. Instead, he turned away and began to pace. Daniel took a step toward Adrianna as Nikita tried to defuse Liam's anger.

"Do you know anything?" asked Daniel, barely moving his lips.

Adrianna, feeling the familiar sensations that came with the Pull, shook her head.

He stepped back.

"She had to have told her something, Thomas," Liam said to the stoic-faced vampire.

"I do not like what you're accusing Kenna of," said Thomas, his tone so calm it was almost icy. "Point fingers at the witch, not Kenna. Or do you believe that my choices are unsatisfactory?"

"She was a damned witch up until a few moons ago!" Liam argued hotly. "They are best friends – *bonded*, best friends, Thomas that does not go away because you turned one of them! Betrayal is a death sentence. If she opened her mouth to discuss Vahir business with some *filthy* witch, I will carry out the sentence myself."

Adrianna's eyebrows shot up but bit her tongue when Daniel sent her a sharp look. *Who is he calling filthy?*

Thomas turned abruptly to Adrianna. His steely eyes gazed into hers searchingly. "Do you know anything about the Maquis attack?"

Adrianna gave him a look. "As if I would *tell* you!"

"Do you even know *what* they are?" he asked.

Adrianna just stared. *I hope he cannot read minds.*

"It's probably just as well," said Thomas.

"Do you know if they plan to attack the fortress?" Liam demanded.

"Why would they not?" said Adrianna.

For the first time, Thomas looked amused at her cheekiness. "Why don't you hand her over to a Rakasha for a night?" he asked Liam. "Maybe they'll get the full story from her."

Adrianna gasped.

"What story?" Daniel demanded.

"This isn't, I have gathered, just about your little plaything knowing about tonight's attack by the Maquis," Thomas drawled.

"One thing at a time," Nikita said coolly. "Liam, calm yourself."

Liam shot him a glare and stopped pacing. He had not looked Adrianna straight in the face since returning, choosing to remain withdrawn and silent. This was not the Liam who had brought Kenna to see her, or kept her entertained with books from Sergus's library. He was a completely different man; she knew it from the look in his eyes.

There was a knock on the door. Thomas went to answer it, leaving Liam glaring at Daniel and Nikita looking pensive. It was a messenger.

"The Maquis have retreated," the vampire said. "They left a message demanding the release of all witches, immediately, or warned that more forceful attacks will come."

Liam sneered. "Those foul-blooded traitors wouldn't last a day against our full forces!"

"Why are the Maquis your enemy?" Adrianna whispered to Daniel.

"Not mine," he replied.

Adrianna frowned. The Maquis were not his enemy?

Nikita looked as if he did not want to discuss anything further in front of Adrianna and deemed that she had nothing more useful to tell them. Quickly following Thomas from the room, he left only Daniel standing as protection to Adrianna. Liam seemed to think better of accusing Adrianna of anything more. "Put her with the others. It's too dangerous to have her around here."

Yes! She shot Daniel a look when his eyes flashed. She wanted to be with her people. There, she would finally be able to live or die beside them.

~

As Lizzette and Collette dimmed the orb-lamps around the stone room, a group of witches sat together at a small obsidian table in the corner listening as Adrianna explained what had occurred above them. The failed rescue attempt was met with sighs of sadness and unsurprisingly, icy quips from Lizzette. "Of course they failed! There is a shield around the fortress. They know this," she snapped. "Stupid men – no wonder they are so lost!" Jess became overwhelmed by the lost chance of rescue and went to her bed crying.

Rosamunda, Adrianna's voluptuous neighbour; Orla, a blonde witch Adrianna had met the night of the attack; Veronique, a robust redhead who was married to the human son of a centaur; Clair, a fair witch the same age as Adrianna; and Peruva, a sorceress, all listened eagerly to her story.

"Why did he change so quickly?" asked Veronique, whose usually immaculate appearance was now dull and simply kempt. "Why would Liam send you here when he kept you above to save you in the first place?"

"I do not know," said Adrianna. "But his demon has been showing itself more and more; I think soon he will be lost to it completely."

"I remember him," said Peruva. "I remember all the children taken that night. Gypsy children too were taken, not just our own. Liam was so in awe of Daniel and Mathias, so eager to be as popular . . . there was so much love amongst you. Tobias was naughty, but he doted on Kenna. And now Kenna is one of them . . ."

As Peruva reminisced, memories of childhood flooded back to Adrianna. Why had she not thought of Tobias? Tobias and Kenna were brother and sister. They had been orphaned young and adopted by their mother's sister, who lived in the same orchard lane as Adrianna. Tobias had been kidnapped the same night as Daniel and Liam by the vampires of Sansul Fortress. What had become of him?

"At least Liam cannot hurt you here," said Rosamunda, holding her hand.

"I wanted so much for the Gordgáin to set us free," said Adrianna.

"We will wait until their next attempt," Clair said softly.

"We are well kept here," said Rosamunda. A snort of derision came from Lizzette, who was pacing. "The rooms are clean and they give us rejuvenation potions once a week," she continued. "They want us to do something for them but I cannot fathom what it is."

"So you do not watch over the sleeping?" asked Adrianna.

They shook their heads. "The sleeping vampires are all in the necropolis on the other side of the fortress," said Peruva. "They do not need to be looked after. One or two sorceresses were enough in the old days."

"Perhaps the Council is planning to wake the vampires and we are the blood supply," said Veronique.

Rosamunda shivered. "Do not give me nightmares, this reality is enough."

"She could be right," Adrianna said softly. "What about the warlocks?"

"I heard two of the guards laughing about the warlocks being forced to mine a substance in caves by the seashore. They said many were dying daily," Rosamunda said bitterly.

"Mining what?" asked Adrianna.

"Who knows," Rosamunda replied. "There are a lot of minerals down there. We are only supposed to take what we absolutely need, if that, but the vampires have no such respect for land as we do. The southern cave is full of stones, but the northern caves have sulphur and other minerals used in Black Magick."

"They have killed the leaders of the Warlock Myriad," said Peruva.

Adrianna was beyond being surprised at killings at the hand of the vampires. The Warlock Myriad was the Sansul army. With its membership extended only to men, it was an army spread across all five Sansul clans. Each clan had nominated four warlocks to sit on the Warlock Leadership. In the past, it was the Warlock Myriad that fought the front-line wars and charged rescues, as in the *Massacre of Rilenaville* and *The War Against The Angels*. Now it seemed that the four Wilmota leaders had been murdered.

"There is no point in hoping that their passing was quick," said Clair. "The survivors must be living in worse conditions than this. At least here we are clean and fed, somewhat."

"And raped," said Collette, passing by with a cup of steaming tea.

The change of atmosphere was palpable. Many witches swapped tense looks. Others retreated even more into their own silence.

"How many women have been taken above, other than me?" asked Adrianna.

"Many," Orla said softly. "Some of them come back."

"Some . . ." said Clair.

"Where is Caitriona?" Adrianna asked Rosamunda. "She was not here last I came either."

Jess re-joined them. Her eyes were red and her face puffy. "She comes back now and then."

Adrianna frowned. "Does she return unharmed?"

"Yes. The first time she was taken, it was for feeding, but she returned without any puncture wounds," said Rosamunda.

"I try to ask her about it but she pretends not to hear," Jess said tearfully.

"If you ask me, she has been serving one of those vampires for more than just blood," said Celeste as she came up behind Jess.

"You should not say things like that aloud!" Rosamunda hissed, casting a worried glance at the elders on the far side of the room.

"You know it's true," Celeste retorted. "*Stop* crying Jess, for goodness sake! Pull yourself together!"

Jess tried by taking a deep, shuddering breath and wrapped her arms around herself. Adrianna stood and embraced her. "She is fine," she said soothingly, patting her friend's hair. "Cait is a strong girl. If he is not hurting her, then we should not pass judgement."

"I wish this never happened," Jess whispered. "We are never going to be the same again, are we?"

The women shared a look. Adrianna thought of Daniel and guilt began to bubble in her middle. She missed his presence. The distance between them had made her solemn.

Celeste ushered Jess to bed with the promise of a soothing tea.

"Tea?" Adrianna looked to Rosamunda. "They give you tea?"

"The vampires feed us better than we expected. I mean, they are not starving us," said Rosamunda.

"Not giving us enough food is part of their plan to keep us weak," said Peruva.

"I am much thinner than I was three moons ago," said Rosamunda. "A proper meal is too much to hope for. Honey-bread and nuts do not make for a healthy diet."

"Maybe for birds," said Adrianna.

"Do not remind me," Orla whined, rubbing her stomach. "I keep dreaming of a roast with rosemary stuffing, mashed potatoes, garden vegetables and even peas, which I hate. Cocoa..." She smiled dreamily. "Excuse me a moment while I eat my imaginary supper."

"I will be dreaming about spiced rice and roasted goat," said Clair.

"I doubt the City of Tents trade ships have made any rice deliveries, dear," said Veronique. "Perhaps *they* will have realised something has happened to us since the ports have been abandoned?"

"They would be stupid not to," said Rosamunda.

"The vampires would surely have blocked any way of entry the ships may have," Adrianna said. "Our only hope lies with the southern villages and the Gordgáin."

"When do you think they are going to take our blood?" asked Orla.

"From what I was able to gather," Adrianna began tentatively, "after they wake Henry and he orders the awakening of the rest of Sansul Legion. The Council has plans to take over Azria coven and merge Sansul and Azria into one coven."

"The Supreme Chancellor of the Azria coven is too powerful. It is impenetrable that coven, exclusive only to the most powerful vampires," said Rosamunda.

"Then why is Henry not a part of it?"

"Different beliefs," she said. "When you were in Azria with your cousin Blanca, did you not realise that the people lived peacefully alongside the coven? The vampires there have rules and they live by them."

"I doubt anyone can live *peacefully* beside vampires," said Peruva.

"Besides all that, the Azria Chancellor and Henry are ancient enemies," said Veronique.

"Why?" Orla asked curiously.

"I do not know the whole tale, but the Supreme Chancellor of the Azria coven was formerly the Commander and Chief of the Vahir Legion, a position Henry always wanted," said Rosamunda. "My mother always said that if the vampires did not have a leadership dispute, the vampires would have won *The War Against The Angels*."

"Perish the thought!" said Peruva, twisting her long, brown hair into a knot on top of her head.

"Citron and Bruniér are allied with Azria," said Rosamunda. "They obviously know which coven is the better. The vampires in the Bruniér Mountains have not come to help Sansul . . ."

"But they haven't helped *oppose* them either," Veronique said reasonably.

". . .because they keep to themselves," Rosamunda finished, as though there had been no interruption.

"It sounds to me like it is everybody and nobody's business what Sansul does," Orla said with a sigh.

A while later, after a meagre meal of honey-bread, dried fruit and water, all but two witches began to fall asleep. Orla and Adrianna lay side by side on the floor. Tucked into their blankets, they faced each other. There were not enough beds to accommodate everyone so they all took turns sleeping on the floor. The witches slept heavily at night. Their consciousness partly separated from their bodies to shield them from the Darkness. Peruva the sorceress had taught them how to use deep meditation to protect their bodies from the Darkness and rejuvenate. Because of this, hundreds of witches remained alive over their three moons of captivity.

Orla smiled at Adrianna. "I am glad you're here with us," she whispered.

"Me too," Adrianna said truthfully. "If I am going to die, I am going to die with you all."

Orla took Adrianna's hand and held it. Sadness filled her bright eyes, a tear slipped out. Adrianna stroked her hair, holding her closer. "Everything will be all right." Though she did not know whether she believed it herself, Adrianna felt that words of comfort were more necessary than words of truth.

"A few weeks after you were taken," Orla whispered, "one of the guards," she paused for breath, ". . . he ordered that I be taken to his quarters."

Adrianna's stomach turned.

"I thought I was going to be killed," Orla whispered, her tears flowing freely. "I wasn't scared of it. I just didn't want him to touch me. I . . . I was brought to his room and one of the women tried to make me change into a gown. I refused. I knew if I did, I would be . . . never mind . . . I knew what he would do. I could not allow one of them to touch me."

"I understand," Adrianna whispered kindly. "You are so brave."

"He walked in as the woman was threatening me. I told them I would rather die than have anything to do with them."

"You did well."

"They had me branded."

"*What*?" Adrianna's heart skipped a beat. She stared at Orla in horror.

Orla undid a button and slid her dress down from her shoulder, revealing an ink marking of the Sansul coven insignia and the name 'André' on her shoulder blade.

"Why did they do that?" asked Adrianna.

"Because I rebelled," Orla replied, covering herself hastily. "I told him that no matter what he did he could never break me. They did this to try to prove they owned me, or that *he* owned me."

"You are away from him now."

Orla scowled. "Until he returns."

"Did he . . . I mean, sorry, I should not ask."

"No, it is all right. He did not rape me. I might kill myself if he did."

"No," Adrianna whispered urgently. "Orla you cannot. *Please*, promise me you won't. Promise me."

"You are lucky none of the vampires raped you. We thought for sure they had. Rosamunda was terrified," said Orla.

"I would rather suffer the Laboratory than that."

Adrianna hoped they had a means to escape before Orla was sent away again. She knew that other than her constant failing health, she'd had an easier time being Liam's prisoner than a captive with her clan. She could well imagine their constant fear, knowing that life was now fleeting. It was not in a witch's nature to allow others to dictate her life, but the vampires now controlled them all, whether they liked it or not.

Closing her eyes, she listened as Peruva softly sang an old folk song by the small, white fireplace. The melody filled the room, her voice soothing them into sleep.

Adrianna looked up to the ceiling and her thoughts drifted to Daniel. Was he pacing as he usually did when he was thinking? Perhaps he was at his desk, writing to those he was in contact with outside of Sansul?

Who are you exactly? If he was aiding people outside the fortress, then his loyalty to Sansul coven, his coven, was doubtful. But how could a vampire betray his own coven? It was practically unheard of, and what would happen to him if he were discovered? If he could order the assassination of a Councillor, just how far did his powers and influence extend?

As she drifted off to sleep, she wondered how long it would be before their fate became clear.

~

The next few days progressed without incident.

Adrianna spent her time trying to remember the outline of the building in which they were imprisoned and talking with the others about their experiences during their long moons in the underground chambers. Celeste the herbalist and elders, Lizzette and Adalina, continued teaching the younger witches. Even though they had no tools to work with, they were able to study theory. Rosamunda explained to Adrianna that they continued the lessons in witchcraft so as to stay mentally sharp.

"Idle minds make for weak people," Margarithe recited.

True, thought Adrianna. The lessons not only kept them from boredom, they kept them in practice for whatever might happen next.

Many of the witches were skilled at various forms of spells, explosions, mind control, projection and manipulation of elements and solids. Adrianna knew that if the Maquis attacked again, causing a distraction, they would have a chance at escaping using their own powers. Most of the witches in Adrianna's group had received their Element. Unfortunately most were either water or air. Had there been more earth elementals they may have been able to manipulate the structure of their prison but there were not nearly enough of them to exercise that kind of power.

During a particularly restless evening, Rosamunda, an air elemental, created a small tornado in the room during her sleep. Her consciousness was separated from her body, floating a few inches over her form like a shimmery haze. Adrianna shook her awake, which was difficult considering the tornado was blowing the witches into the wall.

It was only pure luck that none of the vampires sensed it.

On the day before the full moon which would mark the fourth moon since the capture and imprisonment of the Wilmota people, Sergus, more commonly known as the Librarian, arrived in the underground chambers looking for a new victim; a test subject.

The terror Adrianna sensed coming from the others was palpable. Jess stood against the wall with her hand clamped over her mouth, trembling so awfully that Veronique was forced to elbow her. "Stand still," she hissed.

An eerie feeling crept up inside Adrianna as Sergus walked along the line of witches. When he paused in front of her, Rosamunda wrapped a protective arm around her shoulders. "You cannot do this!"

"Step aside."

"Choose someone older!" said Rosamunda, her voice quivering. She did not meet his eyes, but it was clear she would continue to argue.

Calm washed over Adrianna. "Rosa…" she said softly, her mother's words repeating in her mind: "'Death for our people is a chosen path.'" It was time to put her words to the test. "I will go with you," she said to the Librarian.

~

Adrianna woke with a throbbing headache. With a soft groan, she lifted her head from what felt like ice-cold stone and immediately regretted it. She fell back with a cry as a piercing pain shot through her brain to her eyes. Her head felt as if it had been cracked open.

A blurry, greyness greeted her when she opened her eyes. She made to rub them, but could not move her wrists from her sides. She realised her hands were shackled. Confused, she struggled against the bindings fiercely. "Where am I?" she called out weakly. Her throat felt so sore surely she must have swallowed rocks. "Release me!" In an attempt to clear her vision, she squeezed her eyes closed and reopened them but it was to no avail. If anything, her eyesight became worse. Panicked, she pulled and yanked her wrists to force them free.

"It is no use," said a bored voice, "you'll never come loose."

Adrianna stopped struggling, panting. "Where am I? Who are you?" she demanded, her voice shaking.

"*I* am Sergus," the voice said, now on her other side. "You are in my laboratory. I took you from the underground chambers."

It all rushed back to her in one terribly depressing memory. Having been taken from the underground chambers to the Laboratory, she was chained to a stone slab floating in the middle of a dimly lit room that had seen endless horrors. Once there, she had taken in her surroundings, from the cluttered shelves to the blood stained walls and floor, the new and old candles, the bolted doors to her left and right, she had the overwhelming urge to vomit. A masked soldier locked her wrists in chains by her sides. She knew then that she was about to join the ranks of thousands of unfortunate souls who had met their end in this terrible place.

I traded the safety of Liam's quarters for this? She wanted to curse herself, but her reality was punishment enough.

Adrianna recalled the soulless eyes that had stared down at her as she screamed. Sergus's grey, tight face was stoic as she fought to resist the burning pain that coursed through her veins.

The last time he placed the Torture Stone on her body she had fainted. Having screamed herself hoarse, her body, too exhausted to resist anymore, collapsed. Whether there had been pain afterwards or not, she would probably never remember.

After the first few hours she had little fear, but she was plagued by a lingering worry that he would discover her secret. He had not yet sought her blood for examination. When he did and subjected it to examination, she was certain he would instantly recognise her true origins.

Please, no.

Adrianna flinched when cold, sharp metal dragged down the length of her arm. Crying out, the blade sliced her wrist open and blood poured onto her hand and down her forearm. Sergus leaned in closer to inspect the incision.

"You should feel your sight clearing," he said, running his long-nailed fingers across the cut. "The blood shines. You are as yet untainted by dark deeds."

Adrianna's heart skipped a beat. "It will cease to shine when I have the pleasure of killing you," she said angrily, glaring at his blurry figure. It was frustrating not being able to see. "Why can I not see?"

"I needed to make sure your magic did not project from your eyes until I had you fully sedated," Sergus replied, taking the blood he'd collected from her wrist and pouring it into a cup.

"Why are you doing this?" she demanded, listening closely as he walked away from her.

"Those of feeble minds do not understand," he muttered. "To be one such as I . . . enlightened of all magic . . . what would it accomplish to explain to one who in a few days will be just another corpse?" He spoke to himself.

Adrianna's mind raced. There was a sizzling sound, followed by a bottle being unstoppered. Was he seeking anything in her blood? Could he be separating its properties? There was no indication that he had found anything of interest, yet.

Hours passed while Sergus went in and out of the Laboratory, tinkering, mixing, hexing and testing. Every time he returned she expected to see a look of triumph on the tight skin of his grey face, but he remained elusively withdrawn. In the late afternoon, when her mind was numb and visions of Wilmota's green luscious fields came to ease her, two soldiers entered, dragging a witch no older than ten and three summers. She was small and skinny with thick blonde hair that covered her face as she struggled violently against the vampires holding her up against the wall. Abandoned, throaty screams burst from the child-witch without end.

Horrified, Adrianna watched helplessly as Sergus placed the Torture Stone on the young witch's chest. The child thrashed, twisted and kicked, her cries never ceasing. She looked deranged, wild. Neither the two soldiers holding her to the wall nor Sergus reacted in any way. Bile rose in Adrianna's throat as blood emerged from the corners of the child's mouth; she had screamed so much her mouth was ripping.

"*Please*," Adrianna screamed, "do it to me, not her! Stop! You must stop!"

Sergus looked at her sharply. "*Why is her life more valuable than yours?*" he demanded greedily.

Adrianna stared at him. "Let her go."

"Why?"

"Because she is a child! Innocent! Can you not see this?"

"Are you not a child too? Why should I spare her life? What importance has it?"

"You are insane! You are not as enlightened as you think if you cannot see the value of *life*," she spat.

Sergus seemed to deem the girl unworthy of life, because a heartbeat later, he buried his fangs into the front of her little neck and drained her dry. The soldiers released their hold, allowing her to fall into the Librarian's grip.

Adrianna choked back tears when the girl let out a choked gurgle. The child's hands clawed at the Librarian's shoulders. Then slowly, her fingers unclenched from his shirt and ceased to move. Adrianna turned away, crying silently, and hoped for the young witch's safe entry to the Spirit Plane.

After the child's murder, Adrianna was depleted. Drifting in and out of awareness, she could not be certain of how much time passed in the Laboratory. It seemed like days, but could have been hours or weeks. At intervals she was subjected to further mental torture. After Sergus realised that her body had not yet broken because of her mental strength, he decided to conquer her mind. He was astounded to find she was still sane and lived through endless instilled nightmares, mind torture and hexes that had been fatal to dozens of his previous victims.

During short moments of lucidity, Adrianna resolved to spite him by staying alive. She had entered the Laboratory knowing that nobody before her had ever left alive. This was a place for endings, not survival. There was no rescue party for her, no absolution. Her mind was at peace with this, but she would not let him take her life without a fight.

After what felt like endless days on the stone slab, the hinges squeaked as the heavy door opened in the middle of her screams.

Sergus looked up, annoyed that his work had been interrupted, but instead of ordering the intruder out, he inclined his head. "Jeith," he said, "welcome, welcome."

Numb from the pain, Adrianna did not even bother opening her eyes. She lay there, grateful for the intrusion as her body throbbed.

Jeith's enormous bulk filled the doorway. Yellow pupils glowed against the backdrop of his black eyes. Ferocious and unmerciful, Jeith had made his name through the ages as a Bounty Hunter for the Demon High Council. His favourite prey was witches.

"I came to see how your work was progressing."

"This one is stronger than the others," Sergus said in an explanatory tone, "I have pushed her far beyond the rest. She will break soon enough. They all do."

Jeith grunted appreciatively. "Show no mercy."

"Mercy would not benefit my work," said Sergus.

"Does she scream well?"

"Not as much as others may have," Sergus replied. "She tries to resist the pain."

Jeith grunted, but this time it was in annoyance. "Will she be of use much longer?"

"A little while. There is something unusual about her. Since I doubt she is older than twenty her blood does not give me all the answers to my questions," said Sergus. "Do you wish to feed off her flesh when I am done?"

Jeith moved closer to her. "Yes, but not yet. I will listen to her scream."

Adrianna collapsed into a faint. She came to while being carried into a claustrophobic, stone room covered in dry blood.

Adrianna was not the only prisoner and subject of the Librarian's cruel experiments. Three others shared the cramped room: an old man, chained by one hand to the wall on her far right, a witch, who sat opposite her, practically lifeless, and a bearded man who looked as though he had been there far too long. After being tied next to him, Adrianna slumped against the wall as the Librarian left.

The warlock beside her never spoke. A thick beard and dark dirty hair framed his face, sunken eyes and deep gashes began to scar his chest, legs and arms.

"Keep your head still," he said, making her jump with what remaining energy she had. His voice was much kinder than she expected. It was gentle and melodic. "Your body is in shock. Give it time to recover."

Adrianna straightened her head, closing her eyes. "Recovery is not my problem, warlock. Why do you think I am still alive?"

"To show them you cannot be beaten as quickly as they think," he said.

Adrianna opened one eye. "I am a fast healer. Is that why you are still here?"

He shrugged.

Adrianna closed her eye and leaned her head against the wall. "How long have I been here?"

"Eleven days."

"Eleven days," she repeated. The tiny bubble of hope she had for rescue popped. "How is it I have not seen you?"

"You were unconscious every time they threw you in here."

Adrianna lifted an aching, bloodied hand to her forehead. She forced herself not to cry. "So who are you?"

"My birth name is Gabriel," he said casually. "But I am called Hound."

"Well, I prefer Gabriel, so I will call you that if you do not mind," she said weakly.

"Whatever suits you, highlander. What is your name?"

"Adrianna. And you, sir?" Adrianna looked at the man opposite Gabriel.

"I am Ferzand," he replied, raising a weak, bloody hand in greeting. "This is Toby. Though, she is close to the end."

"Hi, Toby," Adrianna said kindly. "Stay alive, all right?"

Whether or not Toby heard, Adrianna did not know. She hoped the witch would not let the Librarian break her spirit. Toby continued to stare off into the distance before drifting off to sleep.

"Why are you called Hound?" Adrianna asked Gabriel when Ferzand began to slumber.

"I like women."

Adrianna could not help but smile. It was the first time she had smiled in weeks. "How fitting."

"It is more now," he said, turning to her.

Adrianna was taken aback. His eyes were the deepest blue she had ever seen. They were a clear, untainted blue. "Why?"

"I am a werewolf."

"A what?"

"One of the Librarians more *permanent* experiments," he said. "I was bitten by a wolf many moons ago. The wolf was poisoned with venom from a vampire fang. When it bit me I began to change into something else. After a few days I transformed into a wolf. The vampires call us 'wolf men'."

"Us?"

"There are a few more," he replied. "We call ourselves werewolves."

"Why?"

"Beware of us on a full moon. We cannot control our blood thirst. Don't look so shocked," said Gabriel, leaning back.

"How can I not be?"

"This is what the Librarian does. They want to make an army of us."

"Do they not have enough demons to do their bidding?" Adrianna said sourly. "They need to ruin other people's lives and make some . . . wolf-army?"

"Now I know why you've lasted so long," he said. "You never just accept things."

"What choice is there?" she asked, rattling the chain. "Nobody survives this place."

"I think you will," he said, closing his eyes. "Sleep, highlander."

~

Kenna sent Daniel a withering look from across the room.

Nikita, Liam, Daniel, Thomas and a dozen other Sansul vampires had convened to hear from a group that had scouted the outskirts of Bruniér and Aires, the two largest villages in the midlands south of Wilmota.

Unfortunately for the Sansul vampires, they were not able to pass the boundaries erected by the faeries. As soon as word arrived via the Gordgáin that Wilmota had been attacked, the shield crystals were illuminated, protecting the villages from vampires who may raid them.

"The Gordgáin and the survivors will be trying to get to Aires," said Liam. "We must cut them off at once."

A man from the scouting party, a redheaded vampire, turned his head slowly to Liam. "We've been doing that but the Maquis are aiding the witches! The Gordgáin are working here *and* beyond the border!" he said through gritted teeth, trying to keep his tone respectful.

"Don't you have people looking for the Gordgáin?" Liam demanded, rounding on Daniel, who was staring passively out the window.

"We located one of their hiding places in the village," Daniel said, not bothering to turn around. "We destroyed them."

"Why was I not informed?" Liam demanded.

"You were," said Thomas, sitting elegantly in a high-backed chair. He swirled the contents of his glass before taking a sip. "You were feeding at the time."

Liam arched an eyebrow. "How many were there?"

"Six," Daniel answered. "Four men, two women. One was a nymph. None divulged any information. They had taken a Blood Purifying Solution so there was no chance to read their blood."

As the group fell into conversation about the best ways to cut off free witches from reaching Aires or Bruniér, Kenna moved toward Daniel.

"Why did you not stop him from taking her away?"

"I do not have to justify myself to you."

Kenna glared at him. "She is my best friend," she whispered. "My only family. You must feel something for her. You kept her alive. You protected her."

"Vampires do not *feel*."

"Yes we do," she said bitterly. "It just takes longer to understand."

"She is safe while in the underground chambers."

"She is in the Laboratory," said Kenna. "Being tortured . . ."

Daniel seemed to spring to life at this news. Uncrossing his arms, he turned to Kenna. "How long has she been there?"

"Over a week," said Kenna, acting as if they were having a casual conversation. "I tried to get in but the guards would not let me pass." She watched him closely, sensing his inner struggle.

He was trying to stay emotionless in the situation, to be loyal to his kind while Adrianna, their oldest friend, was being tortured down in the Laboratory.

Kenna did not know what it was that made Daniel so sensitive when it came to Adrianna, but she knew it was serious. Daniel had watched many innocents die without so much as blinking, yet he was clearly affected by the knowledge that Adrianna was in the Laboratory.

"Then," Daniel said finally, "then that is how it must be. There is nothing I can do for her."

Kenna did not believe he was speaking the truth. "You told me you were protecting her!" she hissed furiously. "You spoke those words to me!"

Daniel wore a cool look of indifference and glanced behind them. "Perhaps I changed my mind."

"*Oh my goodness*," she whispered, disgusted. "You *used* her, did you not? You sick, heartless . . ."

"Drop it."

"I will not!" She struggled to maintain her calm illusion. "I cannot believe you are capable of this . . . this *filth*."

"Then you have a lot to learn about vampires," he said as the redheaded soldier passed them slowly. "She was good entertainment and very *sweet*," he added meaningfully, "but she is not my problem."

Kenna stared at him.

"Thomas is watching you. Return to your Maker."

"I could care less. Do you know she used to leave flowers outside your house after you were kidnapped?" she demanded in a low whisper. "I told her it was stupid, especially after all the cruel things you used to do to her when we were children but she would not listen. Every week she left a fresh batch on your doorstep, and on your birthday she would go to the sea and light a candle for you. When Mathias told her that you were most probably a vampire, she said she did not care, just as long as you were alive and happy. How can you discard someone who would do that for you?"

Daniel did not reply right away. Instead, he turned to her as the meeting ended, and looked at her with the most condescending expression she had ever seen. "Kenna, I will warn you once. Stay out of my business. And as for Adrianna and her *tokens* of good will, I never asked for them."

"Kenna," said Thomas, coming up beside her. "Daniel, we will be going now."

Kenna took the elbow Thomas offered. "Think carefully about what I said," she told Daniel meaningfully before leaving on the arm of her Maker.

Daniel turned back to the window and looked out to the blossoming spring.

CHAPTER NINE

Mathena

KENNA STOMPED HER FOOT on the trapdoor that served as the secret entrance to the Gordgáin sanctuary.

"Do these people not know the meaning of the word 'emergency'?" she demanded furiously. Her last few visits to the sanctuary had not been pleasant, but she needed their help. There was no choice in the matter. "Why are they taking so long?"

Cursing, Kenna began to pace again, walking with her back to the open doors of the temple. Her hood was low, covering her porcelain face. Mid-step, she cast a quick glance to her right where Daniel stood, unmoving.

Adrianna's life force was fading.

Daniel leaned his back against the wall and crouched down, balancing perfectly with Adrianna's body in his arms. His silver eyes were soft as they gazed upon her bloodied face. Lifting a hand to her cheek, he ran his fingers over the dried blood beneath her nose; her blood, stolen in the most brutal way.

Kenna watched, fascinated. Daniel had never been so gentle, not even when they were children. Something emerged from them, a sort of energy, but she could not find the right word for it. Adrianna was unconscious and broken in his arms, yet she seemed somehow soothed by him.

She must care for him, Kenna resigned herself to believe. *Something happened between them.*

Daniel wrapped the blanket even more tightly around Adrianna's body. "She is dying."

Kenna ran her hands over her own face, closing her eyes. It was true. She could feel it. "Daniel, can you . . ."

"Never!" said Daniel, his eyes flashing.

"If you bit her, she would live," pleaded Kenna, softly. "Please do not let her pass to the Spirit Plane."

Daniel's hold tightened protectively.

"You would let her die?" Kenna whispered brokenly.

Kenna waited for his answer, but it never came. Instead, the trapdoor opened. Daniel raised himself to his full height and watched as Simo, gypsy and leader of the Gordgáin, and a fair-haired witch, appeared.

"Time is of the essence," was Kenna's greeting. "Quickly."

Hesitatingly, the blonde witch stepped toward Daniel and gasped. "What kind of demon did this? The girl looks dead," she said, visibly sickened.

"No, but she urgently needs aid," said Kenna.

"Well, she must have been tortured for weeks because her wounds have begun to heal!" the witch argued, pointing at the cut on Adrianna's cheek.

Kenna looked up to Daniel. "These are the people I told you about. They will take care of her."

The witch extended her arms toward Adrianna. "I will take her."

Daniel did not make any motions to release Adrianna.

"Who are you?" he asked coldly.

"My name is Mathena," said the witch. "I am skilled in healing but this girl is dying. If I do not treat her now I cannot keep her from passing to the Spirit Plane. I will do everything possible to save her. I give you my word. On the life of my clan, Collusus, I will do my utmost to save her."

Daniel looked her in the eye and stepped forward. Slowly, he placed Adrianna in Mathena's outstretched arms. "Make sure you do," he said, his voice promised dangerous repercussions if she failed.

"Take her down immediately," said Simo.

Mathena nodded and carried Adrianna through the trapdoor with the help of a warlock waiting at the bottom of the stairs. Kenna thanked Simo sincerely.

"If only this could be done for the rest," said Simo.

"Take care of her," said Kenna. "I may never see her again."

"There is always hope," Simo said kindly. "Thank you, for your actions," he added to Daniel.

"Thank you," Kenna said once more before following Daniel out of the temple. Raising the hood of her coat, she walked with him to the fortress where they would learn whether Adrianna's disappearance would be questioned or ignored.

~

Adrianna began to open her eyes. Slowly, pushing through the sting she saw clearly for the first time in days. She stared at the wooden ceiling, taking in its colours and textures as if it was the most beautiful thing she had ever seen. Her mind and body no longer throbbed and the taste of blood was gone from her mouth.

Am I dead?

Adrianna lay completely still, struggling to understand. Gradually, she became aware she was no longer shackled on a cold stone slab; instead she was lying in a bed, covered with soft white blankets, her head supported by a fluffy pillow. It was the most comfortable she had been since before the attack. The scent of rose candles floated through the air and the gentle sound of something bubbling came from the other end of the room. Cautiously, she lifted her head an inch off the pillow and was met with the most common sight in a witch's home: a cauldron. She smiled.

A long, white curtain was drawn over the window beside her bed. The cauldron hovered a few inches off the ground over a green fire in the middle of the room. Beside it were a small round table and two chairs. On the far wall was a fireplace, flanked by two shelves.

Looking to her right, she realised she was lying on one of two beds. Between them was a side table on which sat a silver hairbrush, a mirror, a vase full of deep blue orchids, and a cup of water.

As she lay her head down again, the door opened.

A blonde woman with a kind, pretty face entered in a flurry, threw a bunch of bay leaves into the cauldron and smiled at Adrianna. "Welcome back," she said brightly, moving the chair at the foot of the bed to sit beside her. "How do you feel?"

"Like a new person," Adrianna said croakily, taking in the woman's Collusus accent. She had a gentle way of speaking and a less broad accent than the northern one with which Adrianna spoke. "Did you heal me?"

The woman smiled. "I didn't think it was possible when you first arrived," she said. "You were broken far beyond anything I had ever seen."

"How long have I been here?"

"Almost two weeks. You slept most of the time. Though there were times I thought your dreams were doing you more harm than the Laboratory. A lot of things have happened since you came."

"Has my clan been freed?"

"No, nothing so wondrous. But the Maquis rescued the warlocks being held prisoner in the mines beneath the sea."

"Really?" Adrianna asked excitedly. "So they can help to rescue the others in the fortress!"

"In time."

"Oh, I am sorry. I have not even asked your name?" said Adrianna, suddenly feeling sheepish.

"My name is Mathena," the witch replied. "And there is no need for apologies. To be honest, I am surprised you can even remember your own name. You had quite a bit of Black Magick forced upon your mind, not to mention some serious spells. It is by the strength of the Light you can even speak."

"How did I get here?" asked Adrianna, unable to remember any of what Mathena spoke about. She barely remembered the Librarian, and though she knew she had been in the Laboratory, her experiences were mere flickers in her memory.

"I was contacted by Kenna. She and another vampire were able to sneak you out of the fortress."

"But how could she get me out of the Laboratory?"

"I do not know. You are the first person to ever survive it."

"The Librarian does not like for us to die too quickly," said Adrianna. "What about the others? There were three others with me."

She hated to think that Toby, Gabriel and Ferzand were still locked in that horrible place.

"I do not know anything about them," Mathena said apologetically. "Kenna and the man only had you."

"What man?" Adrianna asked timidly.

"He was a vampire. Tall, blonde . . . he was reluctant to leave you." Mathena gave her a knowing look. "I guess some vampires are still able to do the right thing."

Adrianna nodded and looked to the bedside table for a handkerchief as tears blurred her vision. Feeling ridiculous, she put her hands over her eyes as she cried.

"I am sorry."

Mathena placed a hand over hers. "It is all right. There is no shame in crying."

Adrianna was finally free. No longer would she hear the suffering of her people in the underground chambers or need to dream of being out of the fortress. She was no longer a prisoner. She felt a deep, agonizing relief, but then the shame of her own freedom made her reprieve feel sullied. She had liberty, yet others suffered still. She imagined Rosamunda, Orla, Peruva, Caitriona and Jess locked in the underground chambers, separating their consciousness from their bodies to keep themselves free of the Darkness.

Adrianna nodded and wiped her cheeks. "Thank you," she whispered, plucking the handkerchief from between Mathena's fingers.

"It must have been terrible."

"I had an easier time than many. I am so grateful to be free of that place, but so many of those I love and care about are still trapped. Kenna, the vampire who brought me here, she is my best friend. The closest thing I have to a sister." More tears flowed from Adrianna's eyes. "They turned her and now she is forever trapped there, while I am free. I would suffer the Laboratory again if it meant she was spared that."

"Soon, we will free them too," Mathena said, encouragingly. "With the warlocks no longer in the mines, we can push forward." She tenderly stroked Adrianna's arm. "There is no need to feel guilty for your own freedom. And as for Kenna, your bond will never break. Certainly for her it is not for she freed you. Hold on to that."

Mathena went to stir the cauldron and after a quick taste test, with a complicated wave, the liquid content lifted itself from the cauldron and landed neatly into a cup as though poured by an invisible spout. "This soup will keep your strength going," she said, handing it to Adrianna. "I have not been able to feed you solid foods, so I think it's best to begin slowly. I would like to get you walking a little, now you're awake."

"Will it take long for me to be normal again?" Adrianna asked, sitting up with Mathena's help. Her body was stiff and a little sore from lying in such awkward positions for so long. As soon as she swallowed a mouthful of the delightfully smelling soup her stomach growled. "This is amazing."

"Thank you. It's a family recipe. It should not take long for you to return to full health," Mathena replied kindly. "We need to work on nurturing your body before you begin to use magic, because over exertion will only weaken you again."

Adrianna nodded. "Where are we?"

"The Gordgáin sanctuary. We are far underground, beyond the reach of the vampires. The only way in is through the trapdoor beneath the altar in the temple. Gypsy curses and Protection Spells protect it. The only other way out, for us that is, is through the underground tunnels. But I doubt we will have to use those. I had you moved from the infirmary hall last night. This is my bedroom. It is bigger than most others, so I had you brought in here. When your body started responding to the Reviving Serum I needed to be able to look after you properly night and day."

"This room is wonderful," said Adrianna, leaning her head back against the pillow. "I feel so clean."

"Yes, the Darkness does tend to make us feel dirty," Mathena said agreeably. "You were about to go into a cocooned state when I brought you here. Your body began to protect itself," she added at Adrianna's confused expression. "Your consciousness was drifting from your body in an attempt to keep itself from being affected by the Librarian's evil, and your body was forging a protective shield around itself. That is a very risky thing to do. It requires a lot of power. You must be very strong."

No, just hereditarily fortunate. "I was not aware I was doing it."

"I believe it was triggered by the torture you went through," Mathena said softly. "The Librarian caused you so much pain that your body went into shock. And your mind, to keep itself from breaking down, just separated itself from your body."

"How did you stop it from happening?"

"I took away your pain," said Mathena. "When your body was soothed, I began to talk to you, coaxing you to come back."

"I cannot thank you enough. You saved me."

"I do what I must," said Mathena. "And you helped save yourself. Your will to live really is quite extraordinary."

Adrianna smiled and finished her soup. Mathena busied herself with tea, which she put into a wooden teapot. She let it sit for a few moments and then poured it into a porcelain yellow cup.

"So, what exactly have the Gordgáin been doing?" Adrianna took the cup and blew into the liquid, cooling it.

"Everything," Mathena replied. "I am a member. We sneak heralds in and out, smuggle stragglers out to the southern villages. There were a number of families living here, but they journeyed to Aires. It is difficult being underground...especially if you work outside for a living. We even aid the Maquis when they need it, though I think they only requested help once, and that was because they had no other choice. They do not like outsiders interfering. We attack any vampire who re-enters the village. Recently, some Inter-Plane messengers under Simo's orders have been trying to communicate with the angels."

Adrianna gave a low whistle. "That is a lot. "Why have the angels not helped us?"

Mathena shrugged. "Trouble in one corner of this great Plane is not going to rouse the interest of the angels. We are an island amongst great nations, and our disruption here has barely caused a ripple of news across the ocean, let alone in the Celestial Plane."

"No one across the seas knows of our plight? Not Citron or the City of Tents? How can that be?"

"Communication has been limited because the vampires of Sansul have blocked the ports. They stop us from crossing the borders to Bruniér and Aires. The only knowledge others have about what is going on is what we, the Gordgáin, have risked our lives to smuggle out through orbs and the underground tunnels. News will have travelled over the ocean, but without confirmation, how can they help?"

"The angels have other means of knowing though. We came to their aid when they warred against the vampires. *The War Against The Angels* took just as many of our lives as it did theirs."

"Yes, but they believe themselves to be above our problems. They blame us for the creation of the vampires, so why should they help us?"

"Who said we created them?"

"It is one of the many theories, one which the angels seem very happy to accept and remind us of whenever able. We cannot rely on the angels. I have told Simo so many times. We must look to our own strength to find peace again."

Begrudgingly, Adrianna stayed in bed for another few days, rising only to take short walks around the room with Mathena's help. Mathena had a unique mat she used to stretch Adrianna; bending her legs and arms, rolling her neck and even using her own body's energy to awaken Adrianna's spinal nerves.

"Did you know you had Ridge-back Bat venom in your blood?" Mathena asked one afternoon as she used her thumbs to massage the pulse points on Adrianna's temples.

"No. I could not even tell you all the things the Librarian put in me. Is it out now?" asked Adrianna, sighing as Mathena's fingers soothed a particularly sore point.

"You vomited it out. I redirected all the dirty things he put in you and you brought them up."

Adrianna cringed. "That must have been disgusting. Sorry."

Mathena laughed. "All part of the healing process."

There was a knock on the door. Adrianna straightened her clothes as Mathena went to answer it.

"I am not expecting anyone," she muttered, wiping her hands on a cloth as she went.

Mathena opened the door, revealing a tall witch in a black and green dress. "Mathena of Collusus?" she asked pleasantly, extending her hand.

"That is I," said Mathena, shaking hands.

"Lovely. I am Joan of the Wilmota Assembly. May I come in?"

"Yes, I suppose," said Mathena, though not enthusiastically. "I am with a patient at the moment."

Joan entered and smiled at Adrianna. "I am here for your patient. Hello there, Adrianna," she said brightly, striding to Adrianna's bedside.

Adrianna gave Joan a small smile. Joan was a career-driven member of the Wilmota Assembly who followed Witchery Lore to the letter. She had lived only a few lanes away from Adrianna in Walnut Grove, where her long line of ancestors had lived before her. She invited herself to sit beside Adrianna's bed and pulled a small notebook from her satchel.

"I am glad to see you escaped capture," said Adrianna, watching as Joan flipped a few pages in, found a blank one, and finally looked up. Mathena hovered over Joan's shoulder, looking apprehensively at the notebook. "So, you are not here socially?"

"I have a duty to you and to our clan," said Joan. "I am here as your friend, neighbour and representative."

"Is this an interview?" demanded Mathena.

Joan's expression hardened for a moment, and after taking a deep breath she looked up at Mathena. "I am here to speak to Adrianna about her experience and to offer any help that may be necessary. This is usually done confidentially, but since we are within Gordgáin jurisdiction here in the sanctuary, you are required to be here. Unless," she said, turning to Adrianna, "you waive that right and choose to continue this in private."

"Do not take this wrongly, Joan, but I have not even agreed to speak to you," said Adrianna.

Joan's cheeks went pink. "As a member of the Wilmota clan, you are obligated to attend any meeting when summoned by the Assembly."

"I have not been summoned."

"No, but in our present climate, not all protocols can be fulfilled," said Joan, who was becoming visibly annoyed at the to-and-fro.

"Granted. But I was given no warning of any such intentions by the Assembly," said Adrianna. "You do not seem too concerned about my health or willingness to speak to you about my 'experience'."

Mathena crossed her arms, nodding in agreement.

"I am not going to beat about the bush with you, Adrianna, we have known one another too long for that," said Joan. "My title in the Assembly is Secretary for the Determination of Vahir Expansion. My job is to keep vampire influence in our lives to a minimum. I work with everyone – from the Warlock Myriad, neighbouring clans, faeries, elves and centaurs – to keep vampires out of our way, and in doing so, keep us all safe."

Adrianna looked her in the eye. "And what does your job title have to do with me?"

"I need to know everything you went through as a captive of Sansul Fortress."

Adrianna understood her game. Joan was appealing to Adrianna's patriotism. By confirming her job title and exactly what her mission was, she was playing the clarity card. Adrianna had no doubt that she had more than one trick in her deck. She knew what the Assembly was capable of doing to people they thought were becoming sympathetic to vampires. History could be an evil cycle of repetition.

"I understand," said Adrianna, looking away from Mathena's shocked face. "But now I am going to extend the same courtesy as you did me. You are here solely to determine if I had any relationships with vampires. Coming here under the flag of the Assembly is disgusting, especially considering that most of the Assembly is either captive or dead."

"You are being uncooperative!"

"Call it whatever you wish. What do you intend to gain by questioning me?"

"A better insight into the inner workings of the Sansul vampires. Are you going to be obstinate to your own people?"

"How dare you!"

"You cannot act like a child anymore," said Joan. "And rebelling against authority will only land you in trouble. Nobody will thank you for acting the rebel. It is foolish."

Mathena's mouth fell open.

"Foolish?" Adrianna let the word roll over her tongue. It was almost funny. After feeling terror and standing on the edge of death in The Fortress, being chastised by a bureaucrat of the Assembly was comedic, but still hurtful. The vampires were strangers to her, but the Assembly were her people. "I do not think you know what you are talking about. You know nothing of the way we suffered. And you come here demanding that I perk up and tell you? Why? So you can determine if I was intimate with them. Because that is why you are really here, is it not, Secretary for the Determination of Vahir Expansion? Which section of that office are you from?"

"Section?" asked Mathena, looking thoroughly confused.

Adrianna kept her focus on Joan, whose pale face was growing pinker by the minute. She knew Joan was calling upon every bit of training, every ounce of patience and professionalism to keep from slapping Adrianna hard. "Is it the Social Division?"

"How do you know this?" asked Joan, her voice calm. Her hand quickly jotted Adrianna's words in her notebook.

"The Social Division of your office is supposed to regulate and if need be interfere in relationships between clan members and vampires," said Adrianna. "They determine if dhamphir children will be allowed into the clan upon birth, depending on how cooperative the mother has been. They also 'actively discourage witches and warlocks from befriending vampires' for fear of creating sympathisers."

"You think that is wrong?"

"No, but I want you to tell me what exactly it is you would like to know. Treat me like a person, because I am not the fool you accuse me of being. Do not ask me about my whole experience, because you could care less about it. Ask me the questions you were sent to ask by your superiors."

"Very well . . ."

Less than half an hour later, Joan left Adrianna to rest. Mathena insisted on ending the interview as soon as Adrianna grew dizzy and sleepy. Adrianna gave Joan the bare minimum of her time in captivity, focusing on her time in the Laboratory. She mentioned nothing of Liam, Daniel or Kenna. She knew better than to give the Assembly reason to believe she had been compromised.

After five days in bed, Adrianna felt strong enough to leave the room, albeit with Mathena's help. She was curious to explore the Gordgáin sanctuary. All her life she had lived above this manmade structure, completely unaware of it. She had always imagined the Gordgáin sanctuary as one enormous room with bunk beds and an escape hatch; but just like her imaginings of the fortress, she was wrong.

Glorious was the only way to describe it. The atrium was in the shape of a pentagon. Each of the five corners was an opening to a narrow hallway. Off each hallway were dozens of small lodging rooms.

Emerging from the third hallway, Adrianna looked up in awe. Only a few heads above hers was the ceiling. It glittered with what looked like stars, but upon closer inspection she realised they were actually small glow-worms living in the earth above them. Enchanted to keep from imploding, carved wooden pillars seemed to go deep into the soil above them and into the wooden floors beneath. Torches and fire-globes lined the walls, hung from the pillars. Tea-light candles lined the two long tables in the middle of the vast room.

The fifth tip of the atrium led to a small circular hallway. It differed from the other four in that it did not continue into a hallway. Instead a heavy brass door blocked it. It led to the entrance and exit passageway to the temple above.

But it was the people who made this place a very real sanctuary in Adrianna's eyes. They bustled about: eating, chatting, some walking determinedly from one area to the other. She noticed a pointy-nosed man with a perfectly curled goatee. Adrianna recognised him as being a trader from Bruniér. She watched as Brenna, one of the village healers dumped a heavy load of linens into the arms of a tall, thin man. "And make sure they drink *all* the Blood Purifying Solution," Brenna said bossily. "We do not know what the warlocks inhaled down in the mines."

"Where are the warlocks?" Adrianna asked Mathena.

"Some are in the watchtower, others have already been sent to Aires," she said. "It was too dangerous to keep them here because of what they may be carrying. The mines have many toxins."

"Do you have names of the warlocks the Maquis saved?"

"Not yet. You must be anxious for your friends."

Adrianna nodded, thinking of Cedar, Caitriona's brother; and Mathias, whose sisters Maisy and Mara were still prisoners in the fortress. Fradrik, her guardian, Ralphus who harboured a passionate love for Kenna, had they all been captured and enslaved in the seaside mines?

"Adrianna!"

She jumped in surprise and turned to see a curious group of people at one of the two long tables. They had all turned to stare when her name was called. In front of them stood Renauart, formerly her nearest neighbour, and the husband of Rosamunda. At almost ninety years old, he was thinner than his voluptuous wife, and much loved by his clan for his kind, fair nature. He also went against highlander tradition and did not grow facial hair, which set him apart from the bearded men of Wilmota.

The sight of him brought tears to her eyes.

"You got away!"

Renauart embraced her. "You were brought here almost dead. I thought you would pass to the Spirit Plane."

"I do not let anyone defeat me! You know that," she said, wiping an escaped tear.

Renauart put his hands on her face. "I have been holding onto a wish, that I would one day see Rosamunda again."

"Last I saw her, she is alive and in good health."

The relief on Renauart's face was unmistakable. He bowed his head. "Thank you. It is a relief to know."

Mathena led Adrianna to the group. "I believe you all wanted to see our latest miracle," she said proudly.

Adrianna took a deep breath to steady her nerves. These people were war heroes. They were famous amongst all witchery clans, even though nobody knew their names. Their past sacrifices, their triumphs during *The War Against The Angels* were legendary, and here she was, a mere student, a survivor, being introduced to them for simply surviving torture.

Simo, the lilac-bearded leader of the Gordgáin, placed both his hands on Adrianna's shoulders. She felt an instant sense of kindness from him and knew immediately that they would get along. "Welcome. We were overwhelmed to hear of what happened to you. Your strength and will to live have touched us all and I know many here have been concerned over your progress and will be thrilled to see you up and about."

"Thank you."

"No one can best Adrianna," said Onoria, one of Wilmota's most famous witches. She winked.

Onoria was famed for her handcrafted hair decorations and dagger hilts but even more-so because she was married to the Spellmaker who created a charm that left houses dustless for a month before the charm needed to be cast again. It also added to her allure that her husband had been what witches called an 'Eternal Bachelor' – a man had who publicly announced he would never marry. Never one to back down from a challenge, and true to form, she had dragged him from his comfortable self-imposed eternity alone and married him.

Adrianna smiled. "I knew *you* would be doing something to take on the vampires! But I did not know you were a Gordgáin!"

Onoria grinned. "I like a good fight. Let me introduce Eglantine and Gralam."

Eglantine was a dark eyed, heavy browed woman with long, blonde hair, styled with braids, ribbons and twists. She smiled prettily at Adrianna and spoke in an unusual accent that suggested that she was not from Sansul. "I am so glad you are well, *maya*."

'*Maya*' was a foreign term used in Citron, a country across the Pearl Line. A term of endearment meaning 'dear one', it was usually spoken by older witches to young witches.

Gralam, a heavily bearded man, inclined his head but made no welcoming gestures. He was a short warlock with deep creases between his bushy brows from constant frowning, but to Adrianna he seemed affable enough.

"A pleasure," said Adrianna.

"You'll be joining us then, young one?" asked Gralam.

"Adrianna is not completely healed," Mathena said protectively. "She needs more time to rest. Don't promise him anything. He'd have every able young witch and warlock out there attacking the fortress day and night if he had his way."

Gralam snorted. "Mother hen," he muttered.

As they sat around the table, Adrianna learned that Renauart, Onoria, Eglantine and Gralam were each leaders of their own assault groups, though Gralam was planning to step aside once Fradrik returned. "He's got the brains for tactics," he replied when she asked why he wanted to leave his position. "Me, I'm a field man. Get me in front of a few vampires and I'd happily turn them do dust, but I am not going to sit and *plan* it all. Not me. No."

"How do you know my guardian?" asked Adrianna.

"I was the first friend he made when he and his ship arrived on the Wilmota shore. I knew your father too, girl. Good man, though not one to cross."

Adrianna searched his face for indications of falsehood. Gralam looked as true and rough as the beard on his face, but she suspected he did not completely trust her.

Eglantine had just returned from her stint on the Aires border where she stopped a small troop of Sansul soldiers from infiltrating protected ground.

Onoria surprised Adrianna the most. She had worked with the Maquis on their recent attack on the fortress.

"It did not work," Adrianna pointed out light-heartedly.

"The Librarian was using shield crystals to keep us from entering," Onoria explained. "He had reversed the neurone energy so that instead of shielding from vampires and demons, the way ours are supposed to, they protect the vampires from witches, warlocks, dhamphir and *all* folk of the Light."

Adrianna drummed her long fingers on the table. "So he keeps busy between torturing people. How wonderful for him," she said snidely.

Mathena cleared her throat and shook her head at Onoria.

"I did not mean to mention him," Onoria said apologetically.

"It is all right. I have to get over it. So, why are the Maquis so important?" asked Adrianna, pointedly changing the subject.

"They are *very* powerful people," said Onoria. "The power of the Darkness and that of the Light flows within them in perfect balance."

"Most do not ally themselves with the Darkness, but they still possess the traits and power of their fathers," Simo added.

"Maybe it is time for you to ask Adrianna some questions," said Mathena. "She will need to rest soon."

"I want to help you to free the others," Adrianna said eagerly.

Renauart and Mathena shared a look. "You are too young to be engaging in combat with vampires," he said.

"I do not think the vampires cared about my age when they kidnapped me. I have been living in a nightmare for four moons," said Adrianna, determinedly. "You have no *idea* of what the others are going through. I do. The murders, the feedings, demons ripping witches apart; do you know what it is like to watch people you grew up with leave the underground chambers and never return? Knowing that they were either turned or drained? My best friend was made into a vampire, and I was lucky enough to survive it for a reason. I should be allowed to fight with you."

Eglantine paled during Adrianna's description. "You can help me," she said, clearing her throat. "I convey messages between the sanctuaries and meet with the Maquis regularly. Even though they make us feel about as welcome as a bad smell. I will teach you what I know."

Adrianna nodded. "Thank you."

"We need to know everything you know about the fortress. Entrances, exits, portals . . ." said Gralam, pulling out a large map of the fortress. "This is quite old, but it is the only map of the fortress we have."

"It needs to be updated," said Adrianna. "The residences are in this area of the fortress." She pointed to the east side. "The Laboratory is here." She pointed to the middle building. "And the witches are imprisoned at this end," she added, pointing to the area close to the vampire residence halls. "They will be spread out along many chambers."

"How many have been killed?" Simo asked.

"A few dozen. There are more alive than you think. They were holding us to feed on when Henry wakes the rest of the army."

"Henry is not awake," Renauart pointed out.

"He will be soon," said Adrianna. "That is the Council's plan."

"*Vermin*," hissed Gralam.

CHAPTER TEN

The Maquis

As Adrianna's head emerged up through the trapdoor, Eglantine motioned for her to stay quiet and knelt down to help her.

Once through, Adrianna covered it with the old, dusty carpet, and wrapped her scarf around her neck to protect herself against the evening chill. It was raining heavily outside.

The once beautiful, small structure was now a blood-stained mess. The front door had been blown off its hinges by the vampires during the night of the attack, and the basilica shaped interior had been ransacked on their master's orders by the small and vicious grey-bodied goblins. The altar was smashed to pieces and ritual objects were damaged beyond repair. Blood had dried on the far right wall, and a fire seemed to have travelled along the left side, leaving behind a scorched stain.

"It must have been a wild fight in here."

"It was," whispered Eglantine. "This was the first port of retreat for those in the Gordgáin and the vampires hit us hardest here. Some did not enter for fear of what may have attacked them, but others . . ." she looked to the bloodied wall, "kept coming. Goblins came and desecrated everything. We could not salvage much."

As a cold wind blew through the temple, Adrianna lifted the hood of her coat over her head. "They were thorough."

"Quickly now," said Eglantine, leading the way through the mess.

Adrianna stumbled over a fallen candlestick. They stood against the front wall, beside the door-less entrance. Eglantine peeked around the corner and immediately drew back. Footsteps and a crude laugh drew near. Eglantine lifted a finger to her lips, motioning for Adrianna to remain absolutely silent.

"Heard they are going to wake up one of the ancients," a man's voice spoke.

"The Council does not know what it is doing, that is why," said another. "They are going to *vote* on it."

"Eh," the former said carelessly, "what does it matter to us?"

"Nothing I suppose. It's bureaucracy no matter who's in charge. But I still think they should have woken Henry before the Council decided to kidnap the witches. Did you hear about Rex?"

"Assassinated in his *bed*, he was. Always playing with fire . . ."

To Adrianna's great relief, the vampires passed the entrance of the temple without looking in.

"How did they not sense us?" whispered Adrianna.

"We set spells around the temple to block them from sensing us," Eglantine replied.

Eglantine checked again and this time the coast was clear. Motioning for Adrianna to follow, she ran through the pelting rain to an old, charred home that still, fortunately, was able to shelter them from the downpour.

Whipping off her hood, Adrianna's heart fell. The cottage was formerly that of Celeste the Herbalist, one of the many trapped in the underground chambers. Like the temple, it had been completely plundered. Inside, everything had been taken or searched; only a wooden stool and a small rag doll lay on the dusty floor. No longer were the shelves lined with jars, boxes and vials full of herbs, dried and fresh, potions, lotions, shampoos and medicines. The mosaic partition behind the shop counter had been smashed, so that hundreds of colourful shards littered the ground.

Adrianna picked up the rag doll and wiped some of the dirt from its face. It only smudged. Had the child who owned this doll escaped the vampires? She smiled meekly, remembering her heartache at finding her own rag doll missing as a child. Lillypad was her name, because at three years old it was her favourite word. Daniel was always the culprit of Lillypad's continuous disappearances, but she usually turned up within a day or two, sometimes with a missing limb.

"Why are we here?" Adrianna asked as she stroked the doll's woolly hair.

"A Maquis is supposed to meet us," Eglantine replied. "This is our point of contact. They should arrive any moment now."

Eglantine looked anxiously out the back window as Adrianna pocketed the doll. It was eerie. Complete silence surrounded them except for the rain outside. A storm was beginning; she could hear the distant rumble of thunder in the far pastures.

The night had always been Adrianna and Kenna's favourite time. With no parental supervision, they would sneak from their beds to follow the faeries and watch the centaurs spar in the forest. Adrianna smiled at the memory of moonlight mushroom picking with Kenna, Caitriona and Jess. She remembered picking up their skirts to wade through mud to find the largest, most magically potent White Mushrooms before the mud-pike ate them. Back then the air had seemed alive and everywhere they looked there was the Light. Now, there was nothing.

"Quickly! Get down!" Eglantine hissed, pushing Adrianna to the ground.

They huddled in a dark corner beside the front door, directly beneath the window. Eglantine wrapped her arms around Adrianna and slapped her hand over her mouth as a sharp, high-pitched squeal sounded from outside.

Immediately, Adrianna was overwhelmed by the sensation of her head being slowly crushed. She tried to block her ears but it was in vain; the squeal penetrated. As the pressure built, hot blood dripped from her nose. Clutching at her nose, she tilted her head back as Eglantine pressed a handkerchief to her face.

"Pinch tight," Eglantine said in her ear.

Adrianna craved for the sound to end.

After a few agonizing minutes there was silence. Adrianna and Eglantine looked at one another, holding their breath. Eglantine pressed her finger to her lips and moved to look out of the window above their heads. She lifted herself up but did not get far. The screeching resumed as an enormous figure ran swiftly past the cottage. Its heavy footsteps shook the ground. Adrianna cringed, holding her nose even tighter. She wanted to scream for it all to stop.

The cry did not last as long. When there was silence once again, Adrianna sat with a ringing in her ears.

Eglantine wasted no time. She looked out through the doorway and saw the creature responsible for the ear-piercing screeches, a Rakasha demon. By all standards it was forbidden, much less, impossible for a demon to walk the Elemental Plane. The only way this demon could be there was if its essence was in possession of a vampire's body and the vampire took its demons form.

"A Rakasha," Eglantine whispered as she returned to sit beside Adrianna.

"I have fought one. On the night of the attack," said Adrianna.

"This isn't good for us. Vampires do not usually morph into their demon form, but nothing surprises me anymore. How is your nose?"

"The bleeding has finally stopped," said Adrianna, holding up her blood-ied handkerchief. "But we need to get out of here." Running her hand over her face, the blood disappeared, leaving her clean.

"And not a moment too soon," Eglantine added.

A shadow reflected in the back window. Completely covered by the night, it motioned for them to follow. Adrianna trailed Eglantine's lead hesitantly. When they came through the back of the house, the tall figure that cast the shadow turned and began to walk away.

The cold Adrianna's her face tingle. She followed behind the stranger and Eglantine until they reached the outskirts of the village. The man, whom she took to be a Maquis, wore a long, patched coat and heavy hiking boots. She could not see his face.

"Where are we going?" Adrianna asked Eglantine.

"The Sleeping Forest."

"Who is he?"

Eglantine slowed and fell into step with Adrianna. "His name is Gyde," she whispered as they entered the forest. "A member of the Maquis. He is the son of a very powerful vampire."

"How do you know we can trust him then?" asked Adrianna, watching Gyde closely.

"Because we have a common enemy," Gyde's deep voice said when he stopped walking.

Adrianna thought of only one word when he faced them: soldier. Though he had a commanding presence and fine features beneath his cropped beard and thick, dirty hair, he seemed to her like a wild man. His patched hunting coat and worn black boots signalled thorough unkempt-ness. Though he was pale, his skin was not like that of the vampires. His brown eyes stared at her, down his long nose. "You are the witch set free by the vampires?"

"Yes," Adrianna replied softly, her hands trembling.

"Why would they release you?" asked Gyde. "Vampires never free their captives."

"I cannot remember," said Adrianna. "I was locked in the Laboratory for many days. One day I woke and found myself with the Gordgáin."

She could tell what he was thinking. He believed her to be a spy for the vampires, or in the least, an untrustworthy witch.

"I can assure you," Adrianna said confidently, "that I am working on my own free will. No vampire controls me."

Gyde looked sceptical. "Your assurances benefit no one. But I do believe the Gordgáin would have thoroughly checked your loyalty."

Adrianna stared at him in disbelief. A half-vampire was questioning *her* loyalty?

How dare he?

"Gyde, please, her allegiance lies only with her people," said Eglantine.

Adrianna glared at the dhamphir. She was sick of men like him - pompous, powerful and righteous about their own circumstances or agendas, but distrustful of others. Perhaps it was vampiric nature or maybe all vampires were emotionally flawed; even their offspring.

"She is too young to have other loyalties," Gyde said to Eglantine. "Perhaps you were just fortunate, young one."

As they went further into the forest, Adrianna realised she and Kenna had never come this far. They had always wanted to see the unexplored places inside the Sleeping Forest. They had snuck away from the village earlier each passing night so they could go further and further in, yet they had never quite made it as far as the place she now walked.

Gyde stood on the edge of a large clearing and waited patiently for Adrianna and Eglantine to catch up. His strides were much longer and faster than theirs. At one point Adrianna thought he had disappeared. She could hear a waterfall as they stumbled up behind him, their skirts covered in twigs and leaves, and their faces red from the hike.

Stepping into the clearing, Adrianna beheld a stunning sight. She felt as if they had just entered into another world. The rain that was pounding down on Wilmota seemed not to reach them here. An enormous multi-tiered waterfall was on the far side of the glade, around which stood large circular stones each one ten feet apart from the next. In the middle of the stone circle were horses, some with foals, eating and sleeping. Others strolled along the lake's edge.

It was luscious, green and alive. The glow of the waterfall lit their path toward it. But another light also caught Adrianna's eye. The trees shimmered with a glittery luminescence of a multitude of colours.

Adrianna gasped. She had finally found the dwelling of the Forest Faeries.

"Eglantine!" Adrianna grasped her arm. "Have you *ever* seen anything so amazing?"

Adrianna made sure not to go too close, but as she neared a white willow tree, she was able to look upon a faery residence for the first time. A tiny spiral staircase wrapped around the tree from root to tip, lit with glitter captured in crystals. Doors were on many levels of the stairs, some open so that she could see into the spacious hollowed out homes. Two faeries, each holding an end of a wicker basket filled with nuts, flew down onto the staircase, landing outside a leaf-shaped door and smiled at her. Were it not for the beautiful, green-toned wings on their backs and their size, the faeries looked exactly like warlocks.

"Greetings!" called the man, dipping into a bow.

"Oh! Greetings," she said sheepishly. "Sorry to disturb."

"Not at all," he said charmingly.

"Adrianna, some other time," said Eglantine.

"Of course. Goodbye," she said.

"Pleasant evening!"

Adrianna smiled triumphantly. "I have always wanted to see their homes!" she said proudly. "Kenna is going to be so jealous when she..."

"What is it?" Eglantine asked worriedly.

Adrianna shook her head sadly. Gyde and Eglantine shared a look. "Kenna is probably never going to see the faery trees, is she?" she said bitterly. "It was her dream, but it's always going to be just that."

"I am sorry for the passing of your friend," Gyde said sincerely.

"Thank you, but Kenna has not passed into the Spirit Plane. She was made into a vampire," said Adrianna.

They moved through the clearing, stepping into the circle of stones, passing the horses and walked along the lake. Adrianna paused and peered over the bank where she caught sight of strange things glimmering at the bottom. Nothing swam in the water: not fish or mer-people, not even frogs. Clear, untainted water cascaded from the fall to the lake, but as she looked closer, she realised that thousands of pieces of jewels and gold littered the river floor.

"Eglantine," Adrianna called. "Look!"

Eglantine's eyes widened. "How did it get there?"

Gyde had stopped when Eglantine answered Adrianna's call. He was waiting for them by the tip of the fall.

"What is all this?" Eglantine demanded as they caught up. "Where does all that treasure come from?"

"It has been there for thousands of years," Gyde replied. "No one touches it."

Adrianna was beginning to dislike the Maquis. She felt as if she was going to meet more vampires. Would the others be like Gyde - purposefully evasive and conveniently mysterious?

When they reached the crease between the waterfall and the cliff, Gyde turned to her. "Do not speak unless spoken to," he instructed.

Adrianna glared at him as he disappeared into darkness. The waterfall flowed down on her left, blowing a harsh wind into her face. She followed him, with Eglantine right behind her. A moment later, she found herself climbing steps. *This is so bizarre.* She counted four steps and then felt as if a curtain had been blown into her face.

Adrianna stood rigidly, her whole body tense, her eyes tightly shut, expecting something unnatural to occur. When nothing happened, she slowly opened her eyes. Gyde stood before her looking mildly impressed.

"The Arch has let you pass," he said. "You are trustworthy."

Adrianna shot the Maquis soldier her fiercest glare yet. "Well, *thank you*," she said sarcastically.

The Arch?

The moment Adrianna turned to look at what Gyde was talking about, Eglantine bumped into her as she too came through the secret entrance. Surely enough, a stone arch was engraved in the cave wall, though *how* they had passed through, she did not know. The centre of the arch was not open, but made of the same rock-face as the wall.

"Gyde!"

A blonde, pixie-haired woman stalked through the stone foyer with a stern expression directed at Gyde. She was not tall and had an ink marking of a pentacle star on her left cheek. Though she was very pretty, Adrianna could tell immediately that she was no wallflower. This woman was quite capable of putting people in their place if need be.

"You were supposed to be here a long time ago," she said sharply, her hands on her hips. "What kept you?"

"Vampire guards," he replied. "And Rakasha."

"Rakasha? Are you all right?" the woman said disbelievingly.

"Obviously. My delivery is made." He motioned to Adrianna and Eglantine. "Now they are your problem." He departed without sparing another look to the witches.

The woman smiled at them. "How are you, Eglantine?"

"Very well, Wynneth," said Eglantine, unbuttoning her coat. "This is Adrianna. She is going to be partnering with me on my duties."

"Welcome, Adrianna," Wynneth said kindly. "Please, excuse my husband."

Adrianna blinked. "*That* man is your husband?"

Wynneth laughed. "He is indeed. I apologise for anything rude or offensive that he may have said. Gyde was born without tact, you see. But there is no man more honour-bound and selfless, I promise you. My goodness, you are *very* pretty. You have such lovely eyes."

Adrianna blushed. "Thank you."

Wynneth looked at Adrianna intensely. "You survived the Laboratory."

"How did you know that?" asked Adrianna.

"I feel your pain."

Even though it was not a real answer, it would do for now. Wynneth motioned for Eglantine and Adrianna to follow her. The lair's entrance was large, open and smooth around the edges. Along the right side of the room was a stone ramp that followed the shape of the wall and went up to a second landing in the cave. It was lit with torches like the ones used in the Gordgáin sanctuary.

"This is our Wilmota lair," Wynneth explained. "We use it when we are travelling between towns, but our headquarters are in Aires."

"It seems . . ." Adrianna stood at the foot of the ramp and looked up. "Suitable," she offered sheepishly. She could see light on the second landing where Gyde had gone. Perhaps the lodging rooms were there? She hoped they were not as hoary and monochromatic as the cave entrance. It would be terribly dull to live here if it were so.

Wynneth laughed. "I find it uncomfortable, but as soldiers, decoration is not our strong point. Our lair in Aires is a much more pleasant place, but these sturdy walls have saved us on many occasions, and for that I am grateful. Please come and meet the others." She started to lead them further into the lair then paused, mid-step and turned back to them. "Did you tell her anything about us?" Wynneth asked Eglantine.

"No."

"Right," said Wynneth. "Well, Adrianna, just be mindful of my people. Erik, our Captain, is a great man, but he has been quite stressed and not very . . ." she hesitated. "Well, you met Gyde, and when Erik is tired they mirror one another in personality."

"Perhaps it is best I remain quiet and in the background," said Adrianna, looking to Eglantine. "You are the messenger, after all."

Wynneth smiled. "It may be difficult for them not to notice you. Still, let us see how things proceed."

Adrianna and Eglantine followed Wynneth toward a long table on the far left side of the cave. A dozen men and women spoke in hushed tones around the table. It was littered with scrolls and papers. Some looked like maps, and others were lists and letters. As they approached, a small jug tottered across the table to the outstretched hand of a Maquis and poured a golden liquid into the cup he held.

"Did he say when they were waking him?" asked one of the Maquis.

Adrianna could not see the man's face; he had his back to her.

"He does not know," said another at the head of the table. "Until we hear from, Nikita."

At that, Adrianna frowned.

"Attention people!" Wynneth called as she walked to the table.

The Maquis stopped their discussion and turned to the three women. Adrianna understood now why these people were so feared and revered. Their presence was incredible. She could sense their power from where she stood. It was their inner strength, their balance of dark and light. The promise of pain and their equal ability to do good made her wonder why they forced themselves to live in secrecy.

They were regal and confident yet physically, all were unique. Some, like Gyde, were obviously hunters, with rough exteriors while others were more vampiric; pale with distinct features like turquoise coloured eyes and incisors that one sensed could lengthen to fangs.

A flash of metal caught Adrianna's eye. As she looked closer, she realised that a metal spike was protruding from the head of a rather feminine featured

Maquis warrior. She leaned toward Eglantine and whispered, "Are you seeing what I am seeing?"

Eglantine smiled. "That is Alexjander," she whispered. "And yes, before you ask, it is drilled into his head."

Adrianna saw that he had caught her staring and she looked away hastily, her cheeks burning pink. Not just one but five metal spikes in his head created a Mohawk unlike any she had seen. Gypsies and foreign warlocks often visited Wilmota with strange hairstyles. Some she had even appreciated, but never had she seen, nor had she known anyone, who would forcibly drill metal into his head.

The man at the head of the table had an especially imperial presence. He was magnificently built, with broad shoulders showcased by the red jacket he wore. His short, black hair fell elegantly into hawk-like eyes that swept over Adrianna and Wynneth as they neared.

"Everyone, Eglantine is here with a message from Simo, I presume," said Wynneth, looking at Eglantine for confirmation. When Eglantine nodded, Wynneth smiled and added, "And this is Adrianna. She is the Gordgáin's newest member."

The Maquis seemed taken aback. The man in the red jacket and the turquoise-eyed man beside him shared a look. Sitting in the middle of the group was a bearded Maquis who had not bothered to get up when Wynneth entered. He was cleaning his nails with the tip of his dagger, but spared Adrianna a glance when she was introduced.

"She is just a young thing," he said, going back to his nails. "What is she supposed to do for the Gordgáin?"

"You do not have your Element, do you?" The turquoise-eyed Maquis spoke. "I am Orion. You need not be afraid of us."

"If you say so," she said. "And no, I do not have my Element yet."

"She will only be accompanying me on some of my missions," said Eglantine, rounding on the Maquis soldier. "What *we* do is none of your business."

Orion did not look at all moved by Eglantine's reaction to his question. He observed them coolly, obviously deciding to remove himself from a possibly hostile argument. But not all the Maquis took kindly to Eglantine's tone.

"No disrespect," said the Maquis in the red jacket, "but I have watched many women like her go out on missions and never return. You should look after your young ones instead of sending them to fight and be heralds. Do you not think it irresponsible to send a witch with her looks out of the safety of the sanctuary?"

Eglantine's cheeks turned a deep shade of red. Adrianna could feel the fury radiating from her.

"Erik!" said Wynneth, staring at him in disbelief.

"I chose to help the Gordgáin," said Adrianna, annoyed that he spoke as though she were not in the room. "Those who otherwise would be here are imprisoned."

"And how can you help them?" asked Erik. "The Gordgáin is a serious, rebel group and its members are expected to go to great lengths to fulfil their missions."

Adrianna blinked. "Excuse me, but firstly, I did not come here to be lectured, and secondly, I am not the one who failed their attack on the fortress. Look at your own abilities before you question mine."

"Attacking the fortress is no simple feat," Erik snapped, his eyes flashing.

"Neither is surviving it," she replied as a great surge of anger rose in her.

Orion rested his hands on his hips, sharing a look with Alexjander.

"Erik, she survived the fortress *and* the Laboratory," said Wynneth. "If you weren't so busy attacking her, you might *ask* her about it."

Adrianna arched an eyebrow when Erik looked at her. She had the distinct impression that he would rather suffer the Laboratory himself than request information from her, but the malicious spark in his eyes seemed to dim as they regarded one another.

"We do not need help from a child," said Erik, turning back to the table. "Your messages, witch," he said, holding out his hand to Eglantine.

Eglantine's mouth fell open and her chest seemed to swell with all the unleashed obscenities she was about to throw at him.

Suddenly, scuffling and cries of pain erupted through the cave, slicing through the tense air.

Adrianna spun around and watched two Maquis carry their wounded comrade through the Arch. The injured man swore loudly as he was placed on the ground.

"Joa, Leena, Durand! What happened?" said Wynneth, rushing to them.

Adrianna stood aside as the Maquis surrounded the trio.

"Rakasha," said Durand, the tallest of the three, as he pressed hard on his friend's wound to stop the bleeding. "They were everywhere. They came down on us in a pack."

Two women rushed down the ramp with Gyde at their heels. The first had long, curly red hair and the other looked particularly worried as she tied a white apron around her waist.

"How far out?" Orion asked the woman, Leena.

"Two leagues," said Leena, pressing her sleeve to the gash on her cheek. She swatted the hand of the woman who attempted to check the cut. "They are gone now – Joa saw them headed to Sansul fortress. After they wounded him, that is."

Joa was gritting his teeth as the red-haired healer slowly pulled aside the material of his shirt to check his wound. Adrianna's stomach squirmed and she clasped her hands over her mouth.

"Not so bad," said Gyde, standing over him. "We've all had worse."

Joa did not share his humour. "They've got some evil lurking in that place," he said in a tense voice.

"What do you expect, dhamphling?" asked Orion good-naturedly. "Bunny rabbits?"

Joa scowled at him and groaned when one of the healers placed a wet cloth over his wound. "It hurts, Mairan!"

The red haired woman, Mairan, smiled. "What a child you are! Come on; let us get him into a bed so I can heal this."

"What is a dhamphling?" Adrianna asked Wynneth.

"A young dhamphir," she replied. "It is a pet name but it shows how young a dhamphir is to be called that. Dhamphling are usually difficult because they are trying to balance their energies, and Joa is our little moody one."

"How young do you have to be to be called that?"

"Under one hundred," said Wynneth. "Joa is only fifty."

"It is such a cute name," said Adrianna.

Wynneth laughed. "I think so too." She looked over her shoulder at the group as they took Joa to the infirmary. "Listen, I apologise for Erik's behaviour. He is not usually so abrupt, and he really is a nice man but . . . the times have been stressful and, well, he is under a lot of pressure."

"Believe me; I dealt with worse than Erik. I have never met Maquis before. I realise how sheltered I was in the fortress. But I will and want to help in any way I can."

"Are the witches able to hold on a little longer? Until we are able to find a way to release them?" Wynneth asked. "Our last attempt was disastrous, impatience on both our part and that of the Gordgáin led to a useless attack."

"My people's ability to survive is strong, but I fear the Council will wake Henry. If he is awakened, I do not want to think of what will happen to them."

"We *know* they are planning to wake Henry," said Erik, coming up behind them. "The staunchest supporter of that plan, Rex, has been assassinated. So for now . . ."

"There are others who want him awakened," Adrianna interrupted. "And . . ." She turned to face him, frowning. "How do you know Rex was assassinated? That was a secret."

"There are no secrets in this world," Erik said plainly.

Obviously not. Adrianna remembered hearing Daniel order Rex's execution. How could the Maquis know of it? Unless the Council let it slip, which she doubted, or Daniel was somehow in contact with the Maquis, which she doubted even more. Perhaps the assassin, Vascus, had somehow informed the Maquis of Rex's death. Something was off . . .

"Do you have messages for me?" Erik asked Eglantine.

As Eglantine handed him a small pile of sealed notes, Erik asked, "You are the witch who was smuggled out of the fortress?"

Adrianna had the distinct feeling that he already knew the answer to his own question. If Gyde had known, surely Erik did also. "Yes, I am. How do you know that?"

"Did you see or hear anything that perhaps we should be aware of?" he asked, carelessly opening the first note.

I really do not like you. Adrianna looked to Eglantine, desperately wishing to leave. Eglantine nodded encouragingly, though it was not enthusiastic.

"Well, maybe one thing." Adrianna made sure she had Erik's full attention before continuing. "They are making an army of wolf-men."

"Wolf-men?" His pupils shrank, making his eyes appear blank, yet completely focused.

"Yes. The Librarian's newest creation: werewolves."

Erik narrowed his eyes. "If this is a jest, witch, I suggest you renounce it quickly."

"It is no jest," she said seriously. "Quite soon you will be fighting not only the Sansul vampires, but also the strongest creation on this Plane. Fortunately for us though, they maintain their intelligence and their ability to see right from wrong. So perhaps they are not a lost cause."

"What is it these wolf-men do?" asked Wynneth.

"They take the form of wolves," said Adrianna. "But unlike vampires, they bloodlust on the full moon, not every day."

"*Every* full moon?"

"Yes. I think the Council made them as a gift to Henry, to add to his future army."

CHAPTER ELEVEN

Sleuther

"**I** WILL RIP THAT Maquis half-caste from limb to limb as his traitorous father watches!" Liam seethed.

Daniel paced before the fireplace as Liam threw a map into the air in frustration.

Thomas, who sat calmly at the end of the table, rolled his eyes at Liam's behaviour. They were all accustomed to Liam's fits of rage when things did not go according to the Council's plan, and since the last two moons had been disastrous for Sansul coven, Liam's temper was in a permanent state of fury.

Daniel was deaf to Liam's irate drivel. As he walked, he thought of Adrianna, as he had every day since sneaking her out of the fortress, ultimately setting her free. Was she still in the care of the Gordgáin? Was she even in Sansul? Perhaps she had gone south over the Aires border to safety? He wished he knew; he wished he could feel her. The emotions evoked in him by the Pull were as distant to him as she was. Unbalanced, strange feelings and that sensational tingle in his body were replaced with a dull ache and a sadness he could not shake off, not matter how he might try.

He carried the loss without complaint; Adrianna was free and would not suffer any longer. Kenna had leaked a convincing story of Adrianna's tragic death at the hands of Sergus the Librarian. Daniel made sure to destroy all evidence of the Librarian's experiments on Adrianna. After his mission was complete he made a point of discreetly informing Sergus that Adrianna had been taken by Jeith and murdered. This kept Sergus from going to the Council with complaints.

Liam had had the decency to look guilty when he was confronted with the news through Nikita. The moment passed quickly. He proclaimed her to be 'yet another casualty of war' before ordering a seventh Vanguard Contingent to be sent to the Aires border.

Halting his stride, Daniel wondered how Liam had turned from the mild mannered vampire who wanted to protect Adrianna, to an unfeeling shell in a matter of moons. He had noticed the change but paid it little regard before Liam ordered Adrianna be sent to the underground chambers. *I should have stopped him.* Everyone knew the Laboratory was a death sentence.

"Those mongrels are getting into everything!" roared Liam.

"Have patience," Thomas drawled.

"What good will that do?" asked Liam, frustrated. "Anything moving between here and Aires has been cut off, stolen or killed and our lines between here and Bruniér no longer exist. We are being boxed in!"

"It's your own fault," said Daniel. "Now that the warlocks have been freed they have the ability to block anything leading out of here! We knew this would happen."

"It never would have happened if we'd killed them on the first day!" Liam argued. "How the Maquis managed to find the warlocks is beyond me."

"Everything seems to be beyond you," Thomas said coolly. "Even that little witch you gave up to the Librarian – she was far beyond your reach too. Until your demon killed her."

Liam's dark eyes flashed menacingly.

Thomas waved him away dismissively as he headed for the door. "Your grip is loosening. Daniel, I'd like a word in a few moments."

Daniel was left wondering just what Thomas wanted to speak to him about. They had never had much to do with one another, and there was nothing they had in common which needed discussing. Standing stoically, so as not to make Liam suspicious, he hoped that Kenna had not told her Maker of their rescuing Adrianna. Liam was very unforgiving of activities unknown to him and Daniel had no doubt that if Thomas knew what they had done, he would soon inform Liam.

It would not be long before Henry was awakened; and Daniel knew he could not stop the very thing he had been sent to prevent. Even more dangerous than it was before, the need for a strong, formidable leader was ever more desperate for Sansul coven.

"The wolf-men," said Daniel, as he headed for the door. "You might consider using them to block the paths out of Wilmota."

Liam looked contemplative. "Who would lead them?"

Daniel arched an eyebrow. "You."

Thomas waited for him at the end of the corridor, as he pulled on a pair of black silver-seamed gloves. Without a word, he led Daniel through the residential halls and across the balcony over the main hall. Below them, vampires sat talking and drinking, all seemingly oblivious to the perilous position their coven was in.

Kenna glanced up, sensing her Maker's presence, and watched him cross the gallery above. Though Thomas did not look down to acknowledge her, Daniel did; she gave him a small nod. Both knew they would never be friends, but had cemented a kind of alliance on the night they saved Adrianna from the Laboratory. It was their secret to keep until death.

Thomas led him down a flight of stone steps and outside to the gardens through a guarded exit.

Daniel lifted the collar of his jacket, his hair whipping his face as the wind blew ferociously from the sea. They were on the northern most point of Sansul, facing the cliff in the fortress gardens. White, though it was from the winter snow, green had begun to peak through, signalling the beginning of spring.

"Liam has big plans," said Thomas, walking across the garden path to a smaller, stone building. The black structure was perfectly square. A single vampire who stared directly ahead guarded the only door.

"Like what?" asked Daniel.

"I will show you," said Thomas, smiling awkwardly. It seemed that he knew something Daniel did not, and he was taking great amusement in the secrecy of it all. "It has been a 'project' for both Liam and Sergus. The Librarian is very happy with the progress."

"More monsters? How many more beasts will come from the Laboratory?"

"None of us was very impressed by the blood-drinking goblins," Thomas said in agreement. "I was in charge of destroying that project. It was messy, to say the least. But the fire-breathing gargoyles will work in our favour."

The soldier stepped aside for Thomas, inclining his head.

The door opened with a heavy groan and torches sprang to life. Inside, there was nothing but a single door in the centre of the room. It was mangled and had many claw-inflicted scratches on the surface. But the door was missing one component common in all things that opened; it had no handle.

"Let no one else pass," Thomas told the soldier.

"Aye," the soldier replied. "Mind them today, sir. They are noisier than usual."

Thomas removed a brass, paw-shaped handle from his pocket. As soon as he inserted it into the keyhole, the handle sprang to life releasing a beast-like roar. The paw turned, a click sounded, and the door swung open to reveal a lengthy, narrow room lit by a long river of fire in the centre.

"Impressive, isn't it?"

"Clearly," said Daniel. "A lot of work has gone into this."

"A few spells here and there," said Thomas. "Nothing too bold. Come."

They were instantly met by a horrible smell; damp, decay and something else Daniel could not quite place. Staying away from the stream of fire, he stepped to one side of the hall, as Thomas took the other. He found himself next to some sort of rail blockade. There were dome-like hovels on both sides of the room, all of them blocked off by bars.

Thomas watched Daniel closely. His eyes gleamed through the dimness as Daniel slowly pieced together the puzzle. A slow rumble echoed around the room, the shuffling of feet and rattling of chains.

"Come to pay us a visit then?" spoke an obnoxious voice beside Daniel.

There was not enough light to see inside the cell.

Daniel's eyes dilated, the black pupil quickly ate away the colour of his iris and the whites of his eyes. Turning to the voice, he saw past the darkness of the cell to the shadowy figures inside. Vampire vision was at its best at night; everything with life glowed white. Whatever had blood was visible by the way veins glowed florescent blue. The scent of a woman hit his nose and his eyes locked on her body.

The woman stood by the bars of the cell. Against the far wall sat four men.

When the woman's eyes locked with Daniel's, her expression changed. She whipped her filthy blonde hair from her face, her eyes narrowing.

"I know you," she said softly. "You took a witch from the Laboratory!"

Daniel arched an eyebrow. "Did I?"

The woman looked confused, but she did not back down. "Did you save her?" she asked so softly only he heard.

Thomas came up behind Daniel. "I see you have met, Toby," he said, conversationally.

Toby shrank away from the bars, as though repelled by Thomas' presence, though she did not take her eyes off Daniel.

"Toby is the latest to survive the change," Thomas continued. "She was in the Laboratory, dying, and Sergus decided to make use of her instead of having another body to dispose of. We added her to our collection." He motioned for Daniel to follow and began walking the length of the hall. "These beasts, the wolf-men or 'werewolves', as they like to call themselves, change form at will, but on the full moon the change occurs whether they want it or not. It is also when they are at their most ferocious . . . when they are at their best."

He stopped in the middle of the hall and looked into the cell before him. Raising his palm, a sphere of fire formed and floated through the bars, resting in the middle of the small space, showering it with light.

A lone wolf stood inside. Twice the size of the average highland wolf, it was covered with thick, black fur, heavily muscled and a long tail trailed behind, promising great pain to whomever it struck. Slowly, the wolf turned to face them, pinning them with unnaturally bright blue eyes that narrowed menacingly. It roared, revealing sharp, canine teeth.

Thomas was completely unfazed. "This is Gabriel, one of the first to be turned. He is the leader of this pack."

"How are these ones different to the wolf-men we have out now? They are to be part of the army?" asked Daniel.

"At present we use the early experiments. They hunt on our orders, but they have no minds. And they do not change back to their former human forms. We will be putting these new ones to use, their changes were more successful. But we cannot have them formally as part of our fighting forces. They are beneath us, little more than wild animals. Like the gargoyles, they are an added weapon. Think of how the numbers will grow once we release them onto the Light folk." He smirked. "It is the gift that keeps on giving."

The wolf was morphing. Daniel's mind flashed back to his own change from child to vampire as he watched the fur moult and the body shrink, painfully so. The wolf's howls became groans as Gabriel's bones snapped into place; his snout shrank, replaced with a perfect, long nose and human mouth. Panting, Gabriel shook his matted dark hair from his face, stretching his still rippling body so that his back muscles bulged through his skin. When he turned, his blue eyes stared directly into Daniel's.

"A social call?" asked Gabriel, turning his gaze to Thomas.

"Of sorts," said Thomas. "I am showing Daniel the brilliance of Sergus's work."

"I wouldn't call it brilliance myself," Gabriel replied, nearing the bars, unashamed by his own nakedness. "More like a disgusting accident brought about by a senile vampire with too much time on his hands."

"What the lesser minds do not understand, they blaspheme," said Thomas, casually.

"Preach to your followers," said Gabriel irritably.

"How many of you are there?" asked Daniel.

"All together? About four dozen," said Gabriel. "A few died in the beginning, when the Librarian was still experimenting, but we are strong."

"Why women?" Daniel asked Thomas.

"Breeding," said Thomas. "A social experiment. It does not work."

"Why not?"

"We are not rabbits," said Gabriel icily. "While we are still part human we maintain our minds and social decency."

"So you see," said Thomas. "Not just a pack of rabid wolves. While they keep their minds they can take orders. They will scare off the Gordgáin quite well – even the Maquis. I have had enough of the stench. Let us leave them to rest; they will soon be put to work."

As Thomas walked ahead of him to the door, Daniel moved closer to the cell. "When the opportunity comes," he said in a low whisper, barely moving his lips, "follow the seaside path to Azria. I will contact you."

"Did she survive?" asked Gabriel.

Daniel locked eyes with the man who had been supporting Adrianna's battered body in the Laboratory when he went to save her. Daniel would never forget the rush of fury he felt when he saw Adrianna sleeping in Gabriel's arms. He nodded once, giving the wolf-man the confirmation, and followed Thomas from the prison.

As the door slammed shut, Gabriel's eyes glowed neon blue.

~

Adrianna was savouring the last sip of ginger tea when Renauart came to inform her that a meeting had been called.

"And I have to be there?" she asked, surprised.

Simo wants you to be part of his assembly, at least until we rescue those who used to be his advisors."

Adrianna frowned. "But I am in no way qualified to council Simo on anything."

"You have seen and heard things that could help us greatly," said Renauart. "We know you can add a realistic voice to our plans by what you have experienced."

"And you are in favour of my doing this?"

"I would like nothing more than to know you are safe in this sanctuary at all times, but you will not sit still," he said with a smile. "Not after being locked in the fortress for so long. You can help us. As much as I want to keep you safe, I know there is only so much I can do."

"You are just waiting for Fradrik and Rosamunda to come back and boss me around," she teased.

"Exactly. Come on or we will be late."

Renauart led her away from the pentagonal-shaped atrium and down the second hallway.

"Six women arrived at the temple requesting sanctuary this morning," he said. "They had been hiding in their houses alone for moons before finding each other. Fortunately, they were from Upper Wilmota, there are many more places to hide there. The vampire patrols had made it impossible for them to come here before now. One of them narrowly escaped Jeith's clutches."

"Jeith!"

"You know of him?"

"Know of him? Renauart, it was he who kept me prisoner! Liam is host to Jeith's demon essence."

Renauart stopped walking. "*Liam* is his host? I . . . I took them for dead. All of them. When those children were kidnapped . . ." He could not go on.

"They are not dead, at least not all of them. I never saw Tobias or Adrik . . . I rarely saw vampires, but of those we knew, there were only Liam and Daniel, then Kenna."

"Did Liam hurt you?"

"He sent me to the Laboratory," said Adrianna.

"*Filth.*"

"Do you still think about it? The night they were all kidnapped, I mean."

"It will forever be etched in my mind, Adrianna. Not only did we lose half the village children, never to see them again, but we very nearly came close to being slaughtered," he said as his eyes glazed over with sadness. "I watched my brother die, and it was the only time I ever discarded the Lore and used my Element to kill. I would gladly see the fortress set alight and burned to its foundations. And now you say Liam is carrying one of the most feared demons in recorded history. The cycle of death never ends. Look at us . . . living underground like moles."

"Feel sorrow for those who live in the underground chambers," said Adrianna. "And the mines."

Renauart looked ashamed. "I apologise."

Adrianna smiled at him. "There is no need."

They came to a red door. Adrianna noticed that it was smaller than the two on either side of it.

"Invitation Charm," said Renauart, as the handle turned green beneath his fingers. "It allows only the summoned to enter."

"I know, Fradrik put the charm on our cottage," said Adrianna. "He wanted to keep me safe from vampires and 'uninvited men who may prey on my solitude' when he was gone."

The small room was packed with people. Squeezing through the door, Adrianna saw that a large table took up most of the space. In the middle of the table was a small indiscernible object, covered with thick white cloth. Mathena, Onoria, Simo, Eglantine and Gralam welcomed them inside. Adrianna was introduced to Simo's two daughters, Dahlia and Rose.

Dahlia was a haughty looking witch with curly black hair and a crooked smile. There was something in her brown eyes that made Adrianna feel awkward. When Dahlia did not get up, Adrianna assumed she felt that a glance was welcome enough. Meanwhile Rose smiled brilliantly and shook Adrianna's hand enthusiastically. She had the same long, dark hair as her sister and brilliant brown eyes. Adrianna thought her beautiful.

"Father told us about your escape from the fortress," Rose said sweetly. "You are so remarkable, Adrianna. We are very glad to have you with us."

Adrianna felt a heat rise in her cheeks. "Thank you," she said, unable to think of anything else. "It was really pure luck."

"Surviving the Laboratory is more than just luck," said Rose. "We lost our grandfather to that terrible place. Please, sit next to me."

Adrianna took the empty seat and smiled at Dahlia. She noticed that Dahlia's hands were covered with rings and henna markings. Numerous bangles and bracelets adorned her arms and at least four pendants hung around her neck. It made sense for a gypsy to wear so much jewellery, and Simo being the leader of his tribe, the Rhoxolani, would make Dahlia an important woman amongst her people, but Adrianna could not understand why she wore a skull ring and a tigers-eye pendant.

A witch never wore a skull because it symbolised mortality and a tiger's-eye deflected curses but also added strength to the Darkness. Black Magick witches wore them because they believed it brought their causes good fortune. Whatever the reason, Adrianna knew it could have nothing to do with Black Magick, surely Simo would never let his own daughter affiliate with such things.

Rose was not as heavily adorned as her sister, and wore a simple handcrafted bangle on her right arm and a moonstone ring.

Adrianna made a mental note to ask Mathena about Dahlia's trinkets as Simo stood to address the room. He ran a hand down his lilac beard and gave a weary sigh.

"This is an emergency meeting," he said, all the pleasantness in his voice disappearing. "The vampires almost found the sanctuary entrance. If it were not for quick thinking, we would be conducting an immediate evacuation." He spared a glance at Gralam who arched an eyebrow in return. "This," Simo continued, pulling off the white cover in the middle of the table, "was found in the temple last night."

Adrianna jumped in her seat.

It was a cage. Inside was a black and yellow striped snake that hissed when met with their surprised gasps. Slithering around, its head followed the circle of people around the table. When it reached Adrianna, she saw two black, gaping holes where the eyes should have been. She looked at Mathena in surprise.

"What is it?" asked Rose, revolted.

Dahlia stared eagerly at the cage.

"It is a Sleuther," Simo explained, sitting down. "A snake possessed by the Darkness, bent and forced to do the will of the person who captured it. They are so common now that they breed, becoming a race upon themselves."

Adrianna still did not understand. Why did it not have eyes?

"A Sleuther is used as a spy," said Gralam. "They are perfect for the job; small, dark and absolutely loyal to their masters."

"They do not know any different," said Onoria. "Once something is raised, bred, to fulfil a purpose, it knows not that it is a slave to a deranged master."

"Who uses them?" asked Adrianna.

"Vampires, Black Magick witches," said Simo. "Hags even use them to search for their victims. This one was sent by Sergus."

Adrianna's stomach lurched.

"Sergus can see everything the Sleuther sees, and hear everything it hears," said Simo. "We removed the eyes of this one to break the link."

Adrianna cringed. The snake rolled around in its cage, staring at each of them as though its eyes were still in its head.

"Can it still hear us?" Adrianna asked. "Did you not say Sergus could hear us as well?"

"We have taken care of that," said Gralam, his small eyes locked on the snake. "It cannot hear or see."

"There must be many more out there," said Eglantine, leaning back in her chair. "But we did not see any when we went to the Maquis." She looked at Adrianna for confirmation.

Adrianna shook her head. "No, nothing."

"Did you see any . . .?" Gralam paused and shared a look with Simo.

"Any what?" Eglantine demanded.

"Did you see any creatures that resembled a wolf?" asked Gralam.

The hairs on the back of Adrianna's neck stood up as memories of the attack on Wilmota flashed through her mind. The fire . . . roars . . . wolves bursting into the fray . . . why had she not noticed how different these beasts were to the highland wolves that peacefully prowled the hills?

Her hands gripped the sides of her chair: pain shot through her knuckles. Gabriel, a wolf-man, had been in the Laboratory with her for many days and was himself an experiment of Sergus the Librarian. Gabriel could not help the hunger he felt for live flesh. He was guilty of being cursed, not of being evil. How many others were like him? How many more went unwillingly wild on the full moon? How many went willingly? She shuddered to think.

Eglantine had been with Adrianna as she explained the existence of the wolf-men to the Maquis. She looked as disturbed by the mere mention of them at present as she did with the Maquis. "I saw no wolf," she said, her voice thick.

"He said a creature that *resembled* a wolf," said Renauart. "Adrianna?"

Adrianna realised she was holding her breath when everyone turned to look at her. She snapped out of her paralysed state when Mathena began to release her nails from the wood of the chair. "Sorry . . ."

"You're all right," said Mathena.

"You have seen them," said Simo.

Adrianna looked him directly in the eyes. He was desperate to know. He wanted her to speak of what she had seen and witnessed in the Laboratory. It was why he had invited her to the meeting, not to get her opinion on their future plans. There was no way she was going to tell the story. Going through it once had been horror enough.

"The wolf-men are cursed," she said softly, pulling herself away from every-one. "They were just as innocent as the rest of us. Excuse me, I have to go."

~

Mathena looked over at Adrianna as she threw dried crow's feet into the cauldron. Adrianna had sat silently on the sofa staring at the ceiling since rushing out of the short-lived meeting the previous evening. She refused to speak to anyone and became completely introverted. Knowing better than to push, Mathena mixed her potion in silence, knowing that Adrianna's physical recovery was bound to be faster than her mental recovery.

Unfortunately, Gralam's return from an early morning scouting mission had brought with it bad news. Dozens of werewolves roamed the land now, acting as the vampires intended: hunters, spies, and assassins.

"Are you hungry?" Mathena asked, placing a lid over the cauldron.

"No."

Mathena rolled down her sleeves. "I know how difficult this is. I understand how much you just want to go back to life the way it was."

"I cannot be of help to the Gordgáin," said Adrianna.

"You can, and you have been an immense help this past week," said Mathena, kneeling down beside her. "Do not let fear undermine your strength."

"I promised them," said Adrianna tearfully. "I promised I would get them out, but I have not."

"What could you have done? You are a young witch who was enslaved by *vampires* and lived to tell of it! Not many can say the same."

"It had nothing to do with strength. I lived because someone took pity on me." Adrianna wiped her cheeks.

"You are not weak," said Mathena sternly. "And I don't want to hear you saying so again."

Adrianna sighed. Mathena placed a comforting hand on hers.

"If it would help to talk about it . . ."

"They were innocent people. Harmless. Maybe even with families of their own and now they just want to kill," said Adrianna. "The vampires only . . ." Tears blurred her vision, but she made no effort to wipe them away. She let them trickle down her face. "They only want to destroy things. It is all they know how to do."

Mathena dabbed her cheeks with a handkerchief. "And what about the two who saved you?"

"I do not know. They cannot *all* be the same, can they?"

"No, they are not. There are vampires who are capable of kindness, as was proven by Kenna and her companion. Is there anything about these wolf-men that I should tell Simo?"

"Only that they were created the same way as vampires," said Adrianna, wiping her cheeks. "I was told that the Librarian was working with an alchemist."

"Which alchemist?"

Adrianna shrugged. "I do not know. Someone unknown, I suppose."

"So, if a wolf-man bites someone, they too become wolf-men?"

"Yes. They have venom in their teeth, like vampires. The venom reacts to blood and changes the victim."

"How would they apply that to wolf-men though?" Mathena asked curiously. "Would they bite the victim first, and then mix their blood with wolf blood?"

"I believe the vampire venom was applied to a wolf, which then bit a victim and the victim was then changed."

Mathena frowned. "So the vampires have created another race."

"No, the Librarian and a rogue alchemist created another race," said Adrianna.

Mathena stared at her intently for a long time. Watching as Adrianna prepared dinner for them both, she began to understand Adrianna's mind. She sensed depression inside the young witch. It was deep and painful, but she kept it dormant. Mathena knew this complicated feeling lay there because of the loss and suffering, but she also sensed something else, something only another woman would be able to understand. Part of the sadness was that Adrianna did not let herself succumb to the natural way of mourning. She had not spoken of her captivity, or her relief, or her grief; it was all locked away.

Mathena sat down at the table as Adrianna ladled soup into two bowls.

"You know you are safe with me," said Mathena, "don't you?"

Adrianna sat down and smiled. "I do. I want to ask you about Dahlia."

"She is unusual, isn't she?"

"Yes."

"Dahlia has always been a little eccentric," said Mathena. "I notice that men seem to react to her. She has a kind of . . . seductiveness about her."

"She reminds me of vampires actually," said Adrianna. "She has that same haughty sort of personality."

"I suppose she does," Mathena said agreeably. "She is the eldest of six. Simo has six daughters with his wife, Alysax. I think Rose has always been his favourite daughter, and that made Dahlia a little rebellious."

"Rose is so lovely."

Mathena smiled. "Rose is the sweetest woman, and never says a cruel word against anyone. Now that I compare the two, I do see what you mean. But Dahlia is a valued and honest member of the Gordgáin, if not a little in her own world at times."

"I did not mean that she is untrustworthy!" said Adrianna hurriedly. "I just thought she was unusual . . . fascinating even."

"Fascinating?"

"The way she moves and sits, and when she looks at you, it is like she is looking into your soul," said Adrianna. "Now I just sound stupid."

Mathena laughed. "Well, she *is* a gypsy. They are all dark and mysterious."

"What happened to Simo then?"

"He is probably circus folk," Mathena teased. "Which would not surprise you, if you ever saw the inside of his office!"

Adrianna finished her soup while Mathena told her about her children, Laura, Ide, Vivien and Huon, all of whom, to Adrianna's horror, were imprisoned by the Sansul vampires.

"We were visiting Wilmota," said Mathena. "You see I am originally from Collusus. My brother and his wife live in Wilmota and we were visiting for Samhain. We had only just arrived when the vampires attacked."

Adrianna's stomach squirmed guiltily. "Mathena!" she breathed. "You have not said anything about them! You never mentioned them to me."

Mathena blinked away tears. "It is too painful. I keep hoping they are alive but . . . looking after you has made me feel needed again."

"I am so sorry for your children."

"Thank you. I know I will see them again. My husband...all my little ones, though they're not so little now. They are your age, but even when they reach one hundred they will always be my children. My arms will be full again one day soon."

Chapter Twelve

True Colours

ADRIANNA PUSHED PAST THE pain in her legs and continued to run. The werewolf was on her heels, its pounding footsteps closing in on her position. Vampires were not far behind. Hard and fast, she sprinted through the overgrown Wilmota tulip field, ducked into the farmhouse on the edge of the pasture and collapsed against the back door.

"Go round!" called a soldier.

"Burn it down, Wylder," ordered another. "Do not let the running fox escape."

Panting, she clutched her aching chest and crawled through the dark to the kitchen. Making sure to stay away from the view of the windows, she collided with various objects and felt her way around tentatively. If she could just make it out the front door, she had a chance. As she reached up for the door handle, it began to shake. Heavy pounding sounded on the other side.

Adrianna scrambled backward toward the kitchen counter. The vampires had been too quick for her. They were waiting. She sensed three vampires and a wolf, but there was also something else. Another presence was nearing. Extending her hand, she used every ounce of force in her body to keep the door locked.

"There is someone in there," said a voice outside.

Adrianna held her breath. She knew they were powerful enough to fight through her magic and invade the house. Upon hearing fire-spheres hitting the panels, she crawled back further, waiting for the spheres to blast the door to smithereens.

"What is this?" spoke a deep, coarse voice.

Adrianna froze, staring ahead. *That voice . . .* She looked around the room for something to wedge against the door, but upon quick inspection, with the faint moonlight streaming inside through the window, she realised the only object available was a rather feeble looking chair; the dining table had been smashed. Her force field would not hold against the vampires much longer.

"Sir, we have a witness inside," said the vampire who had given the order to have her hunted down.

"Then kill whoever it is and *move on*," the former demanded.

"The witch is holding the door against us. She raised a Protection Shield," the vampire said, maintaining a courteous tone.

"Move aside!"

A sharp pain shot up Adrianna's arm, forcing her to relinquish her hold on the shield. With a cry, she clutched her stinging arm to her chest, and before she could run for cover, a loud bang shot through the house. Splinters of wood, flames and debris showered her. Three vampire soldiers entered the house, fanning out to block her exit.

"Found her!" said the middle soldier. His teal-blue eyes focused solely on her and a small smile formed on his thin lips.

Adrianna felt her chest clench. *Do not show fear. I am strong. Strong . . .* Doubt momentarily entered her mind. *Who am I trying to fool?* Still she stared defiantly ahead, ready for whoever was about to enter.

A shadow came first. The sound of heavy boots on the wooden floor preceded the silhouette of a vampire so tall he had to bow his head to walk through the doorway.

For a moment, Adrianna thought it was Liam and prepared herself for an uncomfortable reunion. She rose slowly from her spot on the floor as the vampire's face came into view. *Farewell world . . .*

Staring back at her were two impassive eyes contrasted against a face so pale it glowed, framed by waist-length, straight, black hair.

Nikita, a vampire infamous for his lack of humanity and bloodlust, arched an eyebrow at the sight of her. "Well, this is a surprise."

Adrianna glared back. Her heart began to race as Nikita looked her up and down. This was not how she wanted to die. Not at his hands, her blood drained, body discarded the way so many others had been.

"Leave us," Nikita ordered of the soldiers.

"But . . ."

"Now!" Nikita roared. He locked eyes with Adrianna as the soldiers hesitatingly moved out. "I prefer to feed alone."

Taking a deep breath as dread crept up her spine, tears formed in her eyes. Nikita made an elegant and complicated gesture toward the empty threshold and in its place formed a thick wall of vines.

Nikita smirked.

"You look like a cornered rabbit, little witch," he said. His rich, rough voice made his words so much more resonant.

Adrianna did not reply. She took small steps toward the back door.

"I am not going to kill you."

"Then what do you want?" Her body began to shake involuntarily.

"Nothing from you," said Nikita. "I myself am leaving this township. I have no need for any information you might have on the Gordgáin. You'll find the path to the forest clear." He nodded to the door.

Adrianna was even more confused. "Are you not afraid I might tell someone?"

"I am only afraid of one thing, little witch," he said, "and you and what you might say is not it. You are free to go."

"How do I know this is not a trap?" she said suspiciously.

Nikita tilted his head. "You do not."

Adrianna stared wonderingly. What went on inside the mind of a vampire? How did they reason? They were more confusing to her each time she saw them. Even though they lacked compassion, remorse, or the ability to feel emotions, sometimes, just like Daniel had, they proved her wrong.

"Why? Why would you let me go?"

It would have been safer to kill her and leave.

She almost thought he was not going to answer her, but as he turned to leave through the vine-wall, he said, "I think of it as preserving a valuable item, for someone I deem a friend. Now go."

Adrianna grasped the handle to the backdoor and left. She ran around Badger's Hill and up the gravel path to the village where she slipped into the florist's shop. There, she waited for Nikita and his men to leave the village before sneaking back to the temple where Mathena was waiting for her by the altar.

Hearing her footsteps, Mathena unclenched her hands from her hair. "Oh, thank the Light!"

"I ran into some vampires," Adrianna said breathlessly.

"Did you get the list from Onoria?"

Adrianna pulled a crumpled piece of paper from her pocket. "You will never believe what happened to me," she said as they climbed down the stairs to the sanctuary.

~

Adrianna stood on her tiptoes beside Mathena, trying to see over the heads of the people in front of her. Her heart beat rapidly with anticipation.

The warlocks were finally returning to them.

A small crowd of Gordgáin stood in the pentagonal-shaped sanctuary, cheering as the warlocks entered two at a time. Some were sickly and injured; others merely looked exhausted, but all smiled when engulfed by the excited crowd.

Some lucky few were welcomed back by their family; wives, children, brothers and sisters. Others returned to friends, faced with the knowledge that their wives, daughters and sisters were still imprisoned in the fortress or dead.

None returned unchanged. Many carried the scars and emotional torment of their moons as slaves to the vampires, but there were those who proclaimed their immediate support and will to serve in the Gordgáin forces.

It was then that Adrianna spotted a very familiar face. Her heart skipped a beat and a surge of excitement rose within her. "Mathias!" she screamed over the crowd.

The tall, dark haired warlock was being patted on the back and welcomed warmly, but he was visibly searching for his family. Adrianna stood upon the nearest table and cried out his name, crying with joy. He spun around and upon seeing her, pushed his way through the people.

Adrianna jumped down and flung her arms around his neck, holding him with all the love that she possessed. Mathias lifted her off the ground in a backbreaking embrace, sobbing his relief into her ear. His words were indefinable, but this usually composed man was crying on her shoulder; that was all she needed to know. His relief was as great as hers. They were free, but their friends and family were not.

"Mathias," she said, putting her hands to the sides of his gaunt face, "what happened to the others? Ralphus, Cedar, Lachlan? Fradrik?" She wiped the tears from his cheeks with her thumbs. A thick beard covered half his face. His eyes were circled by browning, sunken skin; white hairs streaked his young beard. His hands were cut, chapped and dry. "My goodness, you look so tired." The mines had not taken away his spirit, but the change in his dark eyes told of the toll slavery had had on him.

"We are alive, Adrianna," he said, clutching her as though his life depended on it. "All of us survived. We looked them dead in the face and defied those vermin. We lived when they told us we would die."

Adrianna's eyes shined with tears. "All of you? Alive? Where are they?"

"The watchtower. Those at the watchtower needed no immediate care other than food. The rest of us were brought here to recover. I have been desperate to know, all of us have, are you all right? Did you all get away?"

"It is such a long story, Mathias," she said. "But we were all captured. I was, Kenna, Cait, Jess, Phoebe, Maisy . . ."

"My sister!" He grasped her arms. "And Mara?"

Adrianna swallowed at the mention of his sisters. "They were alive last I saw them, and that was not long ago."

"How did you escape?"

"Might I tell you in private?" she asked softly. She looked around the room at the happy faces. "Not all know about the truth of what happened at the fortress."

Mathias gripped her shoulders. "Were you harmed? It is all I want to know."

"Just a little."

"Mathias?" Renauart came out of the crowd and clapped the younger man on the shoulder. "Welcome back."

"Glad to see you, Renauart," said Mathias, smiling. "Have you been looking after Little Anna in our absence?"

"Little Anna knows how to handle herself," said Renauart proudly. "But we will always look after her, when she allows us to."

"Did Rosamunda not escape?"

"No." Renauart shook his head. "Soon . . . soon they will all return to us."

"Mathias, this is Mathena," said Adrianna, turning to her. "She saved my life and we have become good friends. Mathena, meet Mathias. He is one of my oldest friends."

"A pleasure to meet you, Mathias," Mathena said kindly. "Adrianna has told me many stories about you and your friends. I am also a healer, should you need anything to aid you in your recovery."

Mathias extended his hand to her. "Any friend of Adrianna's is a friend of mine."

It did not take long before the reunion turned to mourning for those warlocks who did not return, and for those men who returned to no one. Adrianna had helped in preparing what was now being called a Wall of Flames. Hundreds of candles were placed against the third wall of the pentagon so that Gordgáin members could light them for their fallen loved ones. For each life there was a flame, lighting the way to the Spirit Plane.

As the crowd began to break, Adrianna turned to Renauart. He stared at the Wall of Flames, determinately avoiding anyone's eye. She knew he was thinking about Rosamunda, his best friend and most beloved wife.

"You will see her again," Adrianna told him.

Renauart looked as if he was holding back tears. "What if I do not? What if one day I place a candle on that wall for her?"

"You will see her again."

"We cannot know for sure. What if she is gone?"

"You cannot think like that. It will ruin you. You must be strong for your daughters."

Renauart turned to her. "They ask me for her every day. I ran out of excuses a long time ago."

Mathena drew Mathias aside. "Has a healer assessed you yet?" she asked, drawing Mathias's attention away from the conversation.

Adrianna placed her hand on Renauart's arm. "I know it is difficult. Kenna was my family. Believe me, I know your pain."

"Does it not bother you?" Renauart asked.

"What?"

"Kenna being a vampire?" he replied. "I know you believe her to still be the same person she was before she was turned . . ."

Adrianna was very grateful that Mathias did not overhear Kenna's mentioning. If word got back to Ralphus that she had been changed, she shuddered to think of his reaction.

"She is!" Adrianna insisted.

"How do you know?"

Adrianna stared. *How could you ask me this?* She never knew him to be a pessimistic man. Kenna proved through her secret visits and dealings with the Gordgáin that she was still the same rebel she had always been. She was a vampire, yet she tried to save witches. How much more proof was needed? Inside her heart, Adrianna knew Kenna was not exactly the same, but she was still the Kenna who Adrianna knew and loved.

"If Rosamunda was turned," Adrianna began, "if she was, would it bother you?"

Renauart's shoulders slumped. "I am sorry. I see my question is unanswerable."

"You cannot answer it because you are not faced with having to," said Adrianna. "I know you would love her in any form she came. Kenna is still my friend, so long as she does not serve the Darkness."

"I would not count on everyone being as tolerant," said Renauart, motioning to the people around them.

"Tolerance is an ugly word. I do not know if I tolerate vampires, what I do is accept they are here and a problem. I tolerate taxes and heat waves . . . but vampires?"

"Adrianna, Renauart," said Mathena. "I am going to show Mathias to his room – he will be sharing with Finn and Cameron. I will see you in the meeting. Simo has just called it."

"Perhaps you should go ahead of me," said Adrianna. "I can show Mathias the room. You are more important than I am."

Mathena shook her head, smiling. "We *both* have to be there, anyway. Simo is sending us out."

"To where?"

"We are going to help the Maquis in their next strike."

"Really?" she asked, not at all thrilled about seeing the Maquis again. Once had been enough for her.

"Yes, and Bruniér and Aires have sent help," said Mathena, smiling even more broadly now. "We just received word that they have just won a battle against the vampires Seventh Contingent and they are going straight to the watchtower."

"We can meet here for supper," Adrianna said to Mathias, trailing behind Renauart.

"All right." He looked worried. "Do not commit to anything dangerous, Adrianna."

Adrianna smiled at him over her shoulder, and, feeling very light-hearted at knowing her friends had returned alive, she followed Renauart to the second hall.

The conference room was very small and cramped. A large table and a dozen chairs were in the middle of the room. Candelabras stood in each corner and a dozen candles floated over the table, illuminating a large map that almost covered the whole surface. Around it sat Eglantine, a messenger, Simo, the leader, Gralam, a withered, grumpy veteran, and Onoria, a linguist who worked with all factions of Gordgáin both in and outside of Wilmota. Renauart took his place beside an empty chair and Onoria motioned for Adrianna to sit down next to her.

Simo smiled at Adrianna and continued speaking. "The Warlock Myriad will have to fight the vampires on the border so we must inform Aires that Sansul vampires may penetrate the border patrols."

"I can do that," said Onoria.

"I am yet to receive the Maquis final plan, but I think it involves a direct assault," said Simo. "With the Warlock Myriad fighting the Sansul soldiers further south as they try to invade Aires, it does not leave many to come with us. The fortress has been quiet, so with the Gordgáin, the Maquis and a dozen of the Warlock Myriad, we should be able to pull this off."

"Excuse me," said Adrianna. She blushed when everyone turned to her. "But I think this is underestimating the power of Sansul coven."

"In what way?" Gralam asked.

"Well, this plan of shifting their attention is very clever," Adrianna began, "but they will have expected it. They would not run the risk of leaving the fortress guarded solely by old gargoyles, goblins and a bunch of soldiers. Vampires are *very* well organised."

"They will use these wolf-men, it is what they were created for," said Gralam with a dismissive air.

"Partly," said Adrianna, feeling frustration rising. "Look, you *still* do not understand vampires, do you? You take them for mindless blood-suckers but they are much more than that!"

Mathena and Renauart shared a look; Gralam opened his mouth to argue, but Adrianna continued. "Vampires are patient, methodical and efficient, but they also have things they need to protect. They will not leave the fortress without ample protection and you should know why!"

Everyone looked confused. Eglantine tapped her pen on the table, her expression one of deep thought.

"She has spent too much time in their company," Gralam growled. "*This* is what happens . . ."

"Perhaps you could explain further," said Simo.

"Well, everybody knows that the necropolis is the most secure and protected place in any vampire coven," said Adrianna, remembering the book she had read in the fortress. "Sansul fortress has a necropolis at its very heart, underground."

"What do you know about the vampires there?" asked Onoria.

"They are very powerful, very old and very dangerous. I did not realise any of this until a few days ago, it just did not click. The entire time I was in the fortress I wondered *exactly* why we were being kept alive. If we were kidnapped just for revenge because of things done during *The War Against The Angels* then they would have just killed or turned us."

"Feeding!" Gralam said as if it were obvious.

Adrianna shook her head. "No. Feeding for vampires is boring if there is no hunt. Without that, half their enjoyment is gone. They would not kidnap us so they can have their 'food at the ready' so to speak. There were many rumours . . . including, that we were going to be used to feed the soldiers Henry would ultimately awaken, but that story does not stick because of what I just said; vampires like to hunt, especially soldiers. Two witches who returned to the underground chambers told us that in the necropolis, they were forced to make sure the vampires' entire entities were kept as whole and perfect as they would be if they were awake. Though, they never actually told us what they did."

"I still do not understand," Simo pressed. "Why would they need protection like this? Vampire's go into a mode of . . . of stasis while they sleep. They need no more shelter than what they have!"

"Exactly," said Adrianna, becoming excited at her own brilliance. "There are *thousands* of vampires in the necropolis, ranging from soldiers to civilians to some of the most powerful warlords of our recorded history. These particular vampires are protected not only because of who they are, but whom they *host*!"

She looked around the room hoping they were beginning to understand.

"I say I only realised this a few days ago because I recognised three of the vampires in one of the books here in the storage room in the fourth hall. The vampires are all extremely old. I mean, they were old during *The War Against The Angels*, imagine now!" said Adrianna.

Simo and Gralam looked at each other. "There are so many . . . Leopold the Angel Hunter, Ingar the Torturer, Syther . . ." said Simo, swallowing heavily.

"For goodness sake, even the vampires are afraid of Syther. Nobody would awaken him!" Eglantine cried.

But Simo continued as through there had been no interruption. "And Henry carries one of the most powerful demons ever known."

"That is right," said Renauart. "Odad, the former Head Chancellor of the Demon High Council. Odad alone was responsible for the deaths of hundreds of angels *and* he led the massacre of Rilenaville. After *The War Against The Angels*, Henry was put to rest in a secret location."

Gralam grinned. "And now we know this secret location."

"Not with certainty," said Onoria.

"Which brings me back to my first point," said Adrianna. "They will not leave the fortress unguarded to fight those in the south."

"You think there is truth to the rumours? Henry and the rest of the sleeping might be awakened?"

"I hope not," Adrianna said gravely. "The witches they have at the fortress are many, but if they wake Henry and a regiment of the old Sansul army, the blood they have there is not enough. They will spread further south. These vampires are thousands of years old. I did not see names, but I know a few from my studies of our history and I am sure one of them was awake during the *Pact of Assin Termin Arta*."

"That was signed three thousand years ago," said Onoria.

"Then the vampires will be in their flush of youth," said Gralam.

"We cannot take the chance," said Simo. He looked much older, the lines around his eyes seemed to have deepened in the past few minutes, and there was certainly a green tinge to his skin.

"Did I overwhelm you?" asked Adrianna, watching him worriedly.

"It is better to know than be faced with an impossible task without warning," Renauart said comfortingly.

"Very good thinking," Eglantine said in agreement.

Adrianna smiled.

Simo stood. "Nothing leaves this room. We shall adjourn this meeting until after supper. We shall meet again four hours past the sunset."

At that moment, the door flew open and Mathena rushed inside. "Sorry, sorry. Did I miss anything important?"

~

"Come in!" Kenna answered to the gentle rap on her bedroom door.

"Would you join me in the sitting room?" asked Thomas. "Some unexpected news has arrived."

Kenna followed him into their shared reception room and sat in the wingback chair by the fireplace.

Thomas took his time, carefully removing his coat. He knew Kenna was eagerly waiting for him to speak. As he poured himself two-fingers of highland whisky, Kenna dug her long nails into the arm of the chair.

"The Gordgáin are on the move," Thomas said finally.

"To do what?" she asked coolly.

"Attack us," he replied, turning to her. "Not that they will succeed."

"How could you know this?"

"I have my sources, Kenna," said Thomas, "as do you."

Kenna's expression darkened. "Back to this again?" she asked irritably.

"I know it was you who smuggled that witch out of here," said Thomas, though not accusingly. His eyes narrowed slightly as they bore into hers. "Do not deny it."

Kenna rose. "I do not. She was my friend and I could not see her die here."

"She is not your friend!" he said harshly. "She is a *witch*. You are better than that now. You are one of us."

"*Better*? Do you hear yourself when you speak? What do you want from me?" Kenna cried. "You want me to give up *everything* I knew and was!"

"Yes!" he roared, throwing his glass in the fire. "Do you not understand the ways of vampires by now?"

"I do not understand you or vampires." Kenna had never seen him lose his self-control before.

Thomas grabbed her by the shoulders. "If *anyone* finds out you freed her, especially Liam, they will not hesitate to kill you. *That* is *our* way," he whispered fiercely, his eyes glowing brightly. "If you are not careful out there in the world beyond these walls, you will be killed simply because of what you are. The vampire world, our history, is drenched in blood. Any step you take requires that sacrifice, but if you make mistakes, the blood you sacrifice will be your own."

Kenna stared back. "You want me to stay alive by forgetting everything I was and believed in?"

"I want you to embrace who you are now. Be loyal to your people."

"And to you?"

"Yes, and to me."

"What is it you would have me do?"

The bond between them was unusual. As her Maker it was his duty to teach her the way of the vampires, to protect her from their enemies while she was still fresh from her change and cement in her mind that her loyalties lay with her coven.

Thomas knew that Kenna's lack of fidelity toward the vampires and her blatant disrespect for the rules was reason enough to kill her. Her mistakes reflected upon his capacity to turn an outsider into a loyal vampire to join the coven. Any mistake would result in dire consequences. The moment he had tasted Kenna's blood he knew the bond between her and Adrianna was strong, near unbreakable. He knew her spirit strong, and her resolve, her will to live was stronger than most. It had been why he was so drawn to her.

Kenna was an exhausting, trying and exciting challenge for Thomas. If the times were not so difficult, he would have allowed her the room to find her own feet in their world, but in these times he could not be so generous.

Kenna could not see herself as a loyal vampire, but as she focused on her Maker's eyes, she realised there was no turning back. Things would never be the way they were. This truth cut her deeply.

Thomas caught the tear that escaped her eye and wiped it away. He was her family now. The coven was her home. She knew what needed to be done.

"I want you to put the past in the past," Thomas said softly. "Let it remain a wonderful memory."

Kenna lowered her head and began to cry. Her tears were a sign that her full transformation was still in its infancy. Vampires were rarely capable of such deep emotion. To their people, tears were a weakness and weakness was not tolerated. They lead to pity, sorrow, revenge, disloyalty and loss of power.

Thomas lifted her chin. "Tears are another part you must forget," he said. "You must strengthen your emotions. Cast away any and all feelings of sadness, mourning, fear and sympathy because they will only make you amiable to the cause of the Light."

"Is this only about becoming a loyal vampire?" Kenna asked, stepping away. "Or am I to become a servant to the one thing I was raised to fight against? Am I to become an unquestioning slave to the Darkness?"

"No vampire is unquestioning," Thomas replied. "Most of us have never served the Darkness loyally our whole lives."

"I am so confused I do not know where to begin," she said, rubbing her temples.

"All you need to begin with is the shedding of your past and embracing your new life. I, too, was like you: questioning, wondering, unwilling to give up my past life."

"What was your past life?" she asked. "What made you just forget your past the way you want me to forget mine?"

Thomas squared his shoulders. "It is unimportant."

"On the contrary."

"When it comes down to it, Kenna, you *must* choose. Life or death? Learning my past will make no difference to the choice you must make. I cannot protect you in the future if you so brazenly go off and help our enemy. If you are willing to save the life of the witch I cannot stop you – I will not stop you."

"It will not be easy."

"It never is."

"Who were you?" she asked. "*Please*, tell me."

Thomas sighed and poured himself a cup of blood. He drank slowly, as though it would help to fortify him against the memories. "It is not something I have ever spoken of and after this," he said, turning to her, "something I will never speak of again."

Kenna sat down and waited breathlessly for him to begin.

"My past was simple. I was born the son of an alchemist in a small village called Rilenaville," he began, spinning the glass in his hand over and over. "I had a normal childhood, a happy family. I also had two brothers and a younger sister. I followed in my father's footsteps and studied alchemy, earning my way to becoming an alchemist. I married a woman who originated from the City of Tents. Her name was Rayca. We travelled to her home village to live. There we had two children. After they were grown and my father was dying – he was one of those who chose to age and go naturally to death - we decided to return to Rilenaville and begin a new life. Within days of our arrival we were attacked."

Kenna closed her eyes as thunder rolled along the hills outside. Thomas sat down in the chair opposite her by the fireplace. He extended his legs and leaned back.

"Demons and vampires swarmed the village and began their massacre," he started again. "I put up protection around my house to defend my family as I fought the intruders outside. Within minutes my children lowered the Protection Shield and took to the fight. They never obeyed as they should . . ." Something almost warm flickered in his eyes, but just as quickly as it happened; it disappeared, leaving Kenna believing it to be a trick of the flames. "My son, Valcan, died trying to save his sister. My daughter, Tosela, fought gallantly by my side but she was cornered by a demon named Odad. As I fought two vampires I saw Odad transform into a vampire named Henry. He offered her life, but she refused him, knowing exactly what kind of life it would be. My mother threw herself before Henry, blocking his lethal blow to my daughter. Rayca grabbed Tosela and dragged her back to the house while I battled Henry. Nothing I did mattered, no matter how large the energy-spheres or how strong the spells, Henry just blocked them with ease. I was so engrossed in my fight I did not see the Rakasha demon cornering my family. It attacked my wife first. Tosela managed to kill it, but not before it wounded her. I remember pulling them both inside the house."

Thomas looked toward the fire as his hands clenched and unclenched.

"That is where they both died in my arms. None of my knowledge or my *years* of training and power could save them. Nothing I had learned could save my family, nothing I believed in seemed to be able to stand up to – let alone defeat – the Darkness. When they released their last breaths I was consumed with every emotion you could think of. I was filled with rage and blasted away everything in my path. I destroyed the house. I could care less about the battle outside.

Drenched in the blood of my wife and daughter, I collected my son's body and that of my mother. I felt nothing when I came face to face with Henry. He deemed me *worthy* of life and he made me into a vampire. I did not fight it. After all, I had lost everyone who meant something to me; I could not save them as a warlock or as an alchemist. The Light *betrayed* me. But even when I was changed into a vampire I could not give up the memory of them. I clung to them fiercely, and even returned to perform the Ritual of Passage when I was strong again. I burned their bodies just before the dawn rise and sent their ashes to the grassy pastures they loved in life. The night they died became famously known as the Massacre of Rilenaville. Less than a dozen of us survived."

Thomas raised his eyes for the first time to look at Kenna.

"How did you put it behind you?" she asked, her eyes shining with tears.

"My two brothers married women outside of our village and returned after the massacre," said Thomas, his voice quite even. "They returned to help put the dead at peace. As I made my own memorial for my family in the privacy of my garden, they witnessed it. They saw what I had become. They did not attempt to fight me but vowed that should we ever cross paths again, they would not hesitate to kill me. They were matter-of-fact, casual, about it. My change seemed not to cause them any grief, but they made it clear what my fate would be should we ever see one another again. They both died many years later, both at the hands of Bruniér vampires. My own brothers could not recognise me for who I really was, they only saw the vampire I had become. Change was necessary if I was going to survive. There were times when I wanted to walk into the sunlight and be reunited with my family. To touch my wife again . . . to hear my daughter laugh and my son recite his poetry . . . at times the thought of death was bliss. But life slowly became . . . bearable."

Thomas turned to Kenna. "It is never to be mentioned again," he warned.

"But your family," she said softly. "You lost your entire family in one night."

"The memories are always there, we never forget. But we must adapt if we are to survive."

CHAPTER THIRTEEN

The Watchtower

I N THE DEAD OF night, Gordgáin fighters stood guard around the village. Concealed in shadows, trees and nooks, others remained in plain sight watching for vampires. They were on alert for any disturbance that may trigger an ambush. It was a blue evening, thick with mist that swirled in the moon's rays.

Renauart waited outside the temple for the "all clear" signal from Gralam, who stood unprotected beneath a lamppost in the village centre. The old, hairy warlock stared toward Sansul Fortress with great dislike as he smoked his pipe.

"Are you sure Mathias cannot come with us?" Adrianna asked Mathena as they walked from the trapdoor, down the length of the temple and stopped at Renauart's side.

"He is still too weak. He cannot produce a strong enough fire-sphere and he cannot remember many of the important spells necessary in a fight," Mathena said reasonably. "Rest and recovery is what Mathias needs, not a battle."

"I know, but he wants to fight with us," said Adrianna.

"There will be other opportunities," said Mathena.

"Mathena is it wise to wear such high heeled shoes?" asked Renauart as he rolled back the embroidered sleeves of his shirt.

"We may be in a crisis Renauart, but that is no excuse to wear flats," she replied as Adrianna looked at her feet. Beneath the skirts of her summer dress, she wore purple high heels that matched her nails. "Besides, my husband could be waiting for me in that watchtower and I intend for him to see me at my best. Now, are we ready to go?"

"Gralam just signalled."

"So the pair before us arrived safely?" asked Mathena.

"There have been no disruptions all night. Follow the path directly to the watchtower," he said.

"How many more after us?" Adrianna asked him.

"You are the third pair so, five more to go. Be careful."

Adrianna followed Mathena along the gravel path, passing many concealed Gordgáin, and even a pair of Maquis soldiers. She noticed Mathena was on high alert; her eyes constantly scanned the area. Her fingers were flexed, as if she was prepared to fight at any moment, her strides were long and fast.

Gralam inclined his head as they passed. "Look sharp."

Adrianna grew vaguely aware of a small, glowing object buzzing around her face before it touched her nose. "Whoa!" She swatted the air around her head. The little thing dodged her hand, making her seem quite insane to onlookers. "What is this thing? Go away!"

Mathena laughed at her. "It is a firefly," she said, extending her hand to it. "See, it follows heat. It just wants to be around friends."

Panting and completely flustered, Adrianna whipped her hair from her face and stared at Mathena in disbelief. "Mathena, it is a *fly*," she said. "It is annoying. *Why* are you holding it? For goodness sake, fireflies set fire to hay when they land on it."

"When you capture them in jars or lanterns, they give off light," said Mathena. "All creatures serve a purpose."

"Well, you keep it. Come on, we're almost there."

"Don't listen to her," Mathena said to the fly. "She's just grumpy."

The watchtower was illuminated by the glow of the moon. A white, round-edged structure covered in purple vines, it had only two windows. A beacon-light shone through a small, round window in the cone-shaped roof.

Even though the watchtower was one of the most visible structures of a witchery village, it was also the most unvisited. It was the daily residence of the watchmen. While one remained during the day, he departed in the evenings and another took his place until dawn; though what they did inside was never discussed. Adrianna doubted they sat in the highest room and looked upon the village and sea all day and night.

Adrianna felt a burst of excitement as they neared the double doors. She was finally going to see what many people had only ever theorised about.

Two Maquis stepped out of the shadow of the watchtower. Adrianna smiled. She had met them on her previous visit to the Maquis sanctuary with Eglantine; they were Wynneth, Gyde's pixie-haired wife, and Durand who was the least vampiric Maquis she had met yet with his bright eyes and pink cheeks.

"A pleasure again, Adrianna," said Wynneth, smiling.

"And to you," Adrianna replied. "Mathena, this is Wynneth and Durand."

"Thank you for meeting us this evening," said Mathena.

Durand led the way to the entrance where another Maquis, Alexjander, was waiting. He stepped out and swapped a few words with Durand.

"Oh my goodness, that man is handsome," Mathena said in awe.

Adrianna thought Alexjander was very polite as he pretended not to notice Mathena's eyes widen to the point that she looked like an owl. Her eyes raked his form; from his studded boots, to the shin guards, to his steel-Mohawk. By the blush on Mathena's cheeks Adrianna could tell she did not mind that particular hairstyle one bit.

Adrianna elbowed her. "Control yourself! You are married."

Mathena seemed to snap out of her fascination at the mention of her husband, but it did not stop her from turning to Wynneth and asking, "Can I join the Maquis? Is there a prerequisite?"

Adrianna held back a laugh, although Wynneth was practically doubled over as she laughed. Alexjander seemed to realise he could not pretend to ignore them any longer and introduced himself, reducing Mathena to a breathless mass capable of doing nothing but stare.

"Excuse her," Adrianna said apologetically, "she is not usually so . . . speechless."

Alexjander smirked. "Happens all the time. It's my nymph blood. Still, you'd better get inside so the others can come up."

Adrianna gripped Mathena's arm and steered her through the door. "What is wrong with you?" she hissed.

Mathena buried her face in her hands the moment the watchtower door closed behind them. "I am such an idiot!" she said. "I do not know what came over me, I just . . ."

"It has happened to all of us," said Wynneth. "He is half nymph so his presence evokes all sorts of emotions in people."

"Mostly sexual," Mathena muttered.

"Yes," Adrianna agreed. "A moment more and you would have been drooling on yourself!"

"Do not tell me you didn't have the same reaction," Mathena said testily.

Adrianna blushed, even though she knew her first reaction to Alexjander was nothing like Mathena's.

"I personally never felt that around him," said Durand lightly.

Adrianna laughed when Wynneth gave him a look and rolled her eyes. "Your wife is half nymph," she said.

Durand seemed to stand taller as pride flowed from him.

"Really? Where is she now?" asked Adrianna.

"Azria. Far away from this unhappiness," said Durand, his face glowing. "She is the light of my life."

Adrianna could tell Mathena was glad for Durand, but there was sadness behind her smile. She wanted to find her husband and son, the lights of *her* life. Wynneth instantly recognised the expression. "With any hope, you will be reunited with your other half soon," she said kindly.

Mathena's smile did not reach her eyes. "I cannot wait."

"I cannot believe we are in the watchtower!" said Adrianna. "You know we are forbidden from entering the building without prior written consent from the Assembly."

The whole structure was built on three different levels, all accessible by the winding staircase that stood on the far side. The floors were made from the same dark wood as the doors and long tapestries ran around the white walls. All sorts of contraptions were on the many sideboards and wall-hollows along the stairs. Some twirled; others bobbed up and down and moved in odd yet orchestrated ways. Two glittery spheres floated around the ceiling. On the second landing was an intricate map of the sky.

"This is amazing," said Mathena, staring up. "It never ends!"

"Seems like it," said Wynneth. "Once you get to the third floor you will see the ceiling is merely an inch from your head."

"So low?" asked Adrianna.

"Yes. The warlocks who built this watchtower filled it with all sorts of trickery. You must be careful of what you touch," said Wynneth. "A lot is misleading."

"How long until the fourth pair arrive?" asked Mathena.

"Momentarily," said Wynneth. "Come, we have much to discuss before we launch our attack. A meeting is set for when Gyde returns from his scout."

"How many Maquis are joining us?" asked Adrianna, becoming more aware of a familiar energy. It was subtle and easy to overlook, but she found herself reaching out, feeling for its patterns.

All life on the Elemental Plane emitted energy. The energies of trees, water, air, flowers, and soil being amongst the most commonly encountered. Every form of life released a pattern of energy unique to its species, making it easier for elementals to identify what they sensed. In Sansul fortress, there was little to sense besides the Darkness, and while in the underground chambers, there was nothing but air and the tiny flames that had provided light. Without nature, the elementals would die, as there was nothing to feed their own energy.

"Everyone in the north," Durand said proudly.

"Dhamphir from the south are coming, but they are protecting the Aires border. The nymphs and faeries need all the help they can get," Wynneth added. "Hopefully they will be able to join us in a few days, if not, we must proceed without them."

"What of the warlocks?" asked Adrianna, climbing the stairs to the second level. Pausing in front of the map of the sky, she looked closely at the names of various stars and the times and dates of the forthcoming moons in the margin. According to this map, they had reached the seventh moon of the year.

Being underground made it difficult to follow the moon cycles and the season changes. It had been winter when she was in the fortress, and now the summer was in full bloom. So much time had passed.

Time. Adrianna frowned, turning from the map. "Astronomers."

"What?" asked Mathena.

"That is what the watchers are," she said slowly, looking around the room. "They are astronomers! Look, they calculate everything with these objects. Those things up there," she pointed to the floating spheres. "They are image orbs. You can send them to another part of the land, and have them project images of the sky to the orb you have. It helps if you're following a shooting star, or even trying to calculate the positions of various moons in different parts of the world to time potions and rituals."

"That's very good, Adrianna. How do you know all this?" asked Wynneth.

"My guardian, Fradrik," she said. "He loves astronomy and has all these. He used to be the navigator."

"Of a ship?" Durand asked with slight disproval in his voice.

"Yes, my father's ship," said Adrianna.

Sailors were not a favoured people but they were the ancestors of her father and she had no shame in admitting to being the child of one of the most respected men of the seas. She had not discussed it for years, not since her parents' disappearance.

"Your father was a good man?" asked Mathena.

"He never plundered anything, if that is what you mean," she said defensively. "Nor did Fradrik. He is more of a gentleman than anyone I ever met."

Wynneth smiled and nodded to Durand. "Well, you're in for a great surprise then."

Durand opened the first door they came to and stepped inside. Sitting around a square table was a group of warlocks whose conversation came to an abrupt halt at the sight of them.

Mathena gasped. Adrianna stood in the threshold; her heart skipped a beat.

Slowly, they stood, staring at her as though they could not quite believe their eyes.

"Adrianna?"

"Felix?" she replied, moving toward the baker.

"It *is* her!"

Adrianna fell into the crowd of men, embracing as many as possible in the midst of the happy reunion. Eronud her neighbour, Balfour who tended to the tulip field, Innis, a fellow student, Jules the artisan and his son Symon, all were among the survivors. Standing behind Symon were four young warlocks Adrianna had been hoping to see again.

The tallest, broad-shouldered and blue-eyed Lachlan grinned at her. Lachlan's brother, Adrik, had been kidnapped on the same night as Daniel and taken to Sansul fortress, never to be seen again. Adrianna hesitated as tears filled her eyes. Her world had seemed so cold and lost in the fortress; she did not know the fates of her friends, but now as they stood before her, worn but no less spirited, she felt a great relief and love for all of them.

Lachlan came forward and embraced her. "Crying is for girls," he said.

Adrianna chuckled tearfully. She looked over his shoulder at the others. Gangly and freckled with a mop of curly brown hair was Orlando, beside him was the burly, ginger haired and bearded Ralphus who had a piercing over his left brow; and beside him, standing with an amused expression, was Cedar, brother to Caitriona.

Ralphus wrapped his arms around both Lachlan and Adrianna. "Glad to see you made it through Twigglet," said Ralphus.

Adrianna smiled at them. "How did you all survive?"

"Mostly by keeping our heads down," said Orlando.

"It was hard labour," said Ralphus as Adrianna flipped his hands so as to inspect his palms. Calluses, cuts and scrapes covered his broad, strong hands. Adrianna's stomach grew tense and anger replaced the sadness. She tilted Lachlan's face gently, inspecting the cut on his neck.

"Why has it not healed?" she asked.

"The blade was lined with red-salt," said Lachlan. "It will close, but a scar will always remain."

"Dare we ask what you have been up to with the Gordgáin?" asked Cedar.

"All sorts," she replied, unable to look him in the face. His sister Caitriona was still captive in the fortress, and as far as she knew, had caught the eye of a vampire. This she would never disclose.

Mathena sniffed somewhere behind her. Wynneth and Durand watched the reunion with very satisfied expressions.

"We had a feeling you would be working with the Gordgáin, Adrianna," said Cedar.

"Cannot remember the last time I did not see you with Kenna," said Ralphus, glancing behind her as if expecting Kenna to walk through the door. "Where is she?"

Adrianna's stomach flipped. Telling him Kenna was dead was more merciful than revealing she was a vampire. Since the dark night when Daniel, Liam and many others, including Kenna's brother Tobias, had been kidnapped, Ralphus had held a burning hatred for vampires. Witnessing their flair at destruction first hand as a child he had vowed to help in their annihilation, not realizing that he had circuitously promised to kill his former friends.

"She did not make it," she said softly, looking away from Ralphus's distraught expression.

Cedar gripped his shoulder as the others lowered their heads in respect. Ralphus clenched and unclenched his hands. His face rippled with so many emotions: horror, sadness, anger and sorrow.

"Did you see her? Before she died?" he asked softly.

Adrianna looked to Cedar, unsure of what to say. With tears in his own eyes, Cedar nodded.

"I was taken before her," Adrianna said softly. "I am sorry I was not there."

"You were taken to Sansul fortress?" asked Lachlan. "How did you get out?"

Oh, no! Adrianna's stomach gave an involuntary squirm. "Actually . . ." A large, warm hand touched her shoulder. She froze, looking at the others.

Ralphus turned his back to them, moving away as his shoulders hunched. Cedar followed him, putting an arm around his friend.

"That is a fighting spirit you have, Adrianna," the man said, turning her around.

Adrianna smiled up at her guardian, Fradrik. Ever since her parents, Irina and Michaél disappeared; Fradrik had been not only her mentor, but something of a second father. He had taught her more than just the magic and history of witches, but also the learning's of *their* people. Embracing him, she could tell the gentle giant had been put through his paces in the mines. She took his hands and ran her thumbs over the thick calluses, cuts, scars and splinters. They were never smooth hands, but these were the hands of a man enslaved. There were lines around his eyes and his cropped beard was streaked with grey.

"Joining the Gordgáin is a fiercely brave thing to do, for one so young," he said, holding her face. *"Did they harm you in the fortress? I failed you, daughter of my Captain. I would go through the torture of the mines for a lifetime if it would have spared you that place."*

"What language is he speaking?" Mathena whispered to Durand.

"Oceania," he replied.

"Well, I have to repay the vampires in kind for what they did," she said, joining him in his first language. *"And yes, they did harm me. Others were ruined, but I fared better than most, even in my pain."*

Fradrik smiled tightly. *"They have taken the light from your eyes,"* he said hoarsely.

"Yes, I suppose they have."

The door flew open and a tall, thin young man stumbled into the room, gripping the wall to keep from falling. He looked around wildly, panting.

"Ma?"

Mathena gasped. "Huon?"

The group watched as the young warlock embraced his mother tightly. Mathena held onto the son she thought dead with a vice grip, sobbing with relief.

"Oh, my son," she said tearfully. "Thank goodness, thank *goodness . . .*"

The agonised relief in her voice brought tears to Adrianna's eyes. Fradrik put his arm around her shoulders, holding her close as they watched.

Mathena pulled back slightly, holding Huon's face in her hands and looked him over. "You are so thin, my child. The shadows beneath your eyes . . ." Her thumbs wiped away his tears. "My heart is straining, seeing how they have aged and hurt you."

Adrianna could see the similarities in mother and son. They had the same shade of blonde hair and though he was slightly taller than his mother, their faces were quite the same only Huon had dark eyes.

"Your father?" Mathena asked hopefully.

Huon shook his head. "He was killed in the attack getting Vivien into the forest."

Mathena nodded, lowering her head. Her chin trembled as she gripped her son's shoulders tightly, leaning on him for support. "I thought he had died," she said shakily. "I knew in my heart."

"We are sorry for your loss," said Felix.

"Thank you," she whispered, lifting her ashen face to look at the warlocks.

"Mother," said Huon, "where are the girls? Laura, Ide, Vivien?" He looked around expectantly.

"I do not know," said Mathena. "I have not seen them since the attack. I was hoping to find them when I joined the Gordgáin. They must be in the fortress."

"How do you know they are not...?"

"Because we – the Gordgáin – collected as many bodies as we could. None of your sisters were among the dead."

"We will get them out," promised Fradrik. "We will get them all out."

"Are you strong enough to fight?" Wynneth asked them.

"We are," replied Fradrik.

"It's time for the vampires to get what's coming to them," said Cedar.

Orlando, quiet by nature, nodded once in agreement. Adrianna thought she heard the sound of crackling knuckles from his direction. It seemed that revenge was the one thing on all their minds, but she had a feeling revenge would not come soon or painlessly.

~

Adrianna gasped and bolted upright, finding herself face to face with Mathena. Mathena's hands were gripping Adrianna's shoulders fiercely, shaking her awake.

"What were you dreaming? You almost fell out of the bed with all your fidgeting," said Mathena, her hold loosening.

Adrianna was hot and sweating, making her nightdress cling to her back uncomfortably. "It felt so real."

Mathena frowned. "You were talking a lot."

Adrianna's heart skipped a beat. "Oh?" she said innocently.

"Yes, you kept saying 'Daniel'."

"I cannot remember much," Adrianna muttered, looking away.

It was partly true. She had dreamt of the fortress. In the dream, she was surrounded by open doors. With each step towards one, the door would slam shut in her face. One after the other they closed as she tried to escape, until the last, which remained open. As she ran toward it, terrified and desperate, Daniel appeared in the threshold and asked her for the password.

"Adrianna," said Mathena, stopping her from getting off the bed. "Listen, I know that there are things you do not wish to speak of, and I know you would never keep anything a secret if it meant helping our cause. But if you ever wish to talk, friend to friend, I am here."

Adrianna sat back. "I know. And I wish I could speak to you of this, but . . . what has been forced upon me is something I must confront on my own. At least for now."

The next morning, Adrianna found Fradrik on the highest level of the watchtower, in the mapping room, his eyes glazed with anger and disappointment as they looked onto their deserted village. The pain of their loss was etched in his face. Wilmota was a shadow of its former glory; the buildings stood as ruins, and nature was beginning to grow wild.

"Fradrik?"

The sailor pulled the long pipe from between his teeth and smiled. "Adrianna," he said pleasantly. "You are awake early."

"I hardly slept," she replied, sitting down next to him.

"Bad dreams?"

"Confusing dreams," she corrected. "I came to ask you something."

"I am your guardian," Fradrik said kindly. "No matter how much has changed, I am still that. It is my duty to answer all your questions."

"Well, I wanted to know about . . . the Pull," she said hesitantly.

Fradrik's eyebrows shot up. He looked at her inquisitively, puffing his pipe for a long moment.

"I know you want to ask me why I wish to know," Adrianna said softly, embarrassed, "but *please* . . ."

"You ask of something you should not have even heard of yet."

"A lot has changed."

"Sadly so," he said softly. "Well, the Pull, simply put, is a connection between two souls. When our souls materialise into these chosen forms through reincarnation, there are times when our soul mate does not come with us. When it happens that they do, the Pull allows us to know they are here. Since we do not retain the memories of our past lives when we reincarnate, the Pull acts as a sort of . . . beacon. You see, as far as we have been able to discover, when a soul is formed though the accidental combustions of The Light, it splits in two. These two halves of a whole are but pure energy. When we incarnate, this energy learns, grows, feeds and dies alongside other energy, here on the Planes. At the end of our life cycles, we return to either The Light or The Darkness. Souls can become separated in these events, and they manoeuvre to reunite. Before our times, when the ancient language was spoken by angels, warlocks, nymphs, elves and witches, the Pull was called by a different name. It was called *Eriseda*."

"What does that mean?"

"Literally, it means *the binding*."

"Does it occur often?"

"More often than you would think," said Fradrik. "Sometimes we do not meet our soul mate in an incarnation because we love and grow close to others during different lives. We reincarnate many times, and sometimes soul mates live a life that does not include one another. That does not mean that if we do not marry our soul mate in one lifetime, that the person we do marry is any less meaningful to us. The love shared between two entities can never be taken away. It is all part of the unknown, the *Seline*."

"Can the Pull hurt you?"

"It can, like anything else. It depends on the character of the people involved." Fradrik surveyed her for a moment, puffing his pipe. "Do you love him then?"

Adrianna looked up in surprise, blushing. "I do not know what you are talking about."

He smiled knowingly. "Of course not."

Fradrik leaned back in his chair, and they watched the sunrise together in silence. He knew she had felt the Pull, but he had a sneaking suspicion that this man was not someone she would easily allow herself to love, or even admit to loving.

After a time she spoke again. "In the Laboratory . . ."

"We do not need to discuss it," Fradrik interrupted, "if it will upset you."

"It does upset me, but this is important. I fear it will have consequences for us, for the secrets we keep," she said.

"Did that filth force you to . . .?"

"No, no," she said quickly. "Not that. The Librarian never managed to extract any kind of power from me. At least not that I know of."

"Then what worries you?"

"He took blood."

Fradrik's expression hardened. He did not look at her. "I cannot imagine the agony you suffered at his depraved hands. I hoped you would be spared the pain of the fortress, and if death was to come to you I hoped it would be painless. But for all of that, you were strong and did not succumb."

"I did." She was quiet for a moment.

A tear leaked out from the corner of Fradrik's eye. Shame washed over Adrianna. She reached up and brushed away his tear, wrapping her thin arm around his massive shoulders.

"I did die, Fradrik. I now remember how, when, and the time it took me to return. It all happened quickly, so perhaps the Librarian did not have the time to record my passing. If he noticed he made no indication to me. He took my blood on so many occasions, and I hoped none of it showed my true nature."

"Are you sure you died? Or did you merely pass onto the *void*?"

"Fradrik . . . there came a point where the pain was so unbearable. I had to let go."

"We must never reveal this. Not to anyone. If *they* sensed your passing and return . . . if they knew of you . . ."

"We would know by now," she said, taking his hand. "They are not coming for me."

"They came for your mother . . ."

"They do not know of my existence!"

"How can you be sure?"

"What is most important is that we destroy the Laboratory and *all* the Librarian's evidence that I was ever there."

"How?"

"The mission. When we siege the fortress, we must split from the group and burn the Laboratory."

"Simo will not give permission for that without a reason," said Fradrik. "And we cannot disappear from the eyes of the Maquis."

"Then we must bring it up at the final Gordgáin meeting," said Adrianna. "Perhaps to look for survivors of the Laboratory? Surely, Simo will not deny that."

"If he does, then I will depart from the group to complete this. *If* he analysed your blood and found something, surely he would have told the Sansul Council. He would have sent soldiers to look for you."

"Do you want to take that risk?"

"Never. Now, may I ask you a question?"

"Of course."

"After regaining your strength, why did you not travel to your cousin in Azria?" asked Fradrik.

"Because my clan must be freed. What kind of highlander am I if I leave them to suffer?" She took his large hand in her small one and gave it a gentle squeeze.

"Besides, I could not leave here knowing you were captive. You would never have left me."

"*Never, blood of my truest.*"

Music floated around the watchtower from the hall. As the sun made its way toward the sky, casting a beautiful golden glow upon the land, the song played on a six-string violin, as a welcome to the new day.

Adrianna smiled. She had not witnessed a sunrise like this since the morning of the Samhain festival. Though she could not see it directly, she cast her eyes in the direction of the fortress and wondered if Daniel could see the sunrise too. Was he able to look upon the sunrise before closing his curtains for the day?

Fradrik regarded her from the corner of his eye. He had been the longest standing parental figure in her life. He had been at her side from birth and had taken responsibility for her when Irina and Michaél disappeared. It was his sworn duty to protect her, bound by a Blood Oath.

As the mentor to all the younger witches and warlocks of Wilmota, he was able to oversee her lessons in witchcraft and admired how fast she progressed. Her strength was written in her blood, though Adrianna herself was unaware of the depth of her own power. He admired her compassion and willingness to learn, although she easily allowed herself to be rivalled, especially by Daniel.

Fradrik smiled a little as he remembered fishing a sopping, hysterical five year old Adrianna out of the wishing well after Daniel had lured her in there.

Just like this morning, it was Fradrik who Adrianna went to when she had questions.

"And Kenna?" he asked, scratching his beard.

"It breaks my heart to think of her," she said softly, staring outside. "I love her so much, but she is gone from me. They turned her into one of them."

"Best friends never stop loving one another."

"I could not tell Ralphus the truth. You will not tell him, will you?"

Fradrik shook his head. "No. I have a feeling he will find out on his own one day."

"They were going to date, you know," she said. "Ralphus was supposed to spend the next day with her. He was so excited. Do you know how he expressed his feelings for her?"

"Flowers, I suppose?"

"No. Treacle." Adrianna could not help but laugh. It rose and burst forth before she could stop it.

"Treacle?"

"Yes," she said, grinning. "Kenna loves treacle tarts and he loves it straight from the jar. So he brought her an enormous amount of it and said, 'I will make the treacle, you make the tarts, and *together* we can make sweet, sticky music together'."

Fradrik laughed.

"It was an awful attempt to charm her, but it worked," she said. "I think he skipped all the way home."

"Ralphus wears his heart on his sleeve, poor boy."

"I hope Kenna and I can remain friends," she said honestly. "I could not bear to lose her completely."

Taking a long puff of his pipe, he resigned himself not to contradict her ideas – or more correctly, her *hope* – because hope was all she had left.

~

That evening, Adrianna was called to the ground floor of the watchtower. Gyde and Mathena were waiting for her. Both looked less than pleased.

"There is someone here to see you," said Mathena, opening the front door.

"Who?" she asked.

"It is me," said Kenna, standing a few feet from the watchtower. She shrank back from the light, pulling her collar up. She wore a beautiful deep red dress and glimmering emerald earrings.

"Stay there," Gyde said harshly, stepping out.

"No!" said Adrianna sharply. She pushed past Gyde, standing in front of Kenna protectively. "Do not hurt her! I will curse you if you do."

Gyde glared at her. "I wouldn't protect her if I were you," he muttered.

Adrianna ignored him and walked a few feet away with Kenna. Her face was almost unrecognisable; white as milk, framed by her dark hair. There was no colour in her lips or cheeks. Through her parted lips, Adrianna saw a small glint of white fang. She stood at arm's length, unable bring herself to go any closer.

"I know I look different," said Kenna. "I assure you, it is me."

"You have transformed completely," said Adrianna, staring at her in disbelief. "You look so . . ."

"Pale?" Kenna suggested.

"Different," Adrianna corrected. "This is not you."

"It is. I am changed."

"Why are you here then?"

"To speak to you face to face. I could not just let things go. Not when we have been through so much together."

Tears formed in Adrianna's eyes. Kenna was so far away. In her eyes, in her resolution, she was already gone from her.

"Does this mean you are siding with the vampires?" she asked thickly.

Kenna nodded. "I have chosen my side. Deep in my heart I do not like it, but I am who I am. They are my people now. I cannot betray them."

"I do not judge you for what you are, Kenna," said Adrianna pleadingly. "You know I never would."

"But you will. One day you will come to your senses and hate me like you hate the rest of them."

"I could never hate you," said Adrianna, wiping her cheeks. "You do not have to do their bidding."

"I am not helping them, but I will not go against them," said Kenna sternly.

"That is as good as doing the harm yourself," Adrianna argued. "You are choosing to stand idly by while they kill children and keep hundreds of witches locked in underground tombs!"

"I know what they are doing," Kenna snapped. "I am not here to justify it or myself."

"Then *why* are you here?"

"To say goodbye," replied Kenna. Her eyes softened. "I will always care about you. Maybe, if we both survive this and things turn for the better we can be . . . friends."

Adrianna stared at her. *Who is this person?* The Kenna she knew would never go against her beliefs and betray her own kind. How could she sleep knowing that her people were fighting for their lives? What had made her change so quickly? Here she was, risking her own life with the Gordgáin to free her people, while her best friend, her kindred spirit, was throwing away everything they had. Adrianna was beyond the point of devastation.

"I want to go back to how things were."

"But we cannot. Time cannot be changed, neither can the past."

"But you can change the future," said Adrianna. "You changed my future. I would have died in the fortress but you saved me."

"That is different," Kenna said softly.

"What about Caitriona? And Jess? Anya? Phoebe? Maisy? Collette?" Adrianna pleaded. "Ralphus is up there," she pointed to the watchtower, "mourning you! He cries for you! He has not smiled since I told him you were gone. I doubt he will ever smile again. How can you not care about them anymore? How can you just wake up one day – oh, excuse me – *night*, and cast us aside as though we never had lives that meant something?"

"I never said I didn't," retorted Kenna, her eyes flashed. "But I must be loyal to who I am. Like you are. Do not make it more painful for me."

"Why not, when you are *ripping* my heart out?" Adrianna demanded as her throat tightened with rising tears.

"I only came here to see you," she said gently. "Not to upset you. Daniel said you were well and happy but I had to come and see you for myself."

"Daniel has seen me?" she croaked.

The corners of Kenna's mouth lifted. "You are not completely alone, Adrianna. Who do you think kept the path clear for you the night Nikita found you in the farmhouse? Daniel was by your side the whole time."

"But I was on duty . . . I never saw him," said Adrianna, her heart beating rapidly. "I was so careful."

"You must stop underestimating vampires; especially one as dangerous as Daniel. I hope we can be civil with one another, if not friends."

"Friends? Kenna our 'friends' and neighbours are dead or imprisoned. Do you understand that concept? *Dead.* As in *murdered.* Never to return to this land as the people they died as. What do you expect from me? I love you from the bottom of my heart but you are asking me to do the impossible."

"I am sorry."

"Me too, more than I can say. While you side with my enemy, you are my enemy."

Kenna closed her eyes, looking regretful. "Then it is so."

"Goodbye."

Adrianna turned quickly and ran into the watchtower where Mathena and Gyde were still waiting.

"What happened?" asked Mathena.

Adrianna ran past her. Mathena looked back to where Kenna had stood, but the vampire was no longer there.

Gyde closed the door. "She should have known."

"She is still young, Gyde," Mathena said reproachfully. "They were like sisters."

"Not anymore."

"She is allowed her pain. Adrianna has been hoping for weeks that Kenna would leave the fortress. Their friendship means everything to her."

"You cannot be friends with a vampire," said Gyde.

"This is coming from a dhamphir?"

Gyde snorted.

"Take it easy with her," said Mathena. "Do not judge her harshly."

Chapter Fourteen

Henry the Destroyer

IN THE CRAMPED MEETING room, forty men and women listened intently as Simo outlined the final plan. Illuminated by candlelight was a detailed a map of Sansul Fortress depicting the buildings, paths, surrounding areas and the locations of defences.

Sketches of goblins and gargoyles in their most likely formations lined the grounds and battlement. The underground chambers and tunnels were outlined in blue, the vampire residential halls were noted in red, and the Gordgáin and Maquis attack points were dotted in purple.

The Maquis Captain, Erik, was the least enthusiastic person in the room, continuously staring broodingly at the map, as though he did not quite trust what it showed. Beside him, Orion chose to take a more active role in the meeting. He sat beside Simo writing detailed notes.

Adrianna noticed every time Simo mentioned the warlocks Mathena's eyes became teary. She held her emotions back bravely, but by the middle of Simo's explanation, her eyes were red and puffy. The news of her husband's death had shattered her. Adrianna knew that Mathena was only standing because she wanted to help free her daughters.

"Do you want to go and lie down? I can relay everything to you later," whispered Adrianna.

Mathena shook her head, taking a deep breath. "No, I have to do this. For him."

Dahlia lounged in her chair. She did not seem at all frightened or intimidated by the task ahead. If anything, she looked excited. Her sister, Rose, appeared not to be listening to her father's voice. She stared blankly into nothingness.

As Adrianna looked around at the people in the room, from Renauart to Fradrik, Durand and Gyde, Wynneth and Onoria, she noted they all had the same determination in their eyes. Her heart swelled with pride. The Maquis, people she had only ever heard about before the war, were there to help save her clan. Yet, even with the help of the Maquis and the surviving warlocks, the people of Wilmota and the Gordgáin, their numbers were small. The southern clans of Aires, Bruniér, Collusus and Azria had not sent a single person from either Assembly or Myriad to aid their most northern neighbours. Instead, volunteers from the neighbouring clans travelled through the underground tunnels in order to help the Gordgáin; witches, warlocks, faeries, nymphs and elves signed their name to the Gordgáin Alliance.

"Shameful," Mathena had said, when she remarked on the lack of aid from her own clan of Collusus to their northern neighbours. "Cowardly . . ."

Adrianna did not blame the clans for wanting to stay out of the fray. Aires was fighting Sansul vampires on their own border, after all. But she suspected that the real reason her clan had been abandoned to its fate was because the others all feared the wrath of revenge should Wilmota be overcome. What would the Sansul vampires do to the people who had opposed them? They feared a punishment worse than that delivered to Wilmota. They feared the beginning of yet another Inter-Plane war.

Adrianna took notice of Alexjander, the young half-nymph dhamphir with the steel-Mohawk . . .

His feminine eyes were focused on Dahlia. It would not have been obvious to anyone at first glance, but Alexjander was most definitely watching her. He looked uneasy, even distrustful. Dahlia seemed to take no notice of him. Instead, her full attention was now on her father. Simo, the Gordgáin leader, looked worn, strained. His lilac beard was faded, his hair limp and while his clothes remained pristine and colourful, he seemed to take little notice of himself. Sending people to fight and die placed a weight upon his soul that Adrianna could not imagine. Tomorrow, before he led them to fight, Simo would shake hands and swap words with men and women who would not survive what they now discussed in the small room.

After weeks of painstaking planning, tracking and gathering of supplies, the Gordgáin were ready to take the vampires down with a surprise approach from the inside. Secrecy was imperative. If the vampires were alerted of the impending attack before the majority of the Gordgáin were inside, they would be crushed.

"The goblins will come from here," said Simo, pointing to the front gates of the fortress, "here," he continued, pointing to the hill just in front. "And once we are inside the gates, from all around."

Gyde leaned against the wall, staring at the map with narrowed eyes. "How many do you think there are?"

Simo looked to Adrianna who shrugged. "Hundreds, I suppose," she replied, uncertainly.

Gyde rolled his eyes at her answer.

"The gargoyles will sweep down once they've seen you," Simo continued. "You will have your hands full. Can you handle it?"

Gyde looked to the other Maquis. They nodded.

"This would be easier if the gargoyles were asleep," said Gralam. "Keeping them in their stone forms would save us time."

Simo nodded. "That will be Mathena's job," he replied, turning to her. "When you are close enough, cast the spell. Just make sure none of you are near when they fall from the air. Once inside, we will be relying on you, Adrianna, to lead us to the underground chambers."

"All right," said Adrianna.

"And the vampires?" asked Durand.

"Kill any that cross your path," said Erik. "We need to bring that fortress to its knees. We have the man power and the ability."

"And our exit?" asked Gralam.

"Same as the entry. We do not want to be taking alternate routes because we do not know the scope of the area. That fortress is protected by more than just what we see. If the Librarian has done anything more with its security, we will have some nasty surprises."

"Shield crystals will be the least of your problems," said Dahlia, casting her eyes to the Maquis.

It was an obvious jibe at their last failed attempt to save the witches.

Alexjander glared at her. His lips became a tight, thin line. Orion and Erik shared a hard look.

"And the Librarian?" Adrianna asked quickly, cutting through the rising tension. "Should there not be someone to destroy him?"

"If anyone comes across him . . ." Simo began.

"That is not what I meant," Adrianna interrupted.

"I know what you meant," he said. "But I cannot ask anyone to take the risk of pursuing such a powerful vampire. We must be as unnoticed as possible. In and out."

"We are already taking the risk," said Adrianna passionately. "If anyone of us is caught, the Laboratory is the first place we will be sent. I do not know about anyone else but I personally do not want to go down there again!"

Mathena looked at Simo sternly. Everyone agreed that her words had merit. No one wanted to fall into the Librarian's hands.

"I volunteer to go," said Durand.

"And I," said Gyde.

"I will be the third," said Fradrik.

"The Laboratory is here," said Simo, pointing to the small area on the map on the lower level, directly beneath the library. "Even if you do not find him, burn the Laboratory."

Adrianna and Fradrik shared a glance. Their secret would be safe. For a time at least.

"How do you know its location?" Orion asked curiously, pausing in his notations.

Simo looked at Adrianna with a smile. "When Adrianna was saved from the Laboratory, her rescuer was kind enough to tell us its location."

"A vampire told you?" Erik asked sceptically.

"Yes," Simo replied coolly.

"And you trust this information?"

"Yes, we do!" Adrianna said indignantly.

"Do you not think the source is questionable?"

Fury bubbled in the pit of her stomach. "Are you calling my oldest friend a liar?" she demanded. "Her information has never been *questionable,* and I do not see you coming up with anything useful!"

Wynneth stared at her in disbelief. Onoria choked on a laugh and quickly turned it into a cough. Dahlia looked positively thrilled at the banter. Rose became curiously fascinated with her nails.

Adrianna did not care about propriety or the shocked faces around the room. No one, not a warlock, a witch, vampire, dhamphir or even an angel could question the truth in Kenna's words. Those words were as solid and true as the night was dark and the day was bright.

Erik met her glare. "Are you absolutely sure?"

"Kenna would never lie about something this important," she said steadily.

"As long as you're certain."

You gave up far too quickly, she thought suspiciously.

"What if there are people in the Laboratory?" asked Fradrik.

Simo sighed. "If anyone still looks natural, unchanged, then try to get them out. If not, leave them. Now to the last item on the agenda," he said, checking the list on his right, "is the use of Elements."

"I personally have nothing against using the power we have acquired by birth to defend ourselves," said Gralam. "If the vampires can draw upon the Darkness to despoil and befoul, why can we not manipulate the earth, air, fire and water?"

"Because you would take what should be used in purity and turn it into a weapon," said Rose. "Our Element is not to be used to harm."

"It has been done many times before, sister," said Dahlia. "There is no ill consequence for doing so."

"There is ill consequence to your being," said Rose.

"I agree with Rose, but we have little choice in the matter," said Onoria. "What do the rest of the Gordgáin say?"

"Most agree that we must use whatever forces we have to fight on. Others believe we should not manipulate our Elements to harm," said Renauart.

"Then for now we leave it to the judgement of individuals," said Simo. "This is a point we have no time to debate."

After the meeting, as Adrianna climbed the spiral staircase to the room she shared with Mathena, she heard a beautiful, haunting tune coming from above. She had heard it many times as a child. It was played on a maple-wood six-string violin and accompanied by a Bruniér flute. But this time only the violin played.

"It is tradition to play that song," said Gyde from beside her.

Adrianna jumped.

"I have that effect on most people," Gyde replied dryly. He looked up to where the music was coming from. "It is a gypsy song. They play it before and after battles."

"Why?"

"It is a lament," said Gyde. "Simo is the leader of the Rhoxolani tribe. His people cleanse themselves and prepare for battle spiritually."

"It is a beautiful song," said Adrianna. "But so sad . . . I always thought that."

"It is supposed to be."

"Why is he away from his people?"

Gyde shrugged. "Last I heard they were in the south. Better there than here . . . how do you know this song?"

"My father used to play it," replied Adrianna.

"Where are your parents?"

"I would like to know."

"The loss of them seems not to have affected you," he said. "For an abandoned child you live a pampered life."

"You would know *all* about abandonment sant, would you not?" she retorted, disguising the hurt she felt with a stony expression. For all she knew about her family she might well have been abandoned, but it hurt no less to hear the words said aloud. "I would bet your story is as common as the rest. Well, at least I knew my parents."

Gyde rubbed his stubbly chin. "You've got a bit of bite to you."

Adrianna sent him a withering look and continued to her room as the song ended. She had not thought of her father in a long time. Shame bubbled in the pit of her stomach. She was surprised at how much pain his memory still caused her. In her heart, her parents had not abandoned her, but there was so little explanation for their disappearances that she could not help but feel forsaken.

Adrianna shook the thought from her mind and lit the candle beside her bed. She undressed and washed her face with the rosewater Mathena kept in a glass bowl in the corner. When the war was over she would be grateful for all the space available back in her cottage. She desperately wanted to live in a home where every room had a function and her bedroom was her own.

Adrianna slipped into bed and removed her bracelets and rings. Staring at the flame, she drifted off to sleep wondering if her parents still lived, and if they did whether they thought about her with the same longing as she did them.

~

Adrianna was overwhelmed by what she saw outside of the watchtower.

"'They were young and old, brave and bold. As the clouds formed a sphere of fire and ice overhead, they bid their families goodbye, for the clash of forces would see this their last day to death,'" spoke Mathena from behind Adrianna.

"Adding to the tenseness?"

"It is a quote from a book about *The War Against The Angels*," she said. "I imagine this is what our ancestors saw when they prepared to fight."

"I think this is on a slightly smaller scale," said Adrianna, who pictured the number of fighters in that war to be hundreds of time the number of fighters gathered this night.

Four dozen Maquis soldiers stood together in their traditional armour, grouped according to their regiments behind their commanders. Each man and woman had a sword tied to their waist, and twin swords sheathed behind their back. Alexjander stood at the head of his regiment, garbed in blue. The men and women behind him were the most vampiric of all the dhamphir in the crowd. Their milky skin was almost blue, their hair thick and shiny, and their eyes were the brightest, as though light were shining from behind their irises. Adrianna could feel the Darkness radiating from them the most strongly, but for all of its potency, she did not feel threatened. After all, these people were risking their own lives to help free her clan. Turquoise-eyed Orion came up the line of his team, stopping to speak to each of them.

Wynneth smiled and came to stand beside Adrianna. "I am with you to assist in the liberation."

One hundred of the Gordgáin stood with the same determination in their eyes. They remained distinctly separate from the Maquis. Clouds of coloured smoke surrounded many of the warlocks. They had braided and beaded their bushy beards for the occasion. Others, men who knew they had lost kin on the night of the attack, shaved their faces clean in demonstration of their mourning. Their three-piece suits were impeccable, their boots pristine. But beneath their show of readiness, Adrianna could see their scars, exhaustion and fear. It was too soon for these newly freed men to fight.

"You're going to smoke yourself like a ham," said Eglantine, to a group of men smoking a heavy yellow tobacco as she meandered through them, coughing.

The witches in their company were busily going over the logistics of the liberation. Their focus was unwavering, even though many refused to use their Element in combat.

Adrianna noticed two witches watching the dhamphir in Orion's regiment with such open curiosity it was inappropriate. Leena, the blonde Maquis woman Adrianna had only met once before, noticed and sternly put an end to their stares. "The circus is not in town, witches. *Move on*," she ordered, "or you get a treatment." Her palm opened and a fire-sphere formed.

"Was that necessary?" Wynneth asked as Leena passed them.

"Your husband is looking for you."

"He *knows* where I am."

Onoria stopped in front of a witch who was an unpleasant shade of green. "Gemma, if you are not up to going, then do not," she said kindly. "I know you want to see your sister, but no one will think less of you if you remain behind."

Gemma shook her head. "No. Phoebe needs me," she said resolutely. "I am going to be there when we free them."

"She hasn't got the stomach to be a Gordgáin," Mathena told Adrianna. "Too soft in the head, she is. She won't even emit fire-spheres because she believes it goes against the Lore of Protection."

"I know," said Adrianna.

"Then how does she expect to fight off an attacker?" said Mathena, shaking her head in Gemma's direction.

"They can get over it," Gralam grunted, coming up behind them. "Like nymphs, they are. Cycle of life, protection of spirit . . . nonsense all of it! Do-gooders; they don't know the difference between defence and protection and they join the Gordgáin?"

"Maybe she is just frightened for her soul," said Adrianna.

Gralam snorted. "Soul, my peachy ass! Your soul knows the difference between killing for the right reasons, and killing for enjoyment. Nowhere in Witchery Lore does it state that we must keep from killing because it is an act of evil that leads to supporting the Darkness."

"Doesn't it?" Adrianna arched an eyebrow. "I have not read the Lore myself, but we are taught to disarm rather than kill."

"*That* has led to more innocent people losing their lives. Kill them before they kill you, that's what I say. Fight hard and you may live to see tomorrow."

Gralam went to join Fradrik and Renauart.

"He is a peculiar character, isn't he?" said Wynneth.

"Yes, peculiar."

"If we succeed, our people will be sleeping peacefully with their families tonight," said Adrianna, her heart beating with rapid excitement.

"This is unbelievable, isn't it?" Rose asked her, striding up from her place amongst the Gordgáin. "So many of us coming together for a common cause."

"It is wonderful. Are you nervous?"

Rose slid her hands into her trouser pockets. "Terribly," she admitted. "Dahlia is so curious to see the inside of the fortress; she would fly there now if she could. She's so much more adventurous than me. Well, I am with Onoria's troop. I just came to wish you all luck."

"Thank you. And good luck to you and your group, Rose."

Rose grinned and returned to Dahlia's side.

"Dahlia, adventurous?" Mathena said when Rose was out of earshot.

"Alexjander can't stand her," said Wynneth. "He says she has a strange aura."

Dahlia flicked her long hair over her shoulder and looked at them. Adrianna could not think of anything very strange about her, besides the vast amount of jewellery she wore. When Dahlia cast Adrianna a smile, Adrianna resigned herself to the thought that perhaps Alexjander was being a little too guarded.

Adrianna and Mathena were two of the first to walk the long path to Whistlers Knoll. "Can you cast a Stealth Charm?" asked Mathena.

"No," said Adrianna. "Besides, it would not last long! We are moving too fast."

Each step heightened Adrianna's anxiety and excitement, to the point where she almost forgot the danger surrounding them.

Glancing around, she realised that most of the Maquis were no longer visible.

She spied a copper-haired Maquis woman gliding up to the far side of the fortress on a small cloud, where she was lifted into the air and flipped over the battlements. Adrianna was quite sure no one else saw her; not even a gargoyle. They picked up their pace, walking faster, jogging in an effort to keep up with the rest.

A few moments later, she saw a flash of fire near the battlement gates. Lifting himself high into the air on a bed of flames, much like his predecessor's cloud, Joa flipped elegantly over the wall and disappeared from sight.

"That is *amazing*," said Adrianna excitedly. "How do they do that?"

"They use their Element," said Mathena. "The woman with the cloud is obviously water, and the man is fire."

"So, we can do that too, right?" asked Adrianna, the muscles in her legs growing tired. She turned her face away, slightly so that Mathena could not see her eyes, and took a deep breath, awakening her dormant side, her mother's blood. Her fatigue instantly faded, giving way to a boost of endorphins.

"Yes, but I do not think you will see a warlock throwing himself over a high wall like that," she said.

Adrianna looked toward Gyde, who ran out of sight to enter the fortress from a different area. She felt slightly more at ease; with the Maquis there they definitely had a chance.

A sharp cry from the skies made Adrianna pick up her pace. Mathena pulled her to a small tree.

"Gargoyles!" she called to those around her.

The people scattered, looking for cover.

Mathena stepped out from underneath the branches, in full view of the circling gargoyles. She raised her hands high above her head and a blinding white light grew between them. "*Halo!*" The orb sped toward the tallest tower, illuminating the space between their flight path and the ground. This way the gargoyles were blind to what went on at ground level.

The gargoyles screamed furiously, some retreating and others gliding blindly down toward the people as they made the perilous journey from open space to whatever cover they could take.

"Quickly!" Mathena pulled Adrianna along. They ran up the knoll and directly to the open gates; blasted open courtesy of Gralam. Adrianna saw him duelling with a vampire soldier. The vampire bared its teeth, its fangs long and dripping with venomous saliva, and slashed his lightening whip at Gralam's middle, missing him by an inch.

Gralam laughed. "Stupid animal," he growled, emitting a fire-sphere from his palm.

The soldier clutched his face, screaming in agony and fell to his knees as he burned. His body turned to ashes as Gralam rushed past him, following Adrianna and Mathena along the grounds.

Goblins swarmed them like ants. One by one they attacked, most dying at the hands of a Gordgáin fighter or a Maquis. The Maquis sliced and hexed their way through the goblins easily, barely making a true effort to lift their weapons. Energy-spheres flew left and right, forcing people to duck and leap for their lives.

There was nothing stealthy about this, thought Adrianna. If the Sansul vampires were not already alerted of their presence, she had completely over-estimated them.

From the corner of her eye, Adrianna spotted a goblin headed right for her. She lifted her hand, projecting a shield, and the incoming goblin slammed into an invisible wall, falling back instantly. Joa beheaded the creature before it could stand up again.

"Best to kill them," he offered, slicing through another.

"I will try," she said, hoping she would not have to.

The ground began to shake violently. The sound of crashing stone and heavy echoes enveloped the area. Gargoyles began to land, challenging people to battle. Their forms were enormous. In the air they did not look nearly as domineering and dangerous as they did on the ground. Eglantine had to duck as one of their expansive, leathery wings retracted, almost knocking her over. She cast an ice-tear into its back as it rounded on Orion.

Wynneth slit the throat of a vampire and beheaded another before rushing to Adrianna's side. "You have not stopped the gargoyles," she said frantically to Mathena.

"I am about to," said Mathena. "I was not close enough before. Go ahead; I will be right behind you."

Wynneth nodded. "Lead the way," she said to Adrianna.

Adrianna rushed across the grounds to a grey stone building. This was the location of Liam's residential room: the place she spent four moons as his prisoner.

"This place is very dangerous," she said, thinking of Jeith, Liam's demon.

"Leena, you wait here," Orion ordered of the blonde Maquis soldier who nodded in understanding.

Instead of going up the flight of stairs that would find them surrounded by vampire-occupied bedrooms, Adrianna took the first stairway down to a narrow limestone hallway.

"Nadia, this is your post," said Orion, turning to a curly-haired Maquis woman at the top of the stairs. "Iver, you stay with her."

Adrianna stared at the door in front of them. When she twisted the knob, it would not budge.

"This was not here when I came last time," said Adrianna, pushing. Failure dampened any feelings of euphoria and urgency as she realised her mistake. What if the prisoners had been moved? What if this was the wrong place?

Mathena came forward and waved her hand over the bolt, muttering something softly. Suddenly, there was a loud 'clink' and a grinding. Adrianna and Mathena pushed again but it opened only slightly.

"Allow me," said a large, top-heavy dhamphir. He pushed upon the door with his shoulder and it opened fully.

Mathena held up her palm, a sphere of white light floated above it and led the way down the continuing steep passage. Adrianna followed closely, her heart lifting. Wynneth, Renauart, Gralam, Eglantine and Orion shadowed them.

"It is the first door," Adrianna whispered, lighting her own palm now. She felt something brush past her ankle and jumped.

Everyone behind her froze as she swatted the invisible annoyance.

"Stand still!" Wynneth clutched her ankle. Slowly, she rose, and struggling wildly in her grip was a black and yellow striped snake. "Sleuther!"

Adrianna shivered. "Kill it!"

Fire formed in Wynneth's palm, engulfing the Sleuther. She threw it aside. "The Librarian knows we are here."

"Let's add some speed to this," said Renauart.

As they came to the heavy wooden door, everyone waited silently.

This is it. Adrianna could hear her own heartbeat in her ears. She was almost crying with excitement. She had kept her promise to them; they would be free.

Mathena raised her hand to open the door, but Adrianna grabbed it before she touched the handle.

"No!"

The group looked at her in wonder.

"We must make sure it is them inside," Adrianna explained. "This is how I did it last time. Knock once."

Mathena did so. There was silence.

She knocked again. This time, there was a reply.

Two knocks.

"Now, you do three," Adrianna instructed.

Four knocks was their reply.

"Is it you, Adrianna?" said a familiar, muffled voice from the other side.

Adrianna could not wait any longer and opened the door. They were all waiting.

Rosamunda, Orla, Veronique, Peruva, Jess, Collette and many others were gathered around the door. Adrianna burst into tears as Rosamunda embraced her, crying with relief. They looked much healthier than the last time she had seen them; though they were weak, the vampires had obviously begun looking after them to fulfil their purpose.

"Are we finally free?" Collette asked tearfully.

"It's Adrianna!"

"She actually did it!" cried a voice at the back of the crowd.

"Stay quiet," Wynneth told them. "No talking. Follow Nadia. She is the curly-haired woman at the top of the stairs."

The witches began to file out, thanking everyone in a whisper as they passed. Over Adrianna's shoulder Rosamunda saw her husband. She kissed Adrianna's cheeks and Adrianna looked back smiling at Renauart as Rosamunda threw her arms around him, sobbing with happiness.

"There are more down these halls," Adrianna said to Orion.

Orion, three Maquis women, Gralam and Wynneth moved to the other holding rooms.

Adrianna and Orla turned to face one another.

"I knew you would keep your promise," Orla said softly, her eyes shining with tears. "Thank you."

Adrianna smiled, tears forming in her own eyes.

"Hurry, hurry," said Renauart. "Everyone out."

"Why haven't we come across a vampire yet?" Wynneth asked Orion, casting a concerned glance at the witches as they climbed the stairs.

"That is what is worrying me," said Orion, his turquoise eyes dilating.

"Where is Caitriona?" Adrianna's asked, looking around to Rosamunda.

"She wasn't in the chambers," Rosamunda replied. "She has been gone two days."

"I am not leaving without her!"

"Maybe she is in one of the other chambers," said Orla, but she was clearly grasping at anything to get Adrianna moving.

"Keep a look out," said Adrianna.

The crowd moved out as silently as they could. Returning the same way they came, the witches stepped out of the quiet building into a fray of fighting. Most made it past the gate without much trouble, flanked protectively by Gordgáin.

Leaning against the wall, waiting for every last witch to leave, Adrianna was acutely aware that the inside of the fortress had remained untouched.

There was barely a warlock duelling with a vampire soldier. The only battle had been on the front grounds, but the building itself remained as still as it was when they arrived.

Goblins littered the ground on the path exiting the fortress. Many had been charmed silent by the witches and set to stone. Luckily, the bell had not been rung and no vampire was disturbed from slumber but Adrianna knew this fortress and surely something was not as it should be.

She half expected vampires to come around corners and attack them by now, but everything remained eerily still.

Adrianna helped Orla to walk as they followed Mathena and Wynneth up the passageways from which they came. Gralam, Eglantine and Renauart were waiting for them in the foyer of the main building. Orion and Joa were catching up to Erik, when Joa slowed down. "Wait a moment," he said to Orion before turning to them.

Orla was breathing heavily, clutching Adrianna's hand.

"Would you permit me to carry you?" Joa asked her.

"I can walk, it just hurts," Orla said weakly. "I would only slow you down."

"Everyone is out," he said.

"It will be less painful for you," said Adrianna. "Let him carry you. Thank you, Joa."

Having just seen Onoria's group out the gate, Erik was waiting for them at the front. He passed through the doors, and when the group was almost behind him, the doors slammed shut.

Adrianna's heart skipped a beat. Dread settled in the pit of her stomach. She pulled on the handle repeatedly but nothing moved.

"Oh no."

Gralam pulled her away from the door. "Get behind me. Open your palms."

"I was wondering when you would all come," said a silky voice, reverberating from all sides.

The group congregated in the middle of the grand room, back to back, looking around for the source.

"You are a little later than I would have predicted," the voice continued. "Perhaps you did not plan this out as thoroughly as you should have. Shoddy workmanship. But then, what else can be expected from the Maquis and Gordgáin?"

Adrianna and Wynneth looked at one another as a sardonic laugh filled the room.

"Whatever you do, don't look at any one of them directly," Joa said, nudging Adrianna to the middle of the group. He set Orla to her feet gently.

"Do you smell that?" Wynneth whispered.

"What? No, I smell nothing," Adrianna replied, holding Orla upright.

Them? What was Joa expecting?

"Witches and dhamphir," it said mockingly, "storming the great fortress of Sansul to rescue their kinsmen. How very noble, and yet, so *very* stupid."

"Show yourself!" Gralam growled. "Don't be a coward!"

Orion seemed to sense something and moved swiftly in front of Wynneth, pushing her back next to Adrianna.

"Cowardice is not a trait vampires behold," the voice replied calmly. "But if you insist."

Adrianna squealed as a gust of wind whirled around them. The room was cast into blackness; metal clanged and screams were immediately muffled. She bumped into Wynneth and then felt herself being pulled up and away.

Mathena shrieked.

Something tight wrapped itself around Adrianna's neck and four sharp points pressed into her side. She struggled to release herself but the more she moved the tighter the grip became. She cried out as one of the points penetrated her skin. Her back was pressed against something firm, and a damp breath blew across the side of her face.

Suddenly, light appeared and the room was illuminated.

Adrianna turned her head as much as she could. Gralam, Eglantine, Renauart, Orion and Joa stood in the middle of the room, back-to-back, ready to for an attack.

Vampires surrounded them. On the stairs, by the doors, across the balcony, circling them on the floor, they stared with glowing black eyes and their fangs extended. Garbed in magnificent, embroidered gowns, a row of females stood in the gallery overlooking the foyer with mild interest.

Soldiers held Mathena, Orla and Wynneth at knifepoint. Adrianna knew it was not the same for her. This was no vampire whose dagger-like fingers were digging into her skin; it was a demon.

A tear slipped from her eye as her side began to throb. Orla was crying and made no motion to stop or quiet. She was terrified. Adrianna wanted so much to comfort her.

Standing before the group was a tall, inhumanely beautiful man. Fiery red hair framed his thin face; black eyelashes and perfectly arched brows outlined his cold green eyes. He was clad in black from his shirt to his boots, and a ruby encrusted pinkie ring adorned his left hand. Everything indicated he was the leader of the coven. No one moved without his say so. No one spoke. His authority was unquestioned. His charisma was enough to bring many women to their knees, but his inner evil was such a force that being in his presence for a long period of time was sure to kill.

"Henry," said Orion, his eyes flashing maliciously.

"Who woke you?" Gralam demanded.

The vampire was blank. "I could hear the beautiful sound of innocent screams," he said lightly. "It has been a long time since anyone dared to enter this domain." He looked around to the group. "But times have changed, obviously. Go – you are free to go," he said dismissively.

They did not move. Renauart looked at Adrianna.

"Release them!" Gralam demanded.

The vampire laughed. "I do not think so." He looked Adrianna up and down. "I must keep some of what you have tried to steal from us. Consider these four women my compensation for your theft of the others."

Adrianna felt her stomach drop. She shuddered and looked into the vampire's eyes. Being a slave to this man would not be as simple as sitting in a small dark room; Henry would make her suffer.

"No," said Adrianna.

The vampire touched her face. "I am afraid you do not have a choice. None of you do. Take them to my rooms," he ordered of the soldiers.

"No!" Wynneth screamed, thrashing wildly.

"Get off of me," Mathena screeched, kicking the soldier that swung her over his shoulder. "You beasts! Demons!"

A soft wave of laugher filled the room.

Renauart fought viciously as they were pushed out of the fortress, calling for the women as they were taken away. Gralam stabbed a vampire through the heart, only to be hurled out, landing heavily on his back. Orla screamed for Adrianna as the doors were closed on them.

Adrianna was forced down a familiar hallway. The tight hold on her throat was constricting her ability to breathe, and the claw was still buried in her side. The pain was excruciating. Blood trickled down her leg as she walked. Everything turned into a blur, her knees were failing and Mathena's screams were now a distant echo; her consciousness was slipping away.

"Stop!"

They did. Adrianna opened her eyes slightly, hearing only footsteps coming toward them.

"Give her to me," said the voice.

Adrianna squirmed, feebly punching the demon. She was too weak.

The demon growled.

"There has been a change in plans."

Adrianna watched, dazed, as a pair of boots came closer, and then something cracked. Immediately, the hold on her throat was relinquished and the claw fell away from her side. She squealed, covering the wound with her hand as she fell to the ground. Looking up slowly, she did not see what she expected.

It was Baliath, the demon essence inside of Daniel. Baliath carefully lifted her off the ground. She whimpered from the pain. Her blood was everywhere, spilling out of the holes. She could barely see the blurry red figure looking down at her but the blackness of his eyes was unmistakable.

"Stay quiet," he said, carrying her down the hall.

CHAPTER FIFTEEN

Loyalty

WHEN FRADRIK, DURAND AND Gyde turned the corner, they found themselves face to face with a Vermillion demon. They stared in bewilderment as the towering, red-skinned male took a step back, and to their mutual horror realised that in his arms was Adrianna.

"A Vermillion," said Durand in disbelief. "On this Plane?"

"Adrianna," Fradrik stared at his ward. Unmoving and bleeding, her body completely limp.

Gyde seemed to come to his senses first and raised his sword to strike.

Baliath dodged his blow and with a simple lift of his hand sent Gyde flying into the wall.

"Take her," Baliath told Fradrik, his voice deep and distorted.

Durand froze, his sword mid-air, and stared at the demon in surprise.

Fradrik hesitated.

"She is wounded," said Baliath, holding her out for him to take. "You need to heal her. Get out of here."

Fradrik looked from Baliath's tattooed face to Adrianna. "What did you do to her?" he demanded.

"Do not be ignorant, warlock," Baliath warned. "Take the witch. She may survive if you get her immediate care."

Fradrik took her, slowly, carefully. Adrianna gave a slight moan as her wound was pressured, but she remained thoroughly dazed. Durand kept his sword extended, a fire-sphere ready in his free hand. He flexed his fingers, looking as if he would love nothing more than to strike.

"A warning, warlock," said Baliath, his voice low and dangerous. "Do not allow her to come to harm. My host will be very unforgiving if she is hurt on the behalf of the Gordgáin."

As Adrianna's blood soaked through Fradrik's shirt, he kept his eyes on those of the demon. He had no doubt that Baliath's host, whoever it may be, would go through with the threat. Just who was this demon who spared the life of an innocent? What had Adrianna done for Baliath's host that it would care about her wellbeing?

Deciding that her life was more urgent than answers to his questions, Fradrik gave a simple nod and departed.

Gyde and Durand rounded on Baliath.

"Leave now," Baliath ordered.

Gyde extended his sword. "Who are you? No demon has ever released the life of a witch."

Baliath's black eyes stared at them: assessing, calculating. He squared his thick, muscled shoulders and began to transform. His skin paled, turning from red to fair. Blonde hair grew from his skull. The demon's powerfully built body was replaced by a tall, leaner figure and the black-tattooed face was replaced with that of a man.

Daniel opened his silver eyes and looked austerely at the two dhamphir. Adrianna's blood was all over his middle, legs and hands.

"Satisfied? You are wasting time," said Daniel. "If you want to live, you will go."

"*Why* did you save her?" asked Gyde.

"I don't make a habit of detailing my personal business to people," Daniel replied. "Take your leave."

"Come on," Durand said to Gyde. "No point in persisting. They'll be on top of us soon."

Daniel inclined his head and departed down the hall from where he came. He too was leaving the fortress.

The area was in total chaos. Stone gargoyles lay shattered on the grounds. Bodies of goblins littered the grass, and ashen remains of vampire soldiers were strewn on the path heading toward the village. Instead of hunting down the escapees and their saviours, the soldiers were ordered to remain within the safety of the battlements.

"How did this happen?" André demanded of his men.

André, Commander of the Sansul Vanguard Vahir, had never lost a fight. Losing a battle on Sansul soil to the Maquis and the Gordgáin was abominable, and his soldiers knew it.

The vampire nearest to André wiped a streak of blood from his chin and raised his glowing eyes to those of his infuriated Commander. "Maquis and the Gordgáin," he replied. "They knew exactly where to find the witches."

"And nobody was able to stop them?"

"We received orders, Commander," the vampire said, somewhat nervously.

"*Orders*?" André hissed.

"Yes, they came directly from Henry. They were to be allowed to leave. We could dispatch of a few, but his order was to let them go."

"*Why*?" André said furiously. "They were within these walls, the others could have been awakened with all the blood we had!"

"I do not know. I merely follow orders."

André seemed to come to his senses. "That is correct, you are *just* a soldier. Call upon the Librarian. Tell him he can clean up this mess," he said, casting a disgusted look around the grounds. "And quickly!"

"I think," said a woman soldier from behind him, "that the Librarian has his own problems, Commander."

André turned to her.

"The Laboratory was destroyed," she said, taking a step back. "Everything is ash."

"Henry had better have a good reason for this."

~

On the outskirts of the village, a slick-haired vampire pulled a nervous witch into a long-abandoned cottage and slammed the door closed. They stood silent and unmoving as the Gordgáin retreated to the sanctuary.

"What is happening?" the witch whispered after a few moments.

"Looks like the Gordgáin have finally done something right," the vampire replied. "You must join the survivors."

"What about you?"

"I have to go back to the fortress, Caitriona," he said. "I've got to continue . . . I can't abandon my post."

"Vascus," she said. "What *are* you doing? Why will you not tell me?"

"Because it's too dangerous for ya to know," he replied. "You need to go back to your people."

Caitriona's blue eyes were fixed on his face. "That means we will never be together again," she said softly.

Vascus's eyes flashed. "Yeah we will; when this is over."

"When this is over?" she said incredibly. "When is all *this* going to be over, Vascus? We are going to be at *war*. Real, terrible, bloody war. Henry is awake, my people are free, Wilmota is in a shambles – you cannot expect all to go back as it was!"

"Better you be free without me than trapped in that place," he said. "At least, out here, you've got a chance and I can see you when the danger passes."

Caitriona's eyes filled with tears. "The danger will never pass. Society and tradition will not allow for us to be together. My father, if he is still alive, would see me dead before he would allow me to be with you."

"Then keep it a secret," he pressed.

"There are no secrets," she whispered, crying. "Do you think my father has no means of knowing? Warlocks will question their wives and daughters, how will we lie? How will you keep me a secret from your people?"

"Soon we won't not need to hide," he said softly, wiping her cheeks. "Cry no more, Cait. I know another who took kindly to a witch, and though he has missed her presence, he wouldn't trade the emptiness he feels for anything knowing she is safe and free. Do this for me, Caitriona. Be free."

Reaching up, Caitriona kissed him deeply. Soft, sweet kisses marked the vampire's lips, drawing a euphoric groan from him as he buried his fingers in her hair. Caitriona's grip tightened on her lover. Pressing her body to his, she sought to touch every inch of him within reach as his fingers unbuttoned the back of her worn dress.

Vascus tugged the material down from her shoulders and lifted her full form onto a rickety table. He listened closely to the footsteps of passing people outside the cottage; the last of the fighters were returning to the sanctuary. With his eyes focused on the pulsing vein beneath the soft skin of Caitriona's neck, he shoved the hem of her dress up around her round hips and breathed her in.

Caitriona braced herself on the table, her legs wrapping themselves around his waist, and drew his mouth back to hers. His muscles tensed beneath her fingers as she ran a hand down his middle to the top of his trousers, unbuttoning the material so that she may touch the place she knew so well.

"I'll miss your softness," he said, his voice strained and his breathing uneven.

Caitriona laughed, drawing him closer to her. "And I will miss your moustache," she said, kissing the dark line of hair above his lip. "Now do not make me wait!"

Vascus grinned, sliding his hands up her thighs.

~

Henry's awakening brought with it widespread panic.

Leaders of nymph tribes, centaur herds, faery clans and faun bands arrived at the temple the day after the successful rescue of over two hundred witches from Sansul Fortress. It was reported throughout the sanctuary that a Protection Shield of the strongest force had been raised around the whole of Whistlers Knoll, the mound on which Sansul Fortress stood. It blocked everything from birds to wind from passing its barrier, entombing the vampires.

Nymph tribes that had been forced to go deeper into the forest after the attack on Wilmota now shared land with the centaurs who welcomed the nymphs onto their sacred territory in the name of fellowship. Faeries guarded the Sleeping Forest and made it inaccessible to those of the Darkness. They wished to move to the safety of Aires, a village further south, but were unsure whether to leave the wellbeing of the village to nature's course. They were even more hesitant to leave without the witches and warlocks that they called neighbours.

"Henry's awakening is the beginning of an age of absolute fear," said the tiny blue-winged faery, flittering in the middle of the circle.

Two representatives of each race stood around a pentacle star in the middle of the temple. When their turn came to speak, the representative stepped into the polygonal centre of the pentacle and stated their position.

"The Librarian has raised a Protection Shield around the fortress," the faery continued. "It is my belief that Henry will assess the strength of his forces and if need be, he will awaken more soldiers."

"What of the ancients?" asked a silverback centaur. "Will he not awaken them?"

"That would create too much animosity and power struggles," said Simo. "Henry will fix the mess the Council have made of the coven, and then he will take steps to overpower Azria. Awakening the ancients would also require Black Magick and those people have been quite silent. There has been no word of their rituals or magic for quite a while, so I believe we can rest easily where they are concerned. For now."

"But first Henry will have to overcome Aires, Bruniér and even Collusus before he can think about Azria," said the magenta-haired nymph beside the centaur. She cast her violet eyes around the group and asked, "Has Azria even been informed of his awakening?"

"Yes," said Simo. "The Maquis have seen to that. How much longer will the Sleeping Forest keep your people safe?"

"Not much longer," said the nymph. "The wolf-men already prowl the outskirts. The forest animals have begun their journey southward, and although I am tempted to join them, I shudder to think of what will happen to the course of nature in Wilmota if all the faery tribes were to leave it without care."

"Nature can replenish itself," said Simo. "Bringing Wilmota back to its full glory can only happen once the threat has been defeated."

"But what if the disease of the Darkness is allowed to seep into nature?" asked the blue-winged faery. "It will make us ill. We use the energy of the earth like any other elemental."

"I cannot tell you what to do with your duties," Simo said respectfully. "If fortification of the land and its cycle is a priority, we will respect that and offer our support should you need it."

"Your kindness is welcome," the faery spoke. "I will meet with my people and discuss a necessary course of action. If we can protect the earth Element from being harmed by the Darkness with the smallest of work forces, I will make it so."

"Very well. Aesa?" Simo asked, turning to the magenta-haired nymph.

"My people will aid both the Gordgáin and the faeries," she said. "We have a duty to fight, but also we have a duty to the land on which we live. We must not forget this."

"I will lead my people to Collusus," said the silverback centaur. "The fauns are welcome to come. Anyone of my people who wishes to aid you, Simo, will stay under your command."

"So it will be," Simo said agreeably.

~

The joy of the reunion in the sanctuary was overshadowed by fast spreading rumours and recounted horror stories of Henry during his past reign of Sansul coven as Supreme Chancellor. As families and friends settled in the small, simple rooms of the sanctuary's residential halls, the Gordgáin focus was suddenly diverted to that of healing and hosting. Dozens of families were broken, lineages cut. There were widows, widowers and orphans without comfort, many of whom did not want the help the Gordgáin offered and remained confined to their assigned rooms. Others demanded to be allowed to leave the sanctuary and travel to neighbouring clans. Mothers, fathers, sisters and brothers, husbands, wives, children and grandchildren lit candles on the Wall of Flames in memory of their losses, some too aggrieved to speak. Many warlocks signed their names to the army, the Warlock Myriad, all wanting to 'do their bit for home'.

The witches who returned from imprisonment seemed to have come to a unified agreement never to discuss their days in the underground chambers. Trauma left many bedridden in the infirmary, quiet and sleepless. Of the fortunate few witches who had not been imprisoned, there were those who tried to pry information out of the survivors. Most were witches of the Assembly, the governing body of Wilmota. They were determined to know as much as possible about the captivity of the women. Many of these Assembly representatives were unhappy with the reaction they received, especially since the warlocks had been so open in their statements.

"There is no shame in what may or may not have been done," said one Assembly witch to Jess, who remained quiet in her bed in the infirmary.

The nurse presiding over the interview stood by Jess with her arms crossed.

"Was there any . . . inappropriate force used upon your person?" asked the Assembly witch, her voice determinedly soft.

Jess glanced at the nurse, then at the next bed where Adrianna lay unconscious. "I was not raped."

The Assembly witch patted her hand and quickly made a note. "We need not be so blunt with our wording, child."

"That *is* what you were asking though," said the nurse. "Why not ask them all at once?"

"I take exception to your tone, nurse!"

"Well, bully for that. I am disgusted by the lack of tact of the Assembly. Coming in here asking questions that perhaps need no answering . . ."

The Assembly witch held up her hand. "Nurse . . . if these women were . . ." she swallowed, "violated, then we must know so as to be aware if any *results* were to show after the fact."

"You are worried they will give birth to dhamphir? *This* is your focus?"

"And their well-being, of course."

"Get out."

"*Excuse me?*"

"Take your papers, your attitude, and get out. I will be making an immediate request to Simo to have all Assembly interviews conducted *after* we clear these men and women for discharge."

"The mixing of bloodlines is a top priority issue for the Assembly, nurse. I have the right . . ."

"No – you do not. What you forget is that in these walls, you are bound by the rules and jurisdiction of the Gordgáin, of which you are not a member. Kindly leave."

Two nights later, Fradrik was given dispensation to visit the women's infirmary as he was Adrianna's legal guardian. He sat by her bed as long as he was allowed before visiting hours were over. Adrianna smiled at him weakly when she woke to find him there, his giant hand holding hers.

"We succeeded," she said.

"Indeed we did."

"When you found me . . ."

"We discovered Mathena, Wynneth and Eglantine being carried toward the Laboratory," he said gently. "Gyde and Durand were able to free them as my only focus was to get you to safety."

"Where are they?"

"Wynneth is with her people, and Mathena and Eglantine have been released from the infirmary. They suffered only minor injuries."

"Did you succeed in destroying the Laboratory?"

"Yes."

Adrianna gave his hand a weak squeeze. "Good."

As the days and nights passed, the tears and wails of loss lessened and people began to talk.

Henry the Destroyer was the topic most discussed. Many older warlocks were hesitant to talk about the days of Henry's power, when even the vampires were at war amongst themselves. Coven had gone against coven, race against race. Friends and allies soon turned on one another, divided by Henry's totalitarian dictatorship. Adrianna was propped up against a mountain of pillows in her infirmary bed when the conversation reached the recovery ward. Her middle was bandaged tightly, making it difficult to move, and the medicines kept her in a sleepy state. Most of the witches were eager to leave but their nurse, a kind, stylish but very firm woman with blonde hair kept them tightly tucked in their sheets. How she worked for ten hours in high heels, Adrianna did not know, but she appreciated the woman's dedication to her profession.

"Fine!" the nurse said when the patients insisted on knowing more of Henry. "Who in here was around during Henry's last reign?"

"Most of us, nurse," said Rosamunda, who sat by Adrianna's bed.

Celeste the Herbalist dusted her fingers of biscuit crumbs. "I'll tell it quickly," she said, still chewing. "Mm . . . excuse me." She took a quick sip of tea. "Sansul coven was controlled by five men and women. Henry the Destroyer was Supreme Chancellor, leading Pandema the Ice Maiden, Ingar the Torturer, Nicole the Seer, and Ioannes the Fair."

"Who gave them those names?" asked Eglantine, who was also visiting.

"Blame the media," said Celeste. "Newspapers liked to name vampires by their chosen vocations."

Adrianna laughed and immediately regretted it. Her side could not take the movement. It tingled unpleasantly. "Gently, gently," said Rosamunda as Adrianna shifted around.

"At that time . . ."

"Was this before *The War Against The Angels*?" asked a witch in the bed opposite Adrianna's.

Even in her state, Adrianna could not help but give her a look of incredulity. Were some people really that uneducated in history? The end of *The War Against The Angels* had been the end of many things, including the dominion of Sansul coven over the north.

"Yes," said Celeste, giving the witch a similar look as Adrianna's. "Very long before that war. Anyway, in the decades before the war, Henry would capture Spellmakers and force them to experiment with ways to allow demons to pass freely from the Demon Plane to the Elemental Plane. Then there was Leopold the Angel Hunter."

"Oh, a scarier man never existed!" said the nurse.

"No? What about Syther?" asked Rosamunda.

The nurse had a look of trepidation. "Terrible days, terrible."

"He was around during *The War Against The Angels*," said the witch opposite Adrianna.

"Yes," said Celeste. "A lot of the ancients were."

"What? What did they do?" asked Gemma, who sat on the edge of her sister Phoebe's bed.

"Leopold was single-handedly responsible for the murders of thousands of angels. He did not bother much with us elementals, but angels . . . they were his career," said Celeste.

"And Syther?"

"*No*, Celeste. That story is . . ."

But Celeste continued without listening to Rosamunda's protest. Adrianna was curious. Who was this vampire that made the nurse blanch and Rosamunda timid?

"Syther was in many aspects worse than Henry. He was a warlord. His bloodlust was so untameable that even Azria coven had him on their list to kill. The vampires in Azria never interfered in Sansul business if they could avoid it, but when Syther's death count rose and rose, he became Priority Number Two. His killings were indiscriminate. Men, women, children, nymph, faery, elf, centaur . . . blood was blood to him. Unlike Ingar the Torturer, who left his victims in agony because he liked the taste of fear and pain in their blood."

Adrianna cringed.

"We tried many times to kill Syther, but always failed. Then we went to the only people we knew could do something to help us. We called upon the Supreme Chancellor of the Azria coven."

"You asked *vampires* to help you kill another *vampire*?" asked Gemma. "How does this make any sense?"

"Vampires are just as varied in character and beliefs as we are," said Celeste. "We went to him with nothing to offer in return for his help but he agreed. With his assistance and that of his men, we were able to capture Syther. I remember him being dragged past me . . . as though it were happening now. He fought his binds like a Baál demon. I remember going cold when the cell door slammed shut behind him."

"You were there?" whispered the nurse in awe.

"I was new to the Gordgáin at the time but yes, I was there. Witches better than I lost their lives to people as manic as that twisted man whose bloodlust sent his mind beyond salvation. The Supreme Chancellor of the Azria coven had agreed to work with us on the condition that Syther be put to eternal rest in the chambers of the Necropolis."

"You mean you did not kill him?" asked Gemma, aghast.

"*The War Against The Angels* had forced some of us to acknowledge that sometimes we had to negotiate with the enemy. In return for his capture, we had to agree not to kill Syther. I was there as witches attached the titanium mask across his mouth. He was chained to the walls as they did this. I held the tray that held the mask and bolts . . . I remember standing in the corner, staring at this *enormous* man, pinned to the wall like a beast. He did not struggle as they gagged him, not like he did when they brought him here. He let them do their work, and when the last bolt was set, he looked at me."

The room was absolutely still. Adrianna felt herself growing sorrowful for this murderous vampire. She knew it was wrong, but his defeat reminded her of Liam, whose own descent to madness would likely lead him to his death.

"I thought his eyes would be black, but they were normal . . . and sad. He knew what his fate was, but I also believe he knew what he had done in the name of bloodlust. In no way did I pity him because I had seen the bodies of those he left behind."

"What did you do?" asked the nurse.

"I looked away and carried on with my duties," said Celeste. "He was placed in a sarcophagus, alive. It was bolted with seven locks. Six of the keys were given to the Supreme Chancellor and one was kept by us."

"Where is the key now?" asked Adrianna.

"We destroyed it with blue fire. No chances could be taken."

"And what happened to the sarcophagus?"

"It was delivered to the foot of Whistlers Knoll and the vampires of Sansul will have placed it in the Necropolis," said Celeste.

"I am sure Henry was furious to see Syther bound that way," said Adrianna. "Were the Gordgáin sending them a message by leaving his sarcophagus there for them to take away?"

"Exactly," said Celeste.

There was a collective sigh.

"My mother was one of his victims," said Celeste. "One of the nameless many on his long, blank list."

~

The week after the rescue mission, Adrianna signed herself out of the infirmary. Still dizzy and weak, she could not bear to remain in the closed infirmary any longer, even with the fake window views Mathena had conjured to make it seem as though they were above ground.

Walking slowly, she used the wall to maintain her balance. The daily hustle and bustle of the sanctuary had been replaced with peaceful silence and the gentle strumming of a mandolin in the distance. Oil lamps had been dimmed in the corridors, signalling that evening was upon them, but the atrium was brightly lit.

Adrianna made sure to stay in the shadows so as not to be seen by those congregated around the largest table. There was much animosity and frustration in the faces of the men: Simo, Gralam, Fradrik, Gyde, and the tall, regal Maquis Captain, Erik.

Simo looked exhausted; the lines around his eyes had deepened and his lilac beard was speckled with grey. A deep gash, partly healed, cut through his cheek. The man needed a few days of rest, at the least. Fradrik, the towering wall of gentility, paced restlessly, and Gralam puffed fierce purple clouds of smoke from his pipe. At the rate he was going he was soon to run out of tobacco.

"Staying here is a mistake, Simo," said Erik. "You must take your people to Aires and join the fight to maintain the security of the border."

"We cannot spare anymore to go and fight and the witches are hardly capable of walking!" Simo argued. "They are drained and weak from over eight moons in captivity! Have you *any* comprehension of what it was like for them? One does not simply heal from that in a matter of days, Erik. Perhaps a dhamphir is able, but not a witch."

"Even if we did get there, what will we do with Wilmota?" Fradrik asked reasonably. "Abandon it?"

"For now, you must," said Erik.

"Horse shit!" Gralam spat. "This is not your home; you have no personal ties to this land so you cannot suggest abandoning a place hundreds still call home. You put that suggestion to the clan and they will have your head, dhamphir. I promise you."

"Do not try to threaten me, warlock," Erik raged. "It is only because of the aid my people have given that you still have a village. Dhamphir have also suffered and we will continue to suffer alongside you because your troubles are ours. I merely suggest that you move your people to a place of safety so that we can be stronger with the south."

"What would you have me do?" Simo demanded. "I have called to my people. Gypsy fighters will be here as soon as possible. The City of Tents and Citron cannot get here because the sea has been blocked, so there go more allies. If only the angels were not so cowardly, they too would join us!"

"The angels are not to be relied upon," said Erik. "The moment they are, this goes from being a territorial problem to a universal one. Another repeat of *The War Against The Angels* and we might as well blast ourselves into oblivion."

"Then we are stuck and isolated," said Simo. "I have accepted this as our fate. What we must decide now is our next move. Do we leave the sanctuary and travel south?"

"Families and the ill cannot remain here," said Fradrik, leaning on the back of a chair. "This is no place for children especially. The people will begin to go stir-crazy. If we send them on now, it will free the Gordgáin to deal with the vampires without burdening them as they are now."

"I agree," said Gralam. "I cannot think on strategies with children running around the place."

"And us?" asked Simo. "Should we leave also?"

"Not on your life," Gralam replied gruffly. "This is Gordgáin headquarters and the vampires bloody well know it."

"You are open to attack," said Erik, trying to reason.

"Then they can suck on my fire-spheres when they come calling," said Gralam.

Adrianna almost laughed out loud at the vulgarity.

"My father would help if you asked it of him," said Erik.

Gralam looked thunderstruck. "*Ask* for *help* from a vampire?"

"Gralam . . ." said Simo, rubbing his temples.

"I do not care how respected your father is, dhamphir, but I will certainly rue the day we ask him or any of his kind for *help*," said Gralam.

And who is your father? Adrianna wondered as Erik stared Gralam down. A leader? A rebel perhaps? Did he have connections in high places?

"My father is a man of honour," said Erik. "Which is more than I can say for many of you. Simo, we will resume our discussions in the morning."

~

Adrianna woke early the next morning to the sound of hushed voices on the other side of her bedroom door. Opening her eyes slowly, she waited for her eyes to adjust to the light of the candle. Her body felt heavy, as though she was only awake from the neck up. She rolled onto her side, forcing herself to be alert.

"When did I get so old?" she asked herself, swinging her aching legs over the side of the bed.

"Witches are already being questioned by the Assembly," spoke Fradrik, whose voice was muffled through the door.

Adriana's eyebrows rose.

There was a cold laugh. She recognised it as Mathena's. "They have the Right of Silence."

"Not when it comes to war," whispered Fradrik. "I believe they wish to question Adrianna again."

"I trust Adrianna," said Mathena. "She is a Gordgáin! That girl has given a lot to us . . ."

"I know this," Fradrik replied. "All I ask is that you keep an eye on her – she trusts you. As a female, a witch of her peerage, you can see what I cannot. It would be . . . inappropriate for me to . . ."

"But you are her guardian," she said. "She sees you as her second father."

"An honour I hold higher than anything else, but where we come from, her parents and I, we maintain a level of formality," said Fradrik. "She does speak to me of her feelings, but as a woman you have an insight I do not. Please, if she puts herself in danger . . ."

"I will do this because it is you who asks this of me. You saved me from a terrible fate the other night, Fradrik. I will never forget this," said Mathena.

"I did nothing, it was the Maquis," said Fradrik. Adrianna could tell by his tone that he was being bashful.

"*I trust her*," said Mathena.

Adrianna pretended to sleep when she heard Mathena enter and close the door.

"You can stop it now," said Mathena, smiling.

"I did not mean to overhear," said Adrianna.

"Of course not, but don't you worry about what they say."

Mathena moved to help Adrianna sit up. "Unbutton," she said, leaning over to the bedside table. She picked up a small jar and scooped out a small amount of clear paste.

"There is nothing to discuss, no matter what Fradrik may think," said Adrianna, shivering as the coldness of the paste spread around her healing wound.

"No? I was there when you were brought here by Kenna and the other one," said Mathena. "That vampire held you with such protection . . . it was fierce. He thought you were dying and his last act was to set you free, to let you die amongst your own people. Do you mean to convince me that there was nothing between you?"

Adrianna's vision blurred and warm tears tracked her cheeks. "I have nothing to say. If you were there you would understand."

"All right," Mathena began, wiping her hands on a cloth, "then allow me to illuminate you a little. Vampires are not a caring or compassionate race.

They do not value friendship, honour, love and family the way we do. They value conquests, affairs, blood, and power *and* in the past there has been more than one powerful vampire that has made a sport of seducing good, innocent women."

"But some find happiness, do they not? Like Cora and Ioannes? Their story became a folk tale," asked Adrianna.

"Yes. It was long ago, and one of a kind. But it was also a tragic story," said Mathena. "Often dhamphir are not made in love, which is why so many of them carry that very large chip on their shoulder. You may have noticed it in Gyde. It is rare for a vampire to feel any kind of . . . caring emotion toward another being, let alone love for a woman or child."

"Is it possible?"

"You tell me," Mathena replied. "Does he love you?"

Adrianna held her gaze for a moment. If she answered, she would be admitting to having been close to a vampire.

"I do not know," she said honestly. "I have tried to make sense of it myself – everything that happened, everything he said - and nothing is clear to me."

"Well, how about you tell me your story," said Mathena, pulling up a chair. "I have had *many* experiences with men. Maybe I can help."

"What good would it do?" asked Adrianna. "I will probably never see him again."

Mathena winked. "Never know – do we? Let's start with his name..."

It took Adrianna all afternoon and most of the evening to tell her whole story to Mathena. As her cauldrons bubbled away, Adrianna told the tale; beginning with her capture, her imprisonment in Liam's quarters, seeing the demon Jeith for the first time. Over dinner, Adrianna told Mathena about the Pull. Mathena was intrigued. She clung to every word and sighed dreamily as Adrianna, quite nervously, told her of when Daniel carried her out into the gardens to let her be with nature.

"A *vampire* did that for you?" Mathena looked astounded. "Well, I can honestly say I never heard that before. Weren't you scared of it all?"

"It is uncontrollable," said Adrianna, dipping the freshly baked bread into her stew. "It is almost as if it forces you to be together. But when you are connected the most beautiful feelings overwhelm you."

"How did you cope in the beginning?" Mathena asked, enthralled. "I mean . . . I can't imagine feeling the overwhelming need to kiss a vampire."

"Shock," Adrianna replied, smiling sheepishly. "We were both loathsome toward one another at the time. We truly did not want what the Pull was making us feel."

"So that was why he was so horrible to you that night he tried to bite you?"

Adrianna shook her head, remembering. Liam had been out and Daniel had bullied her until she was finally cornered with nowhere to go and nothing to save herself. Liam's return had saved her, but not before Daniel almost choked her. "No – that was Baliath's influence. I suppose the thought that I might make Daniel remotely sympathetic to me was revolting to him."

"Then why did Baliath protect you?"

Adrianna shrugged. "Who knows how their minds work?"

"Who *wants* to know?" Mathena asked rhetorically.

~

After almost a week of being confined to her bedroom, Adrianna's wounds were almost completely healed. Thanks to Mathena's remedies and loving touch, Adrianna was free to be of use around the sanctuary. She busied herself by organising the newcomers' duties and rooms, and continuing her lessons with Fradrik, where she found herself advanced into a completely new area of study.

It was far more strenuous learning about offensive spells and charms than defensive ones, but Fradrik insisted that while she studied *The Cycles of the Four Elements*, she learn to control her fighting powers. The idea was unacceptable to many of the witches in the sanctuary. To fight offensively with intent to kill was against Witchery Lore, and not only did it create an imbalanced energy structure, many believed it stained the soul.

"If the energy cycle of a witch is not balanced, there is no telling *what* can happen when she gains her Element," Lizzette argued with Fradrik. "How will she control fire, if that were her Element? Or water? Are we to fear a tidal wave on our shores if she becomes enraged? Or perhaps tornados and days of thunder, if her Element happens to be air?"

"You are overreacting," said Fradrik patiently. "Adrianna must know how to defend herself, and I shall teach any witch the same, should they wish to learn. I teach my ward to kill only when attacked."

"Fradrik, you have lived in Wilmota long enough to know that *we* never approve this kind of tutelage," said Lizzette.

"I am a sailor," said Fradrik, "and with respect to you and your clan, Lizzette, our ways are different. We come from different worlds. Adrianna is half-sailor, and I will teach her our ways to better protect her."

"She is a highlander and child of Wilmota," said Lizzette. "We highlanders are rough around the edges, but Witchery Lore is final. She cannot fight to kill."

"That rule is what got you captured," he replied. "You could have avoided imprisonment, but you chose that degrading future instead of killing your enemy."

"And we suffered for our decision. The soul is what we must protect, above our physical bodies. If a being of the Light kills with intent, it stains the soul. Do you want that for Adrianna?"

"The idea of staining the soul, as you put it, it not a proven one. Please, do not take my words wrongly – Witchery Lore is founded and based in honour, but to claim to know for *certain* that the act of killing would somehow change the soul of the person is unfounded and unproven. Again, with respect, I must disagree with you."

Adrianna gladly put up with Lizzette's pursed lips and disapproving looks. Nothing could dampen her mood. Being surrounded by her clan, her friends, and the familiar faces she had grown up with was enough to keep her in high spirits day and night.

She assisted Rosamunda in organising a group of children who had been saved by a gang of warlocks. Adrianna knew all but a few of the boys and girls and had them sorted into bedrooms according to names and ages and appointed them guardians. Sadly, many were orphaned, but a lucky few had family in other villages.

Along with her other duties, she helped Mathena stock the infirmary with potions and healing pastes, and re-energised the moonstones and crystals when necessary. She went out with Eglantine under cover of night to dig up mug-weeds. When cooked, they were used as a sedative for the ailing witches and warlocks in the infirmary. They went out almost every second night to find fresh ginger, as ginger tea was a powerful anti-toxin. The whole of the sanctuary drank it hourly as it aided in ridding the after-effects of being surrounded by the Darkness.

After a busy day listing the names of every witch freed from the Sansul Fortress and detailing whether they had family or friends in the neighbouring villages, Adrianna strolled through the halls of the sanctuary alone, without another's presence to interrupt her thoughts. It was difficult to find quiet moments when so few were able to care for the number of people who now crowded the sanctuary. Her attention was required from the moment she woke up, and it was taking its toll.

Her thoughts were with Daniel. She often wondered about him. She even fell asleep at night with him on her mind. She had so many unanswerable questions. Why had he rescued her from the Laboratory? If she died there, surely it would have been easier for him; he would not have to think about her anymore. Who was he? What was his duty?

She was confused by her own feelings. When she tried to make sense of it all, she only ended up even more befuddled. Her feelings for him in the beginning had been clear. She detested him and what he had done to her and her people, and he had hated her for simply being. But did he really? Pausing, she thought about his kiss and how it made her burn. What they shared was not a kiss between a vampire and a witch, but between a man and a woman. It had made her want to be nowhere but there, with him, touching him.

A little pang went through her chest at the thought of how far he was from her. *There has to be an easy way to get over this.*

She ended up turning into a dead-end hall, far away from the atrium. She heard hushed voices whispering secretively and ducked back, hiding around the corner.

Four women were huddled together at the far end. Adrianna had not caught sight of their faces, but their voices were familiar.

"What are we going to do then?" one whispered.

Adrianna knew in all decency that she should leave, but curiosity got the better of her. Who were these women? Why were they speaking so secretively? Surely nothing they were discussing required them to meet in a far corner of an underground sanctuary.

"There is nothing we can do," spoke a deep-voiced woman. "Other than keep our heads down."

"*Keep our heads down*?" whispered another fiercely. "Anya, we are going to be questioned by the Assembly!"

"I cannot do this," spoke a tearful voice. "I just cannot . . ."

Adrianna felt sad for the crying woman. Was the Assembly now questioning every survivor of the fortress? Were the warlocks to be questioned as well?

"Keep yourself together, Jess," hissed Anya.

"That is easy enough for you, Anya," spoke a fourth.

"Is it? You have no idea what I went through in that fortress, Collette," Anya replied.

"*You*?" Collette asked indignantly. "I will slap you here and now if you even dare to *think* that you suffered more than anyone else. I was beaten, raped. I saw my sister murdered before me," she said, her voice growing furious, struggling to stay hushed. "You remained in the enclosed rooms, surrounded by the Darkness, while others were forced to suffer disgraces that we must keep secret."

"I agree," said a soft, sweet voice. "I have not told my brother anything, nor my father."

Adrianna closed her eyes, leaning her forehead against the cold wall. It was Caitriona. The vibrant, vivacious bombshell Adrianna knew and loved had not returned on the night they were freed. Instead, a sad, depressed and distant witch replaced her. They had chatted, sparingly, but most of the time Caitriona looked as if she was in a faraway place and not at all interested in those around her.

"Jess, darling, please stop crying," Caitriona continued.

"W-what are th-they going to a-ask us?" asked Jess, her voice thick with tears. "I do not w-want to be asked any questions! I want to be left alone!"

"I know," said Caitriona. "I do not want to be questioned either but we do not have a choice."

"What do you think they will ask?" said Collette.

"I do not think they are questioning the warlocks," said Anya. "At least not as thoroughly as us."

"Why not?" asked Jess.

"We may be just as powerful as the men, but we are still easier targets," said Anya, her voice hard. "I bet you a month's wages that the warlocks will be asked about who, when, where and why the vampires went about enslaving them in the mines. Not us."

"Which means they will be asking us questions about how we were treated," said Collette. "Intimate questions."

"I heard Adrianna was already questioned by Joan," said Anya.

"What was she asked?" inquired Caitriona curiously.

"Intimate questions, but she did not answer. Apparently she gave Joan the run around. They have her down as being 'difficult', which makes her suspicious in their eyes."

"Will you tell the Assembly you were violated?" Caitriona asked, but Adrianna could not see to whom the question was directed.

"No," replied Collette. "No, I will take the shame with me to my death. Besides, what good could it possibly do to reveal such a thing?"

Adrianna wanted to reach out and hug them all. There was no shame in what they suffered. They were innocent victims, mistreated because they were indeed easy targets. She was certain that only a small number of women had been violated as Collette was, because rape was considered a disgrace by vampires. Though as with any race or group, there was always a rotten one. Liam could have raped her every day of her imprisonment, as could Daniel, Nikita, Thomas, or any soldier that passed through the fortress, but none did. She wished Collette had been spared the pain and terror.

"Will you tell them about *him*, Cait?" asked Jess.

"Never. We must leave the fortress in our past and promise never to speak of it. Answer the Assembly's questions as truthfully as you can, but avoid discussing anything beyond the underground chambers," replied Caitriona. "I am afraid of what will happen to us if we are too honest."

"The warlocks will be angry," said Collette.

"Worse than that, we could be accused of being sympathisers," said Anya. "Terrible things were done to people who befriended or became lovers to vampires in the past."

"What if someone else gives the Assembly reason to believe we were . . . intimate with a vampire? I was gone from the underground chambers for days at a time," said Caitriona. "Someone will speak of it."

"I will deny the claims," said Anya.

"As will I," said Jess.

"And I," said Collette.

The conversation seemed to be close to ending, so Adrianna left, unwilling to be caught eavesdropping. They were strong women. Adrianna had no doubt they would keep the Assembly at bay.

CHAPTER SIXTEEN

Gypsy Curses

"I SAID OUT!"

With a bang, the mossy green door burst open, and with it, a gaggle of wood-pixies flew out, shouting curses and obscenities as they went.

An old man with fluffy white hair came to stand in the threshold, waving his fist at the retreating figures.

"Don't let me find you squatting in here again!" he called furiously. "You little termites!"

After retreating into the crooked, abstract house, the door rattled on its hinges, as it slammed shut behind him.

"Pesky little . . . they've eaten through half of it," he muttered, examining the table leg.

A series of holes and bite marks now adorned the length, where the pixies had been attempting to create some kind of warren.

Wood-pixies were tiny creatures with leaf-like wings, greenish skin and high-pitched voices. Though they were a cousin race to faeries, the two did not get along, as faeries built their homes around trees and nature's surroundings, and pixies built their homes inside of trees without consideration for the needs of other races. The largest pixie tribes lived in the Bruniér Mountains and the Wilmota Sleeping Forest. They had been forced out of the latter due to the stringent Protective Shields raised by the nymphs and faeries, and the constant roaming of the wolf-men. With no choice but to leave their homes, whole families, sometimes as large as twenty members, flitted from cottage to cottage, squatting in the most convenient of places while hiding from the vampires and their demons.

This was the fifth group the old man had chased from his home this week alone.

He had barely managed to mend the leg, closing the holes and filling the bite marks by using a Replicating Charm that spread the residing substance in the gaps, when a knock sounded on the door.

"Go away!"

"Allan the Spellmaker?"

"Who's asking?"

"I am André, Commander of the Sansul Vahir Vanguard," said the voice.

"Are you now?" Allan replied with mock admiration. He checked the crystals in the lock beside the door, all glowed, as they should. The shield was still active. "Well, I don't talk to vampires, so you can return to the pit that spawned you!"

"I am here on the orders of my immediate superior," André replied.

Allan scowled. "Tell your 'immediate superior' to leave me alone."

"I must relay you a message."

Allan groaned. "Relay away! But I am not listening."

"Henry, Supreme Chancellor of Sansul coven has requested your immediate presence," said André.

Allan froze. A cold shiver ran down his back.

In his mind, he envisioned the beautiful vampiric face of the man whose heart was as black and dense as soot. The clear green eyes were unforgettable, as cold as they were dazzling, as dead as they were alive; Allan would never forget the cursed day he had looked into them.

The Spellmaker's aged skin began to crawl. Sansul Council had awakened one of the most evil vampires in history. Terror and endless bloodshed were Henry's legacy; it was an age in which innocence was born to die. Sickening dread settled in his bones.

"Henry?" The name sounded as hollow as his voice.

"What say you, Spellmaker?"

Allan squared his shoulders. "I say . . . tell your Supreme Chancellor that I will be unavailable, since I will be laundering my socks!"

"That is no reply."

"It's the only one you'll get!" Allan roared. "Be gone! Or I will have the Elements come down on you in a fury you have never seen."

~

"Explode!"

In the middle of the square table, a small glass vial shattered into thousands of tiny pieces and floated in the air, suspended by the witch's hold.

"Mend!"

The shards melded together once more, taking the form of the vial, pristine and untouched, as if nothing had happened to it.

"Levitate!"

The table rose a few inches from the ground, and, following the hand movements of the witch, it hovered from side to side.

"Implode!"

The cauldron on top of the table began to melt; its edges crumpled, falling into the centre like melting wax.

"Very good," said Fradrik, highly impressed. "You can rest now."

Adrianna lowered her outstretched arm and flopped into the nearest seat, drained.

"Now, do you feel the control you have over the materials?" he asked, indicating to the vial, the table and the cauldron. "Projection Power is about *your* inner strength and knowledge of the Elements."

"And this is the elementary lesson," Adrianna said with a sigh.

"It becomes easier once you have your Element," he said. "But that is why we *study* the magic before we control it. You are different. The power to control, to cast and to conjure is in your blood. You know in your body and your senses how to gain what you want and so Projection Power is ingrained in you."

"I can only do those basic things."

"Before you know it, you will be forming those very objects without much effort," he said. "I am proud of your progress."

"It is a pity my power must remain a secret."

"If it does not, others will begin to suspect that you are no natural witch. Word will reach Citron and they will search for you, as they did your mother after she ran away from her home. No girl of eight and ten summers has been able to do what you have. Only one race can perform such complex magic without spells and they *must* be kept a secret, as you must be. You must not seem out of the ordinary, Adrianna. Your life depends on it."

"You have been protecting me for so long. This was not what you expected when you became my father's second-in-command, is it?"

"I promised your father that I would keep you as my own. It is my duty to school and protect you as long as you need it."

Adrianna smiled. "Do you not miss pillaging foreign shores and sailing across open seas?"

A nostalgic look passed over Fradrik's face. "Sometimes."

"I miss my parents."

"As do I."

"What about Blanca? If I am able to manipulate the things around me, shouldn't my cousin be able to as well?"

"Yes. As the daughters of two brothers who married sisters, you should have the same abilities."

"I wish I could see her. She must be so worried."

"Soon you will."

"Do I look like her? My mother, I mean . . ."

"Yes. You have her grace and beauty, but you have your father's personality and his eyes. He loves you more than anything."

"Then why did he leave me?"

Fradrik lifted her chin. "Your parents did not leave you by choice. Never forget that. They protected you and this land we call home when they left. You shall see them again. Maybe not soon, but you will."

"I am scared that one day you will leave me, too. Everyone I have ever loved leaves; my parents, Kenna, Daniel . . . I am waiting for the day my cousin Blanca is gone, and my friends. Am I cursed?"

"No. Never. You must always have the Light in your heart."

"The Light is always here, but good fortune is not. Why did this have to happen to us?"

"We have all asked ourselves at one point or another during these moons, I am sure. The truth is, I do not know. Sansul has always been an unstable vampire coven. There were too many powerful vampires trying to control it in the past. It was believed, when they were overpowered at the end of *The War Against The Angels*, that they would no longer be a threat. But a resurrected enemy is a dangerous, volatile one."

"But we were kidnapped before Henry was awakened."

"There is no point in trying to understand why vampires do certain things, and you know that Sansul Council was planning to awaken Henry with a massive amount of fresh blood, so as to feed the army he would need."

"Then why did he let us go? If he needed all our blood for the army . . ."

"What better way to terrorise the land than to unleash hundreds of blood-thirsty vampires?" Fradrik said simply. "And, also . . ." He looked hesitant, but when Adrianna gave him a look that demanded he continue, he said, "our Assembly meeting took place this morning."

The Assembly was the governing body of witchery clans, and was constituted of elders and elected clan representatives.

"And?"

"The names of all known dead were finally counted," Fradrik said. "Lizzette has a full listing of names of those who perished on the night of Samhain and those who died in Sansul Fortress."

"Are they counting those who were turned into vampires as dead?"

"No. The names for those whom the Assembly know for certain were turned were put on a separate list. Their families were jardinformed privately."

Adrianna blinked. "I do not know if I would want to be informed of such a thing," she said softly, remembering the morning after the attack in which Daniel and Liam were kidnapped. There was no sorrow like that which she had seen on the faces of their mothers. "What is worse? To be told your loved one is dead or turned?"

"Dead, most certainly." The finality in Fradrik's tone made her smile. "For I would love you no less as a vampire."

"Nor I you. But I had to tell Ralphus that Kenna was dead."

"Do you not trust him to love her still? As a vampire?"

"Sometimes, love does not conquer all."

"No?"

"That does not mean I do not wish them to be reunited one day. But Ralphus would not have reacted well to the news. He needs to mourn her."

"Perhaps that was for the best. There was more involved during the Assembly meeting than the sadness of collecting names," said Fradrik, though now he was cautious. "It was agreed upon – with only two votes against – that every witch be searched for . . . telling marks of whether or not they were . . . used or . . ."

"*Excuse me*?" Adrianna's throat tightened. Her disgust must have been obvious because Fradrik hung his head pitifully. "Telling marks? Used by vampires? What does this Assembly think they are doing? Punishing us for something we could not help? Where are the *women* in this Assembly, I would like to know! They were there, they saw, they experienced all of it – and now they want to subject innocent, good women to a 'search'? To what avail?" she demanded. "To satisfy the husbands that might have been regretfully cuckolded? What good would any of that do? All that will happen is witches will be disowned and cast out because of something for which they cannot be blamed!"

Fradrik nodded, leaning heavily on the table. "I voted against the motion. It will not be easy to overcome. You must understand, for a warlock, to know your wife has been with a vampire is the worst possible type of betrayal."

"There is *no* betrayal when the woman has no choice!" she cried, slamming her fist onto the table. The candles flared and the shelves rattled as her temper spiked. "I cannot believe that this has become relevant in a society such as ours! Rape is rape. You *cannot* blame the victim."

"Veronique has spoken those exact words," said Fradrik. "Many people have been uncooperative with the Assembly. Most just believe it is too soon to conduct interviews, but you were all imprisoned for so long it is impossible for nothing to have happened beyond imprisonment. Still, as a warlock who has seen all shades of what society can do for itself I agree that privacy in such a delicate matter is the best course of action."

"It is the witch's business and nobody else's!" said Adrianna. "I doubt any warlock has been in a room with a vampire long enough to know how it feels when your life can be taken from you at any given moment! Would any of them subject poor Collette to such an insulting interrogation? She was in the hands of vampires. She watched helplessly as her sister was murdered. She begged! She begged for them to take their fury out on her, to leave Annie alone. Now, how could anyone ask her to reveal whether . . . 'acts of indecency' . . . had occurred when she went through such terror?"

Fradrik stared at the table.

"They probably did, but what good would it do for others to know? I understand why I was questioned now!" She laughed at the absurdity of it. "It is *nasty* and *hideous* behaviour from our Assembly. That pretentious crow Joan actually expected me to tell her the truth of my time in the fortress."

Fradrik closed his eyes, shaking his head. "I tried to stop it, I swear on my Blood Oath to your father . . ."

"Do not blame yourself. For all that has been thrown at us, being questioned by 'The Secretary for the Determination of Vahir Expansion' is the least of our worries."

Adrianna rested her forehead on her hand and tried to calm down. Now that she had vented her rage, tears built up inside of her, threatening to fall if she opened her eyes. When Fradrik's hand took hers, she gave it a gentle squeeze and tried to force her tears down. Crying would not do her any good.

They sat in silence for a long while, energy radiating between and around their joined hands. *Energy healing*, she thought, opening her eyes to the glow. Calmness replaced the anger and sorrow she felt. As though she was sprayed with cooling water, her gloom was being washed away.

"You should meditate this evening before falling asleep," he said, with his eyes closed and his face calm. "You have a lot of energy that needs to be redirected to the right places. I sense you are worried about other people. You do not trust some of those in this sanctuary. Why? Is this your natural instinct, or your mind?"

"I do not know," she said softly.

Out of nowhere, a great, rambunctious, unearthly noise rolled through the sanctuary. The candle flames turned a deep shade of green.

Fradrik stood slowly. "Intruders."

"What?" Adrianna's question was followed by commotion outside the room.

Mathena barged through the door in disarray. "Come to the atrium!" she said breathlessly. "Intruders in the temple . . . the vampires have passed the first entrance to the sanctuary!"

The inhabitants of the sanctuary congregated in the pentagonal-shaped atrium, staring up at the ceiling. Mute and hardly daring to breathe, they looked terrified.

"What is going on?" Adrianna whispered fiercely as Mathena pulled her though the crowd, Fradrik close at her side.

"They entered the temple and opened the trapdoor," Mathena replied in a shaky whisper.

Simo, Gralam, Renauart, Eglantine and Onoria stood around the exit door. Eglantine turned to Mathena and Adrianna as they arrived and pressed her finger to her lips.

Thoroughly confused, Adrianna looked around at the crowd of people; their faces mirrored the anxiousness of those around the door. If the vampires had passed the trapdoor entrance, why were they just standing around? Should they not be rushing through the tunnels? Setting up a blockade of some sort? Their silence made no sense at all.

Suddenly, a terrible, ghoulish moan echoed through the tunnel entrance. Everyone jumped; children screamed.

"The curse is working," Gralam whispered. He obviously knew what was happening; he looked slightly less worried than everybody else. "They won't make it much further."

Screams erupted in the tunnel; the intruders were in a panic. There was another chilling moan followed by the wild cackling of a hag, sending a shiver of disgust around the room. The high-pitched laughter grew louder and louder until it echoed around the atrium walls. The witches covered their ears.

"Go back!" someone shouted hysterically in the tunnel. "Get out! It is cursed!"

"Be calm!" ordered another. "It is likely the trickery of magicians."

Gralam laughed. "As if we would employ magicians here."

In the midst of the hag's laughter, another grating voice mimicked that of the intruder. "Go back! Get out! It's cursed!" it said tauntingly. "Grind your bones, we will! Come closer, vampires! Let us show you the hospitality of the Gordgáin."

Adrianna gasped.

The tunnel had been cursed to ward off anyone of the Darkness. Once the intruders found the trapdoor beneath the altar they would walk into a pit of curses made to kill. No one would be allowed to leave alive.

At the cries of agony and pleading last words, Adrianna put her hands over her ears.

"Back! Back!" someone shouted at the tunnel entrance. "It's full of gypsy curses!"

"Shut the door!" another ordered after another teeth-grinding cry.

A moment later, a wolf's howl thundered through the atrium and everything fell silent. The occupants of the sanctuary stood still, listening intently. In the crowd, Caitriona stood close to her brother, shaking. Beside her, Jess crouched and covered her ears.

When all was calm, the people began to move, whispering about the curse of the tunnels. Caitriona ushered Jess out of the atrium, Mathias and Ralphus shared a look and Cedar made his way through the crowd to Adrianna's side.

"They came too close to finding us," said Eglantine, her face drained of colour.

"They *have* found us," Simo replied. "Thank goodness for those old curses."

"Are they gone?" asked Adrianna.

"No – they are not gone," Simo replied patiently. "Those unfortunate enough to descend to the trapdoor are certainly dead, but the rest are in the ruins of the temple. The vampires will be angry, frustrated. Their next attempt will be more successful than this one. Vampire's learn from their mistakes, unfortunately."

"How did they get past the trapdoor?"

"It is the Librarian's doing, surely," said Mathena. "He is the only one able to lift the spells that keep the Darkness out."

"Is there not a Spellmaker here?" Eglantine asked. "He could reinforce the door."

"What about Gilleroy? From Upper Wilmota?" asked Renauart.

"Scarpered," grunted Gralam, digging his pockets for his pipe.

"He managed to escape the night of the attack," said Onoria, shooting the wrinkled warlock a stern look. "He went to Azria and tried to convince the Assembly to send people north."

"Fat load of nothing that did."

"What will happen now?" asked Adrianna, cutting in before Onoria could retaliate.

Wearily, Simo ran a hand through his hair, looking as though he wanted nothing more than to disappear.

"When the Sansul vampires took control of Wilmota, they ransacked every cottage, ripped apart every scrap of wood and linen to find our secrets and weak points," said Gralam. "Anyone in hiding has already been found. There is no going back. Not anymore."

"Yes, thank you for stating the obvious," said Mathena, shaking her head.

"We can try fighting off those in the temple but they will only come back in force," said Fradrik.

"Fighting is not an option for us anymore," Simo said regretfully, scratching his lilac beard. "The sanctuary is filled to capacity. We have sick women, children and warlocks that need aid and we just cannot keep up with the number of people."

Rose pushed through the crowd and grasped Simo's arm. "Father, we must leave this place."

"I know," Simo said gently. "The decision has been made for us." Turning to the crowd, he lifted his hands, calling for attention. "The sanctuary will not provide us with shelter and protection much longer," he addressed the throng. "Therefore, we have two options! Aires or Bruniér – we must travel over a day in the tunnel to reach Aires, and almost two days to reach Bruniér. Now that the vampires know what curses lie here it will not be long before the Librarian is able to remove them."

"No one is powerful enough to remove centuries old curses," someone called from the crowd.

"The Librarian is certainly powerful enough," Simo replied. "Besides, the Darkness is capable of a great many things that we underestimate. And that has been our greatest fault; underestimating our foe. We have a choice to make. A plan will be put together within the hour. All persons over the age of ten and eight summers will convene in the atrium an hour before sunset."

"What about the orphans?" Mathena whispered. "Many are under the age and have no one older to speak for them."

"Anyone under the age of ten and eight summers who has no family will speak to Eglantine and Rosamunda about their destination," Simo added to the crowd. "I request, that any parents who would be kind enough to take in a child for the time being, *please* do so. Until later . . ." He inclined his head and the crowd dispersed.

"You are seriously going to make over three hundred people sneak through tunnels for almost two days?" Eglantine asked Simo.

"What other choice do we have?"

Eglantine's shoulders slumped in defeat.

"I am putting you in charge of the children," said Simo. "Rosamunda, if you would be so kind . . ."

"Of course," said Rosamunda. "But we will need more than two people – there are over twenty children without supervision. Most of them have family members in other clans, but we will have to sort through them all."

"Put together a group," replied Simo.

"Adrianna?" Rosamunda asked hopefully, looking around at her.

"She has *other* things to do," said Simo. "She's been a productive member of the Gordgáin."

Rosamunda looked shocked.

"We will convene in an hour," Simo said to the group. "Gralam, a word."

As they dispersed, Rosamunda rounded on Adrianna. They had not had any time to talk seriously since returning due to Adrianna's wound.

"You should not be doing any more favours for the Gordgáin," she said sternly. "You have done enough!"

"I have tried to make her see reason," said Fradrik. "As usual, she does not listen."

Adrianna looked apologetic. "I have been helping them for a while now," she replied, prepared to stand her ground.

"But you are still just a child!" Rosamunda argued.

"No, I am not. I may be young but I am *not* a child. I know it is a surprise but I really have been able to help."

"Half of what we have been able to do would not have been possible without her," Renauart said proudly, wrapping an arm around his wife. "She is the reason we were able to rescue you."

"She's a strong girl," Mathena added.

"Strength has nothing to do with it," Rosamunda snapped. "No Element, no training and no heeding of danger! You are too young to be in the Gordgáin, Adrianna, no matter how grown up you feel."

"I am not running into battle," said Adrianna. "Kenna would do the same if she were here."

Rosamunda did not argue further, but by the withering look she gave her husband, they knew it was not the end of what she had to say.

~

The meeting room in the second corridor was more crowded than ever before.

Renauart ushered Adrianna into the room.

"Ren, I do not think I will be entirely useful in this instance," she said in a low voice, as people bumped into her. "Our clan is free. Have I not outlived my usefulness to the Gordgáin?"

Renauart shook his head as he tapped the shoulders of two broad warlocks who moved aside so he could squeeze Adrianna through. "You wanted to be in the Gordgáin. You're in."

"Yes, but helping in the organisation of a mass of people is not what I expected to be included in!" she replied, smiling sheepishly at a broad-faced witch with a nose piercing whom she had accidentally bumped. "I am *so sorry*."

"I did not know we were recruiting children now," the woman in a clipped, light accent that Adrianna recognised instantly as being that of the Azria people.

"Leave it be," Renauart said as Adrianna opened her mouth to retaliate.

Really, she thought, scowling at the witch. *So rude!*

A map of Wilmota was suspended over the round table, rotating slowly. Like the map they had used before launching their attack on Sansul Fortress, important village points were illuminated. In red, the watchtower, the temple and the village square; in blue, homes and cottages; in purple, all the paths and roads, the beginning of the Sleeping Forest was in the corner and the tips of the main roads leading to Aires and Bruniér could be seen peeking through the bottom of the map.

Marked in glowing green were the underground tunnels leading from a small sketch of the temple.

Simo removed the map, replacing it with another. This time it was of the sanctuary. They found themselves looking at a very detailed pentagonal shaped image. All five halls were visible, the main door at the tip was marked, important rooms like the meeting room, the infirmary, food storage, kitchen and holding rooms were highlighted, and also the exit tunnels.

The tunnel on the east side ran south to Aires, and another, to the west, extended to Bruniér. South of Bruniér was a township called Collusus, which was connected to the Bruniér underground tunnel. There was no tunnel connecting Aires and Collusus.

"Those wanting to get to Collusus would need to go to Bruniér," said Simo, staring at the map. "It would be best to send all the children to Collusus."

"It would get them far away from the danger," Rosamunda said agreeably.

"The Bruniér Assembly have sent extra people to help Aires protect the border. We all know that if the vampires cross the Aires border then Azria will have to intervene," Simo replied. "At the moment they are holding this line." He traced directly above Aires over the open terrain and to the hills that stood before Bruniér. "Those vampires in the Bruniér Mountains may side with Sansul, the ones further south will likely remain loyal to Azria."

"Why are the vampires in the south not helping those in Sansul?" asked Adrianna.

"Vampires do not aid each other in conquests because they are of the same race," said Onoria.

Gralam snorted. "Same race, same filth."

"There is one powerful coven in the south, whereas here, in the midlands and highlands, we have different factions according to towns and areas," Simo replied. "Azria coven is very organised with its people. They live as peacefully as is possible beside people of the Light. They do not bother the folk and the folk do not bother them. The Supreme Chancellor is, for lack of a better description, a very reasonable man who has no loyalty to Henry. That is good for us."

"Vampires are a very complicated race," Mathena said with a sigh.

"And we haven't even encountered rogues yet," Onoria added.

Adrianna had a vision of grey skinned, blood-mad vampires running wild. Rogues, vampires without conscience or coven, were mindless killers who lived to feed. They had no minds of their own, no thought or reason for being. If they did not frighten her so much, Adrianna would have felt pity for them.

Mathena shuddered.

"Don't make me vomit," said Eglantine. "I just ate."

Simo returned the first map to the table. "Hover!" It rose into the air, rotating so it was visible to everyone.

"Returning to the plan," he said, clearing his throat. "All children will be taken to Collusus. Rosamunda and Eglantine I am leaving you in charge of getting a group together and escorting them there. I will send with you a letter to take to Yonus, one of their elders. In the meantime, it would be best to have all able-bodied witches and warlocks in Aires. I am hearing that the daily attacks from the vampires are becoming less frequent. Bruniér is where families, non-Gordgáin and the sick will stay. A small contingent of nymphs and fairies has decided to remain in the Sleeping Forest and the outskirts of Bruniér to look after the Elemental Cycles of the earth. I won't pretend to know anything about it; but I would like for them to be properly informed by you Onoria. You speak the nymph language better than anyone of us . . ."

Staring at the map, a particular green line caught Adrianna's attention.

"What will I tell them?" asked Onoria.

"I will send a note with you, but for now, just inform them that we will be in Aires," said Simo. "This is their home as well and they had better help fight for it."

"Excuse me," said Adrianna. "What is that? Is that another tunnel?"

"Where?" Simo asked, turning to the map.

"The one leading from the sanctuary to the fortress!" Adrianna said. "It looks like all the others."

"It *was* a tunnel," said Simo. "It's caved in."

"Can the vampires not excavate it?" asked Adrianna.

Gralam grunted in the corner.

"They would not bother," said Simo. "Besides, I doubt anyone living knows about it. This map is hundreds of years old."

"Why did you not try to excavate it when we were in the fortress?" asked Adrianna. It seemed a legitimate question. If the vampires were not using it, because they did not know about it or simply could not be bothered, why had the Gordgáin not used it to gain the upper hand? The tunnel would have saved them time and lives.

No one answered immediately. Mathena frowned, looking at the map then Simo. Adrianna looked around the room waiting for an answer. Eglantine looked baffled, but Onoria seemed as though she was remaining silent for a reason. Rosamunda leaned forward to take a closer look. "It must run from the first corridor . . ."

"It would not have taken long," said Adrianna, becoming angrier as the silence continued. "It cannot be all caved in. Why did no one try to get in through the tunnel? You had more than seven moons!"

"Adrianna," Simo said sternly.

"*No!*" she said furiously. The flames trembled. "I have always been honest with you people and you had a way in and did not even bother trying! Hundreds of us suffered and you *didn't even try*!"

"It isn't as simple as that," said Gralam.

"Oh?" said Adrianna. "Moving a bit of dirt is harder than facing demons and being smothered by the Darkness is it?"

"Now, see here, girl," Gralam said angrily, getting to his feet.

"Don't you yell at her!" Mathena cried, standing up. "She has every right to ask questions!"

"Not to be impertinent!" Gralam replied defensively. "We are all fighting here!"

"You know that tunnel is not just caved with dirt," Simo added looking at Mathena meaningfully.

"So it has bodies of the dead in it," Mathena retorted dismissively. "They are *dead*, they won't mind. It isn't sacred ground!"

"It is sacred ground to many," said Renauart. "There are even angels down there."

"Not to the living whose only way out it could have been," said Adrianna. She stepped away from the table and looked at the map in disgust. "Get your own information. I am done."

"Adrianna," Fradrik called as she closed the door.

Simo sighed and slumped back down in his chair. "What is happening here?"

"You shouldn't have yelled at her," Mathena told Gralam sternly.

~

Adrianna passed Cedar and Anya hastily, ignoring their curious stares.

"You all right, Adrianna?" Ralphus called, setting down his candle on the Wall of Flames.

"Yes," she replied, without looking back.

How could it be that the Gordgáin knew of a way to reach the fortress and did not try anything? Why did they let her and so many others risk their lives to attack head-on when a few days of excavation would have allowed them to sneak in and save dozens of extra lives? She had believed the Gordgáin was made up of powerful, courageous people, but more than that she believed them to have honour. There was no honour in leaving innocents to die for the sake of preserving supposed sacred ground.

But, if it was 'scared ground', what had happened there? Renauart had mentioned angels; did their bones lie alongside elementals? If so, how had they died? What tragedy had stuck these immortals in the tunnel, leaving them in an untouched tomb?

While not far from her room, she was distantly aware of someone calling her name. Thinking it was someone from the meeting, she ignored the voice until the follower placed a hand on her arm.

"Are you okay?"

Adrianna snatched her arm away, whipped around; ready to yell at whomever it was, only to sigh with relief. "Orla."

Orla looked slightly healthier than she had in the fortress, though the light in her eyes was yet to return. Adrianna felt a rush of emotion for the witch and embraced her.

"Sorry. I just came from a bad meeting. My nerves are on edge. Honestly, I do not even know why I was invited . . ."

"You are in the Gordgáin?" Orla asked in surprise.

"Yes, not on an official basis. I am not old enough, you see, but I help."

"So why do you look as though you're about to burst into tears?" asked Orla, patting her back.

"My life."

"I think we are all in that predicament," she said sweetly.

Adrianna could not help but laugh. "How are you? You look much healthier."

"The healers have been very good with us. They only allowed me to leave the infirmary yesterday. Most of us are back on our feet, preparing for this big move through the tunnels. And how is your side?" she asked.

"It is almost fully healed," said Adrianna. "Thanks to Mathena. She is so good with potions."

"I know a lot of the mothers have been giving lessons again for those who are willing to continue studying," Orla added. "I think they want to return to a normal life. As much as can be possible down here," she added, looking up at the low ceiling. "I feel now that I know how moles feel underground."

"Would you like to come to my room? I was about to make some tea," said Adrianna. "After that meeting I need something to calm me down."

"And someone to talk to?" Orla asked sympathetically.

"Is it pathetically obvious?"

Orla looked down at her hands. "The truth is I haven't had anyone my age to talk to for a while," she said softly. "With my sister gone . . . and since I am not originally from Wilmota, I don't really know anyone."

Adrianna patted her back gently.

"I feel like *such* a weakling," Orla admitted, annoyed with herself. "I *never* cry. I do not want to burden you."

"Nonsense," Adrianna interrupted. "The truth is I am a little lonely too. My best friend was made a vampire, and I feel like a stranger to all the others. Being in the fortress changes us like that, I think. Everyone I have met has been very kind, and Mathena is a great friend, but somehow I feel even lonelier around people. Like two peas in a pod, are we not?"

Orla smiled, nodding.

"Where are you from?" Adrianna asked, leading her along to her bedroom.

"My father is a gypsy," said Orla. "We travelled a lot when I was very little but when my sister was born my family settled in Azria. I was visiting my sister, she was betrothed to a man from your village, and they were celebrating their first

Sabbat together when the attack happened. She would still be alive if it weren't for that."

"What was her betrothed's name?"

"Keiran," Orla replied. "Nice man . . ."

Adrianna's smile faded.

"Are you all right?" Orla asked worriedly.

"I knew him," Adrianna said softly. "He was the son of Celeste and her husband Ronan. You will have seen them around. She helps in the infirmary now that she has healed."

"Yes, I met them only briefly, but our families were to meet two days after Samhain."

"Kieran was the best of all of us, and I know he would have made a wonderful husband to your sister. He was ten years older than me, but he was the kind of man who was a friend to everyone, from a child to the elders. Did your sister ever tell you how he came to have that deep scar on his face?"

"No."

"He saved his best friend's sister. She was being lured away from the village by a goblin . . ."

Orla gasped. "You don't mean . . .?"

"Yes, he was trapping her for the Black Annis," said Adrianna. "Kieran found her walking with it, obviously under some kind of spell, and leaped into action. I do not know how he did it, but it worked. She ran and the goblin slashed his face before disappearing. Another good person killed for no reason," she added bitterly, turning to her room.

"I am glad Peta chose someone so brave. Though, somehow, it feels like they have been gone a thousand years," said Orla. "I hope we do not forget the dead."

"Your sister was marrying very young. Come to think of it so was Keiran," Adrianna said as they entered. The room awakened instantly; the fireplace came alive, and the window, charmed to illustrate a garden, allowed natural light to enter the otherwise small room.

Walking in reminded her of just how luxurious her home in Wilmota was. Spacious, lush and open, it was quite the opposite of the bland, limited accommodations now available to her. But with a sigh, she admitted to herself that this was much better than the fortress. A tree house was more welcoming than that prison.

Adrianna motioned for Orla to sit at the table beside the window. "I share this with Mathena. Her daughters are still in the infirmary unfortunately."

"I love that you still try to keep the natural elements even though we are underground," said Orla, staring out to the realistic though synthetic view. "It looks so real."

Adrianna smiled. "Mathena did it. I described exactly what I see from my bedroom window at home . . . well, what I would be seeing, and she charmed the window." She placed a teapot on the table.

Orla looked at her curiously as she poured the tea. "So what happened when you were taken to the Laboratory? I thought you were dead for sure."

"Awful things," said Adrianna. "I was tortured but the Librarian was prolonging my death. I met a wolf-man in the Laboratory prison."

"Really?"

"Yes, he was kind to me," Adrianna said softly, remembering how he forced her to keep her heartbeat even so as not to bleed out overnight. Every time she lost consciousness on the stone slab, she woke to find his blue eyes above hers. They were sad eyes, pained. "I hope he did not die there."

"Wolf-men are dangerous."

"Very," Adrianna agreed. "But they are made that way. Wolves usually do not bother us if we do not pose a threat to them. We have many wolf packs around Wilmota."

"Oh?"

"These are the highlands, mountain lands. Wolves have lived here peacefully for centuries. Wilmota people often rescue orphaned wolf cubs."

"You highland people are fearless," said Orla, sounding somewhere between a laugh and a scold. "So you do not fear the wolf-men?"

"I am terrified," said Adrianna. "Soon the wolf-men will become territorial; and I have a feeling they will not remain loyal to the vampires for too long."

"I hope you are right," said Orla, sipping her tea. "This is good tea . . . the smell is so soothing."

"Thank you," said Adrianna, grinning. "It has sweet pippa seeds and gypsy tea leaves in it."

"Gypsy tea leaves?" Orla smirked.

"It is a gypsy recipe – I do not know the leaves by name."

Mathena entered without knocking, her expression grave. Without a word, she sat down at the table, and rolled her neck as Adrianna poured her a cup. Adrianna introduced Orla.

"Pleased to meet you," said Mathena.

"All is not well?" asked Orla. "You look exhausted."

Mathena sighed. "Well, let's just say that a room full of desperate people trying to make decisions is not the most relaxing environment. Be grateful you stormed out when you did Adrianna."

"I had to. I couldn't face them after seeing that tunnel."

"You're right – and they all know it," said Mathena.

"So what has the 'honourable council' decided?"

"Well – all children are to be taken to Collusus," Mathena said. "Rosamunda is rounding up a group as we speak. All willing fighters are to go to Aires; and families and the sick are to go to Bruniér. A small group will remain here as spies and there will be four groups of three in each clan to act as correspondents between the towns."

"Hasn't that been done already?" Adrianna asked.

"Not with all the townships acting as one," said Mathena. "This is a huge operation."

"Glad to hear it," Adrianna said darkly. "Let's hope no one crosses sacred ground or else we'll all be done for."

"They should have tried the tunnel, knowing how much people were suffering," said Mathena.

"What tunnel?" asked Orla.

"There is a tunnel running from here to the fortress," said Adrianna. "It leads *directly* inside. If the Gordgáin had excavated it we might have been freed moons ago. We could have even used it in the last rescue; it would have been completely secret. The vampires would not have known a thing."

"That is why you stormed out?" asked Orla. "Good for you."

Mathena smiled. "Adrianna is quite headstrong."

"Aren't all women?"

"Yes, but Adrianna has quite a temper beneath her lovely exterior," Mathena said proudly, looking at the younger witch as though surveying a particularly pleasant watercolour drawing.

Adrianna bowed mockingly. Orla laughed.

"How are your girls? Will they be released from the infirmary soon?" Adrianna asked in a push to remove the attention from herself.

"Laura is almost fully healed," said Mathena. "She did not become as affected by the Darkness as Ide and Vivien. Ide was much like you; she was slowly dying. The more emotional ones are always hardest hit. Viv is leaving today but Laura wants to remain with Ide until she is well enough. I just wish we could all leave this place and see sunlight."

Orla sighed dreamily. "I *love* the sun." She looked out the window at the blue sky and seemed to have forgotten that the window was not real but a bit of brilliant magic. "Still, better down here than in the fortress."

CHAPTER SEVENTEEN

The Tunnel Journey

"COME ON ADRIANNA," SAID Ralphus, pulling her through the back of the crowd. "At this rate, we're going to be left behind!"

A few paces into the cluster of people, Ralphus tapped Mathias on the shoulder. The dark-haired warlock turned expectantly.

"Did you find her?"

"Right here," said Ralphus, pushing Adrianna in front. "Where is Cedar?"

"At the front with Caitriona," said Mathias. "She has been a bit weird about leaving. He does not want to leave her alone."

The torches in the now empty sanctuary corridors began to dim as the remaining Gordgáin grouped around the entrance to the eastern tunnel that would lead them to Aires. While most mothers had chosen to go to Bruniér with their children the previous evening, a large number decided to lend their abilities to the Gordgáin, thus entrusting their children into the care of Rosamunda and Eglantine, who had escorted the orphans down the southwest tunnel to Bruniér where they would take the adjoining channel to Collusus.

There was a collective sense of forced cheer amongst the people. Nobody wanted to show their sadness at having to abandon the land, which was their home. Pockets of people sang traditional folk songs in an effort to maintain a sense of optimism. *On the Steady Path to Marta* was a favourite of the warlocks who frequented the village Lodge. That one put a smile on most faces. When they sang *Wilmota Held Your Daughter* Lizzette tried to silence them. Adrianna blushed and laughed as the warlocks only got to the end of the first paragraph, which was tame compared to the rest.

Faeries hovered above the heads of warlocks, carrying their belongings in little rucksacks. Many were involved in lively conversations with the witches, warlocks and nymphs, the latter of whom had chosen to leave their families behind in the Sleeping Forest and help their neighbouring tribes in Aires.

Mathena, whose three daughters Laura, Ide and Vivien had gone to Bruniér, came to stand next to Adrianna as the ceiling high double doors opened with heavy groans. Bits of dirt fell from the ceiling as the doors swung slowly inward, controlled by two Assembly witches. Adrianna stood on her tiptoes to see over the heads of those in front. Curiosity and excitement rose throughout the crowd. The seemingly endless tunnel was bright and clean, lit with lanterns that hung from the eight-foot high ceiling. It was six-feet wide, for which Adrianna was grateful. She had envisioned them walking in a cluster, cramped and hot through a narrow tunnel with little light besides that which they themselves could provide.

"Those two dhamphir arrived last night," said Mathias, motioning ahead to where Adrianna could only see if she craned her neck.

"Which dhamphir?" she asked.

"Durand and Gyde," said Mathena. "They came through the tunnel, straight from Aires."

"Really? It's so unnecessary for them to come," said Adrianna. "How much trouble can we get into down here?"

Peeking through the gap between two witches, Adrianna spied the two Maquis. Gyde, the rugged hunter, wore a deep green shirt that looked to have been repeatedly mended over its long life. Any witch or warlock worth their powers was able to repair their clothes so that they looked brand new, so why did he not mend his clothes properly? Durand, who seemed to take much more notice of his appearance, wore an embroidered jacket over his navy blue shirt and was deep in conversation with two warlocks who both sported long braided beards.

Mathias noticed her curiosity and cleared his throat loudly. "What are you staring at them for?"

"Just curious," she said unapologetically.

"Your attention please," Simo called from the front. "We are the last group to leave the sanctuary. For now, we must leave Wilmota, the land of our hearts, and hope that nature can protect her from further destruction. Some of our fellows – faeries, elves, nymphs, fauns and centaurs of the Sleeping Forest – have stayed behind to better protect the forest and act as watchers. Our journey to Aires will require over a day of travel. Let us walk swiftly, break shortly, and reach our destination ready to fight from the midlands. We have already endured what would have broken most. There is strength within us yet."

"Naturally," called Ralphus from beside Adrianna. "We are highlanders!"

Simo smiled as the crowd cheered. The colours of the faeries grew brighter. "One day we will return home – Wilmota will not be forgotten."

"Tears of pride," said a stocky, hairy warlock in front of Adrianna to the witch handing him a handkerchief. "Tears of pride, girl."

At those words, Adrianna felt a pang of guilt. She would miss Wilmota and its peace and beauty, the rolling green hills, the scent of the sea in summer and the way the tulip fields swayed in the evening breeze. Judging by the expressions on the faces of her clan, they too were feeling the same as she. Lizzette wiped a tear from her cheek. Departing was almost like leaving a part of her soul behind, condemning the days before the kidnapping to memories.

Slowly following Orla and Mathena, Adrianna entered the tunnel promising she would return home. The walls were smooth and white, decorated with fading murals: countless images of the times when angels walked freely upon the Elemental Plane, symbols, and picturesque visions of Wilmota as a lively village. A short while into the journey, they passed a section of wall with a painted image of a glowing light surrounded by a group of angels. A panel of ancient symbols ran down the side of the depiction that had not faded with the rest of the tunnels imagery.

"It feels like it will never end," Orla said after a few hours. "Doesn't it?"

"If I do not stop soon I am going to collapse," Mathena whined.

"We are moving at a fast pace," Adrianna said in agreement, shaking her legs out as they walked. "Do you think the vampires will be able to get into the sanctuary?"

"Who knows," replied Mathena. "If they do, we will not be using these tunnels anymore."

"I wonder what is going on above ground," Orla muttered, looking up to the ceiling.

"We'll know soon enough," said Adrianna, imagining uniformed soldiers invading what was left of their homes, ransacking the Sleeping Forest and hunting for Gordgáin, assigned to report the intelligence they gathered.

On the first break of the journey everyone but Gyde and Durand collapsed in exhausted heaps. The two Maquis soldiers shared a look as the people muttered grumpily about the journey. Huon lay down flat and leaned against his mother to sleep. Like most warlocks, he despised long journeys on foot.

"I wish we had a Dial Door," he said, closing his eyes.

"Who was the genius who decided not to put one down here?" Collette muttered, massaging her feet. "It would be the perfect place."

Adrianna leaned against the wall as Orla laid her head down on her lap. Though still weak from imprisonment, Orla insisted on going to Aires. "Even if I have to crawl," she pressed when Mathena tried to convince her to go to Bruniér with those still healing, "I am going to help the Gordgáin."

Adrianna closed her eyes and rolled her neck. It felt good to rest, even if it was for a few minutes.

"Don't get too comfortable," said a deep voice above her.

Adrianna looked up at the forever-brooding dhamphir standing over her. She arched an eyebrow in question.

"We will be moving again in a few moments," Gyde added before continuing down the tunnel to the front of the group.

"He is quite intimidating, isn't he?" said Orla.

"A little," said Adrianna, watching his retreating figure.

She began to wonder about the silent Maquis soldier. Had Gyde grown up with his mother? Did he ever meet his father? Did he even know who his father was? Perhaps his father was the reason for Gyde's mother's death. It was not uncommon for dhamphir not to know who their vampire fathers were. Their mothers or grandparents raised most; the unfortunate few were abandoned. The Maquis was a group that valued its secrecy and Adrianna was quite sure many had found themselves fighting their own fathers at times, perhaps unknowingly.

Soon, they were roused and the journey resumed. Gyde remained ahead of the group.

Adrianna linked arms with Orla. Caitriona remained close beside Cedar, quiet and reserved. Her bubbly nature and vivacious banter was gone. Her clothes were plain and her hair pulled into a simple, neat bun, which surprised all who knew she had always been at the forefront of fashion and style. As Adrianna watched her friend walk alongside her tall, comforting brother, she knew Caitriona's loss of love for style and laughter was deeper than the trauma of their imprisonment. There was something else.

Hours later, the whispers of a melodic tune resonated down the long tunnel. The voice was feminine and ethereal, and though soft, it floated in the air all around them. Behind Adrianna, others began to sing the old song in a language long abandoned.

It was an aged, mostly forgotten tongue spoken by witches, nymphs, vampires and angels alike before *The War Against The Angels*.

The melody had a profound effect. Adrianna began to feel calm and warm. Visions of Wilmota in the peacetime flashed in her mind. She smelled the rain in the summer, flowers, the ocean, and then a vision came so strongly she felt transported to a time and place unknown.

A beautiful, ivy laced cottage appeared before her surrounded by a vibrant, colourful garden. Her heart skipped a beat as she stared at her home. She was certain the vampires had destroyed it. Surely she was hallucinating. There was soft grass beneath her feet, thick and green. The wind was slow and hot, the sun strong in her eyes.

Could this be real?

Laughter came from the house; high and innocent, followed by a low, deep laugh that made tears come to her eyes. She caught a flash of blonde hair. Daniel ran around the side of the cottage carrying a little boy under his arm while another sat on his shoulders.

Adrianna gasped.

Daniel looked so alive; so beautiful and happy. His face shone when he smiled. The two boys were young, barely three summers old: one was blonde and the other dark haired. Daniel looked up from the child in his arms and grinned at her. He motioned for her to come to him.

Adrianna smiled and reached out for them when, suddenly, someone grabbed her arm.

"Adrianna!" a voice yelled sharply.

"What?" she snapped in surprise.

Her heart fell. She was back in the tunnels, staring at a wall. Judging by the shocked faces of the people around her, they were as stunned as she. Embarrassment crept up within and she looked away.

Mathena released her arm.

"What happened?" asked Adrianna, wanting to go back to whatever they had pulled her from.

"You fell victim to the *Par intra*," said Durand. "The song provokes certain people into seeing things – past, future, aspirations. But only the troubled ever see anything."

"I am not troubled," Adrianna lied quietly. "I did not see anything."

Durand looked sceptical.

"I felt as if I were sleeping," said Adrianna.

"Why did they sing that song?" Orla asked. "They must have known what would happen."

"It occurs so rarely," Mathena replied. "Maybe you should tell Simo to continue," she said to Durand.

As Durand went to the head of the crowd, Mathena urged those around them to continue with their own business.

"You were staring at the wall for a long time," said Orla. "It was weird."

"What did you see?" Mathena asked secretively.

"Daniel," Adrianna replied.

"And?" Mathena pressed.

"So it was a vision!" Orla said excitedly.

Adrianna frowned. She did not believe in visions, soothsayers, seers or fortune telling. There was such little proof of its accuracy and so much that could be disproved that she discarded that particular branch of magic, regarding it with great reservation. "It was a bit farfetched to be a vision. Daniel did not look like himself in whatever it is I saw. He seemed happy."

"Well, in things like this the *whole* vision matters," said Mathena. "Every detail."

"How exhausting," Adrianna said as the crowd began to move again. "I do not know . . . maybe it was wishful thinking."

Orla laughed. "Some wish!"

"Adrianna." Cedar was going against the flow of people, followed closely by Ralphus. Both looked worried. "Adrianna, are you all right? The dhamphir said you had experienced the *Par Intra*!"

"I am fine," said Adrianna. "Truly. It was just a little daydream."

"Let's keep walking," pressed Mathena.

"They should not have sung that song," said Ralphus, falling into step with Adrianna. "Especially at a time like this."

Adrianna patted his bulky arm. "No harm done. Orla, Mathena, have you met Ralphus and Cedar?"

"No," said Mathena, extending her hand to Cedar. "Adrianna has mentioned you both many times."

"Pleasure to meet you both," said Ralphus. "Any friend of Twigglet's is a friend of mine."

Mathena laughed and Adrianna blushed with embarrassment. "I am *not* a twig, I am perfectly proportioned."

"She is *now*," Ralphus said in an undertone to Orla, "but she was a teeny tiny little girl. She was so skinny that at nine we could fit her in the bucket that goes in the well and lower her down without breaking the rope."

Mathena gasped. "You put her in the well!"

"I was a victim extracting revenge," Ralphus said righteously.

"Tell the truth," Adrianna said over their laughter. "The truth is Ralphus and his goony friends used to do the most *terrible* things to us girls. We did not have a moment's peace and we rarely got revenge."

Ralphus snorted. "You and Kenna were always up to something."

"We liked to think of it as pre-emptive strikes," Cedar added.

"They put bees in my closet once," Adrianna told them. "*Bees!*"

"Oh my goodness," said Orla, horrified. "That is so cruel."

"It was Daniel and Mathias who put the bees in your closet because only Daniel knew how to climb up to your window," said Ralphus.

"But who caught the bees?" Adrianna asked expectantly.

"All right that was me," he muttered.

"I got them back though," Adrianna said proudly, and Ralphus turned red.

"Adrianna," Cedar said warningly, "no . . ."

"We stole their clothes when they went swimming in the ocean," Adrianna said proudly.

Orla laughed, sending Ralphus into an even deeper shade of red.

"They had to run through the village stark naked," Adrianna added triumphantly. "Seven little boys, running like the wind. Ah, the memories."

"Well," Ralphus sniffed proudly, "I had nothing to hide. Perfectly willing to show off my best asset . . . all Kenna needed to do was ask."

"Nothing embarrasses him," Adrianna said with a sigh.

A warlock drifted in and out of the crowd plucking his fiddle. As his tune turned to a happy popular one, a witch began to play her violin and the crowd began to sing.

Up the steady road to Marta,
Through the foothills of Wilmota,
There's a nothing you can barter,
That'll stop me chasing up,
All the nymphs so bright and bare,
With their brightly coloured hair,
There's a secret up in there,
In their scanty underwear . . .

~

It was a great relief to see the enormous, floor-to-ceiling double doors at the end of their journey. The travellers sighed and murmured expectantly as they stopped, waiting to pass the entry way to the Aires Gordgáin sanctuary.

"I am going to sleep for a year," said Caitriona, resting her forehead on Adrianna's shoulder.

"Me too."

"I need a massage," said Rose, reaching back to rub her own shoulders.

Mathias looked as though he was going to oblige her, when Ralphus clapped a hand on his shoulder. "Do not even think about it, pretty boy. We have a duty here."

Simo stood before the double doors for a long moment, scratching his lilac beard thoughtfully, before he raised his hand to the looped knocker and slammed it twice. The sound echoed.

Adrianna expected the wooden doors to open slowly, but what came was a surprise to everyone.

A vivid blue light emerged around the edges and skimmed across the metal work decoration that covered the door, illuminating it for all to see. A blossom tree, the Aires township emblem stood in high relief on the glowing blue metal. It was a remarkable sight. With a loud creak, the doors began to open.

"Finally," Mathena said with a sigh.

Huon wrapped an arm around his mother's shoulders. "Don't worry, mother. A warm bed and a cup of tea, and you'll be good as new."

"Welcome," said a deep, soft voice, enhanced so they all might hear. "Aires welcomes you, dear neighbours of the north."

The Gordgáin poured into the Aires underground sanctuary as Simo shook hands with the leader. Adrianna watched as they bowed to one another.

"That is Connor," Rose whispered to Adrianna and the others. "He is the leader of the Aires Gordgáin, answerable only to my father."

"Come on, Cait," said Cedar. "Let's go and find a quiet place to rest. Lads. . ."

Mathias and Ralphus followed.

Connor was a brawny man, much like Ralphus, but did not seem one bit intimidating. He had blonde shaggy hair, typical of the Aires people, and kind blue eyes. One was decorated with a half-moon ink marking that began over his left brow and finished at his cheekbone.

"My council and some of the Wilmota Assembly," said Simo, motioning to the group behind him.

Connor smiled at them all.

"Mathena, Gralam, Renauart, Adrianna and Rose," Simo introduced proudly. "Elders, Adalina and Lizzette. Our allies from the Maquis, Durand and Gyde."

"An honour," Connor said to the Maquis, inclining his head. "We have only just met with Erik – he was anxious to know of your status."

"He is in town?" asked Durand.

"Yes. He is with the Aires Assembly discussing inter-township communications," Connor replied. "And Simo, your messengers have been in contact."

"Good, good," said Simo, nodding. "Then things are going according to plan."

"We must join our people," said Durand.

Connor nodded. "I will have someone escort you to the exit at your earliest convenience. Ah, Aramé – meet our allies from Wilmota."

Making her way through the crowd of people, where Aires folk welcomed their northern neighbours, was Aramé, a small young woman with fine features and a dazzling smile. Adrianna was instantly reminded of Dahlia, but could not fathom why, since this witch did not resemble Dahlia in any way. Where Dahlia was dark, Aramé was fair. But there was something . . . not quite right.

"Welcome! You must be exhausted. We have rooms prepared for you," said Aramé, her voice soft and kind.

"I could do with a bed," said Orla, leaning heavily on Adrianna.

"I can take these witches to their quarters," Aramé said to Connor.

"Thank you," Mathena said gratefully. "Huon . . ."

"You go, mother. I will go with Ralphus and the others," said Huon. "Do not worry about me."

The women introduced themselves. As Rose extended her hand, Aramé eyed her curiously.

"Rose? Are you Dahlia's sister?" she asked.

"Why, yes, I am. Are you a friend of hers?"

"Yes. It is lovely to meet you."

Following Aramé, Adrianna walked with Mathena, Orla and Rose through the village-like Aires sanctuary. It was quite a change from the pentagonal-shaped, one-level, small-roomed Wilmota sanctuary. Here the large atrium closely resembled a village centre. On the far right was the exit, a small archway that led to a winding staircase. Adrianna noticed that Durand and Gyde were already making their way there.

Aramé directed them past the waterfall, along a series of doors to their left and up a small flight of stairs that opened into two quite identical hallways.

"You get a better view of the sanctuary from here," said Aramé, turning to look at the atrium from the top of the staircase. "Now, the doors on the right are where we keep supplies. Those stores are exactly like the ones we have above ground. You know, the apothecary, potions supplies, herbs and so on. They are always open, and we of the Gordgáin who come down here to aid in the war are always available, so let us know if you need anything. Now the doors to the left," she said, pointing to the strangely shaped entries that varied from triangles, to circles and diamond shapes, "all do different things. Some will lead you to rooms full of things like Staircase Trunks, Disappearing Cupboards, jars of Night Power, and fire-works, but it's mostly storage. One of them is a library, but I do not know which one. It keeps moving!" she laughed. "And *that* one," she pointed to a large triangular green door, "is a Dialling Room. Oh, here we are. An incomer . . ."

The triangle-shaped door began to glow. A moment later, it flew open and a beleaguered looking man with a rounded belly walked out, pulling along an over-packed trolley. "Sigrid! Where do you want this rubbish?" His boisterous voice filled the entire atrium.

"That room allows us to bring in mass amounts of larger objects," Aramé explained. "We simply couldn't get some things down that winding staircase – it's too narrow."

"Why don't you shrink them?" asked Mathena.

"Too many things to shrink," said Aramé.

The whole place was a hive of activity. Witches and warlocks moved quickly from person to person, room to room with conviction and focus. Many carried folders and satchels, others boxes. Witches in calf-length perfectly pressed dresses of purples, blues and reds walked smartly past them. No one looked up to greet them.

"Maggie! Charles needs your report on the Sansul Vanguard *now*," called a thin warlock in a grey suit and checked shirt.

"I can only work so fast, Harry!" replied the witch as she ran past Adrianna and down the stairs in a very tight dress and high heels.

"Efficiency is key to success," said Harry, giving her a stern look.

The witch disappeared from view once she opened the round door in the atrium. A cluster of faeries hovered around the fountain, all talking loudly, drawing the attention of other faeries.

"We have not had time to rest since the attack on your clan," said Aramé. "Each day that the vampires press on our border we are closer to suffering the same fate as you."

"I doubt your *whole* clan will suffer as we did," said Adrianna. "Especially not now that you know they are coming."

"Yes, maybe so. Anyway, follow me. Your room is this one on the left," said Aramé, turning into the carpeted hallway on the right. They saw a long neat row of doors. Between every other door stood a small table adorned with fresh flowers.

Aramé opened a door next to a vase of orchids and the women entered a small white and blue themed room. *'Duplicate!'* she said with an elegant wave of her hand, pointing to the middle bed. It slipped itself in-between two of the three beds on the far side of the room.

"You have really outdone yourselves down here," complimented Rose.

Adrianna helped Orla lay down on the bed furthest from the door. "She is still very weak," she explained, looking up from Orla's pale face. "Do you have any Strengthening Potions handy?"

Aramé nodded. "I will fetch some. It is the most requested potion. Would any of you be willing to help us with the stock? We could use more hands with the potions as we are running low. Everyone in Aires supplies us, but with all the extra people now, I foresee we will be greatly stretched. There are so many things to do around here. The infirmary needs extending, and more rooms need to be made, all sorts . . ."

"Of course," said Mathena. "We did not come to just sit around. Whatever is needed we are happy to help."

Aramé smiled and made to leave but paused and turned back. "This may sound a little odd . . ." she said apologetically.

"It cannot be anything we haven't heard," said Rose.

Aramé looked nervous. "Well, I just wondered if you know any soothsayers."

Adrianna and Mathena shared a look. Orla sat up in a flurry and Rose looked utterly dumbfounded.

"Soothsayers?" Adrianna repeated, hoping she had heard wrong.

"I know it is forward to ask such a thing," Aramé said in a secretive tone. "But many of the Gordgáin believe our side would progress further if the angels would help us. The only way to reach them now is through a speaker of the sooth. We have three here, but if we have more it would mean more power."

"You have *real* soothsayers here?" Mathena asked sceptically.

"Yes, they have been casting bones since the night of Samhain, when the vampires attacked you," said Aramé. "Two are gypsy – one is from a small corner of Aires where she lives on her own. She is the most powerful. You see she is able to connect with demons."

"And you *tolerate* this?" Rose demanded.

"Is that even possible?" asked Orla.

"Is she a demon child?" said Mathena.

"And who is to say the demons she connects to are not using her as a spy?" Adrianna asked suspiciously.

"She is quite loyal I assure you," Aramé said quickly. "I know soothsayers are not popular."

"It isn't the people we frown upon, it's the craft," Mathena said correctively. "Soothsaying is not something we dabble with. It is . . . it is . . . *taboo!*"

"I understand," Aramé replied.

"But we do have one," said Mathena with a sigh. "Unfortunately he is in Bruniér. And he is very demanding, not at all the type of person you would find helpful. I doubt he would make the journey."

"Maybe you can speak to Connor and Simo about sending these three soothsayers to Bruniér," Adrianna suggested.

"We can only try."

Aramé smiled. "I will get the potion and have food sent up as well."

Once the door was closed, Rose quickly put a Muting Charm on the room.

"Well, that was a surprise," said Adrianna.

"Soothsayers!" Rose said with incredulity. "Father will fall over backward when he hears this! They are shunned, even by us gypsies!"

"Soothsaying is about as reliable as a magician," Orla muttered, crossing her arms. "They conjure things that should not be allowed. And some of them try to speak to the souls of the dead."

"Sometimes people go to soothsayers to speak to a passed soul they miss," Mathena said reasonably.

"It shouldn't be done!" Orla insisted. "The soul has passed on! They go to the Spirit Plane. It's not right to disturb them."

"What about the gypsies who can tell your fortune?" Adrianna asked. "I had a gypsy read my palm once."

"What did she say?"

"That I was destined for hardship," said Adrianna.

Everyone laughed.

"She also said I would have four children, one who was not of my own blood," Adrianna added as the laughter died. "I never forgot that."

Orla snorted and rolled onto her side. "Believe what you like, but I am not gullible."

Aramé returned a short while later when Rose was asleep and Mathena had gone to meet Simo. Orla drank the Strengthening Potion and lay down to sleep.

"It works wonders this one," said Aramé, popping the stopper in the bottle. "It is made with dried breight-root instead of the fresh kind, so the seeds have had time to lock the juices inside. I've heard some people remove the seeds altogether, not knowing that is where the potion gets most of its strength."

"You know your potions," Adrianna said admiringly.

"My mother made them all her life," Aramé said proudly. "Some people in her area were too busy or lazy to make their own, so she would do it for them. She ran a successful shop for many years."

"Is she helping here then?" asked Adrianna.

Aramé shook her head. "She died when I was little. Oh, it was far too long ago to get teary about it," she said apologetically, blinking rapidly to stop the tears. "I am such a cry-baby. I cry at anything."

"I am sure she would be proud of you if she were here," said Adrianna.

"I hope so." Aramé smiled. "Well, I will leave you to rest and food should be up shortly. I know you are a very active member of the Gordgáin and have an important mission coming up."

Adrianna nodded. "I am a messenger."

"Brilliant," said Aramé. "I wish I were that brave."

"You are. And there is no bravery involved, I just pass messages."

Aramé looked sceptical, but Adrianna could tell she appreciated the compliment. "Until tomorrow morning then."

"That girl is strange," Orla muttered when the door closed.

"Should you not be asleep?" Adrianna poked her playfully.

"Who can sleep with all this chatter," Orla said with her eyes closed. "She is very . . ."

"Nice?" Adrianna offered.

". . . *smiley,*" Orla said darkly.

After washing quickly and eating supper in silence, Adrianna lay in bed and lifted the covers to her chin. What the gypsy had told her as a child made her think more seriously about the vision from the tunnel. Was it possible that she would have children of her own? And with Daniel? The idea made her a little uncomfortable, especially considering the danger and anger involved in their reunion at the fortress. They had not parted on friendly terms, but confused and unsaid terms. He had seen her suffer the pain of the Laboratory and never contacted her since saving her from certain death in that terrible place. Had he washed his hands of her? Was his act of salvation a last goodbye? Was she to take the vision or the gypsy seriously?

~

Adrianna looked over Orla's shoulder toward the winding staircase where Fradrik was waiting for her. She was set to leave with a pocket full of letters for the Maquis. If only Orla would release her from the embrace and allow her to depart.

"I'll be back before you know it," said Adrianna, patting her on the back.

"It's dangerous out there," said Orla. She pulled back slightly. "Promise you won't do anything stupid."

"I promise."

Orla let her pass and waved alongside Mathena and Rose as Adrianna and Fradrik ascended the staircase, and found themselves in a narrow passageway that appeared incomplete, as though it was in the middle of construction or remodelling.

"Why couldn't they put a floor here?" Adrianna asked as the heel of her shoe dipped into the dirt floor for the third time.

Fradrik gripped her elbow as she tripped, and swung her into his arms. "My goodness you weigh as little as a child," he said as they arrived at yet another set of stairs.

Adrianna waved her hands over her shoes and the dirt crumbled off. The stairs continued up until they reached a trapdoor. Setting her on her feet, Fradrik unlocked it.

"Be on your guard." He climbed through the hole with ease and turned to help as she stumbled.

They found themselves in a small house that by all signs seemed abandoned. It was dark and the air smelled stale. A thick layer of dust covered the bare room, and a large spider web spanned across the far corner. Faint moonlight streamed through the filthy windows.

Adrianna closed the trapdoor and a puff of dust blew into her face.

"Where are we supposed to meet the Maquis?" Adrianna asked, wiping dust off the end of her nose. The tips of her fingers tingled and an eerie feeling passed over her.

"Here," replied Fradrik.

"Then where are they?"

The lamps sprang to life. Fradrik spun around, casting two fire-spheres to the opposite sides of the room, and armed himself with more, ready to strike. The heat of the fire-spheres filled the room. Adrianna ran for the door but it was bolted shut.

"No use," said a thin voice from behind them. "You have been caught. And now we know the location of the sanctuary entrance."

Adrianna quickly gave up on the door and turned to face the speaker. Fradrik pointedly stepped in front of her, blocking her from any attempted attack. His fearlessness in the face of mortal danger made Adrianna admire her guardian all the more.

Liam, Thomas, Kenna and four soldiers stood on the far side of the one-room cottage. Adrianna's heart sank at the sight of her best friend. Kenna stood motionless and blank beside Thomas who looked uncharacteristically haughty. She tried to catch Kenna's eye but it was to no avail. Kenna avoided looking at her.

"Well, well. So the dead do return," said Thomas.

Adrianna felt a rush of hatred. She wanted nothing more than to slap that arrogance right from his face.

Liam stepped into the light. His face was gaunt and his skin tinged with green. This was no man. There was little to see in his face. His eyes were completely black, like glimmering onyx marbles. He was high on power, but Adrianna sensed it was not *his* power. Rather it was that of his demon, the Baál, Jeith. Adrianna she knew it was not Liam looking back at her though those eyes. Liam was gone. "Thank you, Adrianna. You have been helpful."

"You will never get through it," Adrianna spat over Fradrik's shoulder.

"I do not need to," said Liam. Holding out his hand, a large Darkness-sphere hovered above his palm. "All I have to do is burn it."

Adrianna looked to Kenna, desperate that she would interfere. A Darkness-sphere was more powerful than a fire-sphere in that it acted much like a bomb upon impact. Only vampires cast them, and a single launch of a Darkness-sphere had devastating effects. "No!" she cried.

Liam's black eyes narrowed as Fradrik held Adrianna protectively. "Take them to the fortress," Liam barked to the guards. "And this time, Daniel will not be around to keep you alive."

The guards moved forward and took hold of them. Adrianna slapped their hands as they gripped her arms. "Do not touch me!" she snapped as the vampires pushed her out the door. Liam, Thomas and Kenna remained in the cottage, leaving the soldiers to take them away. The cold air whipped her face. Fradrik was brutally overpowered.

"Leave him alone!" Terrified, she twisted herself in the grip of the two soldiers, fighting to get a glimpse of Fradrik. They had punched him. Fradrik spat blood from his mouth as the vampires shoved him forward.

"*Worry not,*" he said in the mother tongue of sailors. "*Do not expose your abilities.*"

Adrianna sighed, frustrated. There were only four of them. If she could summon enough strength from the earth she was certain she could defeat them.

They had not walked far before a blindingly white sphere shot out from behind an oak tree, slamming into the vampire to Fradrik's left. Adrianna squealed and threw herself to the ground when she saw the sharp end of an ice-tear coming toward her. It missed her by less than an inch, only to embed itself in the head of the vampire holding her arm. Pressing her forehead to her knees, she listened to the fast-moving figures, hardly daring to move, until, with a soft *thud*, the last body fell to the ground.

"Your timing could not have been better," Fradrik said as the bodies of the dead burst into flames.

Adrianna looked up in surprise.

Gyde, his pixie-haired wife Wynneth, Durand, and the youth-faced Joa stood before them. Wynneth helped Adrianna to her feet and led them to the tree line of the White Woods where they would not be seen.

"Why did you not meet us in the house?" asked Adrianna.

"We knew they were inside," said Wynneth. "By the time we arrived they were already squatting there."

"They could have killed us inside," Adrianna whispered, giving her handkerchief to Fradrik.

"It was a chance we were willing to take," Gyde said dismissively.

Adrianna glared at him; Durand tried to hide his smile.

Wynneth apologised. "We didn't know how many were in there," she said. "And we were going to kill them, but you arrived."

"Liam is about to set fire to the sanctuary," said Fradrik, dabbing his bloodied lip.

"The sanctuary is well protected against such attacks," said Durand.

"How many vampires are in there?" asked Wynneth.

Adrianna bit her tongue. She did not want Kenna to be killed in that house, even if she had stood by while Liam taunted her. Wanting desperately to object, she did not want to give anyone a reason to think she was untrustworthy. Though Kenna made it clear where her loyalties lay, Adrianna could not ignore the sickly feeling in the pit of her stomach.

"Three," Fradrik answered.

"Why is the village deserted?" she asked.

"It isn't," Wynneth replied. "It just closes down at night. It is too dangerous for people to wander at night."

"We should establish how the vampires managed to enter unnoticed," said Joa.

"The Arch," said Wynneth.

Adrianna frowned. Was the Arch a secret way the vampires travelled, like the Dial Doors used by witches and warlocks? Then, she remembered the first time she had ever met the Maquis. Gyde had led her and Eglantine through the

Sleeping Forest, and in order to enter the Maquis lair, they had to pass safely through the Arch. Were they the same?

"Could be," said Joa. "But how do we stop any more from coming?"

"If they did come through the Arch, scouts would have seen them. It is in White Woods," said Gyde.

"We have to take out the crystal embedded in it, the one connecting to Sansul fortress," said Wynneth.

"I'll see if I can find any tracks," said Gyde, disappearing in the trees.

"We have to stop the vampires in the cottage," said Joa. "Kill them before any more get through."

Adrianna swallowed the lump in her throat. "I cannot . . . I am sorry."

"What?" Fradrik stared at her.

"Kenna is in there," she explained. "I cannot be party to killing her."

"She is a vampire," said Joa.

"She is also my best friend and the best person in the world. I *know* she is not like them but, I think I have a way . . . I have some potions here," said Adrianna, opening her bag. She pulled out a small vial full of a bluish smoke. "It will render them unconscious. You can take Kenna for questioning and kill the rest." She shrugged. "I am grasping, I realise. I don't know how you like to do things."

Wynneth grinned. "She's catching on. Let's go with the first one. Do you want me to . . .?"

"No, no," Adrianna interrupted. "I am capable – I just have to get close enough."

"Let's go," said Wynneth.

Fradrik followed Adrianna to the open window of the cottage. To her relief, she could see that Kenna and Thomas stood in the far corner close together. Kenna's focus was on the front door. Liam stood in the middle of the dusty house, his face tense. His shoulders shook and his head rolled back.

"He is morphing into his demon," Fradrik whispered.

Wynneth, Durand and Joa stood outside the front door.

"I am sorry, Kenna," whispered Adrianna, before she threw the vial through the window. She ducked when it shattered. The roar that followed made her skin crawl. There was a blast and a squeal. Liam, half transformed, stumbled out of the cottage.

Running to the front, Adrianna watched as Durand raised his sword and ran it through Liam's abdomen. She held her breath as Liam howled in pain before backhanding Joa, sending him to the ground, and with the sword still in his middle, delivered a heavy blow to Durand. Liam grasped the hilt of the sword and yanked it from his body. The rasp and squelching noise made Adrianna's stomach turn. Wynneth jumped aside as the sword swung at her.

It came too close.

"No!" Adrianna screamed as Wynneth jumped out of the way of his incoming fire-sphere. "Liam, please *stop*!"

For a single moment she thought he was going to heed her plea. He froze; his hand ready to deliver another blow to Joa. He turned to her, his eyes wide with surprise. Adrianna could not tell if he was surprised that she was alive or that she had spoken to him at all. It seemed as if he was seeing her for the first time. Her eyes lingered on the fire floating above his palm.

"Please," she mouthed, her eyes pleading.

Joa stood, slowly raising his sword to deliver the killer blow. "No!" she squealed when Liam turned sharply and threw the fire-sphere.

Joa was thrown back in an influx of fire.

"*Bind him in air*," Fradrik roared, his hand extended.

Liam growled and fell to his knees as he was enclosed in a small tornado, barricading him instantly. His hands bound themselves behind his back. Like a caged animal he struggled to push through the vortex but Fradrik had a strong hold of his Element.

Adrianna ran to Joa's side. Wynneth cradled him. His eyes were wide and stared intently up at the sky. Badly burned, he had been saved by the protective magic woven into pieces of his clothes. His face was scorched, his flesh blistered and peeling away, and his left hand was blackened. He looked like a rotting corpse. Adrianna put her hand in front of her mouth to keep from being sick. His body began to tremble from the pain; his body going into shock.

"We are going to get you back," Wynneth said softly, holding his good hand.

"Here," said Adrianna, her unsteady hands pulling a small pot made of carved wood from her bag. "It needs to be applied on the burns. It will cool the skin until you get to an experienced healer." She looked at the open door of the cottage. "The safest place is the sanctuary."

"I will go down, explain and return with help," said Fradrik quickly.

"Thank you," said Wynneth.

Fradrik disappeared down the trapdoor. Durand stood guard over Liam as Adrianna applied the paste with Wynneth. As she ran it over Joa's left hand, she felt him tremble with every stroke of her fingers. His flesh peeled away leaving raw, pink skin exposed. He looked agonised but could neither yell nor move for fear of his face falling apart.

A moment later, a breathless Fradrik arrived with a small group of witches, including Peruva and Mathena. Peruva cried out when she saw Liam. They passed him hastily, making sure to give a wide berth around the tornado.

Mathena crouched down beside Joa's head. "It doesn't go past his neck," she said, examining his injury.

"His hand," said Adrianna, lending him a soothing energy as she held his palm between hers.

"Easily tended to," she said. "You're lucky it didn't hit the rest of your body," she told Joa. "We will get you inside and begin immediately. Fradrik . . ."

"*Rise*," said Fradrik.

Joa's body lifted from the ground as a white mist formed beneath him. He looked to be resting on a cloud, and with Fradrik's guidance began to float toward the trapdoor. Mathena squeezed Adrianna's hand and turned to follow the group back to the sanctuary.

"What do we do with Liam?" Adrianna asked Wynneth when all had gone.

Wynneth's eyes flashed malevolently. "We put him where all the rest are," she said, looking at Liam as though he were filth. "The Maquis lair. Where vampires are prisoners."

CHAPTER EIGHTEEN

Eriseda

BY THE TIME ALEXJANDER arrived to help transport Liam to the Maquis lair, Liam had almost succeeded in breaking through the tornado. Adrianna watched with Wynneth, a safe distance away, as Fradrik released his hold, collapsing on one knee in exhaustion.

Alexjander tackled Liam from behind, forcing him face down to the ground. "Give me a reason," he said, "just one . . . and I will kill you."

"Fradrik!" called Adrianna, rushing forward to help her guardian.

"Stay back!" ordered Durand as he helped Fradrik to his feet. "Wynneth, you too, please. This one is too dangerous."

"His demon is very strong," said Fradrik, catching his breath. "It was he who was breaking through the boundary in the tornado. Who is the Maquis holding the vampire?"

"Alexjander," said Durand.

"Alexjander," Fradrik called, striding to his side. "I know we have not yet made acquaintance. My name is Fradrik, and I believe the best way to move this . . . vampire, to your lair is to keep him from transforming. Obviously binding him will not suffice, therefore I suggest another method."

"Which is?" asked Alexjander.

Fradrik opened his palms, but instead of fire-spheres or ice-tears, a long, white cord extended, snapping in the air.

Alexjander looked impressed. "A lightening-whip. By all means, warlock . . ." He took a step back from Liam, who looked up defiantly.

"Stand." Durand yanked Liam up. "Walk. And do not even . . ."

With a snap, Fradrik cast the lightening-whip and struck Liam's back and legs. The glow of the whip was dim and not in full power, but its touch would be enough to send a strong sting through Liam's body, keeping him in his natural form.

Each time Fradrik slashed through the air the sting became stronger, sending Liam's body into a spasm.

Wynneth and Adrianna followed a few steps behind.

"The lair is in the hillside," Wynneth explained casually over one of Liam's more excruciating growls. She pointed to the mound just ahead. "It is called The Sinner's Hill by the Aires people. They say the ashes of those responsible for murders during *The War Against The Angels* were buried in the soil."

"Why?"

Wynneth smiled. "It is just an old folk tale."

The Sinner's Hill was barely thirty feet high and equally as wide. A single maple tree stood steady and proud at its highest point. The auburn leaves, still visible through the darkness of night, were beginning to fade for the winter. The golden shimmer of the maple would weaken, and soon, all of the trees would lose their beautiful colours and turn white for the snowy season. There was no indication that this was anything but an ordinary hill. Adrianna saw no door or outline in the grass. For a moment, she wondered just how they were going to reach the lair, until Alexjander and Durand readjusted their grip on Liam and walked straight into the side of the hill as though it was not there at all. "Where did they go?"

"Maquis just pass right through," said Wynneth. "Normally it only permits dhamphir to enter. The Aires people walk on the hill all the time, but we have made changes to the entrance so that it will also allow you to pass."

"*Could they not simply construct a building?*" Fradrik wondered aloud in his native tongue.

"*It would be much simpler,*" Adrianna said agreeably. "*But perhaps this is a more secretive way to go about for them.*"

As they neared The Sinner's Hill, Wynneth led the way and gave them an encouraging smile over her shoulder. They stepped tentatively into the hillside and felt a rush of cold air. The next moment they found themselves alongside Wynneth in a large, empty foyer.

Directly ahead of them a door opened into a brightly lit room that seemed to be set on a lower level. Durand and Alexjander wrestled Liam into the room, and the door closed firmly behind them. Then, a wrought iron gate slammed shut over the door and locked itself into place.

"Very secure . . ." said Adrianna.

The foyer was a dome-shaped room with highly polished wooden floors, a fireplace on the far left side and comfortable-looking sofas and rugs. The light was kept dim, and Adrianna wondered whether this was because dhamphir were just as sensitive to strong light as their vampire fathers. Wynneth raised her hands and the room grew immediately brighter. Crystals set in the ceiling glowed.

A little dark for my taste, but it is cosy, she thought.

"Here comes Erik," said Wynneth.

The gate through which Liam had been taken opened with a rusty groan, revealing the tall, dark haired Maquis Captain whom Adrianna had clashed with more than once. His scrutinizing gaze landed directly on her and she knew that he too was remembering their last heated argument.

I am not going to argue with him today, she promised herself.

"Are you all right?" Erik asked Wynneth.

"Of course."

"Good. Leena wanted to talk to you when you returned," he said. "Apparently Nadia had another upsetting vision about you."

"I should go and see her then," said Wynneth somewhat resentfully.

"Wait . . . perhaps, we should begin to take her visions a little more seriously," said Erik, with a touch of reservation. "She has been correct a number of times now."

"So, what are you saying? I should abandon my work?" Wynneth asked heatedly. "All because she keeps warning about a *possible* capture?"

"What if it turns out to be true?"

"I do not want to discuss this now. Gyde's putting you up to this, isn't he?"

Erik took too long to answer. "We just think we should err on the side of . . ."

"Keep your noses out of my business. I am a Maquis and I *intend* to do my job. I'll talk to Nadia myself. See you later, and good work," she added to Adrianna and Fradrik.

"That is a great woman you have with you," Fradrik said as Wynneth passed through the gate and walked down a set of steps. "Very courageous."

Erik led them to the sofas by the fireplace. "Yes, thank you. She is a loyal Maquis and a great friend."

Adrianna sat down beside Fradrik, opposite Erik.

"Were you harmed?" Erik asked Adrianna.

"No, I was not."

Erik's eyes wandered over her body for a moment as though to make sure she was not lying.

Adrianna shifted uncomfortably.

"Good," he said, his eyes lingering on her neck.

Fradrik cleared his throat. "I believe you will want to know what happened in the cottage."

Erik leaned back and crossed his legs, moving in the same smooth way as the vampires. "Of course."

Fradrik explained the evening's events. He was very detailed about Liam's transformation and Joa's injuries. He promised the very best care the Gordgáin healers could offer.

"It was best for Joa to be taken in quickly instead of carrying him the distance to the lair," Fradrik concluded.

"Thank you for aiding him," said Erik. "You have further proven your honour with your quick thinking and courage in that difficult situation."

"What will you do with Liam?" asked Adrianna.

"I have sent a scouting party to find his companions," said Erik. "As for the one you brought, he will be questioned and if need be, he will be killed."

"Will you torture him?" she asked, unsure of why she needed to know.

Erik arched a dark eyebrow in question. "Would it bother you?"

Should it bother me? she asked herself. *No, but it does.* Liam was responsible for the deaths of dozens, maybe hundreds, so why should he not be brought to justice? Was it their shared past history? "Well, you see, I knew him when he was a child," she said softly. "He was always a good boy . . ." Her voice drifted away as she realised how feeble her reasoning sounded.

"He is not the little boy you once knew as much as it may pain you to hear it," said Erik. "He is a vampire responsible for many deaths. You will have noticed his eyes?"

"Yes," said Adrianna. "What about them?"

"He has given himself to the Darkness," Erik said coldly. "He is not 'Liam' as you call him, but a willing, *loyal* soldier of Sansul coven. No matter how you may try, how much you want to make yourself believe, *nothing*, not even your beautiful face will break through what he is. Being a vampire is not an ailment simply cured by a potion. Vampires are a race of people; people you would do well to stay away from."

"I understand," she said stiffly. She felt as if he had doused her in cold water.

"I know the loss you feel. Truly, I do, but you will learn to live with it. Forget him."

Adrianna knew she never could forget Liam, but she nodded anyway and pressed on to the messages the Gordgáin had sent her and Fradrik to relay.

Erik too had news. The vampires were not barraging Aires as badly since the witches' escape from Sansul Fortress. The attacks on homes occurred every few days and kidnappings were just as frequent as before, but there had not been an outright battle for over two moons.

"How can that be?" Adrianna asked confusedly. "With Henry awake, you would think they would be giving everything they have."

"True, but we think he is taking his time," replied Erik. "A source has informed us that Henry has been in touch with the Demon High Council. A bigger plan is brewing. I believe Henry is planning to launch something brutal."

"What could it be?" asked Adrianna.

"With Henry, you never quite know," said Fradrik. "But it certainly will be fierce."

"You must also know that the vampire numbers have increased," Erik replied. "Our source confirmed to one of my scouts that another one hundred soldiers are now awake, and more than four dozen vampires have been turned since the attack on your village."

"You believe them to be people from our clan?" Adrianna asked. "Those who did not escape?"

Erik shook his head. "They would have been chosen moons ago," he said. "Vampires rarely turn a person at random. They are selective. Everything is taken into account: power, intelligence, strength, beauty. While you were in captivity, the new vampires now in their ranks were being carefully selected. From your clan and others, they were chosen, assessed and prepared. Then begins a whole process that, thankfully, I am not privy to."

"So they were in the fortress the whole time?" asked Adrianna. "How could we not have come across them during the rescue?"

"They were not in the fortress," Erik replied. "These new vampires were not made there. The Council has reformed their system. It allows them to train their soldiers away from our eyes, to turn people, and for the demons to exercise their power without the Light sensing it."

"That is a frightening thought," said Adrianna. "Where would they get the room for such a place?"

"Your guess is as good as mine," Erik replied. "Which brings me to the most disturbing news. The wolf-men, those now known by some as 'werewolves', have been roaming the lands recently. Free of command."

"They must be the few that the Librarian had in the Laboratory," said Adrianna.

Erik shook his head once. "There are dozens roving the land with nowhere to go and nothing to do but feed."

"Dozens?" Fradrik repeated in disbelief. "How can they make so many?"

Erik shifted his gaze slowly. "The evil genius of the Librarian is not something I have taken the time to study. If these wolf-men are loyal to the vampires then we have an even bigger problem. If they are not, they may be persuaded to join us."

"What if they are loyal?" asked Adrianna. "Is it possible they were released to spy and kill?

"Those would be their main functions," said Erik. "I have men out now following a small pack of them."

Adrianna leaned back as Fradrik handed Erik a letter sent by Simo. Her eyes lingered on Erik's face, watching his lips move as he discussed the letter's contents, though not hearing a word. How did the Maquis kill their prisoners? In all of her life she had never heard of the Wilmota Assembly executing someone. It went against the Lore to take a life, and usually the worst punishment was exile but there had been hardly any call for such things as most people were peaceful.

If trouble occurred, people were capable of defending themselves. Was it right to avenge a death with more death, she wondered? Did the Maquis not fear the repercussions on their souls? Perhaps they did not fear the consequences of murder in the grand scheme of things, after all, to be of the Light did not render you incapable of taking a life. Then again, maybe the Maquis were aware of the cycle of the universe more than the witchery folk.

Did Erik intend to leave Liam in the sun for his crimes? How long would it be before Thomas and Kenna were captured? When Fradrik re-entered the cottage in order to call for help, there had been no sign of Thomas or Kenna. Therefore the potion she had thrown had not worked as intended. For the sake of Kenna's life, she hoped they were out of harm's way because nobody, not even Erik, would be allowed to kill her if Adrianna had anything to say about it.

Gyde emerged through the gate.

The last time Adrianna had seen him, he had left to check the Arch in White Woods and stop its connection to Sansul Fortress. How had he returned before she did? Was there a back entrance to this lair?

Gyde seemed not to notice her or Fradrik.

"You should come through," Gyde told Erik.

"Is it the vampire?" asked Erik.

Liam, she wanted to insist. Why did Erik refuse to call him by his name?

Gyde nodded. "His demon has been sedated. He is talking."

Erik nodded. "We must end this discussion," he said. "I apologise."

Adrianna and Fradrik both stood in acknowledgement.

"I will send word through Wynneth when we have spoken to the vampire," Erik said to them.

Adrianna followed Fradrik out. Just before stepping over the threshold, she turned back to face Erik and Gyde.

"His name is Liam," she told them.

Gyde scowled and disappeared in the direction he came from, but by the look on Erik's face, she knew he understood her meaning. "Liam sent you to the Laboratory and made a name for himself through his ruthlessness. How can you, who suffered so much at his hands, still speak his name?" he asked.

"Some people, including warlocks, believe forgiveness is what makes witches weaker than others," she said. "I do not forgive, and I do see him exactly for what he is. Even though he is what you say, it is difficult to forget what he was. What they *all* were."

"They?"

"It was unfortunate that so many children were captured that night," she said meaningfully. "Some of the mothers still cry . . . even after all these years. Liam's mother killed herself. Do you know what her last words were?"

Erik looked slightly put off.

"I lived to birth a child who will become a killer," said Adrianna. "Just the thought of her only son becoming a vampire was enough to lead her to suicide. I always hoped she would be wrong, but she was correct. That is the saddest part in all of this."

Fradrik wrapped an arm around her shoulders.

"It is easier to think of them as not having lives, as never having a past as ordinary as any of ours," Adrianna said softly.

"I will . . . endeavour to remember," Erik said unsurely.

Adrianna walked with Fradrik into the evening air. She took a deep breath, filling her lungs with the freshness and sighed sadly before following Fradrik down the winding path past the village.

"The village torches are alight," Fradrik observed.

"It is evening. They need to see where they are going," Adrianna replied dully.

"It is not as dead as we were told," said Fradrik.

Adrianna turned her attention to the village. Due to the lanterns, she could see people from where she stood. There were no children, but men and women hurriedly went about their business. No one stopped for conversation, no one looked pleased, and no one seemed to just be out for a walk. Everyone looked as if they had a destination and time was of the essence.

"They seem so worried," she said.

"Because they know it is only a matter of time before the vampires break through the border."

"Aires has shield crystals," said Adrianna. "The vampires cannot pass through those. Wilmota would have been saved if we had had time to raise our shields."

Fradrik patted her shoulder. "We are much better prepared now."

"I hope so. Wait . . ." Adrianna slowed her pace. "If the shields are up, how did Liam, Kenna, Thomas and their soldiers pass the border?"

"Most likely through the Arch the dhamphir mentioned. I assume the Arch works similarly to our Dial Doors," said Fradrik.

"Likely," she agreed.

"By the way, you look pretty in that dress. No wonder Erik could not stop staring at you," he teased.

"Well, thank you for the *half* compliment," she said, smoothing down the folds of her skirt. "I made it in my spare time."

They continued down the path toward the abandoned cottage. Adrianna glanced around with a vague thought of seeing Kenna. *Had she and Thomas escaped?*

Although the perfect autumn evening was cool and still, she could not help but feel as though something was off. It was as if the air was thickening around her, making her skin tingle.

They had reached the end of the path when Fradrik suddenly stopped. The sailor narrowed his eyes, staring between two trees. Adrianna waited for him to continue, but Fradrik seemed to think there was danger there. He motioned for her to remain behind him.

"There is no need to be so protective," said a deep, resonant voice that came from all around them. It was everywhere and nowhere.

Adrianna jumped. She spun around, trying to find the source, but saw no one, only trees and darkness.

"Show yourself!" Fradrik demanded.

"Or what?" the voice asked tauntingly.

Adrianna felt something cold come up behind her. A hand grabbed her arm sharply, holding her still. She took in breath but held it, too frightened to scream. Her skin beneath the stranger's grip began to warm, and the warmth up her arm and into her chest.

"Miss me?" whispered the voice, hot breath in her ear.

"Get off her!" Fradrik roared, opening his palm to reveal an ice-tear.

Adrianna turned around, suddenly unafraid. The familiar sharp silver eyes, smirk and blonde hair made her sigh with relief. She was met with a cheeky half grin she knew was only meant to tease her.

"Are you trying to scare me to death?" she asked, scolding.

"That would not do me any good would it?" Daniel replied. He looked over her head at Fradrik and his grip tightened a little on her shoulders.

"I would not trust him," Fradrik told Adrianna.

"Fine words," Daniel said wryly. "You have not changed. But I am not here to kill you, Fradrik."

"You're a vampire – that alone makes you untrustworthy."

Daniel arched an eyebrow.

"Stop it now," Adrianna said sternly. "There is no need for that!"

"No," said Daniel, looking at Fradrik in the eye. "There is, because I do not intended to stay here with you."

Daniel pulled Adrianna close. Before she had a chance to react she felt herself becoming lighter and her surroundings turned into a blur. She shut her eyes and held him tightly, as she realised she was being lifted away. Then as quickly as the sensation came, it disappeared.

Tentatively, Adrianna opened one eye. The world around her stopped spinning and she found herself in an entirely different place. Slowly, she released her grip on Daniel's arm and sighed with relief. For a moment she felt as though she were going to fall off the end of the earth. It was not a pleasant experience for someone who loathed heights.

"You!" she said furiously, her eyes snapping to his. "What have you done to me?"

"Is that your unique way of saying 'hello'?" asked Daniel.

"And yours was so much better? You have frightened my guardian!"

Daniel looked unmoved. "No one can get to us here."

Here? Adrianna wondered. *Where is exactly are we? What is he doing in Aires?*

Glaring at him, Adrianna noticed how his features had softened. The bright light that blazed through his eyes began to dim so that he looked almost . . . normal.

The room began to spin again. Adrianna put her hands on her knees. "I think I am going to be sick."

"Lovely," he muttered. Pulling her up straight, he placed his hand over her forehead.

The spinning and the floating sensation stopped immediately. "How did you do that?"

"More energy," he said. "I had to use my demon side to bring us here. And you are not used to being handled by that kind of power."

"It was so bizarre."

"Your wound has healed?" he asked, gently lifting her arm to inspect her side.

"Yes," she replied. "Thanks to you. If your demon did not take me away when he did, I would have bled to death. Again."

"I will tell him you said 'thank you'," he said sarcastically.

Adrianna made a face. "Where are we?"

"My . . . home, I suppose you could call it that. I found this place many years ago," said Daniel. "Come . . ."

Daniel led her further into what looked like a large, blue room built in the middle of the ocean. A round crystal floated close to the ceiling, casting a glorious water-toned light over the vast space. It did indeed look like a home. Shelves of neatly filed books and papers lined the walls, and at the far end, over a hand-woven green and gold rug, was an open bedroom.

A large sleigh bed was against the far wall, and a comfortable wing-backed chair faced what looked like an enormous window. Sounds of the ocean filled the room. Adrianna sensed that this place was built in a cliff face beneath the sea.

Adrianna moved toward the chair and saw that the window allowed for a view directly into the sea.

"We are underwater," she marvelled, watching as a school of fish swam by.

"Yes," said Daniel, dimming the crystal's light. "This place is very old. I found it shortly after I was turned. I was sent off to feed, but I went searching. I stumbled into this cave. It is not big, but it is safe. Nobody knows about it but me, not even Liam."

Adrianna felt a pang of guilt. "They have him."

"I know," said Daniel, closer now.

"So, you and he are no longer working together?"

"We have different priorities," said Daniel, standing beside her.

"This place is amazing," she said, seeing a distant light in the sea. "It is so far away from everything."

The familiar tingling of the Pull became more apparent as he remained beside her. There was so much to say, but she did not know where to begin. *How do you start an emotional conversation with a vampire?* she wondered. She was suddenly so tired of thinking, and talking and strategizing and studying. In a romantic way it felt good to be suddenly whisked away to a place unknown. Here, she did not feel guilty about being absent from her duty.

Daniel, I missed you. That was what she wanted to say. But instead, unable to voice the words in her head, she asked, "Do you think it will be over soon?"

"No."

And who cares right now? Adrianna moved closer to him and gently took his arms. With trembling hands, she wrapped them around her and then encircled her own arms around his waist. She could feel he had not embraced anyone in many years, probably since his childhood, but she remained there, comfortable beside him, until he too began to relax into the embrace.

Daniel's aversion to personal contact was just another barrier she knew needed to melt away. It was even more difficult because he was usually so confident.

He moved his face closer to hers, feeling her skin against his. Adrianna blushed as a heat began to grow between them. The incessant tug grew into instinct as they began to move. Daniel held the side of her face in his hand, gently stroking her jaw. Impulsively, Adrianna leaned up and softly kissed the corner of his mouth.

Daniel froze, sucking in a sharp breath.

Adrianna, not put off by his rigidity, kissed him again, lingering. The heat beneath his hands spread throughout her body.

"Daniel, please," she said softly. "Kiss me now."

When she leaned in again, Daniel brought his hands to her face and kissed her deeply. She smiled against his lips. It felt so right, so perfect for them to hold one another this way. The strength of the Pull was there, but the initial shock and disbelief they had felt in the fortress was long gone. Acceptance had made way for their feelings to come free.

Adrianna felt warmth spread in her middle and instinctively pressed herself against him, rising on her tiptoes in an effort to reach all of him. Daniel grabbed her hips possessively, deepening the kiss. Nervously, she ran her fingers through his hair, slowly losing herself in the way he moved.

Daniel pulled away from her lips gradually, as he ran his hands over her hips. His eyes were glazed over with lust and the silver irises shined brightly. Adrianna shivered as his fangs peeked through his lips, and she thought of the way her tongue had brushed against them.

A shiver of anticipation ran down her spine as Daniel stared down at her with a predatory gleam in his eyes. He was so beautiful. His skin and hair were so fair; his eyes so dark and alluring, they held a promise of many pleasurable things.

All thoughts of war, the Gordgáin and suffering were forgotten as Daniel led her to his bed. Adrianna stood still as he walked around her slowly, like a wolf would his prey, his hands gliding over her body. Daniel moved her hair to one side and unbuttoned the back of her dress, letting it fall to the floor. She closed her eyes, and bit her lip nervously, as it tumbled around her feet in a heap. Running his fingers along her neck, down her spine and to her brassiere, he unlaced it. Adrianna felt a rush of nervousness as it joined her other clothes on the floor.

She lifted her arms to cover herself as Daniel stood before her. Gently, he lowered her hands and let his eyes drink in the sight of her. Looking pleased, he ran his hands down her back and across her knickers.

I can do this. Adrianna took a deep breath for courage and pulled off his jacket. She unbuttoned his shirt and ran her hands over his chest before sliding it off. His muscles were incredibly hard and sculpted. Running her fingers over his pectorals, she smiled when his muscles twitched beneath her touch. Her fingers trailed down his muscled middle until they rested on his trousers.

Adrianna hesitated.

Sensing her uncertainty, Daniel brought her hands gently to his front.

Adrianna worked quickly on the buttons, and watched as he divested himself of the rest of his clothes. She had thought him beautiful before, but now he was so much more.

Daniel kissed her softly, taking her bottom lip between his teeth as his hands pulled down her knickers. "You are very soft," he murmured, running his hands over her small waist. With his body against her, Adrianna could truly sense how much Daniel liked her body.

A lustrous white light surrounded them as Daniel lay her down on the bed. Adrianna closed her eyes as he kissed her all over, his hands roaming. Slowly, his lips glided down her middle and he spread her legs. Adrianna squeezed her eyes closed as he ran his fingers over her inner thighs until she began to shake. She whimpered when he dipped his tongue into her navel.

Daniel sensed more about her body than she knew. He knew where to touch her, *how* to touch her. Even when her body shook, he knew how to put her at ease.

The Pull was incessant. The force of it kept drawing them together. Her body ached when his hands were not touching her. Daniel slid up her body, between her legs and kissed her lips, his hand travelling down the length of her at an agonizingly slow pace.

"Open your eyes," he said, the baritone of his voice vibrating.

Adrianna looked at him in the eye and gasped as his fingers touched the sensitive skin between her legs. She squirmed, trying to close her legs but he stilled her with a look.

"You must be relaxed," he said seductively. "Feel the heat from us both." His fangs lengthened slightly.

Adrianna moaned as his touch deepened. Her cheeks flushed with heat. She gripped his arms and arched as his hand worked on her, his eyes drinking in her every move.

Daniel's eyes dilated at the sight of her exposed neck. Arching against him, her head tilted back. His tongue licked a vein that ran from her neck to her breast, stopping at its peak to tease her until her blood became warmer still. His sight locked on her pulse point; her blood hot and thick, he could smell her freshness as her heartbeat raced. His fangs throbbed with the need to sink into her. It would have been perfect, to thrust and bite in unison.

"Do you feel that tug in your middle," he said in her ear as his fingers slowly travelled deeper. "The way your body calls for mine . . . you want me."

Adrianna gasped; her eyes aflame with desire. She nodded.

Daniel scraped his fangs along the tender skin between her breasts. "Say it!"

"I need you," she said, her voice breaking.

Daniel's fangs lengthened fully and his fingers thrust so deep they broke her barrier. His eyes glowed even more brightly as she cried out.

Adrianna dug her nails into his arms while his fingers caressed her after that agonizing movement they had made. A tear ran down her cheek as Daniel removed his hand from her. She moaned, protesting at the emptiness. Daniel's husky laugh made her shiver and open her eyes.

Her blood was on his fingers, and she watched, mesmerised, as he licked the crimson liquid. He delighted at the taste of it. His tongue licked away every red drop before he turned his heated gaze back to her.

"Has the pain gone?" he asked.

The truth was she could not tell. She shook with need; needing to be touched like that again, though without the pain and blood. She was both thrilled and mortified that he had tasted her blood. Whether the physical pain of his taking of her innocence was gone, she could not tell for sure.

"I need . . ."

Daniel grinned, his fangs retreating. "Tell me, Adrianna," he said.

She blushed. "I need to feel," she said as he moved above her.

"This?" he said, pressing himself against her.

"Yes!" she cried, wrapping her legs around his waist instinctively. "Daniel, look at me."

"I am," he said, his hand gliding to her breast.

"With your eyes," she said softly, stroking his face tenderly. She felt so deeply for him, so much more than friendship, so much more than caring.

Daniel's eyes faded to grey as he pressed himself to her.

Adrianna moaned. "*Please* . . . love me."

Daniel did just that, met equally by her tender lust. Each knew what the other needed by sense, as though they had been together for many years before this night.

With her blood coursing through his veins, he was intimately connected to not only her body but also her soul. For the first time in years, he was able to feel emotions. While he made love to her his heart felt open and bare.

Every time she kissed him his heart opened a little bit more. He could feel her blood melding with his, entwining its senses with his own the way their bodies did. He felt raw and exposed. The consummation of *Eriseda* would not be complete without it.

He was surprised that she loved him the way she did. Adrianna met his every move and seduced him as much as he seduced her. His blood burned as he watched her hips move against his, when she screamed for him with a voice so raw with need and love it took all his willpower not to reach the blissful ecstasy they worked toward. As their fever built, the light that enveloped them began to grow.

The bed became a mess of tangled sheets, entwined limbs and sweat.

Adrianna looked down at Daniel's beautiful face as she rocked her hips above his. His blonde hair stuck to his face and shoulders in the most carefree way. It made her smile. All her inhibitions were now gone as she brought him closer to bliss. She braced herself against his chest as he gripped her hips and pounded harder and harder into her.

She stroked his face, gliding her thumb across his lips. She gasped as he took her thumb in his mouth, pricking the soft flesh with a fang. Feeling her blood rush into his mouth, she watched as Daniel sucked feverishly, his eyes darkening.

As Daniel sat up and pulled her mouth to his, she wrapped one arm around his shoulders and with her other hand she laced her fingers with his.

Adrianna cried out and leaned her forehead against his when finally, he thrust up, the white light glowed ever more brightly and their bodies stiffened as waves of ecstasy rushed through them.

Adrianna collapsed in his arms as the light began to dim. They lay motionless, still joined, as their heartbeats slowed. When the light was gone, the seal was forged; the consummation of *Eriseda* complete.

Peeling herself from Daniel's body, Adrianna lay down beside him, but he held her close, rolling onto his side to face her. He wrapped a strong, possessive arm around her slim body and kissed her.

"I knew it would feel good," she confessed, "but that was incredible."

"You surprised me," he said. "Do you regret it?"

Adrianna frowned. "No, why?"

"You are bound to me," he said. "You bound yourself to a vampire."

"I do not think of you like that. You are Daniel and I love you."

"Love."

"Vampires do not feel love," she said, wanting to shut away the pang of disappointment.

"I felt it when I tasted your blood. You gave me emotions I have not felt in too many years. Believe me, I felt it. Truly and deeply. But now that we are not joined, it has faded."

"So you love me?" she asked hopefully.

Daniel looked hesitant. She could tell he wanted to stay it, but his lips could not form the words.

Adrianna placed her fingers over his lips, smiling sadly. "It is all right," she whispered. "I *know*."

Daniel held her close, breathing in her scent. Her body moulded perfectly to his and slowly relaxed against him. With a wave of his hand, the covers moved up over their bodies. Adrianna buried her face in the crook of his neck.

"Daniel . . ." she said sleepily. "I like your underwater home."

His soft laugh made her smile.

Chapter Nineteen

Henry's Council

T HE COUNCIL HALL WAS in danger of frosting.

Surrounded by high indigo walls the black marble floor reflected a dim glow that emanated from oil lamps hanging from four stone pillars. The centre of the marble floor was lower than the outer edge by three steps. The room was stark, furnished with two small tables, each with four seats, which were placed opposite one another at the head of the room.

Three vampires sat at the right table while the left was unoccupied.

The three were on edge, anxiously awaiting his arrival. With their black eyes avoiding one another's gaze and fangs extended so that the tips of their lethal incisors were visible, bursts of misty air rushed from their mouths with every shallow breath. Their silence was as bitter as the cold that penetrated their clothes and sank into their flesh. The thirst for blood had reached a boiling point in the fortress ever since Henry had banned hunting. Blood-thirst was painful to vampires. It gnawed deep, making them think and act like wild animals.

The creaking of the double doors echoed through the room as they opened.

Fully rejuvenated, Henry strode into the Council Hall clad head to toe in black. His tailcoat was crisply tailored. His fire-red hair fell perfectly around his narrow face. His boots made no sound on the marble floor. Behind him were three soldiers and two councillors, Thomas and Pandema.

Pandema was a statuesque woman. With her porcelain skin and tumbling, red curly hair and blood-red lips she resembled a delicate handcrafted doll more than killer. The Ice Maiden, they called her. Her black emotionless eyes locked on the three vampires, making them shiver involuntarily.

"Morgan, Brendan, Hammer," Henry said briskly. "What is the status?"

"We followed your orders and went as close to Aires as possible, avoiding the Arch. The Maquis have removed the crystal from the Arch in the White Wood, preventing us from using it to travel anymore," said Brendan, purposefully avoiding looking at Pandema as she seated herself at the empty table. "Liam is definitely a prisoner."

"Of the Maquis or the Gordgáin?" asked Henry, narrowing his green eyes.

"The Maquis. We got one of those wolf-men to nose around for us," Brendan continued. "The Maquis are holding him in a secret location. Apparently, the witch he used to have in captivity here is responsible for bringing him to them."

Henry frowned. "I have heard too many mentions of that witch whenever Liam is involved. Where is Nikita?"

"Returned to his coven. As did Daniel," Thomas answered.

"Daniel was always a fine soldier, a magnificent male," Pandema said silkily. "But when that *witch* was around he was . . . different."

"Kill her! You deal with it," Henry ordered of Hammer. "Apparently you are skilled at making people disappear."

Hammer inclined his head. "She will no longer be a burden."

"And you," said Henry, turning to Thomas. "I want you to find this Daniel - find him and kill him. When you have completed that task, I want Nikita back here. Make sure it is done before the next solstice."

"How could you possibly convince Nikita to come?" asked Pandema, her voice low and sweet.

Thomas inclined his head to Henry. "There may be a problem. Both Nikita and Daniel are of the Azria coven. They are protected by Blood Bequeath."

"Azria is the most powerful coven in Sansul," said Pandema, "until now," she added hastily when Henry fixed her with a glare. "The Blood Bequeath is strong. Its borders of protection extend to wherever a coven member is. If Nikita and Daniel do not want to be found by us, they won't be."

"Lasso them if you must," said Henry coolly.

"And Liam?" asked Pandema.

"Brendan and Morgan take your men and mount a rescue," said Henry. "Liam knows too much to be left behind."

"How do you know he has not already betrayed us?" asked Thomas.

"I know," Henry replied. "You . . ." He turned to the two soldiers flanking Pandema. "I want every vampire in this fortress in this Council Hall immediately."

As they waited, Henry paced up and down the length of the room. Pandema and Thomas sat unmoving. Morgan, Brendan and Hammer spoke quietly amongst themselves.

"Can you handle the job, Hammer?" asked Morgan.

"Better than Liam could," Hammer replied, earning himself a warning glare from Pandema.

"Rein in your flippancy until you have proven yourself to be worthy of more respect than Liam," she said, her voice low and even.

"Am I not worthy of respect? I sit on this Council," he replied, shooting her a look of loathing.

A placating smile flashed over Pandema's face. "For now."

Henry had just reached the head of the room when the double doors opened and the coven entered in pairs. Hundreds of pale men and women with blood-red lips and stoic expressions streamed through. Kenna was amongst them, her body adorned in a purple lace gown.

The vampires parted in the middle of the room and stood on either side, taking seats on the raised outer platform. The men stood and the women sat. Elegantly, the women were seated on low stools, their backs straight and their appearances faultless. The men stood in perfect formation: one behind a woman and one beside.

Henry moved to the centre of the room when everyone had taken a place. Nobody dared to speak. Their sole focus was the charismatic figure they had awakened to lead them back to glory. "I have called this meeting because of recent events that are due to be addressed," he began. "This coven enslaved the witchery clan of Wilmota, plunging the highlands into a state of war and discord. There was little planned with regards to what to *do* with them once they were captured, and they were left to dwell in the underground chambers. Thanks to the unapproved work of the Librarian, we are responsible for the creation of the wolf-men. *Filthy beasts*, created through the donation of vampire blood. In the meantime, the Gordgáin and Maquis joined forces. In collaboration, they rescued our captive witches from the fortress, warlocks from the mines, and children from the goblin cages."

Henry paused and looked into the faces of his people. "Do you wish for applause?" He clapped three times, neither pleased nor angry. There was just contempt etched in his brilliant eyes.

"If I had not allowed the Gordgáin and Maquis to leave this fortress with the witches, I would not be worthy of calling myself Chancellor. We are not prepared for the inter-plane war that would have resulted. And as much as the angels cower at the sound of the word Vahir they would have taken up arms against us and a repeat of history would ensue! This Council . . ." He pointed to the platform at the head of the room, "is not complete. Four council men and women have lost their lives. Rex, Giulia, Simon and Fiona – all were not protected from our enemies. The murderer will be found, for vampire blood on the hands of another is illegal!"

Kenna looked to Thomas. Both he and Pandema were engrossed in Henry's speech. She had a feeling that things were about to turn for the worse.

"We are due revenge, we *deserve* revenge – but the cost of the Council's failure has been high! Where are the legions? Where are the warlords? Where are the plans? Our allies? After this *shameless* show of failure how can our allies be confident to side with us again?" he asked rhetorically. "We have shown the world that Sansul coven has no structure, strength or honour. We inspired fear in the nymphs, faeries and centaurs, who now cower in the forests. The mer-people no longer come above the water, abandoning the land folk. The City of Tents is too far to give aid. I expect – at the least – if the Council decides to plunge our coven into a war then it will do so with a plan for victory. Every battle must be won. Every opponent must be conquered. Every soldier must have blood. But the plan was flawed. Wilmota was *ours* for the taking and the Council failed! HOW CAN THIS HAVE ALL GONE SO WRONG?"

Kenna began to feel nervous.

Ever since Henry's awakening things had become unbearably strict around the fortress. The vampires who had any persona were now quiet, obedient. They often took the form of their demons and convened in private according to race. The few Baál in the fortress did not show themselves, and if they did, it was only with Jeith in company. Lasé demons remained quiet, tactfully gathering information from the discontented Rakasha who had been forced to remain within the fortress walls on Henry's orders.

Henry was ruthless in making the fortress in his image: ordered, loyal, un-questioning, faultless and brutal. Protection was doubled and all references to elemental magic were prohibited. Talk of their lives before becoming a vampire 'did not exist.'

"My past speaks for itself," Henry said confidently, striding past them. Kenna watched as his eyes lingered on a recently changed vampire named Sara, one of the kidnapped witches and mother to young boys. "I have fought the angels, defeated the Warlock Myriad and come face-to-face with the Maquis and fought their leader in hand-to-hand combat. *I* will lead us back to greatness."

Everyone began to murmur and Kenna finally caught Thomas' eye. Kenna bit down on her tongue. Thomas's eyes shone with pride, relief even. Blood filled her mouth as she held her tongue, fighting the urge to cry out.

"This Council needs reformation," said Henry, turning to face the blanched councilmen. "My first call will be to awaken Byron. With his aid we will return Sansul coven to the glory of its past."

"*Byron,*" Morgan hissed in Brendan's ear. "With him here we will have no power at all."

"We can be great again," Henry addressed his coven. "We *will* be great again!"

~

Their legs were tangled. Adrianna was on her stomach, her dark hair strewn across the pillow she held with her outstretched arms. Daniel had moved her hair so as to better see her face. Now he ran his fingers gently down her spine.

He had spent hours exploring her body while she slept, tracing every curve and line, front and back. She was very ticklish he found when he touched her ribs beneath her breasts. As the moment he put his lips to her neck she melted. He noted that for future use.

Adrianna reached out and touched the 'v' shaped tattoo on his right pectoral. He had a bear paw tattooed on his pelvic bone that she found very alluring, and ancient words were written on his left shoulder blade. The 'v' shape had many curves and points. It was beautifully set against his pale skin. It looked like a figure usually seen in mist or smoke.

"It is very pretty," she said. "Is it a symbol for something?"

"Not really. Adrik did it for me during our combat training," Daniel said casually.

"Adrik? Lachlan's brother, Adrik?"

"Yes." Something flickered in Daniel's eyes. "He stayed much the same, even after the change."

"Well, that is good, isn't it?"

"Not for him. He was the best of all of us, the most loyal man you'd ever know. He drew symbols and images on those who came to him. He said this reflected what I was feeling at the time."

She smiled. "Artists are like that. What do you mean 'he was'?"

"He was killed."

"I am so sorry."

"It was a long time ago."

"I can tell it bothers you."

"It bothers me that decent men die, and those who deserve death live on."

"I am sure Adrik found peace on the Spirit Plane." She lifted her head and kissed his nose. "The words on your back, what do they say?"

"Life is the one you make," he said.

"Poetic. What does it mean?"

"Do not try to kill your soul mate," he said wryly.

Adrianna laughed. "Ah, now he realises," she teased.

"When I was turned, I could not believe this was what my fate was to be. I had it written to remind me that I had the power to change anything."

"You do not like being a vampire?" she asked curiously.

"It is what it is."

"What was it like?"

"A nightmare."

"Did any others survive along with you, aside from Adrik?"

Daniel did not answer immediately. He had a strange look on his face, as though he was sifting through the many memories. "After the change, some died and some went on to have good lives as vampires. Normal lives really."

"Did Tobias live?"

Daniel's jaw stiffened. "No," he said softly, rolling onto his back. His eyes stared fiercely at the ceiling. "No, Tobias is dead. Rightfully so."

"Oh. I cannot believe the misfortune of Kenna's family. First Black Magick witches murder their parents. Then Tobias is turned, and now Kenna. There is nobody left of their line. No cousins even . . ."

"It happens."

"Do you miss your mother?"

"Sometimes . . . emotions like that disappear after the change."

"You mean, you do not care about seeing her again, or you do not know how to?"

"A bit of both."

"She moved to Aires, you know. I do not think she could take the memories of Wilmota anymore."

"Yes, I know."

"In that book I read at the fortress, it said that vampires could lose themselves to their demons," she said. "Is that what happened to Liam?"

"Yes."

"You would never let yourself be overcome, would you?"

"Never. Baliath has no need to take over me or destroy my consciousness. Only weak vampires are destroyed by their own demons. Baliath's powers only make me stronger."

"Is that how we got here? Baliath's power?" She asked because she knew no elemental was able to simply appear and disappear at will, at least, not without magical help. It was quite impossible.

"Two demon races have the ability to project themselves across vast spaces. Knor demons leave a trace of smoke when they disappear, but Vermillion's do not. A Vermillion, that is Baliath's race, can control their surroundings similar to Projection Power, but they do it without words. The Darkness works in a very different way from the Light and their abilities are totally different. The Darkness is in the core of demons and seeps into its surroundings."

"Like the fortress. The Darkness is in the walls and everything . . ."

"Precisely. Demons do not use elemental magic, and not all vampires use it either. The most steadfast vampire will not have anything to do with elemental power because they believe it is not their 'natural' ability."

"But they are elementals. Darkness or not."

"Yes, but they view themselves as separate."

"Does it hurt when you transform into Baliath?"

"Every time. It used to be agony, now it is just a sting. I grew into this body to cope with the change."

"Can you eat normal food? I read that vampire bodies change to accommodate the blood they drink, but I would hate to think you would never eat a pastry again!"

Daniel watched her for a moment. "It really is the simple things in life that please witchery folk, isn't it?"

Adrianna smiled. "Yes. Festivals, fireworks and food."

"Have you beaten your record of ten pastries a day?"

"I am now on five and ten," she said proudly. "I won't be trying to best that. I reached my record on Yule two years ago, and Kenna had to stay up all night and make me take a Stomach Easing Potion."

"*Why* would you eat five and ten in one day?"

"Because Ralphus ate four and ten," she said, as though her reasoning was unquestionably sound. "I could not just let him beat *my* record."

Daniel smirked. "Strange witch, you are."

Adrianna nestled closer to him so their bodies were pressed together. "I missed you a lot," she said softly, resting her head on his chest. "I thought you were dead for so long."

"It was probably for the best," he replied.

"No one locked me in old shacks anymore," she said, smiling.

Daniel held back a laugh, but he smiled at the memories. Her grin startled him. There was no suppression or nervousness in it. Her eyes shone brightly as she looked up at him. She also had the most infectious laugh he had ever heard. He ran his fingers along her ribs and she shuddered and laughed as she begged him to stop. He had not noticed the happiness in her smile until now.

Adrianna frowned at his staring. "What?"

"You're very beautiful," he confessed. Though his tone was not soft and loving, his voice deepened and was laced with satisfaction and something else that Adrianna could not quite name. "Your smile is quite radiant. You should smile more."

Adrianna blushed. They were the last words she had expected to hear from him. She knew he found her attractive. It was one of the things most important to a vampire when taking a lover. "Thank you."

Daniel gathered her up and carried her out of the bed and into a small passageway Adrianna had not noticed earlier. She heard a gentle trickling of water and smelled soft, woody fragrances. It was dark inside but the crystals embedded in the stone came to life upon their arrival, illuminating a small washroom. In the centre was a circular bath-like system. The ground in the middle was hollowed out for the bath, which was filled with steaming water. Perched on the far end of the bath were a few coloured bottles and linens.

Daniel released her when he stepped into the water. The water came up around her chest, and Adrianna only unravelled her arm from around his neck when she was sure it was not too hot.

"Amazing! What is this?" she asked.

"Mineral water," he replied. "This was part of the cave when I found it. Someone had lived here once. Obviously this was used for bathing."

"Where does the water come from?"

"The spout," he said, nodding to the silver tube that was filling the bath. "The mineral water comes through from the Jewelled Falls."

"Remarkable," she said, looking at the glowing water. "How does it stay so warm?"

"I put a charm on it."

Adrianna grinned. "So you use witchery now? You keep surprising me, Daniel. How many more secrets do you have?"

"Many," he replied, running his hands over her hips.

Yet again, Daniel proved himself to be an enigma. His secrets were his own and his honour was unquestionable, yet all of these facets brought forth many more questions. Adrianna did not think there could be another side to Daniel other than the condescending, arrogant, cold and influential vampire who had kept her a prisoner in the fortress, but once again she had been proven wrong. Daniel could never be a sweet speaking, enamoured, sonnet-writing lover but she did not want him to be. She liked him as he was; the man he was when he was with her.

There were so many questions she wanted to ask. Why did he occupy this cave? Why was he not at Sansul? Who was it he communicated with outside the fortress? How did he want to proceed with her? What was he doing in the war? She needed so many answers . . .

After washing and cleansing themselves, the time came for Daniel to return her. It was almost sundown. He waited patiently by the door as Adrianna slipped on her shoes. In accordance with their plan, she made sure to make herself look a little shaken and worn, as if she had escaped from capture.

"Good enough?" she asked, turning around.

Daniel nodded.

"I do not think they will believe me so easily," she said nervously. "Gyde will be able to see through it for sure."

"Fradrik saw your capture," said Daniel. "He will not refute the story."

Adrianna nodded. "Make sure to arrive outside the village. I do not want you to be captured too."

"As you wish," he replied, taking her hand.

Adrianna closed her eyes as a tingling sensation erupted in her stomach. No longer was the cave floor beneath her feet, but grass. She blinked. They were on the outskirts of Aires in the time it took to take a breath. A pale glow was on the horizon. It was just after sunset.

"Dizzy," she said, a little wobbly. "I do not think I will ever get used to this mode of travel."

"Don't move too fast, you will be all right," he said.

As the wind picked up, Adrianna looked around them. "You should go. The Maquis are everywhere and the night-watchers see everything. Well . . ." she said, thinking back to how Liam, Kenna and Thomas had somehow snuck into Aires, "almost everything."

Daniel looked at her for a moment. He seemed hesitant to leave, and then he swiped a kiss, and was gone. The touch of his fingers still lingered on her hand. She instantly felt the separation. It was deep and lonely. She wanted to call him back to take her with him. It felt so sudden. One moment she had his protection and the next she was alone.

Adrianna took a deep breath and walked around the village to the abandoned cottage outside of White Woods. She spotted a light through a group of trees and followed it. Walking as quietly as she could, she found herself outside the cottage within a few moments.

"Who goes there?" someone said sharply.

Adrianna gasped as a group of people emerged from their hiding places. Simo and Durand jumped out of the two trees, landing beside her. Mathena and Gralam came around the side of the cottage, and somebody slinked up behind her. Her arm was snatched and twisted behind her back.

"Stop!" Mathena cried. "Stop – it's Adrianna!"

"What are you doing?" Adrianna snapped at Gyde. "Let me go!"

Gyde released her as Mathena ran forward.

"We were so worried," she cried, holding her tightly. "Fradrik came running back saying you had been kidnapped by a vampire. We've been searching all night and day!"

"I am perfectly fine," Adrianna told her, nervously. "A little shaken, you know, they are not very nice. But I am fine."

Gyde watched her suspiciously. Adrianna felt very anxious. He was a dhamphir. He knew the tactics the vampires used. She had a feeling Gyde would very likely have been able to recognise the vampire scent on her. She had no marks or bruises, her clothes were intact and she did not smell of blood. Adrianna could almost hear his thoughts.

"Let's get you inside then," Wynneth said softly. "We should talk . . . just us girls."

"I am all right," she insisted.

Fradrik emerged from within the cottage, but instead of looking relieved, he was angry. He grabbed her by the shoulders and for the first time, spoke his mother tongue in front of strangers. "*What did he do to you?*"

"*Nothing,*" she replied. "*They cannot know anything,*" she spoke in a broken accent, motioning to those around them. "*All they need to know is one of them took me and I escaped.*"

"*Then you will tell me the truth! What you are doing is madness!*"

"Excuse me, but is it really necessary right now?" asked Mathena.

"*He saved my life . . .*" She gave him a meaningful look.

The anger in Fradrik's face slowly faded, he embraced her tightly. "*Running off is reckless.*"

"*It was not my idea, but I will not go again.*"

"We should go now," said Wynneth.

The heavy, twisting guilt in the pit of her stomach made Adrianna feel sick as she followed Mathena inside the cottage. They all climbed down the trapdoor, into the tunnel and through to the sanctuary where everyone clapped at her return. There were many cheers and whistles as she passed which only served to deepen the shame that had drained the colour from her face. She just wanted to cry.

Mathena led Adrianna up the stairs and down the eastern hall to their room. Wynneth followed, leaving Gyde and Durand with Gralam and Simo. When they arrived, Orla cried out in relief.

"I was so scared," she said tearfully. "I hoped and hoped that whoever kidnapped you did not . . . did not *brand* you, like I was."

Adrianna swallowed painfully. She thought back to the night in the underground chambers when Orla confessed to being branded. Staining the young witch's skin, on her left shoulder blade, was a tattooed image: the Sansul insignia, and the name of the vampire that 'owned' her, André.

"Come on," Mathena urged.

Once inside the room, Mathena turned and spoke in a soft voice toward the door. Wynneth, Orla and Adrianna sat down on one of the beds as Mathena finished the charms that would ensure their privacy.

"Where is Rose?" Adrianna asked, looking at the empty fourth bed.

"I think she is helping with the infirmary stocks," said Orla, watching her closely. "Are you all right?"

Mathena turned to Adrianna sharply and said, "Can we talk freely?" She gave Adrianna a meaningful look and motioned to Wynneth.

"I think so," said Adrianna.

"I can tell already," Wynneth said casually. "And I think it is an unwise thing to continue."

"How could you know?" Adrianna asked incredulously.

"My mother had an affair with a vampire and it caused her nothing but heartache," Wynneth replied. "As a dhamphir I can sense these things, and I can smell the scent of a vampire from leagues away."

"You saw a vampire?" Orla asked softly. "Willingly?"

"Did he hurt you?" Mathena asked with her arms crossed.

"No!" Adrianna said indignantly. "No, he is not like that. Well he is, he's very condescending and brash and cold with people, but . . ."

"Not with you?" Wynneth finished. "It's like my mother. You must stop it! It could hurt our cause and worse, it could hurt *you*. You don't know for sure if he cares about you or wants information."

"He has not asked for any," said Adrianna. "He does not need it."

"Why?"

"Because he is not the kind of vampire to leave himself . . . uninformed," she said, grasping for anything to satisfy their questions.

"I just hope that every time you leave this sanctuary he isn't going to whisk you off again," said Mathena. "I am all for love affairs, the Light knows I have had my share, but not in the middle of a war like this."

Orla looked very disturbed. "You can't trust them," she said softly.

"I do not trust them, I trust *him*," replied Adrianna. "Do not think badly of me!"

"I don't," Orla replied. "I just worry. I know you would never betray us for anything, but you don't know for sure that he would not betray you."

"You will not tell, will you?" said Adrianna.

"No, of course not," said Wynneth. "But I have a feeling Gyde knows. And most of the others. Remember, we have a good sense of these things. Just promise that if the vampire comes around again you will tell him you cannot go."

"All right," said Adrianna. She felt so pressured, so tired and strained.

Mathena grinned. "It was good to see him again though, right?" she asked cheekily.

Adrianna couldn't help but blush. "Of course," she said in a small voice.

"If you think about it," Wynneth said seriously, "it is quite a romantic thought."

Orla smiled shyly. "Oh, yes, being whisked away by someone mysterious to a secret location," she said breathily. "In the middle of a war for a passionate night together . . ."

Adrianna buried her face in her hands. "Stop it, it sounds awful," she said, embarrassed.

"The feeling of danger and excitement," Wynneth said dramatically, enjoying the way it made her friend so embarrassed. "The *unknown* . . ."

"But you knew the strong vampire would protect you," Mathena interjected. "I can just imagine it – the moon above, the two of you talking so sweetly . . ."

Adrianna began to laugh as the three of them gestured theatrically.

"His kiss so cold, and yet so sweet," said Wynneth.

Adrianna clutched her side as tears came to her eyes. It looked so ridiculous; three grown women acting like old gypsy dramatic actors putting on a show. "Stop," she cried, "that is so mean."

Mathena tried to stop laughing. "If you think about it, this whole situation is quite absurd!"

"That did not happen!" Adrianna snapped as the women continued to laugh hysterically.

It was quite an amusing story; she could admit it.

"My life . . ."

"We are going to have to think of a story for why he let you go," said Wynneth.

"I escaped," said Adrianna. "He turned his back and I ran."

"It is too loose," Wynneth said dismissively. "Surely the vampire came up with a better story."

Adrianna sighed. "Pretend he is one of Liam's soldiers," she began. "He stayed back after Liam's capture and took me . . ."

~

There were swift changes occurring in the Aires sanctuary. As warlocks and dhamphir worked closely together for a common goal, acquaintance grew to friendship and misgiving made way for trust. Men and women who would have otherwise refused to eat at the same table as a dhamphir, openly welcomed their new allies. Deep gratitude played a role in this for the witches and warlocks of Wilmota who knew their salvation was in part due to the Maquis. The Maquis, though always guarded, seemed open to the new appreciation and were welcoming of the new bonds that formed.

Ralphus, Mathias and Cedar were especially curious about Alexjander and spent many a meal discussing his steel-Mohawk. "And women like it?" asked Mathias.

Alexjander laughed, though he was slightly bashful. "What do you think?"

"I am getting one," said Mathias with conviction. "Mohawks are magnets for women."

Ralphus and Cedar shook their heads but did not bother to argue with him.

One particular Maquis was around more often than necessary. Adrianna noticed Gyde always seemed to be in her vicinity, and she had begun to suspect the Maquis Captain, Erik, was behind it. Weeks went by, and Adrianna forced herself to ignore him. Until one evening, she had had enough. She slammed her cutlery down, excused herself from the table glaring across the room at him and quickly left the dining room.

"Adrianna!" Gyde called, coming up behind her on the staircase.

"Oh, *what*? Want to search my room for hidden objects? Check my mind to see if I have been tainted? You will not find anything, and I am *sick* of you following me everywhere. *Stop it*!"

"You are a very stupid woman."

Adrianna struck him hard across his face with all the strength she could muster. Her regret was instant, especially as he did not react. Gyde stood before her as though nothing had happened. Her hand stung but she was bitter and did not care. Who was *he* to tell her she was stupid?

"I do not care what you think."

Gyde took a step toward her. "Going around with a vampire is foolish."

"And you know this how?" she asked indignantly, stepping back.

Gyde stared for a long moment, assessing her. "You don't know the true nature of a vampire," he said finally. "You fool yourself if you think he cares for you at all. Don't ruin your life for something like that."

"I am not hiding anything that will hurt anyone."

"I know. You're not a traitor. But you are too innocent to see that you are in love with someone who does not exist."

Adrianna felt a surge of anger at his words. "How can you say that to me?"

"I have seen women like you before. You are fooling yourself if you think you have a chance at a normal, healthy life with that man," said Gyde. "Baliath is strong in him. I was there when he saved you from that demon during the rescue mission. No matter what, a demon is not loyal to anyone. A demon's only aim is to destroy. Make life easy on yourself . . ."

"Well, thank you for your opinion and insight," Adrianna said snidely. "But I do not know what you are talking about." She turned sharply and climbed the rest of the stairs with shaky legs. The truth of his words was heavy, almost painful.

"Wait."

"No, thank you," she said, almost to the door of her temporary, shared bedroom.

"*Wait.*"

"What?" she cried, frustrated.

Gyde did not seem at all perturbed. "You might want to watch that temper of yours."

"Do not tell me what to do. What do you want?"

"The vampire we captured," he said. "He wishes to see you."

Adrianna raised her eyebrows. "Liam? But why?"

"Before a vampire is put to death, we grant them one visit, sometimes," said Gyde. "You were his choice. It is an old custom, not mine. If it were up to me, I would have sent him to the sun weeks ago."

"Put to death?" Adrianna asked numbly.

"The Maquis and the Gordgáin believe this to be the best punishment. His soul will not be tarnished. The demon will be killed when it separates from the body."

Adrianna shivered. "I do not want to know the process. Have you learned all you can from him?"

"Somewhat."

Adrianna nodded sadly. It was an indescribable feeling, knowing that someone was about to die. She did not agree with this practice but she had no right to interfere with how the Maquis worked. "Let me think on it," she said softly.

"I must have your answer by morning," said Gyde. "He dies tomorrow at sunset."

"Sunset?"

"The falling sun is strongest," he said simply before leaving.

Adrianna could not stop tears that threatened to fall. She had held them back when they began to prickle but hearing the date of his death being spoken so casually made her realise that he was so alone in the world. He was evil and heartless, but he had been good once, and he had saved her life in the beginning of the war. She wanted to remember him the way he was before he was turned. After all, he had been turned as a child, against his will.

Adrianna sat down on her bed and stayed there for what felt like hours in complete numbness. She did not hear her friends enter the room and only snapped out of her trance when Wynneth clicked her fingers in front of her face.

"Still with us?" asked Mathena, squeezing her shoulder affectionately.

"They are going to kill Liam at sunset tomorrow."

Wynneth's face fell. "I told Gyde not to tell you," she said, irritated.

"Liam requested to see me," said Adrianna, ashamed that she had slapped this good woman's husband. "That is why Gyde told me. Why are they going to kill him? I know that deep down *he* is not evil; it is his demon. It has so much influence over him." She broke down into sobs and leaned into Mathena as she wrapped her arms around her.

"Maybe you can convince the Maquis not to kill him," Orla suggested.

"He condemned many children to death and sent dozens down to the Laboratory," Wynneth told Orla. "I know he was your friend long ago Adrianna, but he is not that man anymore."

"How can you be so sure?" Adrianna asked breathlessly through her tears. Her face was red and her eyes puffy.

"I saw his eyes," said Wynneth. "Down where we keep him. I saw his eyes and there was nothing left there. When we brought the demon forward he cursed all of us, and everyone we knew to death and suffering at the hands of the Darkness. He swore revenge on us all if he ever escaped."

"Adrianna . . ." Mathena crouched down in front of her. "Liam is evil. Put aside your feelings of your childhood together and see what is in front of you. He sent you to *die* in the Laboratory. Liam, as you knew him, does not exist. He has evolved into something else and must die."

"I know."

"Do you really? Do you really see the reasons why we must destroy him?"

"I do."

Rose entered the room with her arms full of herbs, small boxes and two pitchers. Wynneth went and eased her of the load. Flushed, Rose thanked her quickly and turned around to the three witches on the bed.

"You will never believe what I just heard!"

"What is it, Rose?" asked Adrianna.

"Those soothsayers we sent to Bruniér have been killed," said Rose.

Mathena stood slowly. "What?"

"How?" asked Adrianna.

"They were murdered on the outskirts of Bruniér," said Rose. "One of the messengers said it was the work of a vampire named Hammer."

"Hammer!" cried Wynneth.

"He is one of the Sansul assassins," said Adrianna. She remembered one of Daniel's men, Rowan, mentioning Hammer.

"And a member of the Sansul Council," Wynneth added. "Did the messenger say how the soothsayers were found?"

Rose shook her head. "But the Bruniér soothsayer was nowhere to be found. Apparently he disappeared from the village days ago without a trace. The vampires went to his home on the beach and found it had been abandoned."

"Three dead soothsayers," Adrianna muttered. "One missing. It makes no sense."

"Pity they did not *see* it coming," Orla added, her lip curling. "You would think with all their *foresight* they'd at least see their own deaths."

"One thing does not make sense to me," said Mathena. "How could Hammer know who they were and where they were travelling?"

"It could have been an accident," said Wynneth. "Perhaps he just stumbled upon them."

"No, quite a few people knew that the soothsayers were going to Bruniér," said Adrianna, shaking her head. "Someone must have told."

"How? And who here would tell a vampire anything?"

"Black Magick conjurers, sorceresses," Mathena said as if running down a list, "there are plenty of people."

"I hope they are caught," said Adrianna.

"What benefit would it be to the vampires if a few soothsayers were dead?" Orla asked. "It does not make any sense."

"Soothsayers can point out traitors, can't they?" said Adrianna. "Perhaps the traitor needed them out of the way."

"Everyone needs to be much more careful," Rose said, opening one of the boxes she had brought in. She pulled out a crow's foot, cringing, and dropped it in the small cauldron in the corner of the room.

"What are you making?"

"It's one of Dahlia's recipes," said Rose. "Apparently it rots demon flesh."

"It must be complicated," said Adrianna, going to the cauldron.

Rose added a spoon of slug skins and aged owl blood. The cauldron began to emit a deep red vapour and a woody, forest scent. "It is about to get very unsavoury," said Rose. "You may want to leave for a while."

"Why is she having you do this?"

Rose sighed. "She has other things to do. I do not mind helping, I just wish I did not have to handle animal parts."

"I will help you," said Adrianna, rolling back her sleeves. "Now let's see here . . . powdered Rakasha bones, yuck, and a drop of viper venom after stirring the potion seven times and removing the crow's feet. How disgusting!"

CHAPTER TWENTY

The Demon's Bounty

ADRIANNA STOOD BEFORE THE prison door with her mind set and her heart in her throat. The journey from the entry of the Maquis lair to the prison had led her down a flight of steep stone steps, through a titanium door that locked from the outside with three separate keys and down a narrow, low-ceilinged hall made entirely of cedar wood. Fire-spheres in glass orbs hovered close to the ceiling, providing dim light.

"Are you ready?"

Adrianna hid her clammy hands in her coat pockets and nodded. Wynneth gave her a small smile and knocked on the door. Adrianna's stomach felt heavy and a flutter rose up between her ribs to her heart. "I am not ready," she replied to Wynneth.

The door swung inward revealing a square room made of wood and stone, at the centre of which was a damp, abused figure held in spiked chains. A single orb glowed above the figure, dousing him in pure white light.

Sickened, Adrianna stepped slowly into the room. The Darkness was thick in the air, tingling her lungs. She let out a small cough. Erik and Gyde stood on either side of the door, while the turquoise-eyed dhamphir Orion stood behind the figure to the right and Durand, the left.

Pity poured from her as she gazed upon Liam. The spiked chains that wrapped around his wrists were nailed into the ceiling, keeping his arms above his bowed head. Blood dripped down his forearms and torso from where the small, thorn-like spikes dug into his flesh. He kneeled on the floor, his clothes damp with sweat.

Adrianna looked to Erik, angry that he had been presented this way. They could have tried to keep him in a more dignified manner, instead of the same way in which the vampires incarcerated their captured enemies. Erik looked right back at her, neither apologetic nor interested in her reaction.

Durand dimmed the light of the orb with a wave of his hand as Wynneth closed the door, locking Adrianna in with the four dhamphir and a vampire. As the light faded, Liam began to move. Slowly, painfully, he shifted his slumped figure. The chains rattled and he grunted as the spikes slid in and out of his skin with every move, until he stood tall, towering above them. Adrianna stepped back, her shoulders colliding with the door.

Liam had not been this tall when she last saw him. He surpassed at least a head above Orion, who was the tallest dhamphir in the room. His body had broadened so that his clothes were tight on his green-tinged skin. At last, Liam raised his head revealing blank, black eyes that looked out from a gaunt face. A beard had begun to grow in. Yet with all this change, there was something odd around the temples of his head. Two small lumps on either side were visible beneath his black hair.

"It was not long ago that our roles were reversed, witch," said Liam.

A small frown formed between her brows. His voice was slightly distorted, though he still sounded somewhat like himself.

"It was not before this war that anyone survived the Laboratory and went on to tell of it," he continued, focused solely on her. "I was there when Sergus had you tied to that stone. Inches from death, yet you carried on living when most would have given up."

Flashes of the Laboratory stole her focus for a moment: the pain, the blood, the experiments, the questions of the Librarian. She remembered seeing Jeith before her strength gave out and she lost consciousness.

"Then I suppose our roles are reversed," she replied. "But you will not survive the sun."

"This body will not."

"Why did you ask me here?"

"I was interested to see if you would come."

"Why would you be? You are a demon."

Orion and Durand shared a look. Adrianna noticed Orion shifted his eyes to Erik who stood behind her.

A smile crossed Liam's face though she knew it was not his smile. The smile belonged to his demon, Jeith, the Baál who now controlled him like a puppet. How dead was Liam's consciousness that he had given his body to this terrible demon without a fight?

"I have always had an interest in witches," said Jeith, squaring his shoulders.

"I know."

"I am honoured."

"Do not be. You are a glorified Bounty Hunter who sold witches to demons and were not even half decent at the job."

Liam's face froze for a single moment and she knew she had caught him off guard with her words, even though they were untrue. Jeith was a scourge who had terrified the whole of the Elemental Plane. His hunts were widely recorded. Just the mention of his name was enough to send witches cold, even the fiercest. During *The War Against The Angels* he added angels to his bounty and sold them to demons for less currency than he did witches.

"Now, why am I here?"

"To pass a message to *him*," said Jeith, with a look that underlined that she knew of whom he spoke.

It took her seconds to realise who he meant, and when she did, she was left slightly startled. "Why would I do that?"

"You know why, little girl. There is so much that you know, yet pretend to ignore. I knew that Baliath was on this Plane, yet it took me years to discover the name of his host. *You* led me to him."

"Let us pretend I know what you are talking about," she said her heartbeat racing. "What does it have to do with me?"

"That filthy Vermillion ran from our home Plane knowing I would follow, knowing we would *all* follow," said Jeith. "His seat on the Demon High Council is now owned by his brother; the brother who usurped him, who made him an outcast. How amusing that I should spend years searching this forsaken Plane for him, only to have him show his face in aid of a witch who would fetch me so little currency on the market."

"You took over the body and consciousness of a decent man to freely hunt another demon?"

"And you made for a good pawn," said Jeith. "Why do you think Liam kept you safe? It was on my command! My suspicions were already on Daniel, and what better way to confirm them than to put his little childhood friend before him? All I had to do was wait and watch."

Heat rose in Adrianna's cheeks. It was true. As the Darkness made her sick, she was left in Daniel's care when Liam went to hunt. Had this been orchestrated by Jeith? All this time she believed it was Liam who left her with Daniel because of their shared past, but it was Jeith who had been suspicious of Daniel and wanted to smoke him out! The night Daniel had buried her in soil Baliath revealed himself in order to protect her from another vampire. Had Liam seen this? Was that why he had sent her to the underground chambers after the Maquis failed attack? She had unintentionally revealed Baliath's host and thus was of no further use.

"Yes," said Jeith, and Adrianna realised her thoughts must have been clear on her face.

"You could not have known he would reveal himself around me. That was a fluke!"

"A chance taken by a male so egotistical in his own strength and status that he let his guard down for filth like you," said Jeith. "Were it not for the influence of *his* host, he would have left you to die."

"So Baliath is your new bounty?"

"I will collect his head and add it to the leg of the Skull Throne," said Jeith. "The throne on which he once sat."

"You people are truly disgusting."

"We are the legends you feared growing up. Did you think we were not real?"

"No, but you know what they say about meeting legends. They are not nearly as interesting as the stories told of them."

Liam tilted his head.

"I feel let down, truly," she said lightly. "I mean, aside from being about eight feet tall, which is impressive, you *are* a tiny bit of a disappointment. Especially considering you were captured without much of a fight. At least I killed half a dozen vampires before one knocked me unconscious. But . . . who knows about me? Nobody. Instead, *you* – you are a legend! And yet here you are, chained up by a couple of half-vampires. It's a shame, really."

"If you think you have seen the worst from Sansul, witch, think again," said Jeith. "With Henry's awakening, things have changed. Forever. You will die in more pain than you can imagine. You and these half-breeds."

"Maybe so, but at least we can endure," she said confidently.

"Can you withstand what's coming to you? Your friends will become your enemies. Your enemies will hunt you down. Your allies will abandon you. Your people will live in fear. You will be tested. You will *not* last."

"Maybe not til the end, but until then I will destroy everything you have built," said Adrianna.

"I have angered you."

"Just by being alive," she confirmed, watching as his skin ripped beneath the spikes of the chains. The ceiling creaked slightly. Orion opened his palm and struck the back of Liam's legs with a fire-sphere.

Liam hissed and collapsed on one knee, tugging at the chains that kept his arms above his head. The small mounds on either side of his head grew bigger as his fangs lengthened.

The horns, she thought. Jeith was physically morphing into himself now that Liam's consciousness was dormant. Would it take a complete transformation for Liam to die or would Liam be as Jeith was? Hosted.

"I hope in your next life, you chose a better path than this," she said, turning to leave.

"You did not ask me *why* he lost his seat."

Adrianna looked to Gyde. His usually stoic expression was replaced with one of concern.

"We should end this now," said Orion. "He has talked enough."

"I agree," said Erik.

"Yet, the little witch wants to know," said Jeith, still on bended knee.

Adrianna turned back to him. "Why did Baliath lose his seat? And do not lead me down the garden path, you son of a bitch."

Kneeling there with his arms painfully stretched out, an impassive expression met her angry one. He had not called her to come for anything but to gloat and make sure he had the last word. Liam had died the moment he became host to Jeith. There was no way a child as gentle and as nervous as Liam would have been able to fight the will and influence of a demon like Jeith on the night he was turned into a vampire. Little by little the demon had chipped away at the foundation of Liam's spirit, collapsing him completely so that he, Jeith, could rise onto the rubble and claim possession.

"Because he told them *no*," he said.

CHAPTER TWENTY-ONE

The Letter

"THEREFORE, TAKING A life is an act of the Darkness and taints the soul," Lizzette concluded with a kind of finality to her voice that did not invite any sort of counter argument.

Sitting at the table behind that of the Wilmota Assembly were Adrianna, who had chosen to ignore the infuriating conversation they were listening in on, Mathias, now fully healed and an official member of the Gordgáin, Ralphus, still nursing a broken heart over Kenna's 'death', brother and sister, Caitriona and Cedar, Veronique, the robust fiery witch who loathed the 'To-the-letter' attitude with which Lizzette practiced witchery, and the dark alluring gypsy, Dahlia.

"What a kook!" Cedar muttered, glaring over at the table in front of them.

"That mentality should have been thrown out the window with all the Black Magick books when *The War Against The Angels* ended," said Adrianna, stealing a piece of piecrust from Mathias's plate.

"*She* would have us all succumb to the vampires instead of fighting them," Veronique whispered furiously, cocking her head toward Lizzette. "You should have heard her in the underground chambers! *I* wanted to kill her."

"But Lizzette," spoke one of the warlocks from the Wilmota Assembly, "there is a difference between killing for pleasure and killing in defence. The Spirit Plane, after all, is the place for the soul to rest and live in peace, without the divides of Light and Darkness."

"Pish!" Lizzette cried. "A demon soul is different from the soul of a witch or that of an angel!"

"A soul is a soul, the body is the body," the warlock said exasperatedly. "The physical form we establish at reincarnation has nothing to do with what we are at the core."

"That argument is relative, but a dark deed in life does not stop at the physical, it affects the individual's spiritual balance and energy," said Lizzette.

"Which is why we have the Darkness and the Light," Adrianna said under her breath. "Some souls ascend to the Light, others to the Darkness – that is what the life lessons are for!"

"How do you know that?" Ralphus asked curiously.

Adrianna looked up from her tea. "I read it somewhere," she said lightly.

In truth, Adrianna did not know how she came to that particular conclusion. Something inside of her told her she was correct. While most elementals agreed on the cycles of life and death, there were those who, like Lizzette, believed that demons, angels and elementals had different souls. It was a theory that went against their core understanding for the reasons of reincarnation and ascension.

"Maybe Fradrik mentioned it in one of his lectures," she added.

"Well, I think she's barking mad," said Dahlia, plucking a honey roll from the centre plate. "All her thoughts come from that eight thousand year old guide to witchery. It was written before the vampires even existed, so how can we live by the same rules as when no followers of the Darkness lived on this Plane?"

"True," said Veronique. "Demons did not leave the Demon Plane before a sorceress managed to merge a demon essence with a vampire body, so we had no real need to fight and protect ourselves."

"The other argument is: why do we have the ability to produce fire-spheres and ice-tears if we are not supposed to use them?" Dahlia asked. "Our elemental powers are enough to protect us, should we need them."

"We are not supposed to use the energy and gifts nature gives us to take life," said Caitriona, speaking for the first time at the table. "It is a betrayal of the cycle."

"The cycle of what?" Dahlia asked testily. "Ascension to either the Light or the Darkness is inevitable . . ."

"But to kill is the first step toward going to the Darkness," said Caitriona. "We are taught this from childhood."

"It takes many lifetimes, and all the choices of those lifetimes, to influence which energy you are most likely to ascend to," said Veronique. "Mistakes will be made."

"But who is to say the right way is to go to the Light?" asked Mathias.

Adrianna and Caitriona shared a look.

"Excuse me?" said Ralphus, clearly caught off guard.

"Well, they live in balance don't they? The Light and the Darkness – so, who is to say, ascending to the Darkness is 'wrong'? It's just an observational question," Mathias said quickly.

The conversation on the Assembly's table was becoming heated. Peruva, the sorceress whose guide to meditation had allowed the witches to heal themselves in the fortress, slammed down her cutlery and stood up. "I am not going to sit here, and listen to you tell witches that they should allow themselves to be abused for the sake of preserving a law that was written *thousands* of years ago! With new times come new rules."

Lizzette raised herself slowly, calmly pinning Peruva with a shrewd look. "If you cannot uphold the laws, *sorceress*, then you may resign from your duties. A sorceress especially must put the Elements and Witchery Lore above all else!"

"Do not dictate to me, elder!"

"I will remind *all* who fall out of step," Lizzette shrieked, her curly hair stood on end with the amount of energy radiating from her. "To kill – no matter the circumstances – is abominable! I move to motion for a vote. *Any* actions of violence will be met with punishment."

"What?" snapped the warlock to Peruva's left.

Cedar dropped his knife with a 'clang', Dahlia looked horrified, Ralphus turned a snort into a cough after Lizzette sent him a sharp look, and Adrianna immediately regretted the words the tumbled, quite venomously, from her mouth.

"Well, that is just stupid!"

Adrianna snapped her mouth shut when Lizzette's lined, brown eyes turned to her.

"Excuse me?" Lizzette asked contemptuously, turning her full attention to their table.

Peruva shook her head vigorously, her eyes pleading with them to remain quiet. The rest of the Assembly watched Lizzette nervously.

Adrianna turned her attention to the greying elder witch and felt a rush of dislike for her. Lizzette was everything Adrianna did not want to be, and reminded her of everything that was wrong with their society. She also had no doubts that Lizzette was one of the Assembly members who had suggested that witches be questioned on their 'involvement with the vampires'.

Lizzette knew perfectly well that Peruva had caught the eye of a vampire while in the fortress. She also knew that Adrianna had been a captive of Liam's, and for the elder, they were tainted. No longer purely of the Light, but 'touched' by the Darkness; they were unfit for her clean and pure village.

"I said," Adrianna spoke confidently, her green eyes boring into Lizzette's brown ones, "that is stupid." She heard Caitriona suck in a breath to her right, and Mathias stiffened on her left. "If you seek to punish the innocent for defending themselves, you are committing an act of violence on the innocent. I have killed many vampires in defence, and I would never let someone attack me for fear of a 'stain on my soul'. That is a weak thing to do."

Lizzette's eyebrows shot up. "*Weak*? Child, you speak without the knowledge . . ."

"Ah," Adrianna scoffed, "away and play with your *knowledge*. That kind of mentality is what got most of the village kidnapped! If we had used our Elements we could have given the vampires what they deserved."

"I agree!" Dahlia spoke up.

Lizzette turned to her, her gaze landing on the tigers-eye pendant around the gypsy's neck. She narrowed her eyes; her lips became a thin, white line as she assessed Dahlia. "My girl, Simo would not be impressed by your attitude."

"My father does not tell me what to think," said Dahlia. "He would never agree with what you are suggesting. You have no right to serve punishment on people for defending themselves."

"Please, Lizzette, leave it," said Peruva.

Adrianna took a step toward Lizzette, ignoring Mathias who begged her to back down. A look of surprise crossed the old woman's face for a split second, before annoyance settled once again in her wrinkles. "You are the last person who can dictate to us about violence," she said in a low voice, leaning in.

"What do to mean, silly girl?" asked Lizzette, her eyes now wide.

"I *know* what you did. All those years ago. I *know*," said Adrianna, revolted to be looking into the eyes of a woman who had helped flay an innocent woman just for being a vampire.

"You are too young to understand," Lizzette told them, her voice trembling slightly. "Too young to see that the Darkness does not miss a chance to influence you. Many souls have ascended to the Darkness; its power lies with those who did not hold true to the ancient books. Written by the most enlightened angels and elementals . . . if we are to defeat the Darkness, be true to the written words of the ones who came before us." With that, Lizzette swept out of the room, her white skirts whirling around her.

"Well, if the angels are so enlightened, why are they not here?" Veronique muttered, pushing her plate away.

Caitriona poured more tea, but instead of drinking it, she gave it to Adrianna. "You need this. I can feel your energy vibrations from here."

"How long has it been since you meditated?" Peruva asked them as the Assembly members filed out of the room.

"Ages," said Adrianna. "I cannot sit still long enough to do it."

"Me neither," said Ralphus, rolling his thick shoulders. "I get too deep into my own thoughts and give myself a headache."

Caitriona laughed. "The irony of that!"

Ralphus blushed, looking shyly at his large hands. "Ah . . . you know."

Adrianna felt a rush of pity for him. *He is still thinking about Kenna.* She had seen him place water lilies in the sanctuary fountain and light a candle for

Kenna's memory on the Wall of Flames, back in the Wilmota sanctuary. *But she is not a memory.*

Mathias clapped the big man on his meaty shoulder. "She knows, warlock. She knows."

Ralphus cleared his throat, rubbing his chin. "Yeah, listen, I am going to call it a night. I have to . . . sleep, or something."

"Ralphus, it is not even sunset," said Caitriona.

"I did not sleep last night. See you . . ."

Adrianna sighed, resting her forehead in her palm as he left. *Why does everything have to be so sad?*

"Adrianna?" Mathena's voice drifted into the room. "Anna . . . are you in here? Oh, there you are!"

"We were just eating."

"Why the long faces?" Mathena asked around the room.

"One of the elders, Lizzette, was talking nonsense. It is just upsetting," said Adrianna.

"A clan is supposed to protect its people, not hurt them," said Veronique. "I will not see *my* clan be governed into stupidity by that woman."

"The Assembly does need to reassess itself," said Mathena agreeably. "Adrianna, Simo would like to see you."

"Now?"

"Yes."

"Why?"

Mathena shrugged. "If only I knew. I will take you to his office."

A few minutes later, arriving at a red, circular door in the large atrium, Mathena said, "He wants to see you on his own."

"Okay." Adrianna knocked on the door.

"Come in!" Simo looked up from the mountain of papers on his desk. There were a few more grey hairs around his temples, mixing in with his wind-swept brown hair. His staple lilac beard was longer at his chin than when she had first seen it. He wore an emerald green vest over an orange shirt, tucked into his purple trousers. With black, leather wrist cuffs, and a moonstone ring adorning his left hand, he was the most curiously dressed person Adrianna had ever seen.

"Adrianna, come in, come in," he said welcomingly. "Please, sit."

Adrianna sat in the uncomfortable wooden chair opposite him.

"I have asked you here, personally, because there is something I need done and only trust a fair few people to do it," Simo began, running a hand through his hair. "This letter needs to be taken to the vampires in Azria." He raised an epistle closed with the seal of the Gordgáin.

Adrianna blinked. *He must be joking!*

"But that is so dangerous!" she said. "You wish me to go south on my own and knock on the door of Azria Manor and hand them this letter?"

"Yes," he replied. "Not many people have the courage to talk to vampires, and I need someone who is in my circle, in my confidence, to fulfil this mission. It may be a letter, but it could change the tide of this mess."

"How?" she asked, wanting nothing more than to run away from this gargantuan feat he was asking her to accomplish.

"Azria coven is arguably the most powerful vampire coven in the world. Above Sansul, Bruniér, and even Citron, Azria's closest blood-ally. The Azrians: vampire, witch, nymph, and faery – they live side by side. An unspoken agreement between them has been honoured for centuries. Henry has many powerful enemies, but the one we need to reach is his most staunch enemy; he is Rasmus the Supreme Chancellor of Azria coven. A most revered vampire. If this . . ." Simo tapped the letter, "could reach his hands, and he lent his support, the war will be ours to win."

Adrianna bit her lip, even as she felt a rush of excitement, she was terribly nervous. "We are losing, are we not?"

"The war? We are very close to that point. With Henry and a whole new contingent of Vahir soldiers awake, we will be overrun."

"Vahir?"

"It is the ancient word for 'vampire'. The Vahir Legion is the most ancient vampire army, you have heard of it?"

Adrianna nodded.

"Now, the winter is upon us, and the snow will slow Henry's forces. He will take this season to assess his options, put together new plans and make for an attack on the south in the spring."

"Would that not force Azria to help us?"

"The Azria vampires will only protect themselves. They have no need to help us. But if we request their aid, I am quite sure they will provide it. Through this letter we will hopefully have gained an ally."

"And we will not need the help of the angels?"

"The angels could have stopped all this before it began," said Simo. "But, that is a bitter conversation best left for a longer day."

Adrianna took the letter and looked the gypsy man in the eye. "I cannot guarantee I will get this done."

"You are a true Gordgáin," Simo said proudly. "I know you can."

"My cousin Blanca lives in Azria," said Adrianna, a sudden thought occurring. "I was supposed to travel south the day after the attack on Wilmota and visit her. I know she will help."

"Try to keep your confidants to a small number," he said.

"Of course, but I want to take Orla with me."

"You trust her?"

"Yes. Besides, she is from Azria. I know she wants to return to her family."

Simo nodded. "Very well. Thank you."

Suddenly, there was a hasty knock on the door.

Adrianna looked over her shoulder as the knocking continued. The air became tense. *Something is wrong.*

As soon as Simo answered it, Huon, Mathena's only son, bounded through looking windswept.

"What happened?" Adrianna asked immediately.

"He's escaped!" Huon cried. "That vampire escaped during his execution and he wounded one of the Maquis."

Simo and Adrianna looked at one another, taking a second to process Huon's words.

"Come," said Simo.

Adrianna followed as they rushed through the sanctuary. "How did it happen?" Simo asked.

"Four vampires came down upon them as Erik brought the vampire out to the sun," Huon said hurriedly. "Someone said they saw Henry himself. The attackers grabbed the vampire and disappeared before anyone had the chance to react. Some of the Maquis followed but have not returned yet. One of them is wounded, badly."

"Who?" Adrianna asked.

"Your friend," Huon said as they reached the trapdoor. "The silent one."

Gyde. "Oh no," Adrianna muttered following Simo up through to the floor of the dusty, bare cottage.

"I was also told to inform you that Allan the Spellmaker is one of those following Henry back to Sansul Fortress," said Huon to Simo, keeping his voice low. "Allan was there to oversee the execution."

"Thank you, Huon. Guard this entrance," Simo ordered at the door. "Should you hear anything, go back down and seal it closed. No matter what."

Adrianna and Simo arrived at the Maquis hillside lair just as Orion was closing it off. Many dhamphir were resting on the floor in the foyer sporting small cuts and bruises. Alexjander's shirt was scorched and ripped, and a curly-haired woman was bleeding profusely from her nose. But none was wounded as badly as Gyde, who was being helped through the gate and door by Durand.

Adrianna went straight to Erik. "How bad is Gyde's wound?" she asked worriedly.

Erik was clutching his side. "He will live. He is stubborn. Our best healers are with him."

"What happened to you?" she asked, bending to look at what his hand was covering. Blood seeped between his fingers.

"Nothing serious," Erik said tightly.

"Erik, let me help you," she said. "I am good at this, I don't even leave scars."

Erik looked hesitant but he resigned and walked with Adrianna through the gate and down large, stone steps. "My office is right here," he said, nodding to the first door on the left of the stairs.

Adrianna requested a small pouch of specific herbs and some cloths of a dhamphir woman carrying a basket to those in the entrance. Erik had already pulled off his jacket and dropped it to the ground when Adrianna entered the room.

"Not very patient, are you?" she asked, moving to help remove with his shirt.

"Not in these circumstances," he said darkly.

"Do not be shy, I promise not to stare," she teased, tugging the material over his head. "Sit," she ordered.

"I do not like being told what to do!"

"I can imagine," she said, unmoved by his tone. "Especially by me, a mere witch. Sit still, I have to inspect the damage."

Erik glared at her as the Maquis woman returned with everything Adrianna asked for. "Thank you, Kara."

Kara smiled at Adrianna. "Do not let him get to you," she said. "He's always moody!" Her tinkling laugh only seemed to aggravate Erik more. "Be nice to the witch, Erik," she warned before shutting the door on her exit.

"It is only a flesh wound," said Adrianna, putting her fingers gently to the gash on his side. "You made it worse when you kept on fighting. By the way, I am sorry Liam got away."

"Are you?"

Adrianna did not look up from the wound. "You were right, when you warned me the other night of his true state of mind," she said. "When you lose everything, you cling to the good memories of the past. I suppose I was doing that, even when it was clear that Liam was beyond help." She gave him a small smile. "It is not easy to admit this."

"Sometimes people allow themselves to be engulfed by a larger power or ideology. Liam is not the first or the last to do that," Erik said as she lifted his arm and began to clean the knife wound. "We were prepared for an attempt to escape. We were not prepared for Henry. *I should have been ready*," he exclaimed, slamming his fist on the desk.

Adrianna ran a damp cloth over the offended area and dipped her fingers into a small pot with a clear paste. "It will not hurt," she said, concentrating. "This will not take long to heal. Calm down, now. It was not your fault."

"How did you learn this?" asked Erik. "Do you plan on becoming a healer?"

"No, I haven't the temperament. But I have been learning a few tricks because you never know when you'll find yourself in need. Besides, Mathena insisted and she has been teaching me everything she knows."

Erik gave a small smile. "Thank you." He flexed his arm, testing the movement of his left side. "You will do well. It needs no stitching?"

"No. The paste works quickly, and being a dhamphir, you will heal before morning."

"Great."

Adrianna put the lid back on the ceramic pot. "I am leaving in the morning."

Erik looked perplexed. "Why?"

"A mission for the Gordgáin. I am going south to Azria," she replied. "And I am telling you because I don't want you sending anyone to follow me. This is not for personal reasons."

"It isn't wise to go alone."

"I will be taking my friend, Orla," she said. "We both have family there. I know Orla will want to be reunited with hers. It is something the Gordgáin have asked and I cannot say 'no', not when so many others are doing more dangerous things."

"The Gordgáin are flexible with how they use their young people," Erik said unhappily. "There is much that could happen between here and Azria."

"I know, but it must be done," she replied. "I am in no danger . . . yet."

"Unless I hear of danger, I will not send anyone," he said honestly. "But I will be speaking with Simo about who he sends to pass his messages."

"How do you know I am sending a message?" she asked in surprise.

"I inherited my father's knack for pre-empting other people's actions," said Erik.

Adrianna arched an eyebrow at his sarcasm. "Yes, well, I hope you will be able to put your special skill to work with regards to Henry," she said, throwing the bloodied rag in a basket. "He is going to be difficult to deal with."

Erik pulled on a clean shirt. "Concentrate on Azria," he said. "We will deal with Henry."

Adrianna frowned. "A plan, dare I say?"

"I have too many plans," he said. "This war will turn me grey."

Adrianna laughed and headed for the door.

"Adrianna, wait . . ."

"Yes?"

"When you disappeared the other night," he began somewhat nervously, "we thought Liam's people had taken you in revenge for his capture. I will admit I felt slightly responsible."

Adrianna looked at him curiously. *Surely he knows what really happened. Gyde could smell Daniel on me; he knows I was with him.* Had Gyde kept the previous evening's conversation personal, or was Erik being sly and prodding for information? "I was not harmed," she said.

"Obviously," said Erik. "I am not interested in other people's personal business, Adrianna. It is one thing I pride myself on. But when I heard whispers about the vampire that took you just so happened to be the same one that kept you alive in the fortress . . ."

"What do you want to know?" Adrianna interrupted. "I am not an idiot, and if there is something you want to ask, just ask it. I do not play games."

Erik leaned back in his chair, mildly surprised. "All right. Then I shall do the same."

"It would make things easier between all of us," she said, "don't you think?"

"Very well. Is he still in these parts?"

"I do not know," she replied.

"There is no . . . force?"

"Dhamphir seem particularly worried about that kind of thing."

"History demands it."

"No, there is no force," she said.

"I do not take you for a liar, nor do I take you for a fool. But you *must* be careful."

~

The plan was set.

Adrianna and Orla would leave before dawn. Departing immediately would allow for them to get a head start on the cold weather. Winter was upon them and Adrianna was determined to get to Azria before she was knee deep in snow.

Orla was thrilled to be invited to go and promptly packed a bag and was ready to leave before Adrianna had finished placing an Illusion Charm on their coats.

In the privacy of their shared bedroom, Mathena began a long, one-sided discussion about the right roads to get to Azria. "Do not walk on Joining Road," she said pleadingly, "and don't forget to remain a hag!"

Orla went cross-eyed and turned to Adrianna in a huff. "I am *not* travelling as a hag!"

"It is the safest way," said Adrianna. "I have already charmed the coats," she added, holding them up.

It came to light centuries ago that vampires did not attack hags. The hideousness of the deformed women repelled vampires from their blood, and the mere viciousness and strange natures of hags was disgusting to vampires. Witches, inspired, soon began to use this knowledge to their advantage. They would use an object to instil the Illusion Charm, whether it was a coat, a crystal or a broach, something that was always on their person and allow them to seem, outwardly, like a hag.

After a few more minutes of arguing, Orla relented. "But I am not going to be terribly hideous."

Mathena and Adrianna shared a look.

They were going through the last of Adrianna's clothes when a knock sounded on their bedroom door. Orla slid off her bed and answered it. It was Ralphus and Mathias.

"Hello lads," Adrianna said pleasantly, noting how Mathias winked at Orla. "What brings you here?"

Orla blushed and went to continue packing.

"We need to talk," said Mathias seriously.

"I told you to let me handle this," Ralphus said, uncrossing his arms.

"Talk about what?" said Adrianna.

"What you've been doing," said Mathias. "There are rumours going around about what happened to you in the fortress."

Adrianna crossed her arms. "Really? Do enlighten me on these 'rumours', Mathias."

"It isn't about the rumours," said Ralphus, "at least not the bit about you. We heard it was Liam that kept you a prisoner."

"It was."

"What?" Mathias stared at her in disbelief. "Liam?"

"Yes."

"Why didn't you tell us?" Ralphus said indignantly.

"Do you both know him?" Mathena asked them.

"They were Daniel and Liam's best friends," Adrianna told her. "Mathias and Daniel were very close."

"Adrianna, what do you know that we don't? What is going on?" said Mathias.

"Do you want the truth?"

"Of course!"

"You mean they don't know?" asked Mathena.

"Know what?" asked Ralphus, suspicious.

"I was Liam's prisoner for a few moons, I ended up in the Laboratory, and then Daniel rescued me from it and brought me to the Gordgáin. Since then I have been a messenger," Adrianna confessed. "No, Mathena, they did not know because I never talked about it. There was never time."

There was a pause.

"How is he?" asked Mathias.

"Who?"

"Daniel. Is he . . . is he all right?" Mathias asked, somewhat sheepishly, as though asking about the wellbeing of a vampire was shameful.

"He seems to be. He can look after himself."

"Where are you going?" Ralphus asked, nodding to the things on her bed.

"Away," Adrianna said with a sigh. "No one can know where I am."

"You are going alone? I do not like this."

"No, I am going with her," said Orla.

"We can take you wherever you need to go," said Mathias.

"No, I have to do this alone."

"Why?"

"Mathias . . ."

"You're too young to be doing all this on your own," Ralphus said in agreement. "The Gordgáin shouldn't be sending you out there. You'll be fodder for anyone. Look at what happened to Kenna! You could die too."

"Now listen up!" Adrianna said furiously. "I have looked after myself just fine for many, many years. I am not going to get into any trouble."

Ralphus took her by the shoulders and stared down at her. "What if you end up like Kenna?"

"I will not."

"If you keep putting yourself out there, you are going to get hurt," he said in a hollow voice. "You never let anyone help you. It's how you get into trouble."

"I have to do this."

"Why?" Mathias demanded, moving Ralphus aside. "Why is it so important that *you* need to go off? Why not someone older? More experienced? Haven't you thought of that? Don't you think that perhaps the only reason the Gordgáin is sending you out to do this 'secret' mission is because you can use your looks?"

Orla gasped.

"And you think I would stoop that low?" Adrianna demanded.

"I think you are too innocent to see you are being used. Can't you see that the Gordgáin know exactly why you were kept alive? Like Caitriona and Jess? The villagers have been talking about Peruva and some vampire named Raphael for *weeks*. They know vampires are attracted to you!"

"I think I have had enough of being slapped in the face," said Adrianna, taking a step back. "Thank you for the concern, but I have packing to do."

"No, Adrianna . . ." Ralphus put his hand on her shoulder. He looked as if he was going to speak, but instead, he embraced her tightly. "Do not do anything dangerous."

"I promise." Adrianna smiled and patted his back. She looked at Mathias and he stared defiantly at her for a moment. "On my honour as a witch, I will do nothing stupid," she promised.

"If there is any trouble . . ."

"You will know. Everything is going to be all right."

"You have the most unusual friends," said Mathena, shaking her head as Mathias and Ralphus left.

"Let's finish packing and get out of here," said Orla, opening Adrianna's bag. "Okay, you charmed our coats with the Illusion Charm, so we should put them on only when we get outside. Now, brush, pins, shawl, leggings, trousers . . . check."

"Remember, if you get lost, walk east to the shore line and follow it down to the south," Mathena told Adrianna. "Once you take the Dial Door to Collusus, make sure you are not being followed. The vampires will be watching all entrances and exits. Should you not be able to use the Dial Door to get to Azria, there are plenty of signs to direct you but I suggest you follow The River Pike past Stag Forest and then hop onto the main road."

Adrianna blinked. "Right . . . did you get all that, Orla?"

Orla looked up from Adrianna's lace chemise. "Get what?"

Adrianna laughed and Mathena shook her head amusedly. "I shall write it down."

"What are you doing?" Adrianna asked Orla.

"This is so pretty," said Orla, running her fingers over the lace.

"I made it. It is quite simple once you master the spell to move the needles in the pattern you want," said Adrianna. "I can make one for you if you'd like."

"Would you? Oh, thank you," she said excitedly. "My mother does not believe in lace. She thinks it is frivolous."

"Nonsense!" Adrianna scoffed. "You are so pretty you should wear it all the time. Lace on undergarments and shirt edgings is beautiful. Some women go overboard with it but a little here and there is charming. My mother used to mix it with silk."

"So does mine," said Mathena. "She puts frills on the tops of her socks with silk too. Her *bustiers* were lace extravaganzas!"

"I do these little lace edgings," Adrianna said, lifting her skirt to her thigh, revealing a cotton sock. "You can fold the lace over and thread a silk bow through it too if you're feeling a little mischievous."

"You have to teach me all about this!" Orla said, enthralled. "My mother would *never* let us do something as that!"

"Really?" Mathena asked. "How do you seduce a man then?"

Orla blushed. "Well . . . I have never really come to that . . . my mother says, 'Lace is for the loose'."

"Really?" Mathena's eyebrows shot up.

"I believe your mother may be a little afraid of pretty things," said Adrianna. "Lace simply adds decoration to clothes. *All* women use it."

"My mother is not all women," Orla said. "But I would love it if you made me some of these. You could teach me."

"Of course!" Adrianna grinned.

"Quickly now," said Mathena, clapping her hands. "Let's finish packing. It is almost sunrise."

Within the hour, they were packed, dressed in warm clothes to protect against the winter's beginning, complete with gloves, scarves and hats, and prepared for their journey. Mathena and Fradrik walked with Orla and Adrianna to the entrance as the sanctuary slept. She embraced Adrianna for a long time before finally letting go.

"Be safe, and never forget your path," she whispered. "Keep this . . ." She pulled off a ring from her middle finger. It was silver and wrapped around the length of her finger like a snake. At the tip of the ring that ended at her nail sat a small yellow stone. "My first husband gave it to me. It has given me a lot of good fortune. I give it to you, my sister, and wish you the best of luck for this mission."

Adrianna cried as Mathena slipped it on for her. It morphed itself to fit her, and the stone glowed. "Thank you." She kissed her cheek. "We will see each other again soon."

Mathena smiled. "You have Simo's letter?"

"Yes."

"Be careful my darling," she said, embracing Orla. "Keep each other safe. All the best to your family."

"Thank you," said Orla.

Fradrik leaned his forehead against Adrianna's. "*If you find trouble, turn back or call for me in the wind. I will come, even if I betray the Gordgáin.*"

"*They need you here,*" said Adrianna. "*I love you more than I can say.*"

"*And I you daughter of my truest. Now go, before I lose my courage to see you walk out into danger.*"

Adrianna kissed his cheek. "Look after him, Mathena," she said. "Look after each other."

"No doubt about it," said Mathena, linking her arm with Fradrik's.

The two witches climbed the rickety stairs up to the dusty, abandoned cottage, in which, only a few weeks ago, Adrianna found herself facing seven vampires.

"I am glad to be travelling with you, Orla," said Adrianna.

"I feel the same."

They would each be reunited with their families, but for how long?

With too much to lose on either side, the war would not have a swift ending. Something big was on the horizon, something much more dangerous. Everyone could sense it. It was what made them shiver when they were alone, what made them want to fight.

How far would each side go to defeat the other?

As the chill of the early morning wind blew through the house, Orla and Adrianna pulled on their coats, instantly transforming into a pair of squatty hags, and stepped out beneath the fading stars.

Glossary

The Light: the force of energy used by elementals and celestials.

The Darkness: the force of energy used by vampires and demons.

Blood Bequeath: A Blood Bequeath occurs during the Initiation Ceremony. When a vampire is inaugurated into a coven, the coven's protection both physical and magical is bound to them.

Lexicon: a spell book that consists of spells, potions and remedies. Each witchery family has a Lexicon.

Ancients: vampires are classified as 'ancients' if they were made before *The War Against The Angels*. Most ancients went into the *Dormazu*, the rejuvenation sleep, after the war.

Maker: vampires who have turned another being into a vampire, and to their subjects they are known as Maker and spend years teaching and nurturing them in the *Vahir* way.

The Maquis: a dhamphir warrior brotherhood.

The Gordgáin: an ancient rebel group that has served on the Elemental Plane since the birth of the vampires.

Necropolis: a secure location for vampires to sleep; it is protected by soldiers and Black Magick.

Dhamphir: a half-vampire. A dhamphir is fathered by a vampire, and the mother may be a witch, nymph or angel.

Vahir: the ancient word for 'vampire'. Literal meaning: 'fallen from seraphim'.

Eriseda: the ancient word for 'the Pull'; a force of power that draws two soul mates together. It is the bonding ritual between soul mates who find one another outside the *Spirit Plane*.